D1431549

The Value of an
Anne Elliot

The Delightful Sequel to Jane Austen's

'Persuasion'

Kate Westwood

Published by Kate Westwood
www.katewestwood.net

ISBN: 978-0-6450494-0-4

Disclaimer

This is a work of fiction. Names, characters, places,
organisations, events, and incidents are either products of the
author's imagination or used fictitiously.

Books by Kate Westwood

A Scandal at Delford

Beauty and the Beast of Thornleigh

A Bath Affair

The Value of an Anne Elliot

KATE WESTWOOD

Acknowledgements

I would like to thank Beverly Swayzee for her invaluable feedback and encouragement, Kim Lambert for her formatting skills and publishing knowledge, and Cathy Walker for her cover design expertise.

Table of Contents

Dedicated to Lily and Connor, across the ocean, but always close to my heart.

'Lady Russell had only to listen composedly... but her heart revelled in angry pleasure, in pleased contempt, that the man who at twenty-three had seemed to understand somewhat the value of an Anne Elliot, should, eight years afterwards, be charmed by a Louisa Musgrove.'

Jane Austen, *Persuasion.*

Prologue

Friday, 26 May, 1815
London, White's Club.

The letter smelled faintly of almonds. What others might have described as a cloying, sickly scent, brought to him the steadying reminder of all that he owed. Family was everything.

He ran his thumb along the edge of the paper. He could not fault the folding of it. It was perfectly executed. As always. On the front, the direction was written in black ink; the sure but delicate hand did the perfect folds no disservice. Turning the letter over, he perceived the shape of a rose imprinted into the black sealing wax. He smiled, understanding immediately. He enjoyed a private quiz, and his sister's singular humour never disappointed him. Oh, how true the old saying that it takes one to know one.

He had understood his older sister from a young age. She was like a cipher, a hieroglyphic, that only he knew how to read. Her spoken word and her meaning were always two different things, and his survival instincts, always strong, had taught him at an early age to learn her particular language. He had learned from her too, that there were always two ways to read things; the way they were presented on the surface, and the hidden meanings that lay below, he thought, eyeing the black rose. There is always, he pondered, something to be found below the surface if one is prepared to hunt for it. A shrewd practiser of the art of obfuscation in his own dealings, he appreciated the same approach in the one person to whom he was closest in life. He had assuredly learned from his sister the art of concealment. Perhaps their characters were too similar, because they almost never quarrelled. Was that a fault? Mim would say that it was. But he could not imagine anyone else with whom he could be of so similar a mind, and in so perfect a harmony.

She came and went at her own volition, following her own will, and he suffered under no misapprehensions; her will was iron clothed in velvet. But he would always be ready to escort her, with the greatest degree of solicitous attention, anywhere she desired to go, in his own carriage, at his own expense, and at a moment's notice. He would do whatever she bade him, no questions asked. He could do no less for the older sister who had fought for him when he needed a protector, mothered him when he was young and motherless. Even now, she always took his part with the fierce loyalty with which two siblings, united by blood then orphaned together and left almost to raise themselves, would most naturally find themselves bound. He had on several occasions got himself into one or other kind of difficulty, and she had always beat him an easy path from trouble's door.

Therefore, if she summoned, he came, and was glad to obey. The symbol of the rose and the scent of bitter almond was her own gentle reminder of the lengths she would go to, if needed, for his sake. He neither needed, nor minded, this conjuring of his memory. He was every day grateful. Family was everything. The *only* thing.

He lifted his eyes. The salon was empty and the air cool at that time of morning. The numerous brown leather chairs which were arranged in comfortable twos and threes around small tables of chestnut and rosewood were vacant, most fellows not having risen yet. Almost nobody ever showed his head through the front door of White's before midday, and even one o'clock in the afternoon was early for those who went to bed at five in the morning after a night of drinking and gaming. For himself, he took great pleasure in being thought singular and made a point of rising early, even when he had been up all night, much to the ire of his sleep-deprived valet.

He enjoyed being at his club. Since his election several years ago he had taken a quiet pleasure in the air of respectful reserve which each member preserved so studiously, while still managing to engage in the usual pastimes found in such halls, in that jovial and 'hail-fellow-well-met' fashion which was the glue which held them together in brotherhood. Along with his other vices, he unashamedly considered himself an inveterate gambler, and it suited both his taste for the tables, and his reticence with regard to his private life, to have a membership at White's. Here he found a gentle camaraderie, mingled with that terribly English tendency to insularity which resulted in never having one's privacy intruded upon. It allowed him an easy existence; welcomed by his fellows, he would pick up the threads of a conversation here and there, and toss off a few of the usual earthy remarks expected in a roomful of males, but he could exclude company just as easily, and without question, if he wished it. And best of all, he never had to talk about his past. Or his present, for that matter. They all accepted him for what he appeared to be, and if anything, they merely smiled at the tales which sometimes followed him through the front door. It was *Town*, after all.

Now, in the early morning sun was only just brushing the furniture with pale gold through the heavy damask window drapery, and he revelled in the quiet of the room. Those morning street noises, the clatter of carts and bustle of self-important servants moving about with baskets of cabbages and fish, the strident calling out of various purveyors, none of these assaults could be heard from the behind the white stone walls separating those within them from the dirty streets. The fetid summer stench of the road, which arose from the mingling of human urine and horse droppings, was also barred from the club by the means of two front doors, and the boot room in between. It was not that he despised the street, but when he entered into the quiet, elegant world behind those stone walls, he expected the street to wait outside, until he was ready, like a servant awaiting his orders.

Leaning forward, he now took up from the table the ornate letter knife which lay there and applied it under the wax seal of the paper. Separating the black wax from the paper, he was careful to leave the rose emblem unbroken, and he opened the letter out.

The heavy, heady scent of almond filled his nostrils. He stretched out in the chair and drew his breath in forcefully, enjoying the rush of pleasure in his temples, and that odd but welcome feeling the scent of her letters always gave him, as if his sister was in the same room with him. The scent of her was like opium vapour, he thought, but without the stupor afterwards, better than the best Macouba snuff.

He read over the letter:

> *Bennett-Street, Bath.*
> *Wednesday 24 May*
>
> *'Haro darling,*
>
> *Well, here I have been for six weeks, and I cannot tell you how tedious it is getting with me and dear Leticia. You know I love my own sister quite as much as I ought but I confess that I am becoming disenchanted with Bath. The place is ill-designed for prolonged stays, with the weather so dreary and the people so bland. It wearies me, so long we have been here, and all the amusements that we ran mad for in the first weeks have palled. I long for your company again! You are always the only person who can relieve my tedium! And you surely must have had your fun in London by now, if I have it right, for I always give you six to eight weeks until boredom sets in. Am I not a canny mathematician? Are you weary of her yet? I know she is young and innocent and sweet but even you must tire of that cloying, sweet innocence sometime! And besides that, you naughty boy, you know it will not be long before the papa finds you out! Pray do not get into another fight, Haro. You cannot expect me to get you out of yet another scrape! Be a good fellow and leave London and come to me in Bath.*
>
> *There is another reason I ask you to come to Bath. Do you remember what we discussed at the*

Parsonage before we parted? Well, I have a scheme to put to you, and even you must approve it! My new acquaintance here, with whom I am on the most intimate terms, is the eldest daughter of a crusty old baronet who has made his home here in Bath, a Sir Walter Elliot. I made their acquaintance almost immediately on my arrival six weeks ago, almost quite as soon as I singled the lady out as a prospect for you.

Elizabeth Elliot is a woman of refined air, good breeding, and is quite marriageable despite her thirty odd years. I can vouchsafe to say, that while I perceive a certain strength of character and a tolerable superiority of mind, she is nothing compared to the strength of two people together, united by blood and a shared past. No indeed, the poor creature, while possessing enough common wit, rank, and superior beauty to make her acceptable in any drawing room in Mayfair, will not, I collect, give us any trouble. She is too distracted with increasing her own consequence to understand others on anything but a superficial level. She is, in short, perfect to our purpose.

Now, since you have solemnly promised me that you will settle down and make me some nephews and nieces to amuse us when we are at E, I have done my part and secured her trust. I have painted her a darling picture of you, and now you must come and play your part in attaching her early affections. She has recently been low in spirits; a young man, who has gone away and married someone else, or some such thing — you know how it is — her hopes on that score were sadly dashed, and you, Haro, can arrive just at the right time to soothe her feelings and pamper the flame of her self-importance until she is charmed and under your spell! I really do think you could have her with a very little effort, and she is quite a beauty, for all her one-and-thirty years.

Yes, I really do think you will approve. There is no tedious piety or false modesty with this one - one Miss FP is enough, I collect, for us both! — do you recall how enamoured of her you once were? — nor is she of a sulking bent as with your spoilt Mrs R; no, this one is quite full of the right airs and manners which a good birth bestows, and she will be tolerably endowed upon her father's demise. And that cannot be far off, for I have never seen so choleric an appearance in a person since our aunt's illness.

I believe, Haro, that an alliance with Miss Elliot would be a match to befit your status, your fortune, and your breeding. Matrimony, my dear boy, is your duty, and you cannot ignore duty forever or it will catch you and have its way. Better to choose than be chosen! And you know we must both do what we must. I, too, must do my duty in turn. We must stem the tide of gossip and besides that, you know that we must preserve E by means of an heir.

Come soon. You must take a house in a good part of town. It will not suit our purpose to be too modest if we are to catch us an Elliot. I shall arrange to engage a house in Laura-place or Williams-street for you directly. Darling boy, I believe you must congratulate me on my genius! Come early next week and we shall have a pleasant coze on it all,

Your loving
Mim.

P.S. Were you not diverted to see the wax seal? I shall adopt it always now. It amuses me excessively!

He put down the letter carefully on the varnished side table near his hand. So, his sister had made good on her word and found him a female, modestly rich, with breeding and airs and pride. He played idly with the condensation on his glass, the expensive ice within shifting inside its little bath of excellent whiskey. If he *must* marry, he thought, that is precisely the kind of woman he should like; a proud, haughty woman would suit his nature well, for he could take pleasure in taming her and making her fall in love with him. He had powers of pleasing enough to put a hole in the heart of any woman he chose. Even cold little Fanny Price had not been immune — he had *almost* managed to cage her up like a little bird, a little bird he would have found much pleasure in amusing himself with — but he stopped himself and gave a short, mirthless laugh. *She* was not worth his time. How glad he was that she had backed out of the engagement! Yes, this one sounded more to his taste. But thirty years old! Ah well, but he could not expect to have all his tastes catered to. Besides, these silly little sweet, young things that it seemed was all London afforded these days, tired him easily. The little innocent he had been dallying with here in town was already becoming a bore to him, but he hadn't quite finished with her yet.

Reaching into his pocket with his left hand, he withdrew a small, ivory carved box and opened its painted lid. Pinching a small amount of fragrant snuff within in his fingers, he placed it on the back of his right hand and bent his nostrils to the powder, sharply inhaling twice. His eyes watered and he delicately wiped away the tears, then the residue, from his nose and hands with a cloth he always kept for the purpose.

He leaned back contentedly in his chair. Three more days and he would do his sister's bidding and get himself to Bath to play the marriage game, but he had some pleasures of the flesh to extract first.

One

Thursday 1 June, 1815
Kellynch Hall, Somersetshire.

'A letter, my dear, just now arrived.'

The gentle, enquiring voice which interrupted his reverie was an intrusion into the quiet morning light of the library, but not an unwelcome one. Putting down his pen and blotting the ink of his correspondence, Captain Frederick Wentworth smiled with tender regard at the open, pretty face of the woman before him. He took the letter from her hand. 'I shall have done in a few minutes. Tell Sophie I will come to breakfast shortly.'

He had been expecting orders any day, although he had hoped fervently that they might be as delayed as would not injure the greater good, so that he might remain at Kellynch as long as possible. But both he and Anne knew what the letter contained, and the risk attending his career had been known to them both before they had married.

His wife stood a moment more, hesitating, her palé blue muslin morning dress providing a pleasant foil to the pink-blushed cheeks and dark hair above. He fancied privately that his Anne was lately so altered in plumpness and in good looks that he could hardly think her recognisable from the creature he had met with last year at Uppercross. 'Go to breakfast, my dear. I will come directly.'

He watched his wife retreat, pondering as he did so often these days, his good fortune. With Anne he had found an unexpected happiness that he had never brooked upon. She was always so right, so capable, so dependable! She seemed so in harmony with his own thoughts and so sensible of his wishes, that he marvelled not for the first time that he had gained such a creature!

Very lately married, he had come to value ever more the quiet, gentle soul which was the Anne Elliot he loved! Three months of marriage had taught him nothing he did not already know, except the increasing strength of his passion for the woman who had taught *him* in turn, of the value of abiding constancy in love. All the success he had ever enjoyed as captain of the Asp and then of the Laconia, all the material manifestations of his achievements, he now realised as falsely valued, when compared with the gaining of a treasure such as an Anne Elliot!

Smiling slightly still, he returned to appraise gravely the handwriting on the letter, feeling that he apprehended already the contents of the sealed paper. A minute's reading and his suspicions were confirmed. Rear Admiral Malcom had arrived in the country the previous day and had posted immediately to London to report. Two months previously the Great Powers had declared Napoleon an outlaw and had vowed to destroy his power in Europe. Another war was now inevitable. Each power had deployed one hundred and fifty thousand men on the ground, and Wentworth was certain that there would now be a request for naval reinforcements in Europe. The letter was lowered, and some moment spent in serious reflection, his face thoughtful.

His countenance had never suffered the rigours that other sailors suffered, even while his father-in-law liked to declare, out of his hearing, that his son-in-law was well-looking enough but had not escaped a sailor's ill fortune of always seeming slightly weather-beaten. However, it was a fact acknowledged by most of his acquaintance, that Captain Frederick Wentworth not only had never lost his good looks, but that they had seemed only to improve with the advance of years, despite their being subject to several seasons at sea and enough battles to bring him home a handsome fortune.

Now, happy in love and comfortable in marriage, he might

have been said to glow with vitality, even if that glow was at present overhung with anxiety for the news he was about to impart. He knew Anne would be waiting for him in the morning room, at breakfast with his sister and Admiral Croft, and it was there he made for with reluctant haste.

He leaned his head into the doorway of the morning parlour and took in the charming domestic scene. His sister, Mrs Croft, still sat at breakfast, and Admiral Croft, her husband, had taken up the paper and made himself comfortable. Her own breakfast finished, Anne sat with her husband's socks, darning tools at her side. This task she always insisted was her own, for it gave her, she said, a way to render what small service she could for the husband who had made her happy beyond whatever she could have hoped for only six months ago! With Anne, her pleasure was to always give way, her joy was to serve. He marvelled, smiled to himself, and entered the parlour. Anne immediately put down the stockings she had taken up and raised enquiring brows.

It was, however, Mrs Croft who spoke first. 'Frederick! Have you come for some tea? Janet, make a fresh pot, if you please. Now do sit, Frederick. You find us lately risen, for poor Matthew has the gout again and we have been discussing the possibility of Bath, for the waters; it did him such good in February, and Anne agrees, but now that Anne is —'

'Ah!' interjected Wentworth hastily, 'that is not good news, I fear! I am sorry to hear of your trouble, Admiral, but I have sobering news myself, I am afraid.'

He proffered the letter first to his wife, who took it and perused it with great seriousness in her large, dark eyes.

Mrs Croft sighed with the resignation only a seasoned sailor's wife could summon, and said, 'I take it you have had news? Has the War Office written to you? Shall they send forces to Ghent after all?' and at the same time, Admiral Croft ventured, 'Ah, so it has come to this, then, aye but it was naught that was not expected. Perhaps you shan't be away long, Frederick?'

Wentworth, however, only had eyes for his wife, who, after looking over the letter, was as composed as she was serious.

She put aside the letter and began calmly, 'It was what we have all been in expectation of, and of course, I shall be well looked after here. I cannot hope for more, and you must follow your duty. But what do you comprehend from this news? Surely you will get orders very soon. Do you expect to be called away today?' Her voice was steady, and her countenance tolerably composed, even though she was to lose her husband only two months after their marriage, to his other wife, the ship which he would command his attention for perhaps several months, or even more!

He admired her composure, and taking her hand, smiled into her dark brown eyes. He could not but help glance at her smooth muslin dress, and the pleasing new plumpness it concealed. 'You are too good, too forbearing,' he replied in a low voice meant only for Anne, 'but it is more concerning to me that I must leave you alone, perhaps for many weeks—'

But before Anne could remonstrate, the admiral, slightly deaf in both ears, had already seized the letter and perused its contents. 'So, Frederick,' he interposed comfortably, so that Wentworth paused mid-speech to Anne. 'What do you make of the news?' The admiral was quite composed, so much acquainted with years of practice in the first alarms of war and letters of summons that he could not but remain unmoved at the idea of another battle. 'I judge that Malcolm's new appointment to Rear Admiral by Wellington was a wise one, and if he is posted up to London so soon after his return, I am persuaded they will give him plenty to do. He is a capital kind of man, quite well enough acquainted with the rigours of working with the army to assist with supporting the Allies. I wonder though, what is the Duke's aim; I suppose they might send the navy to Martinique or perhaps to Europe, although what good can be done by a presence there I cannot tell.'

'Pardon me, Admiral, but I believe the scheme of offering assistance will require Wellington's presence in Ghent or Brussels; on that score, I collect you may be right, Sophie.' He glanced at his sister. 'Bonaparte's advance toward Belgium must be considered a decided threat to that city.'

Anne turned to her husband. 'And we have expected this summons ever since Bonaparte's escape from Elba; I am not overcome by surprise, Frederick. We two will be well looked after, whatever this may mean for the next few months.' She ran a hand self-consciously over her dress, smoothing the fabric over her belly. To his eye, there was the merest hint of a roundedness that he had not seen before, but to others it must be yet invisible.

Wentworth gave his wife the singular glance that only a besotted husband, newly to be a father, can give. 'You must promise me to take care of yourself, and our child. I wish fervently that I did not have to go away—'

Mrs Croft stopped him mid-sentence. 'I despise to hear you talk of Anne as if she were a delicate creature, Frederick, unable to stand an absence of a few months,' she scolded him affectionately. 'Of course, it is always the way with us navy wives, is it not Anne, that there will be a *little* anxiety, but we are made of sturdier stuff than what could only suffer calm waters; I shall be here, and Uppercross not so far distant, and I vouch that the time will pass quickly enough until we welcome you back, brother! Meanwhile, let us not alarm Anne unduly, especially in her delicate condition, for it is but a trifle of news that need not alarm anyone to a great degree until we have just cause to feel it!'

'Sophie, you are quite right,' said her brother placatingly, 'and I still have no definite orders, nor a set departure date, although I apprehend it cannot be long, with this summoning of Malcom. They mean to support the action in some way, and it cannot be more than a day or so before I am called away, I think!'

'Let us hope that the action, whatever form it takes, will be swift and sure then,' added the admiral. 'My dear,' he said, turning to his wife, 'It would be best to delay this scheme of going up to Bath, until we hear where Frederick is to be stationed, don't you agree?'

'Oh,' cried Anne in quick embarrassment to give such trouble, 'pray don't let my husband's impending orders prevent you from taking the waters at Bath, Admiral; you know how they do you good! I could go to Mary, or really, I am quite well enough to remain at Kellynch, until your return!'

'Nonsense, Anne,' cried Mrs Croft kindly, 'we wouldn't hear of going away to leave you alone, and besides, it will only be small delay, until things are settled, and then you might come with us, perhaps! Or we might all go into Shropshire, since my brother Edward has been quite forceful in his entreaties to visit him and Catherine and the new baby. Anne must come with us — I do favour Bath for the admiral's gout — but wherever we are, Frederick, Anne will always have a home, be assured of that!'

His sister was all amiable condescension, all sisterly affection. Wentworth received her assurances gratefully and told her so. 'It is too bad though, to be called away at such a time—' he said, thinking of Anne's impending confinement.

Mrs Croft would not be put off. 'Pray don't think on it, Frederick, we look upon Anne quite as our own family, you know; it would be unthinkable to leave her behind here. No, she shall go to Bath when and if we are satisfied that you are stationed safely wherever you shall be sent.'

Wentworth joined with Anne in giving them his thanks again, and not for the first time had reason to be grateful his sister and the Admiral had offered them a home until the threat of war had passed and he and Anne could purchase a cosy establishment of their own. Now, more than ever, it occurred to him the good in the scheme, for Anne would be close to Uppercross and could have the daily care and attention of her own sister during her confinement. He was both excited by the thought of being a father, and naturally anxious, and his sister's being present to support Anne would be a vast relief to his mind as he went to war once again.

'It quite escaped my mind, but I have had a letter from Mary this morning,' said Anne, breaking into her husband's thoughts. 'Poor Henrietta has come over with a bad cold; it is very bad luck so soon after the wedding, poor girl, and Mary is convinced she will catch it,' she added, suppressing a smile. 'Perhaps I might invite Mary and the children to come here for a few days, if you will say yes, Mrs Croft,' she added, 'It might do Mary good to have a change of environment. All the excitement of change has belonged to everyone else these last weeks, and I think my sister feels as if she has been left out a little.'

Mrs Croft was gracious. 'Why of course, Anne! This is just as much your home as it is ours, and you must know you can never stand on ceremony with us, can she Matthew, or we would be quite offended! You must ask your sister and the children to come away here, before we make for Bath, if we go at all, of course.'

Wentworth said with amusement, 'I collect that your sister has had all the excitement of the Musgrove sisters' double wedding, and a large breakfast, to give her some not so *very* insignificant object to attend lately.'

'Yes, my dear,' replied Anne, 'but you know how Mary disapproves both the matches; I think she still feels it keenly that Henrietta married a country curate instead of a captain.' Her eyes danced.

'Aye, it would be wonderful indeed, if every woman was as fortunate,' he laughed.

'And Louisa Benwick is in Lyme with her husband and the Harvilles, I believe?' reminded Mrs Croft. 'Then your sister must want for company. I collect it will be dull enough at Uppercross for her to welcome a little change of scenery.'

Admiral Croft inclined his head and added his own earnest entreaties to invite them at once, and Wentworth, who was applied to by his sister, agreed it was a good scheme, for it would distract Anne from the thought that he was to go away soon.

'Then I shall write my reply,' answered Anne, 'and invite them as soon as they can come.'

Later, when they retired to bed, Anne sat up against the pillows with her husband. 'I shall enjoy a visit from Mary and the children. Your sister is so very kind, but I confess I shall miss you terribly when you are called away. The children, I am sure, will be a great distraction.'

Wentworth, knowing Mary Musgrove to sometimes be missing those little touches of sensitive kindness toward her older sibling said, 'Don't forget that Sophie is as much your sister now as she is mine! And Edward a brother! You shall meet him in due course. I hope Mary treats you with more than the usual amount of civility and kindness now that you will both have something more in common than only a mother and father!'

'I am afraid, as much as I dearly love my sister, she will take as little pleasure in my condition as she has done in her own! To Mary, bearing children is an inconvenience! But even if my sister is neglectful, I shall barely regard it, for I will have the dear children, and in them I shall have real affection and an object of interest and amusement. Yes, they shall do me good, I collect!'

Wentworth took her hand earnestly. 'I expect orders tomorrow or in the next week at most, but I can only hope, with all my heart, to be home in time to greet our child into the world!'

Anne only squeezed his hand gently, would not weep although she longed to, and leaned over to blow out the candle.

Two

Thursday 1 June, 1815
Bath, Camden-place.

'So, my sister is to provide an heir to the Wentworth name, and so soon after the wedding? Her husband must be congratulating himself. Someone must spend all that head and gun money when he is gone!' A small pause, then, 'Although I am sure my sister's enthusiasm for frugality will never permit them spend _all_ of his fortune! Well, her news comes none too soon, since he must, I am sure, be called to sea again within the month, perhaps never to return!'

Elizabeth's tone was brittle, the extent of her good humour reached too quickly these days at the mention of her sister. Like a wounded ship, she was listing sadly under the wrecking losses she had recently suffered. To her it was a sharp and painful wound to her pride that her sister — dull, mouse-like Anne — had managed to increase her consequence in the world by snaring a Captain Frederick Wentworth with twenty-five thousand pounds and the likelihood of, at the very least, a knighthood, bestowed within a year or two, should he further distinguish himself in the navy. Surely, the man could not gain a _baronetcy_? These new-made creations were nothing with _her_, hardly worth anything, compared to an hereditary baronetcy, but even so, the irony of the situation which now pressed upon her so forcibly made her tone less than warm when she spoke of her sister.

The assumptions which she had so long nurtured, being the older sister and with so much more *right* to a rich husband than Anne, had turned on her viciously. The thought of the fast-approaching danger of her thirty-second birthday snapped at her heels like a little lap-dog too long enduring its master, shocking in its sudden ferocity. The alarming notion of spinsterhood, which she had confidently relinquished on the re-emergence of Mr Elliot many months ago, now tormented her cruelly when she was alone, and more so in the last few weeks, since she had been further humiliated to learn of the shocking marriage of her former friend, Mrs Penelope Clay, to that same scheming, odious gentleman! *Mrs Clay!* The same Mrs Clay who, in company at least, had always reprobated inequality among the ranks! Mrs Clay, who knew her position, and never forgot who she was! Mrs Clay, who could never have been reckoned handsome in her life, with her jutting tooth and unbecoming freckles!

The knowledge of all this had taken its toll not only on Elizabeth's humour but even upon her looks. She was haggard and drawn; she feared it, and she knew it to be so, although her father kindly insisted that she was as handsome as ever, and she daily resented that while *she* had suffered, Anne had only increased in good looks and prettiness.

Lady Russell sat with Elizabeth and Sir Walter in the drawing room at Camden-place, as she did most mornings on her way to the Pump-room. For herself, she could not summon enough of her usual good nature to agree with Elizabeth's remarks on Anne's good news. It was not that she did not feel keenly Elizabeth's disappointments. Lady Russell had made it a point to afford special attention to Elizabeth since the news of Mr Elliot's cowardly defection, as she liked to think of it with angry satisfaction. She fancied herself needed, now more than ever, at Camden-place. Elizabeth had suffered a great deal, her sadly wanting spirits a testimony to the rigours her pride and heart had been forced to endure. It had been shocking, vastly shocking indeed, to hear of Mrs Clay's marriage to Mr Elliot, so soon after they had run off together to London, but Lady Russell privately could guess how Mrs Clay's particular form of cunning had won through, how the lady might have brought persuasion to bear on a man whose vanity and scheming had made it a first object to retain the title he had coming to him by whatever means at his disposal. Even if it meant marrying his competition!

She and Anne had spoken of it privately at the time, out of Sir Walter and Elizabeth's hearing, for the sake of Elizabeth's feelings. Anne, not able to bring herself to open maliciousness, said little on the subject, but Lady Russell was disdainful.

'Mrs Clay has long understood the art of pleasing, and made herself indispensable to your sister and father; you saw it as plainly as did I, and now, I perceive there is no want of understanding with her, for she has, I vouchsafe to say, likely threatened to marry your father unless Elliot gives her the protection of his name, and Kellynch for her daughters. They will have a son, of course, and they will all be provided for. Just as she long planned it, I am certain!'

'I wonder at it,' replied Anne doubtfully, 'for it will be a match filled with mistrust and disharmony — he cannot love her, I think. It is, I am persuaded, a great evil indeed to make a such a marriage connection; to remedy evil with another evil — it cannot bring any good!'

Lady Russell sighed. 'Perhaps they will each be satisfied with their lot; he does not lose Kellynch, and she may be satisfied enough with her new situation in life as to make her tolerably content.'

Now, however, despite her loyal tendency to owe Elizabeth's feelings everything that was due them as the oldest daughter of her dear departed friend, Lady Russell found herself having to turn away angrily for a moment at Elizabeth's callous remarks concerning Anne. She was almost prompted to remind Elizabeth that it was Anne's *frugality,* her good sense and desire for economy, which had done its best to spare the family the degradation of debtorship, before they were forced to exchange Kellynch for Bath. To have her own dear Anne, her estimable, worthy Anne, so little thought of by her family, was a sore aggravation to Lady Russell's heart. But detecting in Elizabeth's tone a note of desperation, and feeling all that was right and just for Sir Walter's spurned and disappointed daughter, Lady Russell let pass the vexation she felt on behalf of Anne, and the callous suggestion that Wentworth's demise at sea might be imminent.

Instead, after a moment or two, she said placatingly, 'Her mother's steady influence while she was alive has always inclined Anne to a greater economy than might be called for in some with such a happy fortune to spend, but I would rather have it that way than any other; they will be comfortable, but without, I think, the pomp and circumstance of those in a more elevated situation and a greater consequence in the world. Wentworth is a steady, sensible man; he is not likely to allow his large fortune to alter his good sense, or his civility to all, nor his amiable and excellent character! These qualities, I am persuaded, must be made only more worthy by his wife's frugality — they will live within their means and in accordance with his natural, modest consequence, notwithstanding her own rank as an Elliot. It would be most disturbing if they were to live as if his station in life were more elevated than it was. Do you not agree, Sir Walter?'

'Gentlemen of the navy,' observed Sir Walter coolly from his position on the sofa opposite, 'often have the most liberal notions of their own importance in general. Of course, my son in law might be found exempt from such a criticism for now, but should he receive a knighthood, I should not like to wager that they will not immediately be buying up a house in Laura-place, or procuring acquaintance among the very best circles. Not that but my daughter, being an Elliot, should be below such circles, and Wentworth by association may bless his good fortune and look forward to perhaps more elevated company to that which he has been used, on account of his alliance with the Elliot name.'

Lady Russell barely kept her countenance at this misrepresentation of Wentworth's character, but solicitous for Anne's being favourably thought of especially in absentia, and desirous for the acknowledgement of happy news of a child on the way, she felt it her duty to solicit the proper feeling and comments due from the family, which she could then honestly convey in a return letter to Anne. It was not much, but she wished for Anne to believe herself sometimes thought of in Camden-place, even if such thoughts were obliged out of them, in the manner of squeezing juice from a very unripe lemon!

Despite her indignation on Anne's behalf, she therefore turned back to Sir Walter with a countenance composed. Speaking with the delicacy of an intimate family friend, and with the well-bred manners required to soothe tempers and hearts of people to whom she had been strongly attached, she gently brought the conversation back to the little Wentworth-to-be.

'It must bring you joy, Sir Walter, to know yourself blessed with a new grandchild.'

'I can hardly count myself lucky, Lady Russell, to know that I am advanced enough in age to be taking a headcount of grandchildren, when I am not yet five-and-fifty years,' replied Sir Walter in chilly tones. 'In all truth, I consider it a deplorable lack of sensitivity on the part of females to shame a father with a hoard of grandchildren before he has reached his fifth decade! However, I must put up with it, I suppose. I hope she will not bring the child here when it is born, for I cannot abide the constant wailing of infants!'

'Now then, Sir Walter,' cried Lady Russell in good humour, 'you must not be so harsh upon females; their job is to produce children — you cannot blame Anne or Mary for answering a perfectly natural inclination!'

'I hold it the very worst of good judgement in Wentworth, to be indulging such inclinations before he has gone away and come back from war — who is to say he will never come home and Anne left a widow with children to support!'

Lady Russell, feeling as if her sensitivities had been quite abused beyond what she could bear, made a barely civil reply, her heart fulminating in her breast. Soon after, the tea things were summoned and the subject which ought to have absorbed them forgotten entirely as if it were merely a fluff-nothing! If poor Anne knew just how little consequence she held with her family when she was absent, Lady Russell was also angrily determined never to make it known to her!

The daily papers were taken up for the arrival notices and soon afterward, a knock at the door disturbed the reading aloud of '"The Annals of Bath" by Sir Walter.

'It must be Miss Crawford. It can only be she, for she promised to come today, before midday, to walk in the Pump-room.' Elizabeth now rose, elegant, composed, smiling, and ready to receive her friend.

Sir Walter stepped to the door himself, all condescending anticipation. He was not to be disappointed, and Lady Russell, who had heard much of the handsome Miss Crawford, lately arrived from London, was now gratified to be able to view her in person.

Miss Crawford, for it was she, was shown into the room. She was attired in rose and cream striped silk and matching bonnet, had an air of assurance about her which was pleasing and a charm which satisfied the discerning taste of Lady Russell. The lady had very pale "English rose" skin which pleasantly opposed her dark, animated eyes and bright, chestnut-auburn hair. The combination was pleasing, and she was acknowledged by Lady Russell to be a beauty, although her style of handsomeness was very different to that of the dark-headed, elegant Elizabeth. Lady Russell in fact considered the newcomer everything agreeable in figure and in address, and found her manners delicate, containing just the right amount of deference to Elizabeth and Sir Walter, without being affected or insincere.

After introductions were made, and the usual civilities exchanged, Miss Crawford seated herself with the familiarity which frequent previous visits invariably incur. 'And how is your cough, Sir Walter? I hope it is much improved? If it is not gone quite away, I shall myself make you up a little elderwine; my aunt's recipe is by far and away superior to any that can be found in Rundell's book! One can add in two or three other herbs and at once its efficacy doubles! Besides,' she added modestly, 'I am quite experienced in making up the few little medicinals and decoctions needed by Henry and me; my mother's sister was something of an expert herself, and I flatter myself I have inherited a modest degree of her talent!'

Sir Walter bowed, and bestowed a condescending thanks. 'I am excessively obliged to you, Miss Crawford; you are too kind, but my own physician, Poole, has provided me with an excellent elixir of his own design; it is a mixture of laudanum, mercury and dark molasses, and whatever other canny medicines he contrives to have put in it. I swear by it for removing almost anything unpleasant. Why, it has quite taken away everything from a sore throat, to freckles and warts, when applied directly to the skin!'

Miss Crawford affected astonishment. 'I can hardly suppose that *you*, Sir Walter, would have suffered from the altering condition of freckles! And certainly not warts! Never! You cannot mean me to believe it! You are too untouched by life, too much in looks! I suppose you must refer to the freckles or warts of some other person?'

Elizabeth at this moment found cause to drop her teacup sharply into its saucer.

Lady Russell, with a wish of altering the conversation to give less pain to at least one of its listeners, interjected soothingly, 'I myself have always preferred Gowland's for the skin. It improves the texture and the colour. The sun is not kind to older women, Miss Crawford, although I hope it may be to you. *You* have all the advantage of youth, and youth has its own kind of beauty. You think not of lines and wrinkles and freckles, and you have many years before you will. But you see how Gowland's has had its effect on me! And the Bath waters, of course, soothe lines and freckles by regular imbibing. I never use anything now but Gowland's and good Bath waters!'

There was a general murmur of polite agreement and Lady Russell considered the moment of danger as passed. Poor Elizabeth would not hear the name "Mrs Clay" ever again, if Lady Russell had it in her means to prevent it!

'And how are your sister, Mrs Grant, and her husband?' enquired Elizabeth coolly, who had never met them, and hoped never to be asked. Miss Crawford's brother-in-law was merely a Dr. Grant, a nobody, although the sister, Mrs Leticia Grant, had enough natural consequence about her to make her a tolerable enough woman, despite her unremarkable relations. 'I hope they continue to enjoy the delights of Bath?'

'They are both very much engaged with visiting Dr. Grant's relations who have just arrived in Bath,' replied Miss Crawford, placidly. 'I have been alone every morning since Wednesday! I was invited to go walking before breakfast with them several times, but I always prefer a quiet morning; none of this walking about early for me! To me, it betrays a kind of rustic sensibility which cannot be pleasing to others who are not used to it, do not you agree, Miss Elliot? I much prefer a quiet, refined morning! I prefer to sit, over walking! But I am wild to see my brother, who arrives tomorrow. Did I mention that my brother is to come to Bath, Miss Elliot? He has been in town, but comes to stay with my sister and Dr. Grant for a few weeks.'

'Oh?' Elizabeth raised a fine brow and said in her cool manner, 'And where does your brother have his seat, Miss Crawford? What is his profession? Is he a gentleman?'

'Why, Miss Elliot, you do not attend me at all,' scolded Miss Crawford laughingly. 'I told you all about my brother only recently! But you are forgiven, for I recollect we were on the promenade at the time, and you were distracted no doubt, by the heat and bustle.'

Elizabeth took the out which had been gracefully offered, and had the wherewithal to try for a look of contrition, but the emotion was foreign to her and unpractised, appeared more like she had swallowed an insect and was contemplating its passage down her insides. Her eyes struggled.

Miss Crawford, however, had forgiven and forgotten the slight. 'Henry has a seat in Norfolk, but I am afraid my brother dislikes any kind of permanence of abode, and can seldom be found there for long. For myself, I much prefer Everingham to town. It is charming in summer and winter alike! However, I perceive, when he marries, which he must do soon,' she added with a careful glance at Elizabeth, 'he will be happy to settle at Everingham with only two or three extended visits per year to town. That is enough to supply every social opportunity a wife might wish for, but with the quiet of the country to return to when the season grows stale. But for now, he has the liberty that the gifts of wealth and singleness together can bestow and is seldom from town.'

'So,' remarked Sir Walter, who had gotten up to stand at the window-box where his figure might be seen to advantage by the room, 'he is man of property and good birth, then? You so often hear of this or that Mr So-and-So, any "Smith" or "Jones", referred to as a "gentleman", and then one discovers upon a short conversation they are no such thing! Perhaps I am too nice, a tad too fastidious, but I feel strongly that a man may only be called a gentleman if he has a title or property, and preferably both, but as to merely a large fortune, one cannot rely only on *that*! Why, in these modern times, where anyone can raise himself up merely by gaining a modest fortune, what is money in the hands of those of inferior breeding but an evil which can do nothing that becomes them and everything to demean them! It gives rise to too many persons of unremarkable birth being raised into positions they were never born to, and makes obscured the clear line which has always existed between gentlemen and working men!'

While Lady Russell murmured indistinctly what may or may not have been a concurrence, Miss Crawford replied calmly, 'Indeed, Sir Walter, I quite agree! But my brother will not disappoint, I think; our father proceeded from the best English stock, and my mother, from some modestly respectable Saxon blood.' Her smile was demure. 'I hope you will allow me to bring Henry to call, for I have told him of you all and he is eager to make your acquaintance.'

Sir Walter looked as if he could easily add that anyone who might call himself a mere Crawford, would thank their good fortune to be acquainted with an Elliot, but was distracted by Lady Russell's reaching forward at that moment to refresh his tea cup from the pot.

'Sugar, Sir Walter? One lump? Allow me... there... and does your brother have a large acquaintance in Bath, Miss Crawford, to bring him here?' enquired Lady Russell as she replaced the tea pot.

'Oh, not a large one at all, Lady Russell,' conceded Miss Crawford blandly, 'only our half-sister Mrs Grant, and one or two others: the Edward-Smythes, and Sir Robert Locke, and the Perrots, and oh, yes, the Kingsmiths. Haro — Henry — was up at Cambridge with eldest Kingsmith boy, and they have always kept the acquaintance up. Do you know Mr Francis Kingsmith, Sir Thomas's older son?'

Elizabeth said faintly, 'We have not yet had the pleasure.'

'For my part,' continued Miss Crawford, 'I require so little for felicity in life — I am content with one or two intimate friends, such as *you*, Miss Elliot, to walk together with in the gardens, and meet in the evenings at assemblies, but my brother is of such an amiable, magnanimous character, that it is difficult for him to keep his acquaintance very small, for he finds everyone as agreeable as himself and declares he must pursue almost every acquaintance he makes!'

'It is fortunate then that he is a gentleman, for that will afford him a natural discernment, which will prompt his desire to preserve the natural order, and separate him from those without any true claim to distinction.' Sir Walter removed from the window and came over to the table.

'Quite so,' remarked Miss Crawford blandly.

Sir Walter was comfortable enough with their great cousin Lady Dalrymple's esteemed attentions to find himself *almost* unmoved by the mention of some of Bath's most venerated company, some of with whom he was only on bowing terms. He had wished to be on terms with the Kingsmiths since he had come to Bath. However, he comforted himself privately with the thought of his cousins, and with the certainty that any association with the brother of Miss Crawford would not mean any disgrace to himself.

He now swept a hand towards the window which overlooked Camden-place and addressed his oldest daughter. 'I perceive it will rain, soon, Elizabeth; if you are to walk, I think you had better go at once! Lady Russell is going to the Pump-room; you had best walk together, under her umbrella; it would be convenient for her to escort you! If you don't object, Lady Russell?'

'Not at all, Sir Walter.'

'You are very kind, Sir Walter,' remarked Miss Crawford who had stood and was arranging her dress. 'By tomorrow, we shall have my brother to escort us; I can speak for him and assure Miss Elliot it will give him the greatest pleasure, for he always is so attentive to these things! Good day, Sir Walter!'

Elizabeth and her friend, arm in arm, were followed from the room by Lady Russell who was not sorry to be going on to her own friends in the Pump-rooms. An hour at Camden-place usually never failed to give her some pleasure, but today the visit had been a source of vexation to her, and the only relief to her feelings was the addition to their company of the genteel Miss Crawford. She hoped great things for the friendship of the two women, for she saw in Miss Crawford and her promised brother a means to bring Elizabeth out of herself, and perhaps into raised spirits by the time a few weeks had passed!

Three

Friday 2 June, 1815

Kellynch Hall.

Anne sat alone upon the bed in her chamber. The last pale sunlight of the day made long shadows through the window dressings. She soberly examined the prospect before her now, of the many weeks, and perhaps months, she might spend at Kellynch without her husband, and felt the sudden and unwelcome pangs of self-derision. Her natural inclination to cheerfulness and even to stoic acceptance she had until now unwisely allowed to overcome any occasional thoughts of what a long absence would mean for her as a naval captain's wife. Such an inclination to think only of the good and to repress the worries and anxieties which might be attendant upon any separation, and especially one in which personal danger represented an additional threat, had protected her from considering the real effects of such a separation so soon after their union.

She had been foolish to think her strength and forbearance would be enough to carry her through such an absence! When she had been propositioned to change her name to Wentworth, sailor's wife, she had not given the ramifications of such a role any serious thought. She had assumed herself equal to the position it put her in, that duty to her husband and to her country would be enough to fortify her, and she had comforted herself in any private moments of misgiving, that she might even follow her husband to sea, just as Mrs Croft had done. But her pregnancy had prevented such a scheme, and now her usual tendency to cheerful acceptance trembled weakly at the prospect of months without the man she loved at her side. She could only find comfort in the promise made to herself, most fervently, to avoid such self-delusion in the future.

Frederick had left that morning, having received his orders the previous afternoon, the very same day on which they had received the letter from the war office, and just as suddenly as the letter had come, she had bid him tenderly goodbye, and kissed him perhaps for the last time. Mrs Croft and the admiral were extremely solicitous, so very kind in their comforting her, and they bid her several times during the day not to be anxious. But the look in Wentworth's eye, the regret he felt to be leaving her, and in such a state, would not soon be dismissed from her memory.

She was interrupted from this reverie by a gentle knock at the door, and one of the housemaids looked in. 'Pardon me, Ma'am, but Mrs Croft desires me to say young Dr. Thorpe has examined the admiral and is gone away again, and that Mr Shepherd and his wife are come.'

She sighed. Were they constantly to be reminded of the unfortunate events of the last months? She did not feel equal to a meeting with the Shepherds just now, but she said quietly, 'Thank you, Liza. Please tell Mrs Croft I will be down shortly.'

She waited until the girl had gone away and went to the glass. Her eyes were not too much reddened from her earlier tears, and she was pleased to see a tolerably calm countenance. She would not like to give her sister-in-law more anxiety than she already had caused. She tucked a stray dark hair behind her ear and descended the stairs, resigned to a half hour of conversation where she would have been happier to be alone to contemplate the evils of deliberate ignorance!

Mr Shepherd was a civil, courteous man, and had been her father's lawyer for many years. Although he was timid in the presence of Sir Walter, and had a tendency to be persuaded quickly to whatever the prevailing opinion of Sir Walter and his eldest daughter might be at that moment, he was kind hearted and sensible. Despite his tendency to obsequiousness, his deference for both Sir Walter and his daughters was not studied or affected, but born of a real desire to serve the family, and these attributes together had increased Anne's estimation of him as time went by. He was a quiet, unassuming gentleman, and although his daughter had brought much evil to the family, and done her sister a great mischief, Anne found that she could not hold the father responsible for the sins of the daughter.

On receiving the news of his daughter's change of abode from her father's residence to a prestigious London residence under the name of William Elliot, Mr Shepherd had been astonished and mortified. Once the shock of Mrs Clay's defection from the ranks of the Elliots had subsided, a sober Mr Shepherd had hastened to Bath for an audience with Sir Walter. He had made his abject apologies and had assured Sir Walter and Miss Elliot that he had never guessed Penelope's object, and was nothing but provoked and mortified by the events of the last weeks. Sir Walter had maintained a wounded silence on the matter, but Elizabeth, who had been many times forced to defend her former friend's motives with great indignance, suffered vastly in having been proven wrong after all, and it was some time before she could condescend to admit Mr Shepherd at Camden-place without feeling a strong resentment.

Anne privately agreed with her older sister's sentiments, shared when they were alone, and comprehended all the shame that her sister must have suffered. Only with something approaching a great force of bitterness and regret could Anne think of *that woman*, the same Mrs Clay who had insinuated herself into her sister's affections and trust, as the future mistress of Kellynch!

She put this thought aside now however, and was able to meet both Mr Shepherd and his wife with a gentle, welcoming smile and accept their polite enquiries into the health of her father and sister.

'I thank you, I believe they are both well. I had a letter last week and understand that my father is much taken up at the moment with our cousins in Laura-place, and a new acquaintance that Elizabeth has made and which keeps her busy.'

'Oh, yes,' inserted the always congenial Mrs Croft, 'I am eager to hear more of this new person that engages your father and sister so fully. I hear this Miss Crawford is very handsome, and lively in character. Your sister's last letter, which you read to me Anne, induces me to think your sister so much more herself since meeting this paragon!'

'I am vast glad to hear it,' sighed the tiny figure of Mrs Shepherd from the sofa where she sat with Mrs Croft. 'I hope after her dreadful disappointment — well!' She stopped mid-sentence, struggled admirably, then began again. 'I do hope that her spirits are soon much improved — I always find myself that amiable company and plenty of engagements are the very thing to take one's mind from one's troubles.'

'I have just been telling the admiral the very same thing,' exclaimed Mrs Croft, ready and eager to smooth the way, 'Now, that young man who was just here, the new doctor, agrees with me that my poor husband would be much improved by a visit to Bath, not only for the good the waters always do him, but to take his mind from his poor leg!'

Mrs Shepherd concurred. 'That may be true, Mrs Croft, but do you think you ought to take advice from such a young medical man as Dr. Thorpe? I hear he is merely a year from his studies and brings from town the most questionable methods! My sister says he treated her fever last month, not with leeches and calomel, but with ice baths, and strictly forbade alcohol! Heaven knows what he might recommend for the poor admiral's suffering!'

Admiral Croft, who had been sitting with his bandaged limb elevated by an elegant ottoman stool, managed to look cheerful despite his discomfort. 'I have great confidence in Thorpe, Mrs Shepherd. He seems a well-informed gentleman by all means, and I fear nothing in his cure, which was no more sinister than an order to rest and a ban on cook's rich sauces! Aye, Sophie, it is true that a month in Bath always does me good, if only the getting there did not half kill me!' He laughed good-naturedly. 'After thirty-four years at sea, I shall never become used to travelling by horse-power!'

'But it must be worth the journey, when such friends might be met with as take one's mind entirely away from the worries and cares of the day!' Mr Shepherd kindly remonstrated from his place next to Anne on the chaise.

Anne concurred, reflecting on the wisdom of that thought in application to herself and she resolved that this very day she would delay no longer but write to Mary, to invite her and the children to stay. Her young nephews would be just the cure for her own low spirits.

With Mrs Shepherd and the Crofts now engaged in a discussion of diversions of Bath, Mr Shepherd addressed Anne again in a low voice. 'Pardon me for mentioning it, and do not answer if it pains you, but I feel very much for you at present, Mrs Wentworth, for this new and sudden situation in which you find yourself, for to be alone and separated from one's husband must be barely tolerable to one so newly married. Pray, where is Captain Wentworth gone to be stationed, and from which port does he sail?'

'Thank you. You are very kind to think of it,' she replied warmly. 'But it gives me little pain to speak of it, only a very *little* anxiety! My husband is gone to embark from Deal, but not for some days, he thinks. He is awaiting more detailed orders, but I believe he will equip two ships and man them fully before they sail, at Rear Admiral Malcolm's orders. They expect to sail in a week's time.'

'I see! Well, you have some very good friends to keep you busy,' Mr Shepherd remarked helpfully. 'Perhaps you might go up to Sir Walter and your sister, presently? Just now Bath is in very good looks, upon my word! There is nothing so cheering as a view of Bath in the summer, with the wonderful chimneys and spires in relief against the green hills behind!'

Anne could only smile faintly, and turn her attention to the others. She would not, if she could at all help it, go to Bath for a kingdom! Especially without her husband, the only person who could render Bath a pleasant experience for her. With Frederick by her side, she thought she should enjoy anything at all! But, without Frederick, Bath was a dreary place for her. While the town itself was barely tolerable enough, a return to her family was a return to all the things she disliked most, and besides, Bath had never been kind to her, except to bring her a captain!

That she had been in Bath at school when her Mama had passed away did nothing these days to enamour her of the place. And her father's house in Camden-place, where he and her sister were now so happily settled, wanted in the comforts that would make Anne completely satisfied. While her father and Elizabeth took pride in fine drawing rooms, in the style of the fitting up and in every modern addition, and especially in their having so much consequence in Bath as cousins of Lady Dalrymple, Anne felt her wishes and needs were situated entirely in an opposing view of things. She wanted quiet where her family wanted engagements, she wished for cosy fittings over the large, cold drawing rooms of Camden-place, and she yearned for musical evenings and the theatre, whereas *their* every delight was in large assemblies and card parties and parading in the Pump-rooms. Living at Camden-place, she thought, was akin to sitting on a very hard chair, with a prickly wool cushion beneath her. She could fidget and adjust the chair tolerably, but she would never be truly comfortable!

The Shepherds left them an hour later, and Anne was able to spend an hour at the pianoforte, then to retire to her room to dress for dinner. She looked, she thought, unusually solemn in her dark green silk as the reflection in her glass stared back at her. Sighing, she pulled out her writing desk, penned a note to Mary and sealed it, and gave it to the footman to see away to post. Then she made her way down to the dining room.

It was a lonely meal they made that evening, their usual merry little party now reduced by one. Admiral and Mrs Croft made special efforts to distract and entertain Anne, the admiral by encouraging her to take some of his madeira, the pride of his cellar by way of its having passed over the equator 'thrice, my dear, thrice; I suppose I may be a proud fellow but Sophie agrees it is the best she has tasted yet!', and Mrs Croft by talking of what might be done to amuse Mary and her children.

'I think a party could be organised for a picnic, since the weather has been so agreeable.' Mrs Croft consulted her husband, then in worried tones remarked, 'But Anne, do you think it too hot to be outdoors? We must not have you fainting, or I will discharge my duty to my brother very poorly! But do write to your sister immediately and desire her to come on Sunday. It is only three miles, although I admit it will be a vast poor hour in the carriage, with two lively boys, but she might put them up with the driver, to everyone's satisfaction.'

'Perhaps not to *everyone's* satisfaction,' remarked Anne thinking of the poor driver with a smile. Although she loved her nephews, she had a sound knowledge of their propensity for mischief. 'I wrote to Mary before dinner. I daresay she will come at once, given that she dropped large hints that she wished to be invited. But I do hope you would tell me if the children are too much,' she added anxiously, 'for with the admiral's gout—'

'Nonsense, my dear,' interrupted the admiral himself. 'I am not so unwell that you must alter your plans for my sake. Sophie and I welcome the patter of small feet. Do we not, my dear? Having none of our own children makes us more amenable, I daresay, to having other peoples' around us! It will bring some life to the place to have the young 'uns running about! That young Charles is a fine, uncommon lively lad!'

'Yes my dear, but you insist upon making them seasick by jogging them about on your knee until they threaten to cast up their accounts!' scolded his wife.

Anne was about to venture a suggestion that the children not be permitted to eat quite so much cake before such a rolling voyage on the admiral's knee, when the sound of a horse and rider insinuated itself into the quiet evening air, paused, then after some fuss at the front door, could be heard departing again at speed, into the night.

Mrs Croft raised a lively brow and said, 'I do hope nothing alarming has happened!' to which Anne could say nothing, taken by surprise herself, and assailed suddenly by no small amount of anxiety on account of her absent husband. Moments later, Robertson the footman appeared silently, a letter on a salver in his hand, which he presented not to the admiral, but to Anne herself.

'Thank you, George. Oh, it is addressed to Frederick! I think, Admiral, I must open it, since it came by such urgent delivery. Do you not agree, Mrs Croft?'

The admiral assured her she must stand on no ceremony with them, but open the letter immediately.

'Certainly, you must open it, my dear,' similarly urged Mrs Croft. 'I fear it is something alarming; who would be sending letters at this hour unless—'

But Anne had already lifted the wax and opened it up. 'Oh,' she cried in astonishment, 'it is not from Frederick at all, Mrs Croft, but is from your brother, Mr Edward Wentworth, in Shropshire! How odd! But the direction is to Frederick! Oh, I see! Your brother addresses his letter to Frederick, thinking he is present at Kellynch.'

'Well, do go ahead, my dear, and read it, for the admiral and I are agog to hear what my brother can mean by sending such an urgent message at this time of night!'

Anne skimmed, then read aloud:

> *Hawton House, Shropshire*
> *1 June 1815*

> '*My dear Frederick,*
> *You will forgive me the impertinence of such an urgent delivery, but I hoped to catch you before you were called away for the sake of King and Country; I pray I am not too late, or else I regret that I must beg dear Sophie and the venerable Mrs Wentworth for an audience in my brother's place. Sophie, I am sure, will understand at once how it is with me!*
> *As you know, my daughter Julia, from that most foolish first marriage of my youth, is the only consolation I have had over these lonely years, the only comfort I have had in losing her mother so young. I admit to my foolishness, in marrying when I ought to have waited, but Julia has been the joy in a joyless life, that is, until my dear Catherine came to me.*
> *When Cathy and I married a year ago, Julia resented the union bitterly and as you know, I sent her away to a good school in London, thinking the*

distance would finally soften the resentment which had risen between us.

But, a fool I am twice! Not only does my daughter tease me cruelly with an absence of that correspondence which she would once have never denied me, but now I hear reports of her being in frequent company with those beneath her, and worse, that she has been accused of climbing out of the window of her dormitory in the evenings, to attend establishments which are less than reputable, in the company of ladies who ought not be called such! I fear, Frederick, that Julia is much like her mother in temperament, more so perhaps than I had ever suspected. The school matron is beside herself and demands Julia be taken away immediately.

I cannot bring her home to Shropshire, for I fear that will cause a rift as will never be mended and such an atmosphere would be injurious to the baby and to Cathy. I ask, I beseech you, as her uncle and aunts, will you post to London directly and bring her at once to Kellynch, until such time as I can come into Somersetshire and try to win back her familial affections?

This is much to ask, and yet, from brother to brother, I ask it, in the name of the blood which binds us. Catherine is still in such delicate health from her lying in that I cannot leave her and the new child; my only hope lies with you, Frederick, if I am not too late, or with the good Admiral Croft and my sister Sophie, begging the pardon of Mrs Wentworth, on whom this untenable situation must have an effect also.

Write to me immediately, with your assurances that my Julia will be safe, at least, from herself, or I ought to say, from ruining her own character before she is eighteen!

Ever your devoted brother
E. W.

Four

Friday 2 June, 1815
Williams-street, Bath.

'How do I look, Mim? Well enough to impress your Miss Elliot, do you think?'

'Mmmm.' From behind him, Mary's slender arms reached around his neck and shoulders and used the reflection in the glass to guide her hands as she readjusted his cravat. Her hands were white, the milky skin softer than a child's, Henry thought idly, as they grazed the skin of his cheek. Capable. The hands that could do so much.

He submitted to her adjustments for moment, then spun around and caught the same hands. 'Well, sister of mine, will I do? Stop fussing!' She smiled archly, but allowed her hands to remain in his grasp. How much like a silky, purring cat she was, he thought, eyeing the self-satisfied look in her green eyes.

Indeed, Mary Crawford did feel excessively satisfied with her current situation. For one thing, she had succeeded in throwing off another of her sister's kind and well-intentioned schemes of marrying her off to one or other of Dr. Grant's low acquaintance in Bath or town, and all of whom were quite without countenance or air or elegance. The latest possibility was to be the beneficiary of a fine estate. It would so obviously be, her sister Leticia had exclaimed, an excellent match, since the young man in question was to be so rich eventually. Besides which, he was tolerably well-looking, and there could be no objection to his decent, if obscure, family.

But what had been obvious to one sister was not to the other. It was not that she was opposed to her sister's looking out for a suitable match; no, it was Mary's decided object to marry, provided she could marry well and to someone who would give her no aggravation over those little necessities for her felicity such as freedom to go up to Everingham as much as she wished. No, she wished to marry; indeed, it was now *necessary*, but she only differed in her sister's choice as to the rank and character of the intended. She should not be able to tolerate anyone ridiculous, however lenient a husband he might prove! And the latest nomination, the ridiculous Mr Dalbyston, a bob-wigging, obsequious tea merchant, had neither rank and consequence, nor the elegance she required. Her sister deemed it necessary for a beau to possess only a modest fortune and a tolerably handsome face, but Miss Mary Crawford, having as much money as she wished to last her a life time, and regarding a handsome countenance as second in importance to rank and a certain elegance of dress and carriage, could not agree with some of her sister's suggested victims. Either of the Bertram brothers might have done the job agreeably — but she was too late there — she had let herself slip and it was regrettable, but there were plenty more fish in the ocean.

No, the notion of matrimony suited her purpose — it had become a necessity, to supress the murmurs which had followed herself and Haro for some time, but she would not scrimp on her choices or hasten along the natural scheme of things for the sake of necessity; she would certainly have everything she wished in good time. A new scheme had, just recently, presented itself to her mind, and her mind, being of an indulgent nature when it came to entertaining her own ideas, admitted the notion with interest and toyed with it, until it had settled firmly; this was the very thing that would suit her after all. Now she shared this notion with her brother.

'I have decided on a definite scheme of matrimony for myself. I think I will try for Sir Walter,' she informed him, pulling her hands from his and checking her hair in the glass. '*You* may have the daughter. I have thought about it Haro, a great deal, and it answers things very nicely. You shall not want the little fortune which passes to Miss Elliot, for you are as rich as Croesus yourself and have Everingham, and I have my twenty thousand. And I feel I am quite safe from the tediousness of a long marriage since I cannot think Sir Walter Elliot very far removed from his grave, if one notes how he indulges in port and rich things; you will notice when you go there how the colour of his skin is very disagreeable and waxy. A sure sign of rot in the liver! If I cannot have a Bertram, I shall have an Elliot! I think a little setup in Bath will suit me very well once he is gone. I fancy I shall be quite amusing as "Lady Elliot."

She tried on the name for size in the glass, and considering her reflection a moment, said, 'I collect it suits me, does it not?'

'Do not ask me that!' remarked a laughing Henry. 'You know I cannot offer an unbiased opinion! I own my jealously will make me say it shouldn't suit you at all, even though the title has an elegant ring to it!'

Mary smiled an arch smile and contemplated her reflection. 'Pray don't forget that we are to attend the theatre with the Elliots next week. Keep every evening free, for Miss Elliot has not given a firm date.'

'I delight in the theatre!' he cried gaily. 'It amuses me. When I am at the theatre, I feel as if I could play any part just as well as the actors. I fancy myself saying the lines along with the players only with so much more spirit and finesse!'

'You were born to act, my darling boy, but remember the Elliots are overnice about such things and only attend because of their cousins. You must find the theatre a bore, and below you,' she admonished.

'True. Never fear, I shall play my part exceedingly well, I fancy. But tell me dear sis,' continued Henry in a teasing tone, 'how should you like being married to a "crusty old Baronet" as you put it? Won't you find it disagreeable after a time?'

'Oh, it hardly signifies at all, for our time together will no doubt be very short.' Her eyes met Henry's and slid away again. She fingered a trinket on the dressing table idly.

He was suddenly serious. 'Do you really think it wise, Mim? — especially after Mansfield — you said yourself he is all but in an early grave.' Mary did not reply and after a moment he added, 'If you have decided firmly, then I cannot persuade you otherwise, so long as it doesn't make a pudding of my own chances.'

'Why should it?' Her tone was offhand, but there was a hint of vinegar. She picked up one of his snuff boxes from the table and idly turned it over. 'This is pretty.'

He smiled a half smile. 'Why, I believe it is *you* who is jealous!' he drawled. 'Don't, pray, break that snuff-box. It is a great favourite of mine.'

Replacing the snuff box carefully, she did not answer immediately, then said calmly after a moment, 'Of course I'm not jealous. Don't be ridiculous. Why, ought I to be?'

'No, indeed! You know how I adore and revere you!' He reached for her hand, but she moved away a little. He sighed. 'But this scheme of yours — it won't be quite the same with us, and I couldn't bear—' He broke off.

'No. It won't be the same. Not exactly. But we both know what we must do.'

'But, does anything really *need* to change? Don't make yourself anxious, Mim. You know I regard you as superior to all other females.' His tone was cajoling, charming. 'Nothing can *truly* come between us, you know.' This time she allowed her hand to be caught and he kissed it tenderly.

Placated, she gave a little laugh. 'I really am not jealous, Haro; why you should think it I have no notion. Why, you shall marry Miss Elliot and I shall be happy here in Bath. Nothing else need change. You may expect me as a constant visitor to Everingham, for while I am married, I shall preserve the best marital felicity by being as absent as I can from the person of my husband!'

'You know I want you to be at Everingham as often as you can come! I can't really do without you, you know,' he added coaxingly. 'What will dear Leticia say when you tell her you are engaged to Sir Walter?'

'Does it signify? At any rate I shan't scruple to break it gently, not when she would have me marry the most preposterous assortment of ill-qualified bachelors in town. She is still quite determined that I play up to Dalbyston! As if I need stoop to looking at a tradesman's son, however wealthy he might be. I own I am tired of fending off her efforts. It will satisfy me to have done with all that, at least.'

'I wonder she doesn't try for *me*, with all the exertion she has put forth on your own account! If I wasn't so guileless myself, I would suspect a very unsisterly lack of attentiveness!'

He was laughing, and she shook her head. 'I know you could feel more tenderness than you do for her, but on that score, I forgive you for I am persuaded that there lies a mutual share of that same cool sentiment in the bosom of our half-sister! She is by far too ready to bestow her good nature on anyone only half deserving of it, even *you*, Haro! But she is too nice on account of your recent history, and you too naughty, for a perfect good understanding and agreement between you both,' she scolded. 'Your share of that burden must be to smooth things over as much as you are able, and hers must be to make allowances.' She became grave. 'This talk, Haro, must be dampened, or we shall both suffer the consequences of being thrown out of good society, and I have no intention of spending the rest of my life without balls and society dinners!'

'I concede, dearest girl, I do, and I am as anxious for your balls and dinners as I am for my own. Only I detest the notion of having my freedom curtailed, just to please society!'

'You have only yourself to blame if you feel that way, but we cannot leave it any longer — talk is rife. You have been too careless, Haro. For myself, I care very little about what you choose to do in town, so long as it is to *me* you return; in *that* regard you may certainly call me jealous — but you must not be so open about your — vices — to others.'

'Oh,' replied Henry carelessly, 'I shall be more circumspect in Bath, of course; society is more intimate here. But it don't signify what I do in town. I am a red-blooded male, after all!'

'The admiral's bad habits are wiping off on you,' replied his sister scoldingly, returning again to the glass and absently tucking away a stray tendril of hair. 'I cannot think it to your advantage to allow your manners and habits to be contaminated by his own immoral scruples.' She turned to face him. 'No, I see you disagree, but I have said before, you are blinded by loyalty! Being a flirt is one thing, and I see the amusement in a little heart breaking, especially if the objects are young and unformed in their opinions of the male sex; it will do them no material harm, I collect! But Haro, you must beware of becoming too much like the admiral. I know you revere him in a way I cannot, but you see how our uncle is now thrown off by the best of society; his reputation precedes him and I fear it may do the same with you. It is the nature of people to find an unaccountable delight in the dirty laundry of their neighbours; if we do not put a stop to such gossip, it will be your downfall and mine! You must hasten to marry at once, or at most in the next twelve-month!'

Henry, who was indeed blinded to his uncle's immoral ways and had allowed more than a few of his attitudes to pervade his own thinking, felt slightly aggrieved at this attack on their relative. But though Admiral Crawford had been like a father to him, his loyalty was even more attached to the sister who had been everything to him. He reached for his snuff-box and began to prepare a pinch.

'The admiral has his faults, Mim, I agree, but few people would have given me my way half so much as he, and I am grateful for it. And I am not nearly so bad as he,' Henry added carelessly, his eyes watering as he took up the snuff from his hand, 'for I have never installed a mistress openly as he does; I fancy myself a tad more circumspect even if you do not. And if I have broken a heart or two, can you not agree they deserved it, just a little, for being so ready and so willing to be drawn in? Snuff?'

'Like Fanny Price? Or the scullery maid at Mansfield Park?' She adjusted her lace in the glass, then turned and shook her head at the little ivory box Henry held out. 'At any rate, that is nothing to the point, you know! You might be forgiven for being thought an outrageous rake, Haro, but it all the same it would be doing *me* a vast disservice to have Mansfield follow us to Bath! How inconvenient to be obliged to change my scheme now that I have formed it! It wouldn't do!'

'We are fortunate to be admitted in Camden-place; let us hope the talk never reaches Bath! Good old Letty is not one to gossip, I am sure. And I am sure she does not guess *all* our secrets or we

—

would neither of us be admitted. But still, we must be careful. I only hope that damned maid has enough sense to keep quiet!' he added.

'I daresay she does, if she knows what's good for her,' replied Mary coldly, and picked up her reticule. 'She would lose her position; *that* thought will serve well enough to keep her quiet, I collect.'

'Yes, but if she should open her mouth—'

'I shall engage for it she won't. Never expect trouble, my darling — that merely invites it. Let us consider the business over and done with.'

'You never answered me before,' reminded Henry pleasantly, adjusting his tight-fitting blue Bath-cloth jacket in the glass once more. 'Will I do?'

'You look very well,' she replied crisply, 'although no one could say you were handsome in the regular way! But pray don't fish about for compliments,' she scolded him. 'I haven't any that you have not already given yourself!'

'Ah, so you accuse me of vanity,' he retorted, laughing at his own reflection in the glass. 'I own that I ought to be more humble. But when the ladies fall over themselves constantly, vying for one's attention, one's head is apt to become swelled, I collect. It is only human,' he added sagely.

'And not just ladies,' muttered his sister darkly.

Henry shrugged off his sister's suggestion, always loathe to quarrel with her. He finished his toilette. His high cravat in place, and his shoes drawn over the white stockings which clung to muscled flesh above them, he stood up and surveyed his sister. 'You look very pretty. Beware not to eclipse Miss Elliot; we can't have her resenting us. We have work to do.'

She smiled primly in her pale lemon muslin gown and pulled on her gloves. 'We do indeed. Come. Your curricle has been waiting outside these twenty minutes.'

Five

They were received cordially at Camden-place. Henry Crawford was welcomed with as much warmth as Sir Walter could muster, which at first merely heated to tepid his usual cool aloofness with all who were not of what he considered "importance" in Bath. He was welcomed with a little more genuine warmth from Elizabeth. *Her* warmth, being a close reflection of her natural aloofness, in those first few minutes of meeting did not exceed that of her father's by more than a few degrees. But a few degrees was something, and by the time the first fifteen minutes had passed, Henry's wit and unmistakable charisma had broken through her cool reserve and drawn forth something that might be akin to a genuine liking for the charming and well-dressed brother of Miss Crawford. Even Sir Walter was, finally, not immune to Henry's charms, for when Henry applied them, with the confidence of all the history of his successes in mind, he never failed, he *could* not fail, to win those on whom he chose to bestow them.

Lady Russell, too, who had been invited to be present when Miss Crawford's brother called, was much taken with Mr Crawford. His gay and witty manner, and his innate elegance of address and appearance, would, in all surety, be the very thing to draw Elizabeth from her melancholy. And the brother and sister combined, with their animated and agreeable air, might do much for the two disappointed Elliots altogether!

Elizabeth meanwhile watched the Crawfords together, and marvelled at how alike brother and sister were in both appearance and in manner. They each, thought Elizabeth, had the same family trait of being able to adapt to any situation with grace, while effortlessly appearing to flatter and charm those around them. And they were a set, she observed, like a beautiful pair of gloves; they spoke often as one. She had the impression that they could have been twins, for all that the sister was five years older than the brother. They were insular too, both brother and sister maintaining a dignified reticence in regards to personal detail, while managing all the while to seem uniformly agreeable and open. It was, thought Elizabeth, politic of them, for she could never warm to that vulgar tendency she had observed in persons of indifferent birth to reference all manner of superfluous personal details, and which she found so tiresome. The Crawfords, she thought approvingly, seemed as little concerned with tedious personal detail as she found pleasure in listening to it, and she thought better of them for it.

Mr Crawford, she observed, was at pains to please her, although she could never view him as a credible suitor. Indeed, there was only one person whose solicitations to change her name could she ever consider, and that was Mr William Elliot. *He* had represented in his rank, income and air, and his fortunate situation as heir to Kellynch, the only suitor she would ever countenance. Nevertheless, she welcomed the happy distraction which the company of two elegant and agreeable persons could offer her. Overall, she considered the Crawfords obliging, not at all taxing on one's wits, not at all a threat to her own peace of mind, and therefore, she would solicit more of their company, until she felt equal to facing her future impending spinsterhood.

Thank God she was an Elliot, she thought bitterly. Money and rank always made spinsterhood seem more like a choice than a consequence! Her fortunate situation in society would, in the end, salvage her damaged pride, after the loss of a favourite dream she had harboured so pleasantly for many months. Rank and money meant that although she may well be a spinster, no one would dare use the word in her hearing!

After a short time, and some polite conversation, she turned to Miss Crawford's brother. 'Your sister must have told you that my father is to attend our cousins, the Dalrymples, next week, to the theatre. My father does not, as a rule, attend the theatre, since they are generally rather common with regard to those who attend, but Lady Dalrymple has been invited by Lady Hertford, who is to be a guest of the Prince Regent.'

'Oh! I was not aware that the prince was in Bath?'

'I believe he is not. But he is to arrive very soon with a large *entourage*, and naturally, Lady Dalrymple will wish us to attend with her.'

'How very well-connected your family is, Miss Elliot.'

'Our cousin, Lady Dalrymple, has therefore secured us a large box and requires my father to accompany her. There is enough room for all of us. Do you like the theatre, Mr Crawford?'

'Oh, I rarely attend, for I agree with your father's view, Miss Elliot, that in general it is frequented by those who are not considered elegant or fashionable — but I am sure that the presence of your father and Lady Dalrymple will do much to elevate the company. I shall look forward to it,' he added, 'I am sure it will be entertaining.'

Gratified to hear his own sentiments match her own opinion, Elizabeth continued, 'I have heard so much about Everingham, that I am quite curious. How large is the house? What is its style of building and its history?'

With all the knowledge of the history of Kellynch which had been inculcated into her by her father, Elizabeth had understood from a young age the value of one's history and lineage and the importance of being able to boast a seat belonging to several generations. It gave one a solidarity in the world, she had always thought, as if one's name and reputation were rooted more firmly in the world by the material manifestation of its ancient passage through time, and its continuity of place. Since this pride in one's lineage and place in the world was what she had been taught to revere, she was inclined to rely upon the notion heavily; it informed all her attempts to find common ground and connection of mind in those whom she met. The value inherent in a family name could be measured by the number of generations who had lived in its seat, and the more history a house or estate could boast, the more she felt she had in common with its owner. She was not to be disappointed now.

'Oh, Everingham itself is ancient, Miss Elliot.' Henry had been eating tea cake but now obliged her directly by putting half a slice back down on his plate to give the question his attention. 'It was built in the time of Elizabeth. The main part of the house itself is around one hundred and twenty or so years old; well, such portions that have survived to still be standing upright, I ought to say, but the "greats" added and subtracted over the years, according to their own individual, and somewhat singular tastes, so I daresay you might find it an odd-looking thing. Not what you might have been used to at your own Kellynch,' he added deferentially, 'and within, nothing so modern and splendid as the fitting up of *this* room,' he gestured. 'This style is just what I like myself! But I own that the grounds of Everingham are pretty fine. Pater, God rest his soul, had a rather overdone fountain added when he was first married, and our woods hide some of the best grouse and partridges to be had.'

'A pity, then,' added his sister archly, 'that you are never there to hunt!'

Lady Russell heard this speech with a little flicker of disapproval, for she herself held the idea of due respect for one's predecessors in high regard, and did not like to hear of the ancient bearers of a respectable family name so flippantly referred to as "greats", nor Mr Crawford's father spoken of with so little regard. And yet how swiftly we overlook faults when wishing to approve what we like! Lady Russell found herself making allowances for difference of upbringing, and the lack of a father's influence. The absence of a father might have had worse effects, she privately thought. In all other things, the young man seemed altogether a gentleman.

'Everingham must be a grand estate,' inserted Elizabeth condescendingly, although inwardly calculating the house to be not *quite* so fine as Kellynch and perhaps, she imagined smugly, a little run down, but she was not willing to be left entirely unimpressed since she so approved its current owner. The small compliment to this room, and therefore to her own taste, had not gone amiss either. 'And you have lived all your lives there?'

'I have always been of the opinion,' interjected Sir Walter, with all the consciousness of centuries of birth and breeding bearing the name "Elliot", 'that it can do no material harm to leave a place unattended for long periods; it hints at a family aloofness which can only give rise to greater deference, I collect.' He laughed a short guffaw. 'The other day, as I happened to be standing about in Bond-street, observing, and marvelling at the number of wailing children about me, Smithers, the old wine merchant, with whom I have an account at Kellynch, came upon me, much to his surprise. He looked at me as if to say something, then nodding and bowing, went past without so much as soliciting me for his account. No doubt he was too intimidated to do such a thing in the street, but I could see that he was quite in awe, for it has been some time since the fellow has laid eyes on me. Yes, very right of him too; no doubt he could see clearly that with a removal to Bath, there has been no relinquishment of dignity, nor any giving up of those expectations of deference which come naturally to families of long history and consequence.'

There was a little silence in the room, then Miss Crawford spoke again calmly. 'Everingham has been Henry's principle seat although he is seldom there for long periods, Sir Walter,' she assured him. 'As for his absence engendering any larger air of consequence to the Crawford family name, I cannot say. All I *can* say is that he is never at Everingham enough to suit me. He is frequently abroad, or in town. My brother cannot abide being at home all the time, you know! He must have change of scenery and circumstance continually, to satisfy him!'

Henry Crawford smilingly forbore to give this verbal barb the reply it deserved and shook his head sadly. 'You see how my sister teases me exceedingly, Miss Elliot. I am not so intractable on the matter of Everingham as she implies, nor so disagreeable as to *never* go up into Norfolk; indeed, we were there for three months of last year.'

'And I spent four weeks of that time alone, while you were gone away to have society and amusement in town!' cried Miss Crawford in mock offence. 'See how he laughs at me, Miss Elliot! My brother is quite detestable, I declare, for his habit is always to leave me to my own devices while he goes off and enjoys himself until I despair of ever seeing him again!'

Lady Russell had been quiet, sitting with her tea, but observing the teasing familiarity between the siblings, now asked, 'And you spent your childhood as orphans together then, at Everingham? How romantic a picture that inspires! But you must have been each other's support and strength; that is perhaps something that might not have been the case, had your parents lived longer.'

'As to that,' replied Miss Crawford carefully, 'we did not spend a great deal of our childhood at Everingham, Lady Russell; we have since been much of the time after our parent's death with my Uncle Crawford, the admiral, and my aunt, in Northumberland. Henry still calls the place home, when he is not at Everingham. But when our aunt died last year, I felt it — prudent — to have a change of situation, and our sister Grant kindly thought to offer me a home at the parsonage at Mansfield when I was not at Everingham. Mansfield is in Northamptonshire, you know.'

'So then, you have all come to Bath from — where was it? Mansfield? Does your sister have family there? Is it a pretty place? She must have a large acquaintance there if she has been living there many years.' Lady Russell, where Elizabeth was reticent, and cared not for trivial details below her notice, was more solicitous and through genuine curiosity in the newcomers found herself attempting to draw more detail from Miss Crawford, as the brother seemed happy to let his sister answer for them both.

'Why,' replied Mary Crawford blandly, 'Mansfield is equal to any pretty, small town I have passed through, Ma'am. As for acquaintances, apart from a few local families, my sister has few friends there. There might have been one or two families of some small consequence in the area,' she added casually, 'but we hardly saw them apart from the two or three local assemblies. That is what brings the Grants to Bath, you know, for the socializing that my sister misses in Mansfield.'

Elizabeth, now satisfied with the gentility of her friend's brother, interjected with great condescension, 'Since your sister is so taken up with visiting relations while you are left to your own devices, Miss Crawford, I hope you and your brother will sit down to dinner with us soon. And of course, Lady Russell, you must join us,' she remembered in time to include her graciously. 'We rarely give dinners, you know — it is seldom done in Bath on the whole, really — and besides that, on account of my father's retiring so early on nights that we do not have engagements or assemblies to attend, but I shall be pleased to make an exception now — on the occasion of your brother's visit — I hope may we expect you, let us say, two nights from now?'

'How kind!' both the Crawfords answered together at once. Mary added, 'I hope I shall have the opportunity to play for you all; you have a very fine harp here, I see. Henry always delights in my playing; but he is too excessive in his praise for I am but a novice.' She modestly lowered her eyes but directed a beautiful smile towards Sir Walter.

Sir Walter spoke in lowered tone, just for Miss Crawford. 'Pray do not allow *that* to be an impediment, Miss Crawford. I have always preferred an informal performance to a polished one; you must play for us and we shall not pay undue attention to any little mistakes. I am sure you will entertain us all admirably!'

While the Crawfords were graciously accepting the invitation, Lady Russell had cause to smile privately, for she knew that the reason the Elliots rarely gave dinners was due neither to the inconvenient hours of Sir Walter, nor the social customs of Bath, but to a matter more elevated and serious; the fact was that Elizabeth's vanity, and Sir Walter's, could never bear the assault to the Elliot pride if those used to dining at Kellynch now bore frank witness to their lowered state. To reveal openly the difference of style, the reduced number of servants, the quality of the dishes, which had once been their habit, was not to be thought of. Elizabeth could only suffer the giving of dinner invitations to those who had never once been at Kellynch Hall. Lady Russell counted herself fortunate to find herself suddenly included, for she had been in Bath herself three weeks without one such invitation on account of herself.

Sir Walter now stirred, agitated the maid with a complaint about the fireplaces being dirty, and ordered the tea things gone. With this hint, the Crawfords took their leave, and departed with as much calm dignity and elegance as they had arrived. Thus, the first meeting of Mr Crawford and Miss Elliot passed, with a perfect understanding of what must be on one side and no degree of knowledge of anything of the sort upon the other!

Six

Thursday 8 June, 1815

Kellynch Hall

'All that way, Admiral — some two hundred miles is it not? I admire your forbearance, Sir, for it must have cost you some discomfort! And yet I am amazed, indeed, that your leg appears to have suffered no great harm from the journey.'

A handsome young man with pleasing figure and an open countenance had been rebandaging the admiral's gouty foot and now stood back to assess his work. Doctor Silas Thorpe was lately come to the area, but had called three times already at Kellynch Hall to tend the admiral. He was warmly welcomed, always, by the Crofts; his medical knowledge, made extensive by his reading the latest medical journals into the small hours, was eagerly sought by the admiral and his wife. To him, they seemed the most amiable, vigorous, and intelligent pair, and the perfect example of marital harmony, one never to be found far from the other at any time.

Even better, they were not at all the pristine observers of rank which he often endured on attending the gentry. Admiral Croft, he collected, had distinguished himself by hard work, rather than riding on the coat-tails of a rich forebearer and Thorpe admired this ethic excessively. He could not call himself wealthy, although he hoped to be so some day by merit of dedication to his medical calling, nor could he equal the rank of many of his patients, yet he bore his own modest respectability as a medical man and the son of a gentleman, with a quiet, unassuming pride which he had been taught by the example of his own hard-working father.

Recently come down from London and newly graduated, he had eagerly taken the place of his predecessor, who had been unfortunately armed with a veritable arsenal of medical weaponry consisting of every useless universal remedy imaginable! He had spent several months trying to undo the harm caused by spurious concoctions, fomentations, liniments, and so-called tonics containing of all things, arsenic and even lead, though some of the more leading-edge medical journals were just now warning against such things! He admired the Crofts exceedingly, since, for all their advancing years, they were full of the vigour of life, eager to discuss the newest treatments, and having a keen interest in the progress of modern technology and knowledge. In them he had found a pleasing camaraderie and fancied they welcomed him for the same.

With the sister-in-law, Mrs Wentworth, he had had less to do, but he found her a quiet, sensible woman, and suspected her to be in her first months of pregnancy, according to his practised eye. He hoped to engage her in conversation when he had the opportunity, to invite her to confide in him should she need any medical advice.

Now Admiral Croft laughed with his usual frank good humour. 'I am almost my old self again, I assure you, Thorpe; no harm has come to my going on such a journey. Besides that, I could not let Sophie go alone, you know, and it was a snug little adventure we took, all in all! It is our country habits, I daresay you will call them, which makes us fond of being always together, and there is not much that will separate us—certainly not a little journey to London to collect that flighty young niece of Sophie's!'

The young doctor repacked his leather bag. 'And how does young Miss Wentworth go on? I understand from Mrs Croft the lady has taken to her bed these two days. She is not ill, I hope?'

'Oh, our Miss Julia is quite overcome with a *certain* illness, but not of the sort you may cure, for all your new-fangled medical ways, Thorpe! Ay, she is indeed!' Here the admiral broke into a chuckle. 'Nay, it is more a case of blue-devilment, I am certain, not that I am any expert judge on the hearts of young ladies! My wife says I have no notion of what goes on in a woman's head, and she'd be right enough! Am I not right, my dear?'

At this moment, Mrs Croft had, after knocking gently, entered the room to sit by her husband. She took up the conversation. 'No doubt you are, my love, but you must tell me what it is you wish me to pronounce you right about!'

Doctor Thorpe patted the gouty foot gently, having made himself satisfied with the bandaging. 'The admiral has just been telling me that your niece is low in spirits, rather than ill, Mrs Croft.'

Mrs Croft sighed and shook her head gravely. 'As to that, I believe my niece suffers nothing more than a fit of the dismals on account of being removed from the source of her amusements — and by that, I mean from town life and all its enticements. The poor headmistress at St John's seminary was quite glad to see her taken away, for all that Julia is an amiable, glad-spirited creature, or was when we last saw my brother Edward. But she has been through a lot, Doctor, losing her mother so young, and now, having a newcomer to take her mother's place in the household must be a severe trial to her.'

The admiral remonstrated. 'I know, Sophie, that you think on it quite as you ought, for she is your niece, but I also should have thought the governess would have been a sensible woman, enough to keep the child happy and well-adjusted at home. But I dare say I am an old duffer, I am sure, to understand the machinations of a young lady's mind.'

The young doctor smiled. 'I've always been of the mind myself that a good governess or female companion can accomplish much in a motherless girl!'

'Aye, true enough,' agreed the admiral. 'Only look at our Anne, for example! There is no one so good and sensible on the earth as our Anne!'

'That is nothing to the point, my dear,' replied his wife wisely, 'when a young girl, so full of girlish emotion and spirit, is concerned. You must remember that Julia is nothing like Anne, who lost her own mother at an impressionable age and was modest and pliable enough to allow the influence of Lady Russell to be a rule for her behaviour. Although, not always to her benefit,' she added, thinking of the disappointment poor Frederick had suffered when he had first proposed to Anne Elliot nine years earlier and been rejected. Then, Anne had been very much under the influence of the persuading Lady Russell, who had opposed the union and had persuaded Anne to give up the match. She could never quite truly warm to Anne's friend and godmother for that ill-judged advice alone, but Mrs Croft's mild temperament and gentle nature could not allow her not to forgive the woman for encouraging the hurtful slight to her brother.

But Anne herself had already forgiven her godmother, and set the benchmark for gracious behaviour, and additionally, Mrs Croft was an eminently sensible woman, as a captain's wife, and knew where to take up arms and where to lay them down for the sake of peace. 'No,' she continued, 'Julia is made of different stuff, and suffers from a temper and a high-strung constitution; we must expect she will take some umbrage at having her freedom so curtailed, even if it is for her greater good! Although I must say that Edward's sending her to town to go gallivanting around the place after dark without the knowledge of her betters was an ill-judged evil, most certainly!'

Doctor Thorpe concurred politely. There was shortly afterward a commotion heard in the distant parts of the house, and voices in the hallway, and Mrs Croft turned to her husband.

'That will be Anne and the children coming back from the lake,' she reminded. 'Those boys certainly keep her amused, do they not, my dear? And a good thing it is too, for a mind occupied with the present has no part in worrying about the future! My brother, as you know, Doctor, has gone to sea, and his wife is feeling his absence, ever more so since she is to become a mother soon.'

Thorpe, repressing a smile, made a polite congratulation to the pair on adding another charming niece or nephew to the family, and Mrs Croft, gratified with the kind acknowledgement, now took up the conversation again.

'But how does my husband do, Doctor? What may I do for him? I dare say you will not prescribe port and liver, nor Gardener's pills! I am certain they did entirely nothing for my poor Matthew last year!'

Thorpe clicked shut his bag. 'I am not at all shocked to hear it, Mrs Croft,' he noted in open amusement. 'No, the admiral must restrict his port to once per week only, take exercise daily and live temperately with regard to appetite. I have also prescribed tart cherry juice twice daily on an empty stomach.'

The admiral was all appreciation. 'Ah, the marvels of modern medicine! How astonishing it all is! Restrict port! Cherry juice instead! But we have the utmost trust in you, Thorpe. Restrict port, eh? Well if I must, I daresay I must!'

Mrs Croft simply shook the doctor's hand with a great deal of animation. 'How kind, how kind!'

Her husband, still labouring under the new notion of restricting his port, added, 'Aye, we are very thankful, Thorpe! If I have the good luck to live through this attack, it will be only your doing I suspect! Will it not Sophie?'

Mrs Croft, laughing, patted the admiral's hand. 'I hardly think this attack will kill you, my love, if the journey to London and back never managed the deed!'

Thorpe, reaching for his hat, marvelled again that the journey had *not* harmed the foot, denied his was anything other than the usual *modern* advice for gout, *sans* Gardener's pills of course, and then added gravely, 'If there is any other service I can do, either for the admiral, or for that young niece of yours, do please send for me at once. These fits in ladies can turn quickly from dismals to melancholia and lack of appetite. You must keep an eye on her, Mrs Croft, and summon me if—'

'—if I should go into a fainting swoon, or take on in hysterics? I should hardly think I will need your assistance for those, thank you all the same, Doctor.'

Julia Wentworth's high, clear voice rang from the door way, and three heads turned as a chestnut-haired young woman in a light green sarcenet morning dress glided across the room. The gentle tone of the dress was set in relief by the use of a darker pointed lace at the sleeves and a low-set collar, and the hazel eyes of its wearer sparked under the rich brown curls. With her delicate, pale face, she presented a very interesting appearance to the observers in the room, and perhaps one eye above all others rested momentarily with appreciation on the flushed cheeks below the bright eyes.

'Pray, Julia, don't be uncivil, if you please!'

Mrs Croft's tone was a little shocked, and her niece had the grace to look abashed. She dropped a polite curtsy to the doctor. 'Yes, Aunt Sophie. But I am quite well and do not need anyone to "keep an eye" on me, thank you all the same,' she added witheringly, with a glance at Thorpe. 'I have done very well these last years without being mollycoddled!'

The acid in her glance was lost on her aunt, but Doctor Thorpe supressed a smile. 'I was just leaving, Miss Wentworth, but I am glad to have the pleasure of making your acquaintance before I go away. I collect you have been away at school, in London.'

'A ladies' seminary, Sir.' Her tone was neutral, but her eyes challenged. 'A far different institution to a mere school, but I am sure you must know what a seminary is, Doctor. Aunt,' she added, turning away from the Thorpe as if he had never been present, 'Aunt Anne has just come in with the children and is engaged with Mrs Musgrove in getting them changed out of their wet things. She begged me to ask you to go to her at your leisure. I think young Walter caught a pike, or some such fish, in his net, and desires to eat it for his dinner and she cannot dissuade him!'

The admiral chuckled and his wife smiled indulgently. Both were fond of the young boys and doted upon them, having no children of their own. 'Oh! Well done, Walter!' Mrs Croft exclaimed. 'Would you tell Anne I will be along presently?'

Miss Wentworth gave the young doctor a slight bow of the head and retreated, her fast-moving skirts whispering a little rustling objection to being "mollycoddled" in her wake, as the door closed again.

Mrs Croft was anxious. 'My niece is still tired from our long journey, Doctor Thorpe. I hope you will excuse her abruptness. She is a little in want of spirits and I am sure she meant no rudeness.'

'Think nothing of it, Mrs Croft! It takes a great deal more than a cross young lady to offend me! Now, you must summon me if you are at all concerned for your niece. But truly, I saw nothing to alarm, just now, that could not be cured by distractions and amusements here at Kellynch.'

The Crofts saw the doctor off on his mount, and Mrs Croft left the admiral as comfortably arranged as he could be made on the chaise, with his bandaged foot on the ottoman stool, while she went in search of Anne.

Seven

Anne was clutching an armful of wet, muddy clothing when Mrs Croft came upon her and Mary upstairs in the nursery. Little Charles had been taken away by the maid to be bathed but Walter, a young fellow of around seven years, was clutching a large fish which his mother was attempting to wrestle from him.

Mrs Croft, with her natural air of importance and authority, immediately took charge of the fish. 'Why, Walter, what a clever boy you have been! Now, if you like it, I will take it myself and give it to cook to see what she might do with it. Do you want fish for your dinner today?'

'Yes,' replied a red-faced Walter, 'an' Mama says it's a smelly old thing fit for the pigs, but it's not! It's a fine catch! Papa would let me eat it, I know! And I deserve to eat it too, 'cos I fished it right outa the lake and it struggled and struggled afore I got it up the bank, and I ain't giving it to the pigs!'

While Mary clicked her tongue and chided Walter loudly for invoking his absent Papa when she was the present and natural next best authority, Mrs Croft had slipped the offending creature from Walter's grip and given it to Liza who had sidled in to assist. 'Take this down to Mrs Hall, if you will, Liza dear, and see if she can make anything of it.'

'And can you return for these?' Anne added to the servant, dropping the pile of dirty clothes near the door. 'I hope it is not too much for poor Jenny to scrub, along with everything else.' She looked an apology to Mrs Croft. 'The boys did so wish to go fishing from the bridge, and it gave my sister a few hours peace, but I am sorry for the extra work for Jenny. It will be remarkable indeed if the poor girl has any skin left after the mighty wash she will have to do this week!'

Mary, washing her hands at the nursery pitcher and basin, was now able to collect herself and say accusingly, 'Not that but I had *any* rest this afternoon after all, for I have had the most *dreadful* head-ache this last hour; I declare, my head-aches are always worse than anyone else's and cannot be cured by the usual salts and dark rooms!'

'Oh,' replied Anne solicitously, 'I am sorry to hear it!'

'It could be due to my digestion, for you know how I suffer with bad digestion, Anne. It really is too bad of cook to serve such rich sauce with her quails. I daresay I shall have to lie down now — cannot Liza dress the boys and see them to their dinner? Or you, Anne? I am so ill I can hardly stand!'

Anne at once went to her sister, kissed her, and bade her go to her room and lie down. 'You might have said something earlier, Mary, and I would not have troubled you to help with the boys.'

'Oh, as to that, I never mind my head-aches, unless I am bilious with them. I wasn't bilious before, but suddenly I find myself exceedingly poorly with it! I shall lie down as you say; perhaps a few hours rest from the boys will do me good! Perhaps I shall be recovered enough to eat a little dinner tonight. I believe cook said something about stuffed pheasant.'

Mrs Croft politely prevented herself from reminding Mary that Anne had already entertained her nephews long enough and had all the right to a rest herself, given her condition, but a quick glance from Anne forced prudence and she merely shook her head at Anne when Mary had gone away to lie down.

'My dear, you will find yourself quite exhausted if you don't rest more. Pray let me take the boys when they come back from the bath, and the admiral and I will entertain them with teaching them cribbage until their dinner time.'

Anne was grateful. 'You have done so much for my family already, Mrs Croft, that I feel very much in your debt. I am disappointed that poor Charles could not stay a night or two, when he drove them over. He could have helped with the boys. They attend him far more than they do Mary, I'm afraid! Do you think the noise and bustle too much,' she added anxiously, 'for the admiral, I mean, and now that Julia is come?'

'My dear Anne, the admiral and I have seen many more turbulent days and nights at sea than we experience now at Kellynch! I shall not be exhausted for the sake of a little company! And it does the admiral good, I am certain, to have the little boys around him. It takes his mind quite off his poor foot! How is the head-ache? It really was too bad of Mary to forget you had a head-ache too!'

'It is almost gone away,' Anne replied, putting a hand to her temple absently. 'I think I am just in want of my husband,' she smiled ruefully. 'Mrs Croft, whatever did you do when the admiral was away at sea and you couldn't be with him? It must have been very trying for you!'

'I almost always had the best luck to be sailing with my husband; I think it was only once in all the years of my marriage that I ever had to remain ashore and that was a vast trying time indeed, my dear! Depend upon it, you will soon have more to do than will allow you much time for reflection on Frederick's absence, and you must remember that you are not the only one to wish him home, for I can never see him off to sea without wishing my brother on dry land again, safe and sound! The time will pass quickly, you will see!' She patted Anne's hand. 'Now, do give the little boys over to myself and the admiral and we shall entertain them until their dinner time.'

'I *would* like to write a letter to Frederick, Mrs Croft, if you would take the boys for just an hour. You really are too kind!'

Mrs Croft, with her good and generous nature, quickly dispatched herself on the errand of telling her husband that they were to entertain the children before they ate their dinner in the nursery, and Anne found herself at liberty to write her letter.

She entered the familiar library room, the late afternoon light streaming in through the drapes and giving illumination to the dust suspended in the air. This room was a favourite room of hers. It was the one in which she had played as a girl, spent hours reading in with her mother, where she had squabbled over picture books with Elizabeth and Mary, and had gloomily hid within on her first holiday at home from school at Bath after her mama had died. For all the years the room had seen pass, it had not only retained its air of elegance but it seemed to harbour the pleasant ghosts of yesteryear, and Anne felt there was not a room in the house she liked more. That Frederick had been in the habit of sitting here often since they had come to stay at Kellynch, and that she could sense his presence here too, she acknowledged was a further comfort.

She had only that morning received a hurriedly written note from her husband, giving her the news that he was to embark three days from now, on HMS Nightingale, with Rear Adm. Malcolm aboard, and a direction in Belgium where she might next reach him. Being permitted to pick some of his officers, he knew some of the warrant officers by name, and one or two of the midshipmen, he wrote, but he was to have two fellows he did not know for lieutenants, although he liked them both well enough. He was not entirely friendless, however, for Captain Benwick had been ordered to sail behind them, and they would all arrive in Ostend together, in two or three days' time, God willing. Benwick's new wife was to accompany him, at her insistence.

This news gave Anne some pause. Louisa Benwick, who had given up the name Musgrove as recently as Anne had given up that of Elliot, was a lively young woman, with a determined nature which had already cost her dearly, with a dangerous fall from the steps at Lyme Regis only a year ago. Anne could easily imagine the romantic inclinations of the young woman she knew so well having just the right effect on a man who had been left as good as a widower in a previous separation which had occurred while he had been at sea. In light of his previous loss of the young Frances Harville, affectionately referred to as 'Phoebe', whom he would have married, Anne could hardly wonder at Benwick's quick acquiescence to Louisa's demand that she accompany him. Since her coming into company with Captain Frederick Wentworth last year, Louisa Musgrove had demonstrated as fine a naval fervour as any young woman fancying herself in love with a ships' captain might harbour. Supposing such a fervour might work its charm upon an eligible captain, and now that Louisa had found herself just such a one, Anne could not now imagine Louisa's high-spirited character to have taken no for an answer.

Anne also knew, being on such intimate terms with the Musgrove sisters, that had Louisa not been permitted to join her husband, she would not have fared well. Louisa was relatively young, barely twenty years old, and while a generally a good-natured creature, was not much wiser than she had been ten years previous. Merry and animated and ready to be pleased with the world in general, she had never suffered a day's anxiety since leaving the crib. She had been so well protected and doted upon by her father and mother that she had wanted for nothing and barely known hardship. She would, Anne thought, have taken a separation very hard. Perhaps it was better that she had chosen to accompany her husband. And while she may have been overtaken by romantic imaginings of life at sea, her loyalty to James Benwick was quite genuine.

For herself, Anne was grateful that, being forced to oblige the laws of nature and remain at home for the sake of her unborn child, at the least she had been taught by time and circumstances the prudence and the stoicism needed to bear up under the harsher aspects of having a husband whose career was to take him away for long periods. If she felt some tiny stirrings of jealousy that Louisa had been allowed to accompany her husband while Anne had not, she quelled them sensibly.

Now Anne sat at the desk, and drew up some paper sheets, feeling as if Frederick might almost be in the room with her. She took up a new quill, dipped it in the inkwell and was taken up for the next few minutes giving as cheerful an account as she could of the arrival of her sister and the little boys, the poor admiral's gout, and their plans to try for a picnic the following day. She devoted the second part of her letter to the news of Edward Wentworth's letter the same day Frederick had left for Deal, and the hurried removal of his niece Julia from London and her subsequent instalment at Kellynch.

From the account Mrs Croft had supplied her, Anne gathered that Miss Wentworth's removal from the seminary in town had been the cause of a great deal of sulking and tearful pettishness on the journey back to Somerset, and that the young lady had demanded to be returned to town. When Mrs Croft had sternly suggested it was not so much further to take her to Shropshire and put her down at her father's house, however, the affronted young woman had quieted, and agreed to remain for the time being at Kellynch with her aunt.

However, Miss Julia Wentworth had not been particularly happy to enter her uncle's abode without the comfort of a departure date set, and had not been particularly amenable to her new circumstances. 'I was in no danger — it is not as if I am a mere chit of a girl with no notion of proper decorum!' she had exclaimed in low tones, within an hour of meeting her Aunt Anne and suffering to be gently chastised for wishing herself back in London. 'It is insufferably provoking to be dragged away like a child, when I had done nothing wrong!'

Mrs Croft had been astonished. 'Nothing wrong, indeed! Only go about after dark without the permission of the Headmistress, and in the company of some very ill-bred girls! I wonder you do not perceive how close you came to ruining your reputation, and how much anxiety you have given your father!'

'It would not signify, if that wretched Mrs Harris had never written to my father! And then that he should have written you, Aunt Sophie, and told you to come for me! It really is too much!'

Anne, although never having been subject to the unpleasantness of being obliged to welcome a replacement mother, knew what it was to lose one all the same. While Edward Wentworth's first wife had been gone many years, she could still imagine how disagreeable and upsetting it might be to have a stepmother come in between a father and daughter, whatever the advantages might be to Mr Edward Wentworth, and perhaps to Julia too, over time. So Anne had wisely allowed the girl to vent her anger, and after a day or two shut in her bedroom, and refusing to appear at dinner, Julia had finally come down this morning, dressed, eyes a little red perhaps, but composed.

Anne, wishing to meet her halfway and help her niece feel welcome, immediately invited her to join herself and the two little boys to go fish from the pond, but Julia had politely, if a little coldly, declined, and had desired to stay indoors.

'I do not feel up to being outdoors, if it's all the same to you, Aunt. I am a little fatigued and will read here in the little parlour, or help Aunt Sophie with something or other.' She turned away listlessly and sat herself on the window seat.

Anne tried again gently. 'Certainly, if you are not inclined, but some fresh air might do you good. Perhaps tomorrow we might walk?'

'Yes,' agreed Julia passively. 'If you like.'

At least the tears and recriminations had ceased, and tomorrow she would try again to take her niece outdoors. She had looked peaked and pale, and Anne thought fresh air and a little of the medicine she had prescribed for herself, the distraction of Mary's little boys, might do much to brighten Julia's cheeks.

Now, letter done, and folded and sealed with the Elliot crest which stood in the corner of the desk, Anne went downstairs to give her letter to Robertson, her father's aged footman, to take to post. That old fellow had seen forty-odd summers at Kellynch. He was the only remaining of two footmen who had been with the Elliot family when Anne's mother had been alive. Years previously, when the other footman had died of a seizure running alongside the Elliot carriage, when such things were considered fashionable, Anne remembered that her father had mourned three full weeks, and had declared he could never engage another to take his place.

'Ah, William Tate, poor old fellow! Who would have known him to have a weak heart? Devil of it is though, where can I find another six-foot four fellow, with the same build? I cannot abide a mismatched pair, gives a gentleman a vast odd appearance, I declare, having mismatched footmen! Why, last week, when I was in town, Sir Henry had two running by his carriage, one with not a pound of bacon on his bones, and the other corpulent as that old dog of Henry's! Huffing and puffing, poor devil, along the side of the *equipage*, for all that the fellow could only have been four or five and twenty! I said to Sir Henry, "Had not you better put the one on a diet of potatoes and bread and the starve the other?" I asked him. But he only laughed and said he'd given up given up trying to get them each to a tolerable equal weight! Picture to yourselves my amazement! Were they mine, I would insist on their being matched! Ah well, I shall content myself with one footman with the superior gift of a magnificent stature than two odd-sized fellows and be a laughing-stock!'

Poor Robertson, had he known himself to be prized as a "superior gift" on the basis of his height only, may have felt himself justifiably offended, but oblivious that the real value of his service to Sir Walter lay in his amazing stature, merely took a placid view of the world and only sighed with the patience of a saint when he eyed Miss Elliot, coming towards him. 'First Miss Wentworth just now, and so urgent about hers, and I suppose your letter is to be sent directly too, Miss Anne?'

Anne handed him her own letter and scolded smilingly. 'You really ought to call me Mrs Wentworth, now, George. It has been three months since I married!'

'I don't feel I *can* get used to it, Miss Anne! And if I am to call you "Mrs Wentworth", you had best cease using my given name, and go back to Robertson, if you please!'

'You tease me, George, and you know it very well!'

'Never, Miss!'

'Never, indeed!' she laughed. 'Did you say Miss Wentworth gave you a letter? May I see it, please?' She took the paper from the wrinkled hand, and inspected the direction. 'Thank you, George.' Handing it back she let the servant go, and went upstairs again. The letter had been addressed to a "Mr Harry Lyford" at a men's club in London. She could guess the contents. She consulted her sister-in-law immediately.

'It is perhaps worse than we had at first thought, then. To engage in correspondence with a man — it is most provoking, I must say! No wonder she was so very agitated to be taken away from town! She is verily in love!' mused Mrs Croft.

'She would only write to this Mr Lyford if there was an understanding, surely? Do you suppose he could have fallen in love with Julia? Perhaps after all, he is a respectable gentleman.'

Mrs Croft was calm and reason itself. 'Perhaps it is a simple case of calf-love, on both sides, and no lasting damage might be done either of them. But I cannot help but think, Anne, that if he is a gentleman, and has formed a true attachment, then I suspect he will never be brought to respond to a letter sent in such a clandestine manner. He would hurt her reputation.'

Anne was thoughtful. 'I believe you are right, Mrs Croft. A gentleman of honour would approach in person and make himself known, surely.'

'But, my dear, I rather gather this Mr Harry Lyford cannot be a gentleman. If Julia has formed some attachment to him, he must have encouraged it, and that cannot be the conduct of a gentlemen to a young lady. Who would pay his addresses to a young girl who was not in the charge of a chaperone? I think this Lyford cannot be a man of good repute nor must he have a conscience worthy of a gentleman!'

Anne was sober. 'I suspect more must have gone on in town than your brother had guessed, Mrs Croft. Foolish child! But all in all, I see no harm in allowing the letter to go as directed. If he is not in love with Julia, then she shall soon find it out herself by his silence, and if he is then he will write to her and make an offer, or present himself here. Are you of the same opinion?'

Mrs Croft readily agreed with her, and between them they decided to let the affair rest, rather than confront Julia. All would come to its natural conclusion in due course, and Julia would have learned a lesson. Calf love, Mrs Croft had called it, and Anne rather thought she was right. Julia was too young, at barely seventeen years old, to lose her heart to a man, and pray God it would be short-lived, as these attachments so often were.

She looked in on Mary, who was still lying down, then went to the pianoforte for a little while, to practice a new polonaise by Hummel. The distraction soothed as much as did the pretty melodies, and by and by she was able to go to her room and dress for dinner, and go down in a better frame of mind. Remembering Julia's headstrong ways, she was thankful she had sealed her letter to Frederick before they had learned of the young woman's clandestine correspondence. She would spare him as much excitement from Kellynch as she could; he would have enough of alarms and anxious care in the next few weeks!

Eight

Sunday 11 June, 1815

Deal Port.

Frederick Wentworth, captain of his own ship for a good decade, and carrying upon his broad shoulders somewhat of a tinge of much-deserved naval heroism, was well-liked among his men. He was known to be fair and just, ready to laugh, and as dependable in foul weather as in fair. He was well spoken of in naval circles both among the officers and the lower ranked seamen. When many of his former crew had gotten wind of the imminent arrival of Rear Admiral Sir Pulteney Malcom in Deal and that the Rear Admiral was to fly his flag from the HMS Nightingale in a se'en night, and that this vessel was slated to be captained by none other than the venerable Wentworth, they were lined up ready to enlist. Upon his arrival in the town, Wentworth had discovered he had twenty-odd able seamen all eager and ready to sail. He would not, this time around, thank God, have to press for extra men. It was a practice he abhorred and was to be avoided, especially if they were to see action. No commonplace man, pressed into service for the paltry remuneration which was usual, would ever win battles out of passion and loyalty.

There was a second reason the men were pleased to go to sea again under such an auspicious commander; Wentworth had a reputation as lucky. Many of his men, at sea on the Asp and the

Laconia in previous actions, had seen their captain's unusual fortune in both foul weather and heavy battle, and would as soon go to sea again under Wentworth's command for less pay, as for anyone else for higher wages and better grog. Additionally, Wentworth had, from his successive captures, made his fortune and his genius and ardour had seen him on a most prosperous path. His crew, including the lower ranks, had taken home spoil over and above their modest wages. Quite apart from the general eagerness of being employed, many of those men were induced to think it a great satisfaction to be employed under a captain who had never suffered a shipwreck or a defeat in battle and who had made his fortune privateering. To them, he carried an uncommon good fortune, and they now scurried about on board for several days, stowing the victuals, tools, lamp oil and ropes and a hundred other items ready for their voyage, congratulating themselves and each other on their good luck.

The officer's wives, too, were equally were well pleased with their husbands' appointments, not that but there were merely three women aboard this sailing. Rr. Admiral Malcolm, whom at six-and-forty years, was old enough to have learned his naval etiquette under the advises of Nelson, was set against this practice, saying gruffly on hearing of the inclusion of the women, 'Never knew an instance where a female was took to the sea and some mischief did not fail to befall the vessel.' He complained bitterly to Wentworth that he had heard they all liked to practice the washing of their 'dammed fripperies and whatnots' in the ship's fresh water. His own lady, to whom he had been wed seven years, had never once asked to accompany him, he added, and he was thankful for it. Would that other married sailor's wives be just as sensible and stay at home!

Wentworth smiled at this and was placatory. At one time abused for his want of gallantry in professing his unwillingness to admit ladies on board any ship in his command, he had very lately, since his marriage, been obliged to reform his earlier opinion of the evils of carrying women on board a warship. Now, he understood with a deep and personal investment the comfort which married sailors might properly wish for, contingent upon having one's wife aboard. He therefore represented to the admiral the relative harmlessness of the notion, the improvement in industriousness it would bring to the officers involved, and gallantly noted that since there were only to be three women aboard, it could hardly signify as to the washing of their clothes. No mischief could come of merely three females, two of whom were as seasoned sailors as their husbands.

Admiral Malcom, unwilling to dictate and good natured enough for grumbles not to become orders, allowed that Wentworth was in command of his own ship, and would do as he preferred without further remonstration. The ladies were duly given the most well-appointed cabins and Wentworth was satisfied that he had carried out his duty as a married man.

The wives in question were volubly grateful, and the captain, assailed every time he walked larboard or starboard, above or below, quarter deck or fore, was always now hailed pleasantly and taught to hear their thanks for every little provision he had thought of for their comfort. He could have no lasting annoyance at this constant engaging of his time, however, since for the greater part they seemed as knowledgeable and keen as his own sister Sophie. All three seemed eager to be of use with nursing the wounded and looking after the ammunition in case of unexpected engagement.

God willing, they would never have need to defend themselves. Wentworth's orders had merely been to transport Malcom across the English Channel to Ostend, accompanied by the Tartarus, to await his orders there for as long as it took, and perhaps he may be back on British soil within a few weeks. It would be unlikely, and unlucky indeed, if, in crossing the channel, they had any trouble. The Americans had pulled back since the treaty had been signed in Ghent, and they feared nothing from that quarter, at least. But they had the security of Benwick and the HMS Tartarus close by should they encounter danger.

On their arrival into Ostend, Malcom would make for Brussels, the seat of British and Prussian coalition intelligence, by road. There, the Duke of Wellington awaited him. 'All I may do, and it is not much, I collect,' lamented the admiral privately to Wentworth one evening, 'is to inform Wellington of the admiralty's wish to do all in its might to aid the allied armies, should there be another action.'

'Can the navy truly be of use, Sir?'

'Only Wellington can decide that. However, we must do our part and back up our national interests on the ground, for we are patriots, even though we are sea bound!'

Wentworth wondered privately what little the navy might do, apart from remove any wounded if there came about the action which Malcolm had hinted was foreseen by Wellington. His most fond wish was to be home again within a month, by his wife's side, and he longed to write to her. But they might yet be required to ship home any prisoners of war, should action be seen, and he was loath to write to Anne just yet since he did not know how long he would need to harbour in Ostend.

All in all, however, the Nightingale, although she was a sixteen-gun sloop built to fight, did not truly expect to see action, and there was almost no anxiety at all on the part of the crew at the thought of merely crossing the English Channel to Belgium. For his part, Wentworth had gone all over the ship and pronounced her hale enough for a short voyage, although she was, as Malcolm had joked, 'just like myself: greying at the temples.' With good weather ahead and no great dangers likely to present themselves, they were all of them a serene group. The officers had their wives, the able seamen their secured positions on a good ship under an auspicious captain, and the wives had the satisfaction of going to sea with their husbands under circumstances which gave them no immediate cause for anxiety.

It was, therefore, a merry and sanguine ship which pulled up anchor and slid out of Deal harbour into the English Channel at around six o'clock on the evening of June eleventh. The moon, a pale half-circle in the sky, sailed serenely above them. In the officers' mess room, Malcolm and Wentworth, each having gained a degree of mutual respect and understanding of the other, sat with several of the officers and the three females at dinner. They were taking claret, three of their precious but modest store of a superior French kind opened upon the table, and eating their first meal aboard under sail. The claret had been brought aboard by Malcolm, who was fond of a good bottle, and not being at all discouraged by misplaced patriotism or fastidious notions of spurning all things Gallic, he imbibed freely.

'French wine,' he expiated, 'holds nothing to Spanish, and I am persuaded there is nothing finer, despite its being grown on Gallic soil. I cannot stand to be overnice about these things; the French and their grog must be considered entirely separate from politics, when it comes to a good drop!'

'I must own I never expected table to be as fine as that we are enjoying tonight!' Mrs Inchpole, who was at sea for the first time and had been imagining conditions aboard to be so primitive as to be eating their food with their bare hands, was just as astonished at there being table cutlery and silverware, as to discover wine in real glasses.

Mrs Taylor, a sturdy, capable-looking woman with dark curls, joined her voice. 'Confess at once, dear Admiral! Do you have your spies on that side? I will wager such good claret was not gotten by fair means! Do 'fess up!'

'Procured it, let us just say,' the admiral chuckled, 'when I was in Bordeaux last year, Ma'am; I was with the Royal Oak, you know, took a detachment over to North America just before I served as Third with Cochrane. Dammed fine stuff, don't you say, Wentworth? Drink up then!'

The party willingly agreed and quaffed obediently. The air through the open porthole windows was fresh, their having left the fetid stench of the busy port behind them almost as soon as they gained the open waters, but the night was unusually still, even so.

'Well, the wind is not treating us well, Cap'n,' remarked the sinuous, pale first lieutenant called Taylor. He was in his early forties, with a florid complexion and had about him an air of melancholy. 'I daresay it will take us a little longer to reach Ostend, but we'll do our best, Sir,' he nodded to Malcolm who concurred and refilled his own and Wentworth's glasses before the serving boy could run over.

'No matter, Mr Taylor, I have the utmost faith in you all. We may catch a good breeze by the time we have a few miles behind us.'

Wentworth had discovered Rear Admiral Malcolm, for all his naval bluster, to be a clever, well-informed man, with more refined good taste than he had expected in a naval man, and he was pleased with his appointment to transport the admiral to their destination. Besides the quiet air of authority he carried, Malcolm was a thinking man, untouched by ego, and ready to be guided by the wisdom of others before making a decision. His mind was firm and brilliant, and Wentworth looked forward to his company.

One of the ladies, a rather weather-beaten creature of sensible appearance and no particular beauty interjected calmly, 'It is always so, crossing the Channel, I collect. We must always be dependent on the kindness of the wind! Would that we were merely going to Calais! Three hours has not been uncommon I am told, in a good breeze! But I understand we add a full day-and-a-half to our crossing to Ostend. Perhaps we will be fortunate and run into a gale!' She laughed at her own little joke.

The sensible style of the lady's brown French cambric gown was at counterpoint to the insensibility of this remark and Wentworth merely acknowledged the little joke with a cool nod while Malcolm said grimly, 'I sincerely hope we are *not* to have your brand of fortune, Ma'am!'

Her husband, a warrant officer unknown to Wentworth called Cruikshank, was more concerned. 'Aye, Sir, but I don't like the looks of the blue sky we departed under. "Blue sky heralds sunk wind", as they say. But what say you, Taylor?'

Taylor looked unhopeful. 'It is looking very glassy and for this time of year, not unusual to be a little longer crossing, but I hope you are correct, Admiral, and we may be able to get up a greater speed later tonight.'

His lady, not at all put out by the doubtful tone of this remark, turned to Mrs Cruikshank. 'Certainly, a breeze will strike up, my dear Absynthe, it always does as we get clear out into the way of the channel. I have made this trip,' she nodded slightly in Malcom's direction, 'too many times to count, and we always strike a breeze four hours out, I assure you! No need for concern, Admiral!'

In times past, such an assurance from a female, given with such a natural air of authority as Mrs Taylor's, would have invoked a supercilious coldness from an unmarried Wentworth, but he was a new-made man. A fresh humility obliged him now merely to acknowledge the observations of Mrs Taylor with a slight smile and forgive her little impertinence immediately.

Mr Brookbank, the third lieutenant and a particular acquaintance of Wentworth's, addressed Rear Admiral Malcolm. 'Sir, may I enquire how many officers will accompany you off the Tartarus when we reach Ostend?'

'Captain Benwick has got two of my aides on board behind us, and they will travel with me. I shall require a third man. Perhaps one of Benwick's lieutenants, since I know you three are engaged to the Nightingale for the duration. Wentworth, what kind of man is this Benwick? You recommended him to the admiralty for this business — you must be on terms with the man?'

'He is a fine captain, by all accounts, Sir. He served alongside my friend Harville in the last action off the Indies — conducted himself valiantly — distinguished himself and made a decent purse, I collect. He is recently married, too, which makes him all the more careful to get home in one piece!'

'Aye, I'll drink to that,' cheered Mr Brookbank mournfully, who had not his wife aboard.

'You will find Benwick a serious, thinking man, Admiral,' continued Wentworth. 'He recently suffered the tragic loss of his betrothed, the sister of my friend Harville. He has found happiness again with his new wife, but the loss has left him more sober than ever. I think you will like him well enough, Sir. He is a fine Captain and very competent by all accounts.'

'So long as he has a stomach for blood,' replied Malcom. 'We all may have need of that soon enough.'

''Tis a great pity on the state of the allied troops left in Brussels,' remarked Caulfield the purser, 'a vast dubious lot, I'd say, and not to be relied upon if there is a spot of trouble.'

'Aye, true,' replied Malcom. 'Most of the British veterans are still away in North America, more's the pity, or still on ships coming home. We will have to make do, I'm afraid. Still, I think it will only give Bonaparte a small advantage, if any. It will take some doing to overcome the Prussians should he attempt it!'

Brookbank interjected. 'They say, Sir, that Bonaparte has amassed three hundred thousand men. Good, experienced soldiers too, it's reported. Trained and put through their paces every day, just waiting for their summons.'

Mrs Inchpole, sitting with her husband, was open-eyed. Wentworth admitted her to be a fetching creature with an abundance of fair curls framing her delicate face and clear blue eyes, although he preferred a dark eye himself. Like his Anne. His lips curled in a slight smile with the thought. He wondered how old the lady was, for she could not be but more than nineteen or twenty years, he calculated. Well, it would take but one or two voyages, he surmised, and she would be just as seasoned and calm as Mrs Taylor or as his own dear Anne.

But Mrs Inchpole, who had started up with alarm at the very real notion that they may encounter trouble, now enquired tremulously, 'Do you expect trouble then Sir, when you go to Brussels? Do you suppose the French army will really try to attack the Prussians?'

Malcolm looked grave. 'I fear it Ma'am, but I am hopeful that the British and Coalition between them have enough forces to drive them off, if an attack should occur. I will, of course, consult Wellington, and see what may be needed as to taking away any wounded, and so on. We must pray for the best outcome and that Bonaparte may be put off an attack before we are ready. The initial dispositions of Wellington and the Coalition may be enough to counter the French army.'

Wentworth was grave. 'If the Frenchman does move his forces through Mons, to the south-west of Brussels, Sir, he may stand a good chance of enveloping the Coalition. If he is successful, we may have our work cut out.' He did not add that such an event would keep them in port for a good month or two longer.

Some discussion as to the finer points of this manoeuvre were the topic for the rest of the evening and by the end of it, Wentworth was pleased to retire to his cabin and take some rest. Urgent as the journey across to Ostend was, the wind had not yet cooperated and they moved at a speed which meant it would take at least six-and-thirty hours at sea. Through his porthole window, Wentworth could see the distant lights of the Tartarus off the stern of the Nightingale, and he wondered how Benwick was faring. He, at least, had his wife aboard! How strange the workings of the heart!

This attachment to his wife was such that he almost wished that he had allowed Anne on board with them, despite the dangers, so strong was his wish to see her again. A week's separation had been hard; how much harder would the coming months be!

The bosun's pipe sounded the lights out, as if to remind him of his present duty. Shrugging into a white linen night shirt, he retired to his bunk and blew out his candle, finding comfort in the thought that at Kellynch Hall, his wife would be doing the same.

Nine

Monday 12 June, 1815

The following day Wentworth rose at his usual early hour, had his boy bring him warm water and made a hasty toilet. Above deck could be heard the light swish of the sails and he felt a slight rock to the hull of the ship. A wind had sprung up at last. Wentworth completed his morning rituals, left his cabin, and climbed up the steep wooden stairs onto the forward deck. The light wind ruffled his hair and he faced for a moment out towards the bow, allowing the brisk sea air to fill his lungs. Men scurried about under the billowing sails in their distinctive straw hats and blue coats, taking care of their duties as the prow first drew high on the waves then bowed low again into the sea-green swell. On the starboard stern, in the distance, the Tartarus could be seen, sails billowing gladly, just as those of the Nightingale were doing lustily above his head. Beyond the other ship, further out to the southern horizon, he noted some darkening skies. Frowning, he went in search of breakfast and any orders from Malcolm, hailing the odd busy sailor every now and then as he passed by. Cheerful, they saluted him with deference in return.

He consulted his lieutenants at breakfast, found all in order and the ship on course, and was satisfied that they might make Ostend, if the wind was kind, late that night or at least by the small hours of Tuesday morning. The Rear Admiral, who had also appeared and had at once loaded his plate with cold mutton, salted kippers and bread and jam, sat down at the table with him. The smell of strong coffee pervaded the room and mingled pleasantly with the salt tang of the air.

'Ah, Wentworth. Devil of a good wind now, though I am unhappy about those dark clouds to the south of our position.'

'I did note those, Sir. We could be in for some rough sailing.'

'Aye, true enough, but the Nightingale's been in worse. Sturdy for all that she's a tad grey-haired. Reminds me of my wife.' He chuckled. 'After breakfast I shall go over our arrival tomorrow morning. I want your opinion on a few points.' Malcolm nodded to the young powder monkey who doubled as serving boy, and who was sleepily filling cups with the strong black brew. 'There's a good lad — see me right, and your captain too, eh boy?'

They filled themselves and drank coffee until the ladies appeared. Enquiring after their sleep, and wishing them a good morning, the two men left shortly afterward, and spent the morning in consultation with Malcolm's aide and the three lieutenants. They determined after some discussion to stay on course, despite the foul cloud mass in the distance. At midday, however, the wind whipped up to a higher degree and with it, more black clouds came out of the south, obscuring the sun. Soon afterwards, a warm, heavy rain began to spatter the ship and the seas become choppy.

'It don't look good, Cap'n,' cried Taylor, meeting Wentworth on the quarter deck. The wind whipped his voice away and Wentworth had to strain to hear. They were both becoming drenched in the rain which had obscured their view. Wentworth gestured upwards to where Inchpole was at the helm and in conversation with the Cruikshank, and they lurched towards the poop deck.

At the wheel, Wentworth consulted with his lieutenants and they adjourned below deck. In Wentworth's quarters a map was spread out over the wooden table and presently a new course was measured and plotted, which would take them wide of the storm. He hoped.

Taking Inchpole above deck with him, he stared into the greying daylight. Off the stern of Nightingale, the Tartarus could barely be seen and Wentworth wondered how Benwick was faring. He opened his telescope and trained it on the Tartarus. Through the haze of the rain, a sailor on the front deck of the ship was doing likewise, obediently awaiting a signal from Wentworth. Benwick was no fool, thought Wentworth admiringly.

He turned to his second lieutenant. 'Send a message to Tartarus, letting them know our course has changed, and the new coordinates. As fast as you can man, before we lose visibility altogether.'

'Sir'. Inchpole, who was in charge of ship-to-ship communications and was highly experienced in semaphore, nodded obediently and immediately left to gather his flags. Soon they had veered sou'east, and the Tartarus had obediently shifted course with them, although she was barely visible now in the fast-darkening afternoon.

Two hours on the storm had not abated. Waves pounded the ship's sides and washed over the decks and Wentworth cursed the extra time it would take to navigate around the bad weather which covered a wider area than he had expected. Brookbank and Taylor had taken the wheel above deck and Inchpole had gone to do an inspection. There was little the rest of them could do but take shelter below, and most of the able seamen were now huddled in the foc'sle where they had their quarters. When Wentworth approached, a loud roaring from within made him smile grimly in recognition; yells and raucous calls of, 'I demand me good money!' and 'Hold out ye flipper, boy!' issued from the hold. Ducking his head into the narrow space briefly, by the light of a few precarious lanterns, he could see the men were sitting around, seemingly unaffected by the ship's swaying and bucking as it was hit with each wave.

'Captain!' A few of the younger fellows stood, but he nodded them down good naturedly. The air reeked of rum and fetid sweating bodies.

'Joinin' us, are ye then, Captain?' called out one of the seamen with a laugh.

Wentworth shook his head. There was nothing else the men could do but stay as dry as possible and wait for the storm to abate, so he did not mind them taking their portions of rum and playing at games to amuse themselves. For want of anything else to do they were playing at Abel-whackets, and taking loud, cussing pleasure in giving each other great whallops with a knotted kerchief, on the hands of the losers.

'This is for the loss of the good game, this is for the same.' The heavy handkerchief, braided tightly until it was as hard as a rope, came down upon another young hand, and the older men exploded with laughter as the youth pulled up his hand swiftly and in pain, stifling a cry. A few of the younger seamen, greenhorns at only eleven and twelve years old, nursed bruised hands, trying hard to laugh and appear nonchalant, but shocked from the viciousness with which the older men had whacked them. They would learn, Wentworth thought as he left the foc'sle, just as he himself had.

Upon the foredeck above, a few good fellows ran about in the lashing rain, checking all was tied down securely, lurching with the ship as she took heavy blows to her hull from the waves.

Wentworth watched them for a moment then went below to his cabin to dry off and get an hour's rest. Relieved after all that Anne had not had to endure such heavy seas, he wondered how Louisa Benwick was faring on the Tartarus. Anne had not once been ill when he had taken her out for several days after they had first been married, and she had not once complained of being out of countenance, he recollected, but Louisa was of a more delicate disposition, and so soon after her recovery from the fall at Lyme, he wondered if she was taking the rough seas hard. Still, she had Benwick with her. He wondered too, how the ladies aboard his own vessel were faring but being sailor's wives, they would have experienced worse than this. Poor Mrs Inchpole who had been in fright of the French, he pondered with amusement, had more to be anxious about in this gale than in any unlikely enemy engagement!

After a time, he drifted into restless sleep but was woken by the rolling of the ship's hull and wearily cast himself from his bunk. He lurched to his door and wrenched it open, in time to see Inchpole lurching down the hall away from him. 'Inchpole!'

Wentworth raised his voice over the thrash of the waves against the wooden hull.

Over the din of the thrashing waves, Inchpole must have heard him for he turned around and came, with some difficulty, towards his captain. 'Can I be of assistance, Sir?'

'What are you about, and what is the state of the Nightingale?'

'Sir. I've just been in to see the Rear Admiral, but could not find him — he must be above. We are taking on a bit of water, Sir. I've set the men to pumping the bilges; it oughtn't to take long but we can't stand to leave it. The seam has sprung a leak. Not a large one, but large enough.'

Wentworth uttered an oath. He had inspected the seam himself before they had left port and it had seemed sound enough, though the ship was old built. But he had not wanted this voyage to learn that the British admiralty appeared to find, now and then, great diversion in sending three dozen men or so to sea in leaky vessel. 'Have the men plug any leaks they find with caulk and I'll inspect it when we reach port. The seam will have to be resealed with pitch when we reach harbour. Let Caulfield know. Happen she'll get us through 'til then.'

'Yes, Sir.'

'And the sails? Are they all secure?'

'So far, Sir, but I haven't been above for some thirty minutes.'

'I see.' Wentworth had to shout to be heard. 'Get up to Johnson and give me a report on the sails as soon as you can. I shall be on deck.'

'Aye, Sir.' Inchpole retreated with difficulty and Wentworth followed him, listing from side to side as he walked. The rain pelted his face with sharp bullets as he emerged from below. At the helm, he checked to see how they were faring, then went below again, drenched to the skin, to consult the map with Cruikshank and Taylor. It was agreed that they would try a change of course a few degrees wider to the north, which might take them out of the line of the storm's path.

'She's a bucking horse, the ol' Night'ngale,' laughed Brookbank as he was tossed suddenly off his feet. He never feared a storm, and it made him valuable to Wentworth, for the man was unruffled in all weathers and kept his head.

'Did you say a Bucking Whore?' Taylor's smile was mournful as ever, but his eyes were laughing, even as the ship thrashed.

'Only you would know about that, eh Taylor?' replied Brookbank good naturedly. He pulled himself to his feet and rubbed his elbow.

'I'm a married man, and my wife never lets me forget it,' Taylor said, with a half-smile.

Wentworth, indifferent as to the toss and swell of the boat's movements, smiled a little and sent Brookbank to inspect the men, then took Taylor above to find Malcolm. They had only just hauled themselves onto the poop deck, when there was a great roar of wind and a crack like gunshot.

On the main deck below them, men and boys shouted and ran across the rain-lashed deck. One of the huge sails had ripped loose and had begun to struggle violently in the gale. The wooden mast bent ominously in the force of the wind.

'Great God!' Wentworth, a thrill of fear passing through him, dashed forward in the heavy rain, and shouted something but the wind whipped his words away before they had had time to reach the ears of the men below. One of the men, however, had already run to the rigging with a great rigging knife, and had clambered up the mast. He quickly sawed at the lines holding the sail until it caught fully in the wind and ripped away. It swept up and over the waves and was gone.

Malcolm appeared, dressed in a heavy woollen coat, and with him was Johns, the boatswain. They had a short conversation in the rain, then they, too, lurched their way up to the helm. The Rear Admiral thrust himself up and onto the deck and shouted into the wind. 'Near lost the mast, Wentworth, sheer luck young Hobson got to it in time. And there's another devil in your Nightingale; the seam looks in severe need of pitching. Leak in the hold, man.'

'Aye, so I'm told. Let's get below.' Wentworth was none too pleased about the three hours of manpower it would take to empty the bilge and caulk the hole. Once below in the captain's quarters, he spoke to Malcom again. 'Were you down there just now? How does it look?'

'Been below these forty-five minutes, bailing water with the best of them. Could be worse, though. Nothing that we can't remedy by throwing certain be-gowned personages over the side,' Malcolm growled over the storm. 'I'll wager you this is all due to taking females aboard. Dammed pesky creatures, I declare! I'll engage for it that this is all due to that Mrs Cruickshank. Tempting the devil, aye, she did, and he answered too!'

Wentworth only smiled wryly and braced himself easily against another heavy lurch of the ship. 'I will allow that women have a certain air of sorcery about them, but only the kind they invariably use upon the other sex.'

'No, no, Wentworth, I will not have it so! The only kind! You must think the weather to be of the male variety then, since it is quite surely in the power of these dammed females! But I tell you that you have quite mistaken the matter, for the weather is most certainly as female as those we carry aboard this ship, for it is just as changeable, all fair weather one minute and foul the next! No, Wentworth, don't think I can't see you smile at me but it is my considered opinion that women are the very devil on a ship and present circumstances only bear me out!'

'Now then, Admiral,' chided Taylor who was rather partial to his lady, 'you can hardly blame a leaky seam on the females present; why the admiralty has sent us all to sea in a vessel hardly fit, I cannot say, if you'll pardon me for saying so, Sir; why, they are likely casting ballots at our expense as we speak, but it ain't poor Mrs Cruickshanks' doing, Sir. Reckon we got some bad luck is all.'

'Bad luck or no,' intoned Malcolm dourly, 'this has been a set-back indeed, added a good six or seven hours to our arrival, but never mind it now, cannot be helped. Weather witches! I warned you, Wentworth!'

Wentworth ordered the braces and sheets trimmed, in the hopes that they might make a greater pace around the great squall, smiling a little at images of the female tenants of his best cabins as *tempestarii*, able to call up tempests at will. Well, *tempestarii* or no, he had a burden of his responsibility upon him, and he determined not to lose an hour, if one could be spared, in getting the Rear Admiral to Ostend.

Ten

The day dragged but by late afternoon the high winds relaxed their hold on the Nightingale and the waves became less in power. By seven o'clock, the grey clouds had even broken up and the light of the half-moon broke weakly through the misty night. Now the Tartarus could be seen in the distant moonlight, and many knots in their wake. The men had come up from the foc'sle and begun to go about their duties, happier now that they were above board and not breathing the fetid air that eight-and-twenty odd men below deck will soon produce. The light wind stayed with them and they now made good time over the subdued waters. The Tartarus lagged but Wentworth and Malcolm would see them into port the following morning and consult Benwick on certain details regarding Malcolm's transport to Ghent.

Dinner that evening had a celebratory tone. The three married officers all came in with their ladies on their arms, and the party of females was welcomed with due attention. The women were vastly relieved, they agreed, to be out of their cabins and over the dreadful weather they had endured in the channel. Malcolm, who had been much out of countenance over the 'dammed females' and holding a particular grudge against poor Mrs Cruikshank for wishing the gale upon them in the first instance, had become complacent with gratitude, and even conceded to having his claret brought up, and they made a merry enough party as the first sight of land grew closer on the horizon.

An uneventful night brought the sloop limping into Ostend at around nine o'clock the following morning. Wentworth immediately set the men to pitching the seam with tar, under the watchful eye of the boatswain, while Cruikshank was under command to go into town and find materials to replace the missing sail. Meanwhile, Wentworth stood with Malcolm upon the wharf and awaited the Tartarus. As the ship neared port, however, they observed the flag at half-mast and became alarmed. No Captain Benwick was at the helm to bring her in, nor at the prow to watch her progress, and when the Tartarus was finally secure, Benwick's first lieutenant, Blackley, met them with a sober expression.

'It is my duty to inform you, Sir,' he addressed Rear Admiral Malcolm soberly, 'that we have lost our captain.'

Wentworth was forcibly struck, horror making him motionless. 'Captain Benwick? It is not Captain Benwick of whom you speak?'

'Aye, Sir, I do.' The man was apologetic and visibly moved. 'It was the storm, Sir. Our very own Captain Benwick, in his gallant attempt to prevent a sail from being ripped away from the mast, was swept from the ship by a freak wave and was drowned, Sir.' His face was wooden, his voice bland. It was the face that all sailors, met with sea tragedy, assume. 'We tried to find him but he was gone under the waves too quick for us, Sir.'

'Oh God! Wretched, wretched fate!' Wentworth paled, then coming to himself more, asked with urgency, 'Where is Mrs Benwick?'

'Remains in her cabin, Sir. She suffered a bout of hysteria when she heard the news, then fainted dead away. We had to have the surgeon to her; although there is little he can do for the poor woman. He is with her now. It might be well, Sir, if one of the officer's wives sits with her. Perhaps one of the women aboard the Nightingale might to go to her?'

Wentworth gave his immediate assent, but was hardly able to speak, being very much afflicted by this dreadful news. It struck him with horror that Benwick, having only two years ago suffered the tragedy in the loss of his intended bride, had now succumbed to the workings of fate once again. And it occurred to him almost as immediately, that it was *he* who was responsible for Benwick's death, since it was he who had recommended him for the posting!

And now his wife was still aboard the Tartarus. Poor, wretched Louisa! It was not in his power to decide which fate was worse; to be aboard ship and having to face her husband's death after being so lately married, or to be sitting at home in all expectation of her husband's coming home safely. Neither was to be borne! Of all things he had least expected, it was this! And now it must fall to him to give her passage home, and give her parents the dreadful news of Benwick's demise. Perhaps of all people, it was fitting for him to be the one to bring her home to England, for once he had been closely acquainted with the girl. And yet, what an unhappy task! Poor, poor Louisa Benwick!

Admiral Malcolm said everything that was proper and feeling on the occasion, but Wentworth, still suffering under the stupor of shock and pressing guilt, simply agreed with the lieutenant's suggestions regarding the reorganization of the crew to accommodate the loss of the Tartarus's captain. Malcolm gave the authority immediately for Blackley to temporarily captain the ship until another man could be ordered over. The Tartarus was to stay in port with the Nightingale as originally ordered, in case Wellington should have need for the naval support offered by the admiralty, but now Malcolm requested that since Lieutenant Blackley was to be in command of the Tartarus, Wentworth would accompany him to Brussels in poor Benwick's stead.

'It is my strong hope that we shall not be needed — God forbid Bonaparte should make a strike upon our forces here; nonetheless, we must be prepared to give aid, Wentworth. There's nothing for it but you must take Benwick's widow home to England upon our return. I pray it will be a speedy one.'

Wentworth gave his assent to the plan, lamenting privately that this was a fine blow indeed, to take him away from his ship, and the widowed woman he felt responsible for. He must go to Louisa, of course, and offer what small comfort he could, and assure her that he would find her a safe passage home to England at the first opportunity. He must write to the Musgroves, too, informing them of the tragic news. He would write to Anne as well, for of all people, he thought Anne would be a steadying influence on Louisa upon her return, where her mama and papa were prone to those high sensitivities which would make the widow's burden all the more difficult to bear.

But how to get Louisa home! If only Anne had come with them, after all. There was no one so dependable as his Anne. She would know what to do! He retired for a time to his cabin, and leaned heavily over his writing desk, his arms folded and his head hidden, and when he eventually rose from his place, his countenance was pale and heavy, sick with duty.

When soon afterward he boarded the Tartarus and knocked on the door of Mrs Benwick's cabin, he was met by Mrs Taylor, whom he had earlier asked to sit with Louisa.

'How does she go on?' he asked anxiously.

'Oh, Captain, it is a vast poor mite she is, very poor indeed!' lamented the good Mrs Taylor, shaking her head. 'The young lady has taken it very hard, and has only just now cried herself to sleep after I gave her a draught I had about me for my own use. She ought to get home as soon as possible to her friends. How soon do you suppose it can be managed, Captain?'

Wentworth was grave. 'I regret that I cannot give her passage immediately, Mrs Taylor. She must resolve herself to wait in port here, for another ship bound for home, and that could be some weeks.'

'Perhaps the mail packet?'

He conceded but with reluctance. 'Perhaps a mail packet might arrive which had the ability to offer a berth suitable for a lady, if one can be found in these times. Even if it was to found, I fear to send her alone on such a treacherous crossing, without a companion to see to her comfort and safety. It is not uncommon for packets to be set upon in the channel by French privateers, Mrs Taylor. Regrettably, I myself must see the admiral to Brussels. I hope we shall only be a week or two at most but it may be many more.'

'Perhaps another ship then, Captain Wentworth. There must be something due in port soon?'

'I have just this moment made some inquiries and there are no suitable English ships expected in port for the time being. I fear Mrs Benwick must almost certainly wait with the Nightingale and allow me to bring her home when the admiral has finished his business here. And that,' he added bitterly, 'may be as long as two months. You *will* stay with her until my return?'

Mrs Taylor assured him she would do all in her power to serve Mrs Benwick. Wentworth went away feeling the heavy duty of responsibility on his shoulders, to which he could not do justice under his present circumstances, but he was resolved to speak with Louisa as soon as she was awake. Meanwhile, he went directly back to his cabin and took up his quill, to fulfil his duty to the Musgroves.

Half an hour later, his letter to Mr Musgrove written, with all that was feeling and proper said of Benwick, and all sympathies with their poor daughter, all pledges that he would see her home as soon as he could manage, the paper was sealed and the direction written across its surface. Then, after sharpening his quill with the pen knife he reserved for that duty, Wentworth now took up another ironed sheet of parchment and dipped his quill into the ink once more. Here he paused, in sober thought for some minutes, then began.

Tues 13 June 1815

'My too excellent Anne,

> *I write to you under the most tragic of circumstances, and yet I do not wish to alarm you, for I am well, as you see, and we are come to Ostend fully intact. And yet, I must do my sad duty, and inform you of the death of our very good, our very noble friend, Captain Benwick. Yes, my dear, I penetrate that you will be more anguished at this news even than I, for your excellent heart, so loyal and true that it is, will be much moved for a most wretched Louisa, whom set to sea with her husband in all expectation of his safe and happy return and has been made a widow in the face of that expectation.*

I have spoken in the past of the devotion of man, but I own the rightness of your claim that the devotion of women has a strong, more lasting hold on them. Louisa Benwick's devotion to her husband was true and constant and this blow will be very hard upon her. I have not yet seen her, but one of the women here sits with her and informs me she is taking it very wretchedly.

I confess I fear for Louisa's state of mind. She has not your own steadiness, has not your great resources for solitude nor that stoic resignation she might have seen exemplified in you, the epitome of what a naval wife ought to be. No, Louisa has been coddled to a large degree and this new introduction to hardship will be shocking to her, I collect.

I have written to her parents, although at present there is not much they can do until her return, and that, I fear, will not be for some weeks, since no English ships of the quality she would need to carry her home safely are expected to depart Ostend in the next month. Still, I am in hopes of a packet with a suitable cabin, but even then, there is the matter of the risk I take in sending her on such a treacherous journey alone. Mrs Taylor, one of the midshipmen's wives, has promised to stay with her until my return from Brussels. Perhaps our business there will be concluded speedily, in which case it will be my duty to bring her home, or we may find her passage on another ship soon; in any case I shall keep you informed. Once she is home at Uppercross, she will, I hope, find comfort in her own home among her friends; God knows she will need them now!

For my part, I must now accompany the admiral to Brussels, and I fear I know not the likely duration of this journey, how long I will be required in Brussels, nor if the admiralty's offer of assistance will be taken up or not. It all will depend on Bonaparte's movements and the subsequent orders of Wellington.

*Oh, my dear heart, I cannot make up my mind
as to which is the lesser evil; having denied you
passage alongside me, where you might be a comfort
to Louisa, (I cannot selfishly think of my own
comfort now!) or to know you and our child are safe,
but far distant from me. Keep Louisa in your
thoughts and myself near your heart.*

*In the meanwhile, believe me to be your own
fervently devoted*

F. W.'

He added a post-script giving her his direction in Brussels,
though he had already given it to her in the previous letter. Then,
folding the paper, he sat in thought for some time. He felt in no
small way responsible for Louisa Benwick, since they had at one
time been intimate acquaintances, although he had never been
able to bring himself to the point of making her an offer. He had
tried, he had toiled, but his feelings for Anne Elliot he had never
been able to truly conquer. Being in Anne's company day after
day, when he had last year come to Uppercross to visit and found
her there, had done much to throw Anne Elliot, with her fine,
elegant mind and her keen understanding into stark relief against
the backdrop of a mere Louisa Musgrove, pleasant and sweet and
commonplace. Only a year ago he had fancied himself so
irrevocably altered in his requirements for marriage, that a little
beauty, a few compliments to the navy, were all he needed to be
satisfied in a wife; he had been complacent, feeling that a high-
spirited, amiable Louisa Musgrove would do for him just as well
as an Anne Elliot would have done eight years ago.

How wrong he had been then, and how quickly he had
discovered his error! He had had little society among women in
general, to make him nice, and yet, nice he was, for it seemed that
after coming again into her circle, and seeing that she was the very
same Anne Elliot who had charmed him eight years ago, he had
discovered that a mere Louisa Musgrove would not do for him
after all. He had quickly come to his senses and withdrawn
immediately from further acquaintance with Miss Louisa

Musgrove. Fortune had thereafter sent Benwick in his stead, who found in the girl a devoted and sweet wife. As for Louisa's mercurial change of allegiance, it gave him comfort that her heart had so obviously not been as strongly attached as his own heart had been to another!

But now, Mrs Benwick was a widow, and Wentworth could not but feel that it was his own doing, that if he had not suggested Benwick to the admiralty, Louisa would have been spared her loss. The thought struck him cruelly. He must look out for her now, as much as he would wish others to do if he himself had drowned at sea and his own Anne had been made to suffer the very same grief. He would be at peace when the girl was safely in the care of her friends at Uppercross. Her parents were good, steady people, and if Mary Musgrove was wanting a little sense and compassion, he knew Charles Musgrove was a devoted brother. And then, more importantly, Anne was nearby at Kellynch. His mind would be more at ease, if only he knew Louisa was in the care of Anne. No one so proper, so capable as Anne! It was the second time he had been brought to such thoughts, and he painfully recollected the first time, when Louisa had fallen from the steps at Lyme, because he had allowed her to be headstrong — and he had applauded her for it! The burden of his guilt afterward had been heavy indeed. As it was now.

Letters completed and sent off to the post, Wentworth spent the remainder of the day engaged in preparations for the journey to Brussels, getting a team and carriage hired, and in consultation with his lieutenants. At about four o'clock, he knocked once more on Mrs Benwick's cabin door, and was gratified to have Mrs Taylor inform him that 'poor Mrs Benwick' was awake and would see him.

Louisa was a sad sight, however. Her eyes red and swollen, she sat up in a chair, dressed, but pale and sober. She looked up when the Captain entered, and managed a weak smile. 'Captain Wentworth! How kind you are to come!'

He was gratified to see she was calm. He removed his hat respectfully. 'May I offer my deepest condolences, Mrs Benwick. I can only imagine—' He stopped, almost but not quite, awkward and helpless.

Louisa struggled visibly, then became more composed. 'Thank you, Captain, you are very kind. You were always so very kind!' she replied earnestly. 'Please, tell me, when may I go home?'

Never one to be shy or reserved, and having once been on a more intimate footing with the 'Miss Musgrove' of his past acquaintance, he was incapable of awkwardness with her now, and yet he struggled for a moment since it was only bad news he had to deliver.

'It is a great burden to me to tell you so, Mrs Benwick,' he began formally, holding his hat awkwardly at his side, 'since I fear you will quite naturally wish to return immediately to England, yet I cannot find a way to bring it about. The only ship departing for England is the packet which will depart this evening, which carries the post, but I have already made enquires and she has no room for a female. No other ships with any capacity for female guests are due in port for some time. It is my object, and my fervent desire, to accompany you safe back to England, and yet it seems I must discharge my duty here first.'

Louisa was visibly moved by this admission, clearly expecting a prompt return to her own country, but after a moment, she fortified herself and said, 'Oh, but I would not have expected — that is, Captain, if you cannot give me a passage home just yet, and no other ship can do so, then I must be content to wait until it is possible. It does not signify to me, if I must go home in less comfort than I am used, Captain. Pray don't think me so feeble minded or fragile that I cannot bear a rougher type of accommodation.'

Wentworth concealed his astonishment. 'Even so, you will need room enough for a maid, and we must wait at least for a mail packet which might accommodate two females, however crude the furnishings.' He smiled slightly. 'I know you must be wishing every hour to be gone.'

'I don't so much mind for myself,' she replied, faltering a little, 'but my friends at home will be anxious for me. They were excessively fond of James, you see.' Tears remained unshed in her eyes even as she spoke.

She smiled a feeble smile and Wentworth, much astonished at the apparent calm in the young woman he had so recently considered 'commonplace', honoured her immediately for this unexpected maturity. She was no longer an enthusiastic and high-spirited Louisa Musgrove, of unformed opinions and unrestrained spirits, but a grave, moderate Louisa Benwick, married and widowed within a short time. Once, her high spirits and animated conversation had charmed him, briefly, before Anne had reclaimed for her own, his affections and his allegiance. Now he wished those old high spirits back, if only to relieve her of the grief she must feel.

'You will rally, Louisa,' he said in a low tone, and almost before he could prevent himself, leaned forward to take her limp hand.

'Yes.' She gave him no resistance.

Awkwardness made him blunt. 'Did you receive James' personal effects? I am told there were several personal items in his cabin which were parcelled up to be given into your hand.'

She reached for a small fob-watch on the table, and a miniature portrait in a covered pendant. Opening the pendant, she handed it to Wentworth. 'It is of James, of course. He commissioned it before we were married, for another, and it was passed to me. It matches the one I gave him of myself,' she added sadly.

Wentworth's heart gave a small leap and he smiled. 'I remember it well. Your husband commissioned Hargreaves to write to the jeweller, but he had not the heart for it and asked me to write the instructions for its setting instead.' He remembered also the state of his heart as he had written a second note, shortly afterwards, but with more fervour than he had ever written before, since it was a declaration of love, and Anne was to be its recipient. *You pierce my soul. I am half agony, half hope... Tell me not that I am too late!* He returned the portrait to Louisa.

She took it carefully, fingering the chain. 'It's sister, the one I gave to James of myself, he was wearing when he—' she stopped on a sob.

He looked away while she collected herself. 'I have given the matter some thought, Mrs Benwick, and I collect you might wish to remove to the Nightingale — Mrs Taylor is there to keep you company, and Mrs Cruickshank. I may be some weeks — it is not decided yet how long this business will keep me from Ostend. But I shall return as soon as I may, and if another ship has not been commandeered to return you home, I shall accompany you myself, and deliver you to your family. If you wish it, of course,' he added, seeing her countenance pale.

'I am very grateful — it is excessively kind — but may I not go on to Brussels with you, Captain Wentworth? One of the ladies could come with us, and I promise you I would not be in the way. Only, I cannot bear the thought of sitting here for weeks on end, with little distraction to take my mind from unpleasant thoughts, from seeing *his* ship, there in port, every day!'

Compassion gave way to astonishment. 'My dear Mrs Benwick — Louisa! Even if Admiral Malcolm's permission could be gotten, the journey we men will take will hardly be fit for ladies! We leave tonight and will travel all night to Ghent, and then on to Brussels in a short period of time. There will be no stops of the kind required by elegant ladies for their comfort and accommodations. I assure you, it will be an unkind journey, especially with the blow you have been dealt,' he added gravely.

Louisa looked him in the eye. 'I have just lost my husband. If I had not arrived here a widow, I would have accompanied James when he went with Admiral Malcolm. If I truly loved a man, as I did James, I would always be with him. Nothing would have separated us, but for his death. Now I ask to make the journey as if he was still here. I ask you as James Benwick's widow, pray, let me come with you. It was what James had intended. I am not the frail, silly girl I was when you first knew me last year. I can make the journey. I will. I am determined, Captain.' Her gaze was steady but calm.

Wentworth, remembering those very words uttered only a year ago, and their tragic consequences, was hard pressed to admit the rightness of such a sentiment, but he said reluctantly, after a moment, 'I cannot promise anything, but I shall undertake to ask the admiral, and let him decide. If you are of the party, we shall have to take Mrs Inchpole as well, of course, and the admiral has shown already a rather stern prejudice against women present in the course of war business. But I shall make the request,' he added, seeing her countenance fall. 'I will do my best to advance your case. In the meantime, you had better ask Mrs Taylor to help pack your things, for we leave at seven o'clock this evening and you will wish to be ready, should the admiral give his permission.'

An unusually chivalrous Admiral Malcolm gave his grudging consent. 'Only because the Admiralty owes *something* to the widow of Captain Benwick, however unmoved the prospect leaves me personally. I can hardly deny her modest request, since it is yours also, Wentworth.'

The post-chaise-and-four was duly commissioned and made ready for their dispatch. It was determined that Lieutenant Taylor would be in charge of the Nightingale, Brookbank his second, and Inchpole, with the most experience in ground operations, would accompany Malcolm and himself, along with Malcolm's aide, to Ghent and then on to Brussels. Mrs Inchpole was to accompany them, as Mrs Benwick's companion, much to Malcolm's disapproval.

'This is what comes of letting women aboard ships,' growled he, as their trunks were loaded behind the vehicle. 'I'll engage for it the carriage will be overturned on the road! It's all one, ship or coach; women are a nuisance in every situation excepting their being at home in their own parlours!'

Wentworth, who had gone to a great deal of pain to gain Malcolm's consent to Mrs Benwick's accompanying them, said little, but hoped that no accident would befall them on the road or he feared the women would be sent back to the ship directly, middle of the night or not.

They were to travel by night, since the admiral was eager to reach Brussels as soon as it was possible. Mrs Inchpole, who had volunteered readily to come as companion to Mrs Benwick, assured them she would as soon sleep badly in a coach if only she could be beside her husband, as be left behind on the Nightingale, only to toss and turn all night from the fright of his not being there!

The team, driven by a groom and a post boy, was whipped up and the six of them, crushed up together in the post chaise, drove out of Ostend at seven o'clock that evening, and up onto the country road which would take them to Ghent, then onward to Brussels. Louisa Benwick, now dressed in some of the sombre black mourning clothes which Mrs Taylor had procured for her, sat quietly opposite Wentworth, with Mrs Inchpole beside her. They got on fast, with a little conversation among the men at first, but in the fast-falling dusk light, the company withdrew into sombre silence and soon Mrs Inchpole had dozed off on the arm of her husband, and the Rear Admiral, too, slipped into a light doze, next to his aide, Belcher. Mr Inchpole followed them soon after, and succumbed to the rocking of the coach.

When it was only Louisa and Captain Wentworth left awake, Louisa leaned forward and finally addressed him. Her voice was low, so as not to wake the others. 'Last year, Captain, when we became acquainted with each other — I have never — that is, if I gave you any pain, in my choosing James — I never meant to mislead you, only James was always there when I was recovering from the fall, and—'

'Pray, do not think on it!' Somewhat surprised at the mention of a subject that was delicate to them both, he toyed with the blue hat on his knee. 'That is nothing to the point, it never was. It led ultimately to my current happiness. How can I hold a grudge? There was never a spoken understanding between us, Louisa.'

'I'm glad.' She sighed and sat back against the cushions. 'We all love Anne. You know we all wished Charles had married Anne instead of Mary, but now I confess I am glad he did not.'

He inclined his head gravely. 'I, too.'

Louisa turned away again, toward the darkness outside, her face hidden from his, and in a few more minutes her eyes closed. Finally, after perhaps three hours on the road, Wentworth, too, allowed himself to sleep, mostly to give himself some relief from the torment of dwelling on the fate of poor Benwick, and even more so, that of his widow.

Eleven

Wednesday 14 June, 1815

The light of the rising sun was just tipping the horizon when Wentworth stirred and opened his eyes. Louisa was still asleep, resting against the side of the carriage, but in the night, she had covered her face with a shawl, and this hung at an odd angle now with the regular jolting of the carriage. Poor Mrs Inchpole too, slumped against her husband's shoulder and did her best to sleep upright. It was not a journey he would ever have consented to with ladies present, had he been an unmarried Captain Wentworth. He could only feel relief however, that they had met no misfortune in the night by upsetting into a ditch or meeting a highway gang.

But they were not overturned, contrary to the admiral's black predictions, and by seven o'clock that morning had safely arrived into Ghent. On account of Malcolm's having two acquaintances at a certain hotel, he gave the groom directions to drive there in order to bait the horses and bespeak some breakfast.

Mrs Inchpole admired the view from the carriage as they trotted into the main avenue, and gasped over the sight of the famous Castle Gravensteen, which she lauded as excessively imposing. 'I so wish we could go closer and inspect it; Thomas, do you not think we might have time to go and look through it?'

Her husband, catching a look on Rear Admiral Malcolm's countenance, had begun to remind her immediately of the object of their journey, but Admiral Malcolm, all sarcasm and condescending tones interposed loftily, 'My dear Mrs Inchpole, certainly you may look over Castle Gravensteen all you wish. I am at your disposal, and shall drop you outside its gate directly. We will be happy to pick you up on our return trip, say in six or seven weeks' time!' At this, overcome with his own wit, he uttered a short guffaw.

To this attack, poor Mrs Inchpole could not find a reply and only turned her head to the window with a muttered, 'Well! Dear me!' and took great pains to be quite taken up with the view of the streets while her red-faced husband looked apologetic.

Sir John Lambert and Captain Henry Smith had put up at the Reynhardt, and Admiral Malcolm went directly in search of them, Wentworth and the others on his heels. Entering the hotel and getting directions from one of the porters, Malcolm made for the corridor and banged haphazardly on the door which he supposed concealed Lambert behind it. There being no immediate reply, he strode down the passageway, calling out, 'Hallo there, where the devil's the door? Lambert! I say, Lambert!'

An older man, looking to be in his fiftieth decade, popped his head out from the opposite side and uttered an oath, 'Good God, its Sir Pulteney Malcolm if I don't be dammed! Hallo, Sir!'

Malcolm shook hands with him. 'Why, where the devil has Lambert stowed himself, eh? This house is dark as a sheer hulk on a moonless night, can't see anything for the life of me!'

Lambert now appeared in the gloomy corridor and shook Malcolm's hand and introductions were made. Malcolm, suggesting breakfast and desiring the two officers should join the party from the Nightingale, was met with astonishment to be eating breakfast so late since the other men had already taken their refreshments.

'Aye but what's that, by devil! This ain't the Royal Oak, I'll have you know, Sirs, no regular hours here! We are for Brussels and only break our journey here. Come — bear me a hand and get us up some breakfast, eh boys?'

He was now in a fine mood and they enjoyed a jolly breakfast in the dining room together, before Malcolm expressed a wish to press on for Brussels to see his commander, the Duke of Wellington. Louisa, black-gowned and solemn, ate little and said even less, and the two officers were too polite to ask for an explanation or make comment on the widow who was at breakfast with them. Malcolm managed to hiss as they left, 'a widow you know, Captain Benwick's wife who was at sea with him when he died — had no choice but to include her, and Mr Inchpole's lady too — the devil will make me pay for this, I engage for it!'

Wentworth held back from chastising the older man for his lack of tact, for the tragic subject of his horse-whispered comment seemed not to have heard him, or was feigning ignorance, and he was loath to bring her more pain than she was sure to already be suffering.

On the road again, Mrs Inchpole now dared not submit any more requests for sightseeing and the party made good time in getting into Brussels just after midday. Louisa was so quiet as to make Wentworth anxious for her state of mind, but when he enquired, she only smiled gently, and took up a well-thumbed book of Bryon's poems, and sighed every now and then so quietly that only Wentworth noticed. Mrs Inchpole consoled her as best she could, by directing small tidbits of conversation at her, but as Louisa merely sat composed, and said little in response, that lady soon took up her own novel and withdrew into silence.

Brussels was large and bustling, compared with the quaintness of Ghent. Carriages lined the streets and the crush getting on was quite as vexing to the admiral, he said, as any in London. Eventually they pulled up outside a modest establishment, and Wentworth immediately engaged to get them a suite of rooms. Not content to wait, Malcolm went directly on foot with his aide to call upon Wellington at his accommodations in another part of town, taking Inchpole with him. When he returned a good hour later, it was to find them all in a private parlour, taking some tea and refreshments.

'Well, well, I'm glad I find you ladies comfortable,' he began as he entered. 'We shall have to put up here for a few days, Wentworth. Wellington awaits news from the Prussian army as to Bonaparte's movements, and he is yet uncertain as to what aid we might give in all this.'

Wentworth was dismayed at the delay in their returning to the Nightingale. Anne would be disappointed but there was little to be done. His first priority was to find a passage home for Louisa Benwick.

Malcolm continued. 'By the by, Wellington tells me we will have some entertainment while we are here. Duchess of Richmond's here, you know. Giving one of her balls, it seems, tomorrow night. Long and short of it is, Wellington's going to mention our arrival, and I will engage for it that invitations will come to you and Inchpole too, if I know the Duke.'

'I shall not attend, Sir, if you will excuse me,' started Wentworth, looking at the form of a black-gowned Louisa Benwick, 'I rather think—'

'Pray don't make yourself anxious on my account,' said Louisa looking up sadly. 'I shall have Cecelia — Mrs Inchpole — to keep me company. Do go to the ball, Captain.'

He made some further protestations, but at the urging of both Louisa and Mrs Inchpole, who had not any clothes for a ball as fine as the Duchess of Richmond's, and was content to stay with Mrs Benwick, finally conceded to attend with the admiral.

As good as his word, Wellington had them included on the guest list, and by and by invitations found them by that evening, for the following day.

Wentworth found a moment to approach Louisa alone later. After dinner he came to sit beside her on the chaise, and said in a low tone, 'Mrs Benwick — Louisa — I shall be willing to remain behind tomorrow evening. You have only to mention it. If my going on to the Duchess of Richmond's ball would be seen as any disrespect to your husband — to Captain Benwick — then I shall at once send my apologies to Lady Richmond, and be content to be at your service, here at home.'

'Please, Captain,' interjected Louisa calmly. 'I thank you, but I am quite composed. I have Cecelia to stay with me and I have my memories for consolation. I ask for nothing more.'

He paused, somewhat awkward, then ventured to ask, 'If you want for anything, if there is any small sum you might require for your further comfort here, please depend upon me, as you would your husband, to provide for you. It is the least I can do, for both yourself, and for James Benwick, who was my friend.'

'You are very good, Captain Wentworth. Thank you, but I want for nothing.'

'And when you return to England?' He had been anxious for

her provision, since he understood that Benwick was by no means wealthy, although he had not by any means been in low waters when he had died.

'I shall have a small stipend. James made provision for me when we were married. It is not a large one, but it will keep me tolerably. Once I am home, I shall go to my sister, Captain. I have thought about it these last two days and I shall go to Henrietta. I shall be of some use to her, I fancy, when she has a family, and in the meantime, I can find plenty to occupy myself. I shall not die of grief, though it weighs upon me heavily.'

'You are remarkably composed,' he marvelled. 'I can hardly—'

'—imagine it is the same female you met with last summer at Uppercross? And yet it is I, the same Louisa Musgrove, who thought more of fashion and assemblies than of the suffering of those around her, and through her own folly, injured both herself and others,' replied Louisa with a slight smile when Wentworth made a polite protest. 'I have been thinking, Captain Wentworth, and I am wholly ashamed of what I was then! I was a shallow creature then! Now, I am the same Louisa and yet — I feel changed forever, as if have lived and died and come to life again a different person. I feel that I know myself, where I never knew before. Is that not an odd thing to think?'

The eyes that briefly met hers were warm with compassion. 'I cannot say, but I have experienced something like it, I think.' He had thought himself irrevocably altered, after eight years separation from the woman he had loved, but in one moment, on the steps at Lyme, when a gentleman had paid Anne the compliment of an admiring glance, he had felt all his previous feeling suddenly weigh upon him, and it was in that moment that he had understood his heart more fully than ever before. He had come alive again, then, too. But of this he did not speak, and remained silent, not wishing to give Louisa pain by recalling the past and by association, her terrible accident there.

Louisa, perhaps guessing something of his thoughts, grew quiet. Wentworth shortly afterward left her on the sofa, satisfied. He had seen Louisa Benwick quite as composed as he could hope for under the circumstances. He marvelled at it; indeed, he was astonished at it, that this was the same Louisa he had rejected for his own Anne, and yet, in the face of great trial, she had become more like Anne than he had ever guessed was possible. He had a sudden yearning to hold his wife, to place his hand over her swollen belly, to feel the heartbeat of the child which quickened below it. Their progress in Brussels could not be too hastened for him. His guilt sought to pull him down, into the rough, grasping undertow of self-doubt, to drown him. The sooner he could discharge his duty here and return Louisa to Uppercross, the better. Only then would he be able to find peace.

Twelve

Thursday 15 June, 1815

Brussels, Belgium.

The hour was well past ten o'clock the following evening, and as Wellington's arrival must be looked for, Admiral Malcolm had given Wentworth the commission of notifying him when that prestigious gentleman arrived. Wentworth had taken up a station beside one the imposing fireplaces in the large ballroom. Around him the orchestra surged and the couples whirled together in a blur of colour and motion designed, he mused, to make his head whirl in warmth of the room. He shifted uncomfortably in his dress uniform as he bemusedly observed the couples and kept watch for the duke. He was joined, at length, by the admiral. His superior officer, like himself, was in full formal dress, his cravat as high as his ears, and his tufted white hair in slight disarray, giving a distinctly odd appearance to his otherwise stern and aquiline nose and firm chin. For all his advanced years, he was a commanding figure.

'What say you to all this, hey Wentworth? A finer gathering I have not set eyes upon, and yet I auger ill by it, I'll own. But,' he added, downing the last of the liquid in his punch glass, ''tis quite a sight, by all accounts. The prince tells me the rooms here are a converted coach house — pretty a penny spent upon it too, no doubt!'

'The duchess and her husband have certainly spared no expense, Sir. But, perhaps, being in charge of the reserves in Brussels and being its protector, you might say the prince has shouldered a great obligation to keep up the spirits of the alliance. He is as good natured a fellow as he is rich, I collect.'

'You mean he is as rich a fellow as he is good natured,' suggested the admiral with a short laugh. 'Ah well, the place is certainly as ornately decorated as any palace I have ever seen pictured in books.' He held up his empty glass. 'I think I shall drink while I may, Wentworth. I feel ill in my bones, I confess. I've a feeling Bonaparte will advance, if he is wise, and soon. I do not trust intelligence that says otherwise! Drink up, drink up, while you may!'

Wentworth did as he was bid, and soon afterwards the admiral left Wentworth alone again, to stand looking on over the dancers. In addition to Wellington and William Prince of Orange, every other officer of high rank had been invited to the ball. Wentworth was privately a little surprised that with Napoleon so hard by, the greatest of these men had seen fit to abandon their posts for a little while to indulge in revelry. But he collected that all men, even the greatest of them, must have a little diversion now and then, and the tensions ensuing from the possibility of Napoleon's advance across Belgium would well be relieved with a little pleasant company and music. Therefore, the sight of those uniformed officers who paraded past either with their own wives or with the unattached ladies of the very cream of society did not give him undue anxiety. Wellington knew what he was about, and would not sanction attending if any risk was imminent.

Although he had been formally presented to the prince and princesses earlier that evening, Wentworth himself had not been introduced to those of the other higher-ranking officers, and now he looked about himself with a keen curiosity to see with whom he might have a prior acquaintance. Admiral Malcolm had informed him upon their arrival that Wellington was due to arrive later that evening, perhaps around midnight; this was no amazing news since the dancing was expected to go on until at least four or five in the morning. This was, after all, the Duchess of Richmond's ball, the likes of which would be an honour to attend; it must surpass anything and everything ever gone before.

Just then, Georgiana, the prince's sister, whirled past him on the arm of a very dashing young officer who had caught his eye, since the man was dressed not in military garb, as were the majority of the officers, but in naval uniform like himself. Even more surprising to Wentworth was that he sported the uniform of a lower-ranked officer. How did the young man come to attend a ball such as this, he wondered? Besides this anomaly, the young man's appearance was also was singular in that he sported one arm only, the empty sleeve of the right arm tucked out of the way to oblige the eyes of the ladies. Wentworth was amused, however, to note that the absence of his arm seemed not to have any effect on the young sailor's dancing, for he could dance as well as any of the others, and the princess did not seem to notice anything amiss with her partner. The youth was perhaps two or three-and-twenty, and had a seriousness of demeanour beyond his years.

Following the couple with his eye for a moment, Wentworth was suddenly distracted by Malcolm's approach and he stood more upright, ready to receive any orders which his superior officer might commission him with.

'Any sign of the Duke?' Malcolm barked as he approached Wentworth. 'Confounded din, and all these women as free and careless as if nary a worry; I'll hold for it that they won't be so merry tomorrow,' he added portentously, 'I don't like it, Wentworth; this is merely a reprieve many will regret by morning, if my nose has given me the right of it.'

Wentworth frowned. 'What news from the front? Do you expect any difficulty?'

Malcolm shook his head as he looked out at the merry partners now engaged in a spirited French cotillion. 'Aye, nothing but a rumour as yet, Wentworth. Let them have their dancing. I hope for all their sakes they can have tonight, if nothing else.' His tone was grave.

Wentworth, recollecting the threat of Bonaparte's advance towards Brussels and the troops that at this very minute were gathering in answer to that threat, remained gravely silent himself, and stood firmly with his gaze on the door. 'As soon as Wellington arrives, I will send for you, Admiral.'

Malcolm strode away through the crush of ladies and young officers, and disappeared in the direction of the prince, to consult, no doubt, with that gentleman, who recently had been promoted to the rank of Commander, and was in possession of a sizable part of the Prussian alliance at Britain's disposal.

Now, the young man who had caught Wentworth's eye previously came again into view, with his lovely partner, walking sedately alongside the dance floor, having finished the dance. The Flemish princess, to whom he had been earlier introduced, now came very close to Wentworth, and did him the honour of bowing her pretty head gently. He, preparing to bow and allow them to pass by, was unprepared for her gracious 'Forgive my interruption, Captain, but may I present Lieutenant Price?'

'Your Highness, Lieutenant Price.' Curbing open astonishment, he bowed to both of them in return. Perceiving the interest on the face of both the lady and the young man, Wentworth instantly understood that the young man had expressed a wish to make the acquaintance of one of his fellow naval brothers, and with all the consciousness of his being superior in rank, but without any of the ceremony which might naturally attend such a difference, he immediately turned to the young man. 'Can I be of service, Mr Price?'

The princess whispered something into the ear of the young naval officer, and then smilingly allowed herself to be led away by another gentleman, who had come to claim her for the next dance.

The young fellow stood firm and made a bow. 'I do beg your pardon,' he began politely, 'but I was very much astonished at seeing another naval gentleman here, and I do hope you will forgive my impertinence if I might beg to ask you for a very great favour, Captain?'

He was all embarrassment mingled with good manners and Wentworth at once warmed to him. 'I place myself at your service, Sir, although I am astonished at my being in any position to offer assistance. But by all means, pray don't stand on any ceremony, and ask your favour without fear. We are, after all, not on duty, man.'

'You are very good, Sir! My name is Price, William Price, and I have just left the *'H.M.S Invincible'*, under Captain Litchfield, Sir.'

'Litchfield eh? Was she in Ostend, recently, then? I'm sorry to have missed her. A fine ship, the *Invincible*. Fine vessel. I know it well.'

'Yes, Sir, she is. I was cox'n for the *Invincible* for this year past.' He blushed a little. 'I recently took my examination for Lieutenant, Sir.'

'I see. Congratulations. Tell me, how come you to be at the Duchess's ball, Mr Price?'

'I hardly know, Sir! I was given a commission by my captain, which I undertook as a personal favour. The *Invincible* had come back from the Indies and called into Ostend some weeks ago, on account of Bonaparte, with the purpose of bringing provisions for the Prussian troops stationed here.'

'Go on, man,' replied Wentworth, his curiosity stirred.

'Well, Sir, it happened that I was one of the officers who left the ship and accompanied the load of provisions to the north of this city. This being delivered to troops under the prince's command, I was to return here, to deliver a message to the Duke. This is my last duty. I've been given my discharge papers effective tomorrow, on account of my arm.'

He gestured, but Wentworth politely averted his eyes. 'Go on.'

The young lad continued. 'I was to return with my ship to England. But I found on my return to the ship at Ostend, Sir, that *Invincible* had been forced to depart, owing to an urgent summons from England, and my captain left a message for me to return to Brussels, make myself useful to the Prince of Orange, and await another passage. My being here tonight was at the behest of the prince. But when I spotted you, Sir, I immediately saw my possible route home, for I collect you must have a vessel in port at Ostend, and with the very humblest of requests, I offer myself as midshipman for no pay, if only you can return me home to my sister, for she is to be wed soon, and her husband is gravely ill, and I fear she must be looking for me daily!'

Wentworth, seeing the earnestness of the young man's entreaty, was engaged by the warmest feelings, and a desire of doing some small favour for the young lad who had lost his arm. 'I can give you passage, and with the greatest willingness. Only, I regret however, that I am not in a position to say how long it will be before I can myself leave here: I am in the company at present of Admiral Malcolm, and I await his pleasure, seeing as we have urgent business here first. You must, of course, be aware of the threat looming against the city of Brussels by the French armies.'

Price looked his anxiety, and replied with gravity. 'Of course, Captain, and I would be most willing to render any service I may while I wait your departure from here.'

Now Wentworth, his curiosity piqued, thought to ask the boy more probing questions, and began with a query as to the sister he had spoken of earlier.

Price was eager. 'My sister Fanny has been some time at Mansfield, in the south of the country of Northamptonshire, and is to marry my cousin, Mr Edmund Bertram. I am more anxious than ever, since my cousin has been made very ill from poisoning, and the last letter I had from my sister was enough to cause a great anxiety for his health.'

Wentworth was sympathetic. 'Poisoning? But that must have been exceedingly distressing for your sister! How did the poor fellow come to be poisoned? An accidental dose?'

The young man shook his head. 'My sister writes that they are not sure how it came about, but that a servant in the household has confessed to the deed, but will not say any more.'

'Good God! Do you mean he was deliberately poisoned? But to what end?'

'I am sure I cannot say, Sir, but at any rate, I believe my poor cousin is quite done in, and they think he may not recover for some time. Mr Edmund Bertram is a person,' added Price, 'of the highest degree of good nature, manners, and everything becoming. My sister Fanny is quite in love with him, and has insisted that the marriage take place, even though it is doubtful Mr Bertram might make a full recovery.'

'That such things take place in good society is hardly to believed,' replied Wentworth warmly, 'but I can only add my wish that your sister's beau makes a speedy recovery. How does your sister do?'

'She finds that she cannot sleep, nor eat, for Fanny is of a delicate constitution, and has only recently suffered the cruelty of a scandal in the family,' confided the young man. 'At one time, quite recently, she was forced by my uncle to be courted by a man, a licentious and deceiving Mr Crawford. When she refused him, she was made to suffer some cruel injustices, whereby the gentleman, after making his address to Fanny so earnestly, then took up directly with my recently married cousin, Mrs Julia Rushworth. The poor family is still recovering from the scandal. Crawford is a licentious man and used my sister very ill. He dropped Mrs Rushworth immediately and now she must live in disgrace with a spinster aunt. Fanny bears it all very stoically, Sir, but I am anxious for her health with this new crisis and wish to get home just as soon as it can be done.'

Wentworth was grave. 'Of course. You are a very good friend indeed to your sister. I will do whatever I am able to get you passage as soon as I am given leave to withdraw.'

After thanking Wentworth immediately, and praising him as a jolly good fellow, Price wrote down his direction in Brussels, and retreated politely. Wentworth spent some time in silent contemplation of the evils of the world, which despite being at war on a national level, he thought, seemed intent on waging private battles of the vilest nature in parallel.

The music broke now into a style that Wentworth was not familiar with, and he watched in amazement as couples began to stand up and from groups of two, rather than figures of eight or ten. The dance involved having the gentleman directly place his hand upon the lady's waist and retain his hand there and Wentworth was shocked to see that even many of the English women present got up to dance.

When shortly afterwards one of the officers he knew by name drew close by, Wentworth ventured to enquire, 'What is this dance, Hargreaves? I don't believe I have seen it in any drawing rooms in England'

'Oh, I think it very jolly, don't you Captain? It is the waltz – it is said that the prince is exceedingly fond of it, and insists it is danced at every royal assembly.'

Wentworth had little to reply, but watched as the prince's sisters swung by on the arms of high officers, seeming to enjoy the intimate contact with the gentlemen, and the smiles on the faces of their partners were proof enough that the enjoyment was reciprocated. He resolved to relate the evening's activities to Anne; her opinion on the matter would be his own, he thought, for of everything he valued in his wife, her mind, her clever understanding, was the one which he treasured most, as a privateer treasures his spoils.

At precisely eleven o'clock, the Duke of Wellington arrived with a small party, and was immediately accosted by Admiral Malcolm. Wentworth was curious to lay eyes upon the man he had only seen in paintings, and noted that even at four-and-forty, he presented much younger an appearance than Wentworth had expected, with a clear, good skin, a rather aquiline nose, and a shock of brownish-red, tousled hair atop his rather high forehead. For all his youthful appearance, however, he seemed to radiate quiet authority. Wellington and Admiral Malcolm immediately joined the prince and they disappeared for some time, leaving Wentworth to his observations. He was now and then entreated to join the dance, but Wentworth declined, preoccupied with his thoughts, which alternately ranged from the threat of Napoleon's advances, to the poor Captain Benwick just recently lost and who should be here now in his stead, and Benwick's poor widow. He thought too of the comforts he yearned for at home, including the embrace of his wife.

More than an hour had passed in this fashion when the hour struck one in the morning, and at that moment, the prince's aide de camp entered the assembly room. Squeezing through the throngs, this gentleman sought the prince himself, who was still attended by Wellington. Wentworth watched across the room as the prince furtively pocketed a letter handed him by his aide. Wentworth was oppressed by a heaviness of heart, which was unalleviated by the appearance of Admiral Malcolm. The sober countenance conveyed all Wentworth could expect.

'Word is that Bonaparte has amassed one hundred and twenty thousand men on the Belgian border,' Malcolm told him quietly. 'I am not surprised the prince refuses to open that letter in state; he will not wish to give alarm immediately. Look, there, he goes away to open it. It will confirm what we have heard, no doubt.'

The prince now retreated with his aide, and was not seen for some minutes. When he emerged again, he looked strained but appeared to act as normally as possible. Casually, the prince spoke briefly to Wellington, and Wellington in turn summoned Malcolm who went to him immediately. They stood in hushed conversation for some minutes, then the Admiral returned to Wentworth.

'It is grim news, Wentworth,' he said austerely. 'Bonaparte has advanced over the Sabre, even as we danced.'

Wentworth blanched visibly. 'What does the Duke wish? What are his orders?'

'The French have advanced almost into Charleroi, and have paused at Quatre Bras. They must deploy shortly. The prince will give orders after supper is done. He wishes to give the men their last meal before they must charge into battle. A noble but futile endeavour, I fear, and yet I could do no less myself.'

The music in the room around them seemed to Wentworth to fade, although the dancing figures still swirled around them. The prince made no immediate moves, but preceded the company into supper, which was announced only minutes later, but even at table his nonchalance appeared strained, and after a few bites he disappeared into a room behind the supper room. The company stared after him, and only a few resumed eating. The ladies seemed most unaffected, but the men seemed to understand something of import had occurred. They were not long to wait.

The prince emerged from the room; his young face worn with anxious care. He came to stand at the head of the supper table. All fell silent.

'Gentlemen, ladies. It gives me no pleasure to halt this evening's proceedings, and curtail your diversions, God knows you deserve that much. I regret to inform all those on active duty that you are requested to re-join your regiments immediately. Napoleon has advanced upon us; we must meet him this very day, before sunrise, at Quatre Bras. There is no time to waste; make your departure this moment!'

Consternation and dismay were on every countenance in the room as the news circulated quickly. Some of the mothers and sisters began to wail, and many gave way to open horror. There were some heartless young ladies who still danced, until they were led from the floor by their weeping mamas. All was grievous pandemonium; all was horror and abject terror. Mournful farewells were taken, the young men knowing they may never return home, and the mothers and sisters of the men knowing they would in all probability never see their loved ones again. There was not time to change into uniforms, and Wentworth almost pledged to join them, as he watched young men, still clad in evening dress, ride from the city in dread and haste, to meet the enemy. The women could do nothing but return themselves home, while the soldiers sallied forth in grave expectation of a foul and bloody battle to come.

Wentworth now did his best to assist the ladies in calling around their carriages, and helping the weeping females into them. Presently he spotted the young midshipman, Price, doing the same. Drawing near, he greeted him. 'Go to your lodgings, lad, and keep me informed of where I might get a note to you. It is a grim night's end to the duchess's ball, but we all must do our parts from here.'

'Aye, Captain.' Young Price looked sadly after the wailing females he had just seen into their carriage, and saluted his superior. 'God speed to you, Captain. I shall, God willing, see you in Ostend at your convenience.'

After the last of the grieving and distraught women had been seen home, Wentworth joined Malcolm and they, too, returned in deep silence to their lodgings. For some hours they sat in the parlour at the inn, until the day had well and truly broken, for sheer inability to sleep while such a battle was being fought so close by. All throughout the night the distant thunder of cannon fire could be heard, an ominous and dreadful indication of the battle being fought only a mile from the city.

They discussed the women, whom had already retired to bed before they could impart the news. 'It would not do to wake the ladies,' suggested Malcolm shortly after they had arrived home.

Wentworth had agreed. Poor Louisa had been through enough, he thought, and he would keep the dreadful news from the two women of their party as long as possible.

It was not long enough, however, for the two women came down to breakfast already having heard through their chamber maid, and when Mrs Inchpole had been apprised of the details, she fell over in a stupor and had to be revived by salts, administered by Mrs Benwick herself. The latter was calm, but Wentworth detected desperate sadness in her glances.

Later, when Mrs Inchpole had been put to bed, Mrs Benwick and Wentworth sat in the parlour over tea, and she raised her solemn face to his. 'I cannot help but ponder, Captain, the meaning of death in these times we are living in. My dear Benwick died in the midst of war, and yet only by an ill-timed wave, while doing his duty under the orders of the British Navy. And yet these men, too — these good, young, vigorous men — must die in the hundreds. At least *they* will be lauded for their bravery.'

Wentworth could give her no reply, his heart full of the last few hours yet. The cruelty and futility of death was too close to him, and he looked to thoughts of his unborn child, waiting for his return, to give him solace. Benwick, he resolved, would be given the respect due him as a fine captain, who died in service, even if that was the only comfort he could give Louisa.

He left her sipping tea, and went to his room to write to his wife of all that had passed.

Thirteen

Monday 19 June, 1815

Kellynch Hall

Another week brought with it the heat of mid-summer. The admiral and Mrs Croft drove out every morning as was their custom, in the little gig which was wont to overturn in the lane, or suffer some accident to the wheel, more often than it did not. Anne meanwhile did her best to entertain the children, with little help from their mama. Poor Mary invariably was to be found lying upon on the sofa with one of her headaches, made worse by the cloying heat, and no amount of persuading her to walk would tempt her out of the drawing room, if it were only in the company of her own children and Anne.

'You always declare how much you enjoy a long walk, Mary, but now I cannot convince you to move out of this room. Do you not think you would feel so much better once you were in the breezes up in the hill behind us? Will you not come for the sake of your boys?'

'It is too tiresome to hear you talk of it continually; walking up those hills would do me more harm than good! Nobody knows what I suffer! Charles must be made to understand how ill I am, Anne! Cannot you write him and tell him to come?'

'You know there is estate business which makes it impossible for him to return just yet,' replied Anne with patience. 'I am sure he will come as promised in a week or two.' Much used to her sister's complaints and ill humours, Anne could do little, she had discovered, to make Mary more easy in her grievances, for whatever was suggested was most often rejected out of hand. She settled herself therefore to listen patiently, to soften her sister's grievances as much as possible, without giving the younger woman the offence of contradiction or that jolly bolstering of spirits which only caused vexation in the other. 'Shall I get little Walter to run to the kitchen for a cold compress? You always find a lavender cloth soothing.'

Mary was inconsolable. 'Lavender presses only make me bilious. Thank you but no. Pray leave me to rest — I feel so vastly stupid with this heat!'

It was left to Anne to take the boys outside and play with them, and she did so with willingness, glad to be of use to her sister and to have something take her mind from Frederick. He had been gone two weeks, and must have arrived in Brussels by now — perhaps they had been engaged in action with Bonaparte — she could hardly dwell upon the thought without horror. She knew a letter would not come yet, but looked every day nevertheless, telling herself she was foolish even as her eyes went immediately to the hall table every time they entered the house after being gone on calls or to walk in the hills. Julia kept to her room, complaining of fatigue, and began to look so unwell that Anne conferred with Mrs Croft and talked of calling the doctor after all.

Early one afternoon, Anne, who had just sat down to some reading, found her peace disturbed by the early return of the admiral and Mrs Croft. Hearing them all a fluster in the entry hall, she abandoned her favourite novel, *Sir Charles Grandison*, and took herself to the door.

'Anne! Why there you are! The admiral and I have come on purpose to find you directly, for I am afraid we have some news which we did not wish you hear from other sources!' Mrs Croft was all anxiety and took Anne's hand as the admiral followed her.

Anne was at once oppressed by the worst of fears. 'But Mrs Croft, it is not bad news, I hope? Surely it can be nothing so alarming?'

Mrs Croft led her to the chaise in the little parlour and begged her to sit. Admiral Croft stood before them, looking excessively grave.

'Now,' said Mrs Croft with solicitude, 'it is perhaps the best of news, my dear, but I fear it will give you some alarm all the same. The admiral has just been given the very excellent news that Bonaparte has been vanquished at Waterloo in Belgium, and the war is over to all intents and purposes. Yes, my dear, it is true.'

Anne, who could not be more astonished, looked her disbelief, and hid as well as she could her alarm for Frederick. After a fluttering moment she soon found her tongue. 'Oh, but this is very good news, very good indeed, Mrs Croft! Do not suppose I cannot find the grace to be pleased with such excellent tidings, for really, I am quite overjoyed! But, can you give any news of the Duke of Wellington, Admiral? Do you have any reason to suppose Frederick's party to be in any danger?'

The admiral did his best to be jolly. 'Now, I won't have you going about with fears in your head over Frederick, my dear. I have no reason to suppose him in any danger, since he would not likely have been involved in the fighting. But I can tell you, the unofficial news I received by means of a friend of mine who sent a note poste-haste to me just an hour ago, has given me to hold that Bonaparte has done his best to defeat the Prussian army at Ligny. I am advised that Wellington was beaten back, but has held his ground the next day at Quatre Bras, I believe. No more than this was told me, but only that Napoleon was defeated only hours later at Waterloo, and Wellington and Blucher, bless their brave souls, have declared the war at an end.'

Anne, caught up in the vision of such a battle, and prey to her own fears, was pale. 'And when did these events take place, Admiral?'

'The great battle which defeated Bonaparte was fought out on the eve of the eighteenth, I believe, my dear. Three days ago. I have nothing to fear for young Frederick, for he was never part of the ground forces. The navy, you know,' he added kindly, 'have little to do with the militia, and I collect Frederick's only commission was to accompany Rear Admiral Malcolm to attend the Duke; they would have remained well away from the front.'

Anne suffered to have her hand patted continually by Mrs Croft, and did her best to try for serenity. 'I am sure we will hear from Frederick, by and by,' she offered. 'You must have suffered the greatest alarms, Mrs Croft, in the past, and yet you are so serene now that I cannot help but be comforted. You are both very kind!'

Later that afternoon, when all was quiet, Anne took up her pen.

> '*My dearest love,*
>
> *I have been giving myself the foolish hope of seeing you home, or at least of having a letter from you before I write again; I know it was foolish, but I can hold off no more at any rate, for today we have heard of the most excellent news, of the Great Defeat of the French at Waterloo and Quatre Bras. I cannot pretend I was not anxious immediately for your safety with your being so close to the action, but I must give myself the comfort of believing you safe and far from any danger. I could not bear to think otherwise. The admiral and Mrs Croft have been so very kind, assuring me of your safety, and I know I shall hear from you very soon, or, God willing, see you at home.*
>
> *Now I shall command my mind to be content and peaceful, and attempt to give you some frivolous bits of domestic news from home, even while knowing that the cares upon your shoulders must see such silliness as superfluous chatter — but I hope it will somehow comfort you until you return to us, to know of our mundane goings-on here. It comforts me, at any rate, to tell you of them!*
>
> *So, for a start, I go along very well, and your child, who lives inside me, waits with me to see you, to hear your voice once again. I am getting a little figure, your sister tells me, which you will notice even through my muslins, and which feels so strange to me, and yet I rejoice in the feel of the roundness which hides our child. I am not fatigued very much except a little in the afternoons, and I feel almost nothing like the illness which is supposed to plague us women in the first few months.*

Mary and the children came as we had planned. Young Walter is growing into a fine fellow, and little Charles continues to please me with his sweet ways. I flatter myself I am a favourite with him! Mary is very well, or as well as she will admit to being; she is perhaps a little more out of spirits because Charles senior could not join us, but all in all I fancy her more animated and happy for her stay with us, and your sister has been excessively forbearing and everything kind. Admiral Croft has treated the boys quite as his own grandchildren; I am quite charmed by his patience with them.

My sister and father, by all accounts, go on very well in Bath, and they now have the added pleasure, Elizabeth tells me, of the company of a brother and sister of whom they have made speedy and intimate acquaintances; a Mr and Miss Crawford of Everingham, from in the north of this country. Even Mrs Croft declares herself charmed by them although she has only met them in Elizabeth's letters!

She is very keen still to get the Admiral to Bath, and I expect we might remove there for a fortnight or more in the next few weeks. I shall look forward to meeting these Crawfords, for by Elizabeth's account they seem so sensible that I almost hope to see some happy changes in my father and sister; Elizabeth certainly seems more in spirits since she began writing of them, than she has been for some weeks.

Julia is come to us, as you know, and stays with us still—'

Anne continued in this vein for a few more paragraphs, making a tolerable effort at being jolly to keep up her husband's spirits as much as her own, until there was nothing and nobody of any importance left to mention, and the letter was sealed up with the Elliot wax and given to Robertson to post. But if a small tear found its way down Anne's cheek as she gave it into his hand, she wiped it away, and put her anxiety for Wentworth's safety in the same place she had stored her grief at his general absence.

Fourteen

Soon, news of the British victory was the object of all the buzz in the house and outside of it too. *The Gazette* and *The Times*, both of which Admiral Croft took pleasure in subscribing to, published many more particulars on the glorious news of the English victory against the French. Although she took them up in a dread of anticipation, even before the admiral had found time to open either, and scoured the lists of dead and wounded, Anne was gratified to find no mention of the name "Wentworth" among their number, and began to feel gradually less anxiety for her husband. She took comfort in Mrs Croft's serenity and was grateful for their quiet kindnesses which continued to be paid to her. Even so, every day she looked for a letter from Frederick, and it took all her self-command not to give in to wild fears for his safety.

Julia had not been moved very much by the news, and kept very much to her room. Two days after Anne had received news of Bonaparte's defeat, Jenny, the upstairs maid, came down early in the morning, and spoke confidingly with Anne.

'I hope you'll forgive me for the impertinence Ma'am, but I feel as I ought to tell you in case you don't know, but young Miss Julia has been a casting up accounts so to speak, ev'ry morn since Tuesday, and I warrant she mus' be serious ill!'

Anne, paling at once, and with an alarming conviction regarding the cause of the "illness", went upstairs and knocked on her niece's door.

Julia was prone upon her bed, languishing with all the appearance of a terrible affliction, but the appearance of Anne's head around the door at once had the girl sitting up and arranging busily the books and papers beside her bed as if her life depended upon it. 'Do you or Mary need me to mind the boys? I promised Charles I would do a puzzle with him this afternoon. Shall I come now, Aunt Anne?' She looked rather green and Anne shook her head and came to sit beside her on the counterpane.

'Jenny tells me you have been unwell every morning since last week. Do you feel ill? You look a *little* ill, dearest.'

'Oh, no, I am quite well, thank you, Aunt Anne. Its only that I feel so very fatigued most days. It is the heat. I am not used to it. It is cooler in the north, you know.'

Anne eyed her pale cheeks and ventured delicately, 'There are other reasons, Julia, that a woman might become excessively fatigued and suffer nausea. When she is overworked, for example, but you have no reason to complain of that, or when she is — with child. It is quite a common symptom of that state.'

Julia eyed her with horror. 'Pray do not mention the subject! I have not — I declare it is abominable of you to suggest — oh, but how could you say such things!' She stood and strode angrily to the window. 'I declare I cannot abide being mollycoddled, as if I were a child, as if I have not the agency to look after myself! I am a grown woman! Really, this is too much!' Her cheeks had taken on a deep rose.

'How long is it since you used the guard, my dear, if you will forgive my asking?'

Julia stared at her, open eyed and shocked. 'I— I never — I cannot *possibly* be with child — he would not—!' The cheeks that had reddened with shame were now quite pale. 'Two months, perhaps, but that is no reason — that is no proof — oh, *Aunt Anne*!'

The young woman who had only moments earlier been affronted and indignant, had now given in to the alarm which might well follow such a suggestion. Her eyes wide, and her countenance pale, Julia's hand had raised to her heart, and she clutched her pretty muslin gown in abject horror. Indeed, no other prospect could have been as unwelcome to either woman as the notion of a Miss Wentworth, of Wentworth Hall, daughter of a respectable gentleman-clergyman, being with child and *unwed!*

Anne was most ungratified to find her guess confirmed. She was horrified, and yet compassion for the young woman overtook the first inclinations of horror, and she did all she could to comfort the now sobbing Julia. With a little probing, she soon confirmed her earlier suspicions also, for it transpired that Julia Wentworth was in love with the recipient of her letter, and a Mr Harry Lyford was indeed the object of her heart.

'Have you any idea of this man's regard for you? Does he return your feelings? Has he made you an offer, or hinted at such an offer?'

Julia was eager through her tears. 'Oh, yes, I believe so! I mean, never outright, but I thought he would, quite soon! He would never leave me if only he knew I was here — indeed I wrote to him, only last week, but there has been no reply to my letter. If only you or Aunt Sophie might write to him, perhaps you could go to him in London, and find him!'

Anne was sober. 'My dear child, I am very much afraid to say this Mr Lyford is no gentleman. A man does not — dally — with a female, if he intends matrimony, my dear. It is never done.'

'Oh, but Mr Lyford — Harry — is different! He assured me of his affection, he made me believe him in love with *me*, too! I wrote to him at his club! I am certain he will come just as soon as he can. After all, I beseeched him to collect me from Kellynch and take me away! He must be away himself, or ill, or—'

'Julia.' Anne took her hand gently. 'I verily believe he will not come. He has finished with you. I suspect the moment your aunt and uncle removed you from London, he would have forgotten you. I am sorry, my dear, but it is very likely the truth.'

'Oh, no! He will come, my dear Lyford will come, I know it!' She sunk over her pillow in sobs of grief. 'I am ruined, if he does not come, I am *ruined!* You must write to him, or fetch him here! Pray do it at once!'

'Who is he? What are his connections? Do you know anything of his people?'

'He is a gentleman; of that I am sure! His clothes, his manner, his address — all were refined, all pleasing! His family are — oh, I don't know — I collect his family are gone, but he has relations in Bath, or some such place — I did not pay attention! Do not ask me more, I cannot answer you!' Distressed, she sobbed afresh into her pillow, and could not be reasoned with.

Anne did her best to calm the hysterical agitations of the young woman, but shortly afterward left the distraught girl, to enquire with great impatience if the Crofts had returned home from a walk. They had not, Robertson informed her. Mary and the children had gone with them, for the Crofts wished to treat the little boys to ices in the town.

Anne heard this with relief; she welcomed the solitude to think. 'Thank you, George. I shall have some tea in the drawing room, if you could ask Liza to bring some please.'

'Very good, Miss Anne.'

She entered the room, and wandered to the window. What a shocking, unpleasant business now stood before them all. It was not as if such things were unheard of; she knew that young ladies sometimes got themselves into trouble. More than a few were sent away to "school" — the distant aunts, in whose cottages they would have discreet births and then return to society as if nothing had ever ailed them. Some of those girls, of good families, were able to find employment as governesses if the matter had been concealed well enough, otherwise they were destined to live at home as spinsters or go out as companions. A very few found husbands, if their pasts were kept quiet, or the prospective gent could be bribed by a large dowry. Most, however, were spoiled goods, cast from all good society, unable to find husbands, and forced to stayed at home to be a burden to their fathers.

If they could not discover the whereabouts of this Mr Lyford, and force him into marriage, it would spell ruin for her niece. There would be little for it but to return Julia to Shropshire for her lying in, and then she knew not what. Troubled, Anne went and sat upon the sofa, thinking of her own child, only a month further on than Julia's, and the terrible fate of children born on the wrong side of the blanket. They were tainted by their parentage, perhaps farmed out to work, or even left upon doorsteps of parishes. What would be the fate of Julia Wentworth's child?

The door opened, and Anne, expecting the tea things, was

taken aback when Robertson announced, 'Doctor Thorpe, Ma'am.'

A visitor, and at the most inconvenient time! The poor doctor could hardly have known, however, and she sighed. She hoped her cheeks were not flushed, and that her countenance bore no signs of the excitement of the last half hour. She absentmindedly brushed a hand over the blue cambric morning dress which hid the slight roundness of her waist, and rose to meet him.

'Good Morning, Dr. Thorpe.'

'Mrs Wentworth! How do you do? I came to see the admiral, but I am very glad to see you.'

The usual pleasantries were exchanged, the French defeat mentioned and celebrated, and Anne begged him to sit down. The Crofts, she assured him, could only be but a few minutes from coming in, since they had the little boys with them and had only been as far as the village.

Doctor Thorpe however, observing her pale countenance, bethought himself to enquire, 'If I may say so, Mrs Wentworth, you are looking quite pale today, and usually you are so blooming of cheek! I hope you are not unwell? Might I do anything for you?'

'Oh!' Anne paused, then began again in confusion, 'I am quite well, I thank you, only — there has been some rather unsettling news this morning.'

'I am very sorry to hear it,' replied Silas Thorpe with a tactful gravity. He was too polite to make further comment or enquiry and for a moment the two of them sat there in awkward silence, and were interrupted only by the tea things being brought in at last.

While Liza was setting the cups and pot upon the table, Anne had some time to collect her thoughts. And by the time she had assured Thorpe that he was not unwelcome to stay to drink tea, and had poured him a cup, she had made a firm decision. 'Doctor Thorpe, I just now spoke of some news I had been unfortunate enough to receive. Might I venture, if you would forgive me for my impertinence, to put a question to you, since I find that the business in some way might be best answered by a medical man?'

Thorpe placed his cup gently upon the table. 'If there is anything I can do to relieve your anxiety, Mrs Wentworth, I am your humble servant.'

'You are very kind! The matter is of rather a confidential nature — *more* than confidential I am afraid to say — it is something of a scandal and it concerns my niece.'

'I see!' Thorpe, a little astonished, and quite puzzled, waited patiently, and Anne quickly related the facts of the matter, in as few words as she could accurately describe it, and then added her question. 'I find myself wondering at the advisability of sending my niece home to Shropshire when my husband's brother is only lately the father of an infant child. Catherine, his new wife, is in rather fragile health, and because of Julia's unwillingness to go home, and the ill feeling between them, it might be inadvisable for either of them to be in the same house. Are you of the opinion that she would be best to go to her family, or for both their sakes, remove to some other place for her lying in?'

He was silent for some time, and she wondered if he was contemptuous of her, tainted by association with her niece. However, he concealed his disgust, if any existed. 'This is an unenviable situation, Mrs Wentworth, for both Miss Wentworth, and your family. Are you sure the young lady is with child? You are certain?'

'I think so, yes. She is displaying all the usual signs, and once she admitted this Mr Lyford had dallied with her, if you will pardon the expression, it seemed confirmed. She suffers great fatigue, just as I have, and I recognize the heightened colour of her cheeks and eyes, as it has been with myself. Unfortunate though it is for Julia, I have little doubt of her condition.'

He was silent for some moments. 'This is very grave, very grave indeed. And she fancies herself in love, does she? Can the man be discovered and made to marry her? Perhaps the admiral — but no, not in his health. Perhaps someone else might go to London, and see if they can discover his whereabouts?'

'On that score,' replied Anne meaningfully, 'I think there must be little hope, for do you suppose he has given her his true name?'

Thorpe paused. 'Of course — you are right. A most unusual name. I suspect you are quite right. Lyford. Indeed.'

Anne was gratified that she did not have to explain it all to him. 'So, you understand what we are fighting here. It would be well-nigh impossible to discover a gentleman who has given a false name, especially in the throngs of gentlemen inhabiting London. We only know the name of his club, and even *that* may have been given falsely.'

He frowned. 'Yes, I believe you have the girth and height of it, alright. I shall make some enquiries myself, to see if anyone has heard of him, but I suspect we won't get very far.'

Anne was grateful. 'Thank you, you are very kind. Do you know anywhere she might go? Her father will have to give consent, but I believe it must be a respectable house, somewhere away from Shropshire where people will not know the family.'

'There are no other relatives to which the child might go? I suppose she cannot—?' He nodded towards the elegant, green-papered walls.

'Stay here? At Kellynch? I cannot pretend that I have not given it consideration, and I shall consult with her aunt, Mrs Croft, but I feel that it would be better for my niece to remove to where she is not known at all.'

'Of course.' He frowned some moments more, then took up his tea-cup once more. 'You know,' he said thoughtfully, 'I have an aunt who lives very humbly, in a small village in Herefordshire. She is gone down to Bath, just now, but I believe she is to quit the place in few weeks' time. I go up to Herefordshire to visit her at least twice a year. She is something of a favourite of mine, you know; a very kind sort of woman, and good with children. Raised me for several years after my own mother died when I was still in frocks.' He smiled. 'I believe she may be willing to take your niece and harbour her until the child is born.'

Anne was astonished at the thought. 'That would answer the purpose,' she said hopefully. 'You are very kind,' she added. 'We shall of course have to inform Julia's father — Mrs Croft may do that — but it answers very well, very well indeed! Perhaps there might be hope for Julia, after all!'

'I shall write to my aunt this very day, Mrs Wentworth. Let us hope this business may be kept as quiet as possible, to avoid as much further humiliation of the young lady as we can. It is not an easy path she has chosen — but God willing, we may be able to save something of her reputation, although God knows what will be the fate of that poor wretch of a child!'

Mrs Croft, who since their happy introduction had never failed Anne in kindness, gentleness of manner, and sensible advice, had met the unhappy tidings of her niece's situation with just as much good sense and composure as ever, even if it was tempered with more than a little vexation toward the faceless young man who had taken advantage of her niece's youth and silliness.

'I am shockingly provoked! I wish this man very ill, very ill indeed! Can someone not go to find him out? It is a bad business, Anne, I must say. My brother Edward will be greatly distressed by it, and I sincerely hope Catherine is not made ill as a result. She is by Edward's account a delicate creature; she shall suffer unkindly over it. Their name will be tarnished, and the new baby only just come along! Stupid, foolish girl! And the worst of this is, not only is my niece now ruined, but my brother will suffer deeply for his part in the unhappy business, for it was he who sent Julia away to school. His sensitive nature will not support the guilt of having been instrumental in his daughter's ruin!'

Anne could not but agree with her, and the three of them, for the admiral had been informed of the business also, had to confine their hopes solely to news from Doctor Thorpe, that his aunt would take Julia under her wing, and harbour her in a tiny, unknown village for her confinement. It was thought that Mary, soon to return to Uppercross, might be spared from the humiliation which had touched them all, and therefore the news was kept from her. All Mary was allowed to know was that Miss Wentworth had formed an attachment to an unsuitable man, had been withdrawn from school on account of it, and was now suffering from hurt pride.

Anne had not wanted this visit from her niece to understand the great tides of passion that can be harboured in a mere five foot nothing of mortal flesh. Anne's own struggles to contain her past unhappiness at the loss of Frederick Wentworth, to repress it for the sake of others, had made eight years of her life a sore trial, although she had succeeded in supressing the outward signs of unhappiness. The only outward sign that she had suffered had been the loss of her bloom, restored with the return of Frederick Wentworth and their subsequent marriage.

Julia however, having none of her aunt's fortitude, chose violent affliction and gave herself up to the misery of loss. Anne's endeavours to calm and console were met with adamant refusal to be consoled. Julia's other aunt, endeavouring to use reason to bring her around, rather sank the girl further by pointing out the folly of having gotten herself in such a circumstance in the first place. Such advice fell on deaf ears. Julia Wentworth was determined to be afflicted, determined to increase her wretchedness, and admit neither consolation nor reason until she had spent her tears and had nothing left to do but sit dully and sigh every few minutes.

A week or more passed in this manner, the young lady having now been apprised of the plans which had been made on her behalf by her aunts, for a speedy removal to a quiet village in Herefordshire. Doctor Thorpe had already called in and given them the welcome news that his aunt would be very pleased to take Julia, as soon as she returned from Bath, if they would not mind waiting but a week or two more. Mrs Croft and Anne agreed to this proposal, and Mrs Croft, who still harboured a desire to get her husband up to Bath for his health, suggested that they all go up, Julia also, and there she could be given into the care of Mrs Haye, to be removed shortly thereafter.

Julia had refused to see the doctor when he had called. 'I certainly shan't be made to be shamed in front of him,' she cried. 'It is humiliating enough to be carted off like a naughty schoolgirl to some obscure village to hide my face and have a baby! I shan't scruple to tell him so either, if I am made to see him, and I cannot thank him for it, for I would have as soon stayed here!'

Mrs Croft and Anne tried to get the girl to see reason, that to remain at Kellynch was impossible in her circumstances, but she only locked her door and refused to come out, and so Doctor Thorpe went unthanked for all his efforts by the lady he had exerted himself to help.

Julia, still suffering a great deal from the pangs of a now certainly unrequited love, was alternately argumentative and lethargic. Cast low, and anxious for her future, she was altogether struck with fear at her father's reaction when he heard the news. Mrs Croft had written to him, with the full details of the arrangements for his daughter's lying in, but they had not yet received a response, although it was daily looked for with great trepidation and anxiety of the part of his daughter.

The young lady was soon acquainted with her father's thoughts, since around midmorning of the day before they were all to go up to Bath, several letters arrived, one of which was addressed to Mrs Croft in the distinct handwriting her brother. Another two were addressed to Anne, and she almost cried to see Frederick's handwriting on each one. She knew it was too soon to expect a letter from him regarding the defeat of the French, and she yearned to hear of his safety and where he was at this moment. While Mrs Croft immediately took up her brother's letter, Anne took her own two to her room to read in privacy.

She broke the wax on the first letter with a shaking hand. Reading through the contents of the first, she stopped twice to cover her mouth with a muffled cry. The letter finally read, reread, and solemnly closed up, she could hardly remain composed. Captain Benwick, dead! She tried to comprehend it. Poor, poor Captain Benwick, he who had suffered a great deal already in the death of his beloved Phoebe, now to meet the same fate, an early grave unjustified and hardly contemplated! The notion of it was truly cruel, it was unjust, and she felt forcibly all the sadness of the tragic tale. And then, there was poor

Louisa, just married, and her husband cruelly snatched from her.

The second letter lay unopened on her muslin lap, but starting up after a moment, she bethought herself to take it up, eager to hear more of Louisa, and to read more endearments from her husband. Breaking the seal, she opened the paper and eagerly devoured the words therein:

Thursday June 15, 1815,
Brussels.

My dear Anne,

However unthinkable, however difficult it is for me to be so removed from you by distance, and by circumstance, I cannot imagine it half as difficult as what you must be feeling, having received my last. Dear, excellent creature, your tender heart must bleed for poor Louisa, even more than does mine, knowing the family so much more thoroughly.

I take heart, however, for Louisa Benwick, for I am astonished at the great transformation of character which has been effected since her husband's death. You too, will be as astonished as I to witness the transformation from girl to woman, to her great credit. Where once we both knew a young, untried Louisa Musgrove, agreeable and pleasant certainly, but lacking the substance that could ever have made her a true alternative choice, as an eligible competitor for my heart, there has emerged a mature, calm woman, who has accepted her fate, and determines to make the best of it. In this, she reminds me of you, my dear; she becomes like you more each day, and I see the gratifying effect of your influence over her only a year or two ago, which now works to improve her conduct, her attitude, and her demeanour.

In short, I am less anxious for Louisa than I would have been had she remained the coddled, headstrong, carefree girl that she was up until her fall at Lyme. That fall, as tragic as it was, I own cannot fail to have had some significant influence over her nerves, her courage, her character. And then, those changes in her to be shored up so surely by the influence of Benwick himself, a deep, thinking man; indeed, both of these circumstances must have made a difference to her character, but now that she has been tested by providence, with even worse tragedy, she has risen to become something even more — an astonishing young woman — and I own I am gratified to see such changes, although it pains me that she had to be so afflicted by tragedy to effect them.

I shall leave the topic, but such is my astonishment and relief, that I am gratified that you will, too, be able to enter into my feelings with a similar relief, and it is my hope that you will write to her family immediately, if you cannot visit them in person, and give them hope for her mind and spirits after all has passed.

We are arrived in Brussels just today, and are to attend a ball tomorrow night, given by the Duchess of Richmond, who resides here for the duration with her husband. I care not for these things without you to stand beside me, my dearest girl, but Adm. Malcolm wishes me to attend with him and I will do so, even though it pains me. Mrs Benwick is to remain with Mrs Inchpole, one of the officer's wives, both of whom have accompanied us to Brussels on account of Mrs Benwick's distress at being forced to remain in port with her husband's ship. I have left word in Ostend imploring them to write to me directly as soon as packet comes which might be suitable for transporting Mrs Benwick back to England, but if nothing is forth coming, she will accompany the Nightingale when we return, whenever that shall be.

I shall write again as soon as I have word of our departure date, and in the meantime, I remain ever your loving

F. W.

The first letter was not soon to be recovered from, but to be followed by the second! To say that Anne was astonished was an example in understatement; she was utterly astounded. The news that Louisa Benwick, widowed, had accompanied Frederick on to Brussels, that she had impressed her husband favourably with material changes in her character — these things painfully struck her, and instead of giving her relief, as her husband had hoped, worked their mischief on her mind and nerves.

She reread the letter in some consternation. *Lacking the substance that could ever have made her a true alternative choice... she has risen to become something more... an astonishing young woman!* His words played over in her head, until they blurred on the page. He was gratified to see such changes! Was he now regretting his choices? She read again the letter, his dear familiar handwriting the only connection she had to hold him firm in her breast. She chided herself, and told herself her doubts were foolish, that Frederick had long ago chosen herself over Louisa, that he valued her as superior to Louisa, that his devotion had not wavered even over eight long years, despite his resentment toward her. He had come to value her, he had told her on their marriage, over all the treasure he had ever claimed from the enemies he had seized and overcome on the great oceans.

No, she was foolish indeed to allow such thoughts; she was in great error to distrust his devotion now. She struggled, she gained hold. A few more minutes and she was soon possessed of a tenuous tranquillity. She reasoned with herself. Such are the evils of a long separation, so that the mind becomes the enemy, and thoughts can taunt and cause doubt that would never be countenanced otherwise. Yes, she was entirely mistaken, entirely in the wrong, to think what she had thought. She was disappointed in herself. And such was her anxiety for Frederick's safety at this moment, that she could not long be induced to worry at such an insignificant point, she told herself. His safety was paramount to her and must occupy her thoughts. She folded the letter, and put both of them away to be answered when she was more composed, and went to find Mrs Croft.

Julia was now relieved of the misery of the unknown. Mrs Croft informed Anne that her brother Edward had written, and all was made plain. He was shocked and angry, yes, but his anger was not such that his daughter would never be welcome again. He would for now keep it from Catherine, and he agreed immediately to his sister's scheme of putting Julia in the care of Mrs Haye until the child was born. As to the future of the child, he would see to it that the infant was cared for and educated, but Julia was to remain in the care of Mrs Haye for the full duration of her lying in, and until she was well enough to return to school. Then he would, he wrote, see her into a finishing school abroad, and the story given their acquaintance would be that she had been away abroad for the entire duration. She would return home at a later date, to be married if she was fortunate enough, or to remain a spinster if she was not, but at all costs, for all their sakes, they would put the past behind them all. He was most grave and disturbed by the events which had taken place, and felt himself more to blame than Julia, but this did in no way excuse her behaviour and the disgrace she had brought upon them all, and the danger to Catherine's health.

Mrs Croft had already imparted the contents of this letter to Julia and Anne had then only to console a tearful Julia for the umpteenth time over her father's anger and disappointment. 'You only have yourself to blame, Julia! Although I am loath to remind you of it,' she said gently, 'for I collect you have suffered enough already. You could not have expected any less from him, surely? You are extremely fortunate you have been offered a place with Mrs Haye,' she went on. 'She seems by Doctor Thorpe's account a very good sort of woman, and you could have done much worse. You must try to be grateful and perhaps you may enter your father's house again one day, once he has had time to get over the shock of it all. Meanwhile, you now have a chance to recover your character — not all young woman in your circumstances are given that chance.'

'I know, Aunt Anne, its only that I do love Mr Lyford so! If only you could write to him—'

'At what address?' Anne reasoned gently. 'We do not know his whereabouts, nor his direction. Your Mr Lyford was never the gentleman you thought he was; no good can come of writing to him. He has only done what many licentious young men have done — used you very ill, and you must learn a lesson from it, a painful lesson though it must be.'

Julia, quite taken up in a fresh bout of tears, found that recriminations were useless, as were pleas to remain at Kellynch, and after a day or so was resigned to her fate. She took no pleasure in the prospect of a carriage ride to Bath the following day, nor did she care to accompany Mrs Haye onward into Herefordshire. But she had little choice and she passively allowed the maid to place into her trunks all that was thought necessary for a young lady going away to school abroad. None of the servants knew the truth, apart from Jenny, but knowing that good woman as the soul of discretion, Anne had no fears in that quarter.

Mary and her little boys had been collected by her husband the previous day. Anne had shared with her sister the distressing news of Captain Benwick's tragic death, and had been gratified that Mary, so often wrapped up on her own cares, had been very sorry for her husband's poor sister, so that when she learned Anne was to go up to Bath with the Crofts, she supplied them with hardly a complaint, except one.

'Well, and I suppose I must comfort the Musgroves alone, Anne, for you know Charles neglects his duties at home! He is always about on the estate and never has time for me. As for going up the Great House! We were to go to dinner as soon as ever we return, only now I am sure Charles will not go, on account of Louisa's husband. What a pity you could not return to Uppercross with me, but I suppose it will not do to leave Julia with Mrs Croft alone; what a handful she does have in the girl! She might be more grateful to be going away to school abroad, but young girls these days do not know what is good for them! Now Louisa and Henrietta were excessively well educated, and valued their places as genteel young ladies, and would never have dreamed of hankering after a young man as Julia does. Poor, poor Louisa! Well, I suppose it must fall to me to comfort them all at the Great House until she can come home. Pray, did Frederick mention when that might be, Anne?' and without waiting much for a reply, '—I hope it is not too long, for I cannot be expected to spend all my time at the Great House, with my little boys so demanding, and you know Charles leaves me quite alone to manage them with only Penny to help me!'

This little rhetoric done, she lapsed into her usual affronted silence, and did not notice Anne's longsuffering expression. They departed the next day, with as many promises to write to Anne at Bath as sighs at the impossibility of coming to Bath themselves in hay-making season.

Anne was not sorry to see them depart, although she loved her sister dearly. The visit, at first, had had the wanted effect of distracting her from the anxiety of separation from her husband, but since the two letters had come to disturb and agitate her mind, nothing could give her peace and she only longed for the solitude of her room to read and reread both letters, taking alternately both comfort and anxiety from all that had been revealed. She had found a quiet moment to share the contents of the letters with Mrs Croft, although she was careful not to reveal the anxiety she repressed on account of her husband's glowing account of Mrs Benwick.

But something of her thoughts might have been made plain in her tone or countenance, for after quietly attending, and making a small comment here and there on poor Louisa's new circumstances, Mrs Croft said gently, 'I have been a wife of the navy for twenty years, and although I cannot speak for my Matthew, I vouchsafe to say that absence can make foolish mischief in us all. Frederick could not be more devoted to you, my dear, and you will have him safe and sound with you soon.'

Anne, although having outlived the age of blushing, now barely hid a rising self-consciousness, and she hoped fervently that Mrs Croft did not suspect the anxiety in which she had spent the last two days. She smiled a little, and nodded, and said something commonplace, and Mrs Croft, having said enough, patted her hand and left her to her thoughts.

Sixteen

Thursday 22 June, 1815

Camden-place, Bath.

There cannot be a daily meeting of two families such as the Elliots and the Crawfords, one group lofty, dignified, and secure in the awareness of all the deference due them, and other party so ready to give it unstintingly in the interest of future gain, without there being a mutual satisfaction of all parties upon each brief separation.

Miss Crawford was careful to pay all the deference due Miss Elliot, and in return, she was showered with condescending and gracious partiality in public, and intimate confidence in private. Indeed, Miss Crawford found herself filling a vacuum of power which had been left void in the wake of her predecessor, the Mrs Clay who had betrayed the family and run off with the heir to Kellynch. And vacuum of power it certainly was, although poor Miss Elliot had had no view of it thus; if she were to suddenly understand the various means Mrs Clay had exercised to manipulate her friend into letting down her guard, and to insinuate herself into the family, Miss Elliot would have been astonished and vexed at her own foolishness. But being a creature taught from infancy to consult none but her own feelings, and to dwell only upon whatever immediate pleasure might soothe and tickle them into complacence, she was blind to the motives and desires of others.

Since she had been discouraged by her father from any deeper searching into her own character for fear of what she might find in that unforgiving mirror, or into the characters of others for fear of being obliged to cast them off, she had discovered nothing about herself or others at one-and-thirty that she had not understood at thirteen, and could as easily be charged with a lack of hindsight as a lack of foresight.

Mrs Clay, so long her only *confidante* and intimate acquaintance, had certainly left a void when she had turned on her former friend, and Mary Crawford, possessed of as much insight into character and motivation as her new friend was lacking it, assiduously worked her way into this void, filling it in so unpretentious and subtle a manner as to excite no suspicion of creeping toadyism. Miss Crawford had verily become the new Mrs Clay, albeit much prettier and with no jutting tooth, and Elizabeth had no more inkling of danger this year than she had last year. At once both resenting and missing her old accomplice hour by interchangeable hour, she now found herself thinking less and less of the wounding she had suffered, and more and more of the pleasures of again being looked up to in all things, and of being secured of the affections and attentions of a family of tolerable consequence and handsomeness.

Mr Crawford, too, was careful to pay a certain degree of deference to the woman who was destined to become his lady, but knowing the importance of precedent, was careful to temper any deference with a measure of charming wilfulness, as a preventative against astonishment later on, that it should sometimes not *all* go according to the lady's wishes.

Lady Russell, who called in most days, was now pleased to see the effect a handsome, single gentleman might have on the person of a disappointed elder daughter of a baronet. She delighted quietly in the bloom that had now begun to return to Elizabeth's cheeks, and secretly smiled her satisfaction on noting the hours spent at the glass when the Crawfords were to be expected in Camden-place. And the Crawfords too, continued to please her for their own merits; to Camden-place they brought a cheerfulness and a pleasant distraction from all that had gone before, and both father and daughter were looking in more health than they had been for some months.

At any rate, it was soon Camden-place every day with the Crawfords, and their daily intercourse had become a pleasant habit to them all. When they went about town, Henry acted as chaperone to the ladies when it did not suit Sir Walter to accompany them to the gardens, or to parade. Six or seven days had passed however, before Sir Walter had made up his mind, it seemed, to accompany them to every place; it was decided change, noted Elizabeth to herself, which she put down to his enjoying the added advantage of being seen in company with so deferential and pretty a pair as the Crawford brother and sister. It had not yet occurred to her that her father might be harbouring some partiality for her friend, but to notice the motives of others was not Elizabeth's strong suit after all. Henry often accompanied herself, solicitously taking her arm, Lady Russell on his other, while Sir Walter, who had never shown any great regard for escorting a lady before apart from Lady Russell or Lady Dalrymple, now frequently took up Miss Crawford's arm.

'Elizabeth and Lady Russell shall lead, and if we walk a little behind them, I assure you, Miss Crawford, we shall still have a clear view of all who pass on the opposite side. It is of the utmost importance, I have always held, to keep an eye on whomever is approaching, to be prepared to duck off into a nearby shop, or to stop and study the window dressings, if the need is occasioned. It is astonishingly vexing the number of low individuals who think nothing of addressing me in the street to pass the time of day, or who think nothing of being the first to bow; the older ones are not so bad, but the young men! It is so here in Bath, at any rate, and is a prime reason for my preference for town. Why, only last week I was subject to a shocking vexing display from some shopkeeper or other, or merchant, to whom had I had not addressed but ten or a dozen words in all my time here! Poor fellow kept bowing and smiling, and I was obliged to give him my best cutting glance and walk away! It is on one point particularly offensive to me, Miss Crawford, that I must be obliged to be giving cuts to fellows to whom I give my business, for I am obliged then to go elsewhere, and then there is the awkward business of bills and suchlike — I always leave these things to Elizabeth — she handles the accounts quite as well as I could — and I regret that she must feel, by association, the brunt of the impertinence of these people, who ought to know their place. But never mind that, Miss Crawford, I shall guide us apart from such unpleasantness and we shall have a capital walk, I am sure!'

To this speech Miss Crawford had little to reply, but kept her eyes down, and her mouth firm, and murmured something placatory and grateful, while the curve of her upper lip was the only thing which hinted at more delicate and fomenting sensations.

At those times when she joined their party, Lady Russell found ever-increasing pleasure in viewing them all getting along so famously together. If Sir Walter found Miss Crawford to his taste, she could hardly blame him, for her friend had been a widower for long enough. To be sure, the lady was pretty well five and twenty years Sir Walter's junior, but then, Lady Russell herself had been almost fifteen years younger than her own dear husband, and while they might have boasted little in common, she had been well pleased with her situation, and had almost never a cross word to exchange with her husband while he had lived. While a match between Sir Walter and Miss Crawford might seem to have the all the benefit of the match on the lady's side, Lady Russell suspected the delicate feelings of Sir Walter in his predisposition to consider rank almost too highly, in this circumstance might easily be mollified by the addition of the beauty and elegance which would be Miss Crawford's contribution to the match.

How much money Miss Crawford was in possession of, Lady Russell could not enquire without appearing coarse, but Elizabeth had let it slip that she was rumoured to have twenty thousand pounds, which would more than make up for the lack of rank which might have discouraged her friend from the match. No, it was a good match for them both: Sir Walter would enjoy the twenty thousand pounds, and perhaps the elegant good sense of a woman like Mary Crawford would temper Sir Walter's liberality with regard to spending it. In short, Lady Russell had high hopes for the overall beneficial effect of a Mary Crawford upon her old friend.

And then, should Elizabeth be solicited to change her name to that of Crawford, and go away to live at Everingham, she would worry less about Sir Walter if she could be satisfied that he was well looked after by such an agreeable and sensible wife as Miss Crawford would make him. But these thoughts she kept private, for if a little blind to the motives of others, she had learned from the past and would neither make, nor persuade against, a match ever again. And beside this, her character was in every way fashioned out of prudence; she would never countenance a hasty move, for fear it prove false.

Thus, ten or so days passed with a quiet satisfaction brewing on both sides; ten days of coming together and pulling apart, ten days punctuated by brief, regretful separations, and agreeable reunions twelve or twenty-four hours later. One evening they were all to attend a ball given in the Upper rooms, another to see the famous exotic animal exhibition in the Sydney Gardens, and another to meet at noon to parade in the Pump-room. The Crawfords were presented to the Elliot's cousins, the Dalrymples, and seemed in every way to understand the honour done them. Both families were able to enjoy the mutual acquaintance of the Leigh-Perrots, a family of note in Bath who had inhabited it regularly for many winters and were on familiar terms with Sir Walter. They had even dined once with the Leigh-Perrots, laughing afterwards together at the absurdities of Bath's eclectic, and *gauche* society.

Sir Walter had been most eloquent on the topic. 'I have been a good deal acquainted with the family, and on the whole, they are respectable in all things; Lady Elliot, my late wife, was quite intimate with Mrs Leigh-Perrot. She is a great lady, in my estimation, and I believe my wife was invited to Scarlets at least twice in her life. Scarlets,' he added, for the benefit of the company, 'is the Leigh-Perrot family seat, Miss Crawford, in Berkshire. I do not myself go into Berkshire, but I believe it is quite a respectable county. But the relations...!'

'Precisely!' enunciated Henry immediately. 'What did you think, Sir Walter,' he continued in teasing tones, 'of the spinster nieces? The younger one, Jane, might even have amused *your* nice taste, I would have thought, had she not been a sickly-looking creature! But you know, despite that, she seemed possessed of a certain wit and understanding, even if she could never be called handsome compared to the ladies in *this* company.'

Miss Elliot, who felt herself canny and immune to the false compliments paid her by those wishing to gain her patronage, abandoned all her previous suspicion and allowed herself to be flattered. She had missed the little smile exchanged between Mary and Henry.

Contained in Mary's smile, however, was a little warning glance, the meaning of which Henry understood immediately to mean, 'take care not to use an excess of flattery for our object here is a delicate, manoeuvring business.'

'Spinsters indeed!' Mary said gaily. 'Henry, as such they are to be pitied, and you must be more generous, for they did nothing to deserve your derision! A mob cab on an unmarried female I always consider to be the worst punishment! The nieces are to be pitied, certainly, but not teased, you cruel boy! As for their looks, I concur that neither female could be called handsome, but I did not think either female "sickly" — that is much too harsh, Henry! The older Austen female was almost a tolerable-looking creature!'

The Leigh-Perrots had been used to being sometimes joined by the spinster nieces of Mr Leigh-Perrot, Cassandra and Jane, who were both far past the age of marriage. These two ladies had themselves previously regarded the Elliot party with barely disguised amusement on the odd occasions of their meeting, despite their own country style of dress and manners. Elizabeth had been obliged to complain to Lady Russell one time after she had stood just behind them in the Pump-room, that the younger female had made fun of Elizabeth's bonnet, and had added loudly to her sister, 'It is quite detestable for I cannot but think it resembles a dead cat with feathers protruding from the mouth!' And when the older sister scolded, the younger replied tartly, 'Oh, Cassie, since we are poor, there is little enough for us to find amusement in; perhaps they laugh at us too, behind our backs, for our clothes can hardly be considered fashionable! What is left in life to enjoy but to make sport of our neighbours and laugh at them in our turn!'

Sir Walter now replied coldly, 'I can hardly suppose I should find the company of poor, single females a pleasure, unfortunate-looking or otherwise. I have observed such women with great disapproval, Miss Crawford,' he added, turning to Mary, 'for although I am sure it is very good and right for the wealthy to include their poorer relatives from time to time, to give such people a taste of the ranks to which they may aspire works a mischief on the minds of women, who if tempted by untouchable pleasures, must then idle their time away wishing for what cannot be, rather than engaging in useful sorts of work.'

Elizabeth, very aware of Henry's glance resting upon her thoughtfully, laid a hand on her father's arm and said unusually graciously, 'It is the nature of Bath society, I believe, that every sort of person might find a little amusement in it; why should not two unremarkable nieces, of indifferent upbringing and education, take a little diversion for a time? So long as they enjoy Bath in their own time, and do not try to worm their way into the circles of those above them, or in an open and vulgar way try for husbands, what can it signify if two females of little means are allowed to find some diversion before returning to their mundane lives? I have no peculiar aversion to it, I own.'

Mary could not be provoked by either Elliot, and smiled as she said dexterously, 'True! But I never saw in them any behaviour unbecoming, and they are not so *very* unhandsome, and tolerably respectable. No, I am very glad to have made Miss Cassandra Austen's acquaintance, and the sister also. Even if she *did* make sport of your bonnet, Miss Elliot!' she added. 'I confess I cannot enter into your feelings with all the force of your own conviction, Sir Walter, however justified you are in your opinion, I am sure! It is true that to first tempt with, then remove, the taste of a life one may never experience is a cruel and unjust temptation; on the whole however, I saw nothing climbing in either of the ladies, and the older one, Miss Austen, was very proper and kind, so I must forgive them both at once for the possibility of their going home to day-dream instead of keeping their cottages neat!'

Sir Walter, having over a period of a few days' proximity become inclined by personal bias to allow Miss Crawford any opinion that might be opposite his own, with good humour took up the Bath papers and began to read out the visitor section, and allowed the young people their conversation. Soon after, it was settled that a visit to the Sydney pleasure gardens was the order for the following day, and the tea things were then brought in. At the same time, the footman brought in the mail for Sir Walter.

He casually took up the letter proffered on the silver salver and inspected the seal. 'Oh, it is only from Anne. I shall give it to you, my dear. You have more interest in the domestic cares at Kellynch than do I.' He handed the letter to his daughter, who opened it and perused it coolly.

Elizabeth read over the letter. 'Anne and our tenants, the Crofts, come to Bath. They are to arrive the day after tomorrow.' There was at first a certain boredom in her tone, but then abrupt dismay took its place. 'I do hope they don't expect to be staying here, we haven't the room for — oh, no matter, it is all decided; they have taken lodgings in Gay-street — that, at least, is quite respectable enough if we are to be associated with them — and they bring with them Mrs Croft's niece, for a day or two. I cannot,' she added, putting down the letter beside her impatiently, 'conceive of having so many to dine — indeed I cannot — for I am sure we will be expected to give them a dinner. How disagreeable a notion it is!'

Sir Walter added anxiously, 'Do you think that Anne will be expecting to stay on here? What an odd number at dinner — three! I have always disliked three people dining alone. It is so much more cosy, my dear to have just the two of us — but we may make the best of it, for she will make a spare at the card table in any event. And she may accompany us to our cousins, the Dalrymples. Of course, we cannot introduce the Crofts or their niece, but certainly Lady Dalrymple will not have any objection to seeing Anne in her drawing room again. We are Elliots, and *family*.'

'Certainly, the idea of family must not be held lightly. Do not you agree Mr Crawford?'

Before Henry could reply, Sir Walter interjected quite in a momentary irritation because he was thinking again of recent offences, 'It is a peculiar thing to my mind, when those who are fortunate enough to be able to count as family, well-bred people of rank and circumstance, who can claim the additional endowments of handsomeness of appearance and manners, fail to appreciate such connections. Family is honoured most of all by its name and reputation. It is a mark of peculiar ingratitude, I collect, to dismiss one's family connections lightly.'

Elizabeth turned to Mr Crawford calmly. 'My father means it is not ourselves of whom we think, Mr Crawford, but of the standing of the family. Family connections must be honoured!

'I count familial ties as of the most prime importance,' cried Henry with warmth. 'My feelings baulk, Miss Elliot, at the thought of spurning such ties; to refuse to do them justice is to harm oneself, over all things! Mary and I often talk of such matters, for we both hold family very dear, do we not, Mary?'

'Certainly, we do,' agreed Miss Crawford demurely.

Henry turned back to Elizabeth. 'You have expressed things supremely, Miss Elliot, exactly as I would have myself.'

Elizabeth received his charming smile and allowed her feelings to be soothed by it. 'Still,' she fussed, 'it is too bad of my sister to set up an expectation! I do wish they had not said they will come! The dining room was to be new-furnished this week, but I suppose it will have to wait. Do you think I am right to wait?' This to Sir Walter, then she immediately went on addressing the room at large. 'Perhaps a card party — I think a card party, just something small, will do well enough.' Elizabeth was now progressed to a state of happy dismay at the prospect of showing off the Crawfords to her sister and entered into the thought of being obliged to give an evening party with agreeable agitation. She laid an anxious hand on her father's arm. 'Considering Admiral Croft's good standing, his personal consequence in Bath, where he is known intimately, we must be agreeable, Father, but be careful not to appear as if inviting liberties.'

Her father was sympathetic. 'I cannot imagine what Anne was thinking, if they expect to dine here! If it was just herself, but the Crofts! Well, but there was a time I would have said they are not at all the sort of people to be seen with — I hope Lady Dalrymple will not be offended by our giving attention to them — but Admiral Croft is quite a respectable man after all, despite his reddened complexion — even so, they will have to find their own level of society; they surely cannot expect us to have them to dine!'

He was all given up to his daughter's fluster. But in a few moments, it was settled by Elizabeth that Anne could not possibly have expected to dine, and must know how inconvenient a thing it would be to expect them to have the Crofts. A card party might easily be given, which would soothe the Crofts without bringing any real confusion of situation and rank. No, a card party would suffice splendidly and discharge their duty to their tenant, and Anne's new connections, with no great risk to the Elliot name.

Henry now spoke again. 'Your notion of giving a card party, Miss Elliot, is an exceptionally good one! How I adore a card party! Do you not agree, Mary?' he added, momentarily turning to his sister who raised one laughing, quizzical brow at him because she knew very well that he despised card parties. 'An evening party has just the right amount of elegance to lend to a situation which requires careful handling. The Crofts are your tenants, and cannot expect a dinner, but to give them an evening party is the exact amount of deference calculated to not give offence while retaining all the proper considerations of differences of rank and situation. After all, a sea admiral cannot quite be thought of as *not* being a gentleman! It is not so *great* a difference in rank, perhaps, to make you uncomfortable Miss Elliot, even if a dinner *were* given, but an evening party is certainly a perfect compromise where such things might be mistaken by those who seek to take advantage of certain connections.'

'You *perfectly* understand me, Mr Crawford!' Finding herself *sympatico* with one of the more handsome and elegant males she had met, Elizabeth's cool heart had begun to thaw after a frosty winter of hibernation, even if she was yet to acknowledge it. She blushed a little but felt a peculiar light glow about her on receipt of his comment. It was pleasant to be agreed with, and the sensation of being considered correct by Mr Crawford gave her a little flutter within. As to the Crofts, she knew full well from their interactions with the Crofts when they were last in Bath that no such liberties had ever, or would ever, be taken by the admiral and his wife, and that her father had probably thought more often of the Crofts, than the Crofts had ever thought about *them!*

Henry and Mary had exchanged glances but said little more than to murmur their gratitude when Elizabeth now included them at once in the party, which was to be held the night after next. Sir Walter launched into one of his coughing spells at this juncture and Mary leaned solicitously forward to enquire of his health.

'It is only a cough, Miss Crawford. I have run out of all the tincture Poole supplies me; he is inconsiderately gone off to Lyme or Bristol, or some place, and I must wait until his return to get some more.'

Mary was warmly agitated. 'How inconsiderate, Sir Walter! I have two or three very good receipts for some tonics and elixirs, and always have some already made up about me, for Henry. My Aunt on my mother's side, you know, was very good at these home remedies, and she taught me one or two little tricks, if you would please to try one. I cannot hope,' she added modestly, 'to match your Doctor Poole's talent for a remedy, only I cannot bear to think of you in discomfort when you might have some relief with so little effort!' She had placed a solicitous hand on his arm, and now allowed him the liberty of patting it in gentle gratitude. 'Will you allow me to bring you my aunt's cough remedy? A tincture of two or three herbs, and molasses; I have some fresh made; I shall bring it with me tomorrow when we meet.'

'You are too kind, Miss Crawford! I am in your debt.' He smiled his gratitude down at her.

She smiled back and withdrew her hand, for it would not do to be too obvious. 'Then you do me a great favour, by putting my mind at rest for your health, Sir Walter. I insist that you must be made well again in no time at all.'

Seventeen

Thursday 29 June, 1815

The news of the battle at Quatre Bras and the subsequent defeat of Napoleon at Waterloo twenty four hours later, had reached Camden-place as quickly as it had reached Kellynch; indeed, the news had spread within merely an hour or two, from two or three households who could boast captains or majors, to all households, via the great messaging service called the Morning Stroll on the Promenade, and the Pump-room Vine was not to be held any less effective for such a service.

The Elliots wasted no time in making the defeat a topic for conversation among their acquaintance, since they could draw certain attention from it, being possessed of a captain in their immediate family, and when it suited their purpose, an admiral as a tenant. Lady Russell, however, when solicited for comment, could say but little, as her dignified affront over there being made no mention of Captain Wentworth's safety, when it was known he was in the vicinity of danger, could barely be disguised except by silence; Lady Russell found silence could cover very well, on the whole, those times her opinion was solicited on this or that topic, since of all the party gathered at Camden-place her opinion was least looked for among the young people and only by the necessity of civility, rather than because of genuine interest. Her contempt really simmered more for Anne's benefit than for herself on this occasion; while she had not always favoured Wentworth for Anne, now that he was the chosen one, her affection for Anne made Wentworth almost as dear to her as was her god-child, and she sometimes found herself repressing many a pent-up emotion on behalf of them both. But to preserve the gentle repose of the room, and her friendship with Sir Walter, she made all efforts to never let her contempt get the better of her tongue.

The evening before Anne and the Crofts were to arrive in Bath, the Elliots were to attend the theatre to accompany Lady Dalrymple who was invited as a guest of the Prince of Wales, and attend the supper afterwards. This much looked-for invitation had been expected and talked of for many days, having been vigorously hinted at by Lady Dalrymple. The theatre visit had already been put off once, the Prince having delayed his arrival in Bath by a se'en night. But now they were to attend, it was all arranged, and Elizabeth and Sir Walter talked of nothing else for the four days prior, until Lady Russell was vexed and ashamed of hearing it spoken of every time she sat in the drawing room at Camden-place.

As anxious for the good standing of her friend in Bath as any could be, and as able to acknowledge the honour done them as any intimate friend of the family may be, she felt that as much as Sir Walter may be justified in a certain amount of self-satisfaction, in his ingratiating manner she perceived a fawning admiration that even she found distasteful. Sir Walter's notions of his own importance in Bath, she regretted, were not a little elevated beyond what could truly be claimed. She knew, too, that the Elliots usually viewed such entertainments with supercilious disdain, looking down upon those who attended the theatre, and viewing the entertainers themselves as mere fluff-nothings at best, although some of the great actresses were now being accepted into the finest drawing rooms as respected artists. But she held her tongue and graciously accepted the invitation to join them, grateful that Anne, at least, had been spared the sight of her father and Elizabeth making love to Lady Dalrymple for all they were worth!

It had amused Lady Russell too, that for all Sir Walter's disdain of the theatre, feeling it to be beneath him, he was so very anxious for the entertainment on account of Lady Dalrymple's example. Never had he appeared in such good spirits as he had been following the arrival of the invitation. He had formerly dismissed the theatre whenever it had been suggested, but now he seemed to view the prospect of an evening of viewing the boards a respectable diversion.

'Our cousins do us much honour, Lady Russell. I suppose Lady Dalrymple is as unenthusiastic for the amusement as I generally find myself, but if our cousin requires our presence, we must help her to bear it as well as she can! The whole shall be raised up, surely, by the presence of the Prince! I am sure Miss Foote will be as much a lady as one can be in that profession. And to be singled out by the Prince! Lady Dalrymple, I am sure, knows her duty as nobility. We shall attend. Elizabeth and I are in perfect agreement that one does not have the liberty of being nice on these occasions!'

The Crawfords, consenting to being carried to Orchard-street in the Elliot carriage, appeared in the drawing room at Camden-place in good time, Lady Russell having desired to join them outside the theatre, having her own vehicle and preferring to make her own way. Sir Walter, a little overblown but handsome enough in his blue Bath-cloth coat, gold waistcoat, long whiskers, and silk stockings, had checked his appearance numerous times before their guests had arrived, and made sure of walking about the room to appear to the best advantage upon the arrival of Miss Crawford.

Mary, noting at once Sir Walter's movements, and supposing correctly that he was only half in custody of that which would make him fully content, supplied the rest. 'How well you look tonight, Sir Walter. What an excellently cut coat! To whom do you go for tailoring? My brother was just saying how displeased he is with his current man.'

'Oh, I have very good fellow in Conduit-street, in town. Meyer is his name. I shall not scruple to tell you, Miss Crawford, that the Prince has been to Conduit-street for his own coats, and so I am satisfied that I can find none better, if you brother would have my advice.'

'I shall be sure to mention the name to him, Sir Walter. I am sure he will be excessively grateful!'

Mary, dressed in a rich red pelerine gown herself, cap-sleeved and handsomely trimmed, had nothing to be ashamed of in her own appearance. Her brother, in similar-hued, finely-embroidered waistcoat, high cream cravat, cream silk stocking and fine black shoes, gave a charming, understated appearance, at odds with the overblown style of Sir Walter.

None of this was lost on Elizabeth as she viewed the Crawfords from across the room. To Elizabeth's demanding eye, the two of them formed as neat a pair as any two matched greys she had seen. She did not feel intimidated by Miss Crawford, however, for she knew full well the effect she was having on the brother. In her lavender silk-and-gauze, with parma-violet ribbon and French detailing, all in all, she thought, it was as charming a gown as she had ever worn under his eye, and was gratified but not surprised, to see his eyes rest upon her pretty bosom momentarily before they slid up again to meet hers with undisguised warm admiration. Elizabeth did not consider herself a vain woman in the sense that she spent more hours before a mirror than any other female of quality, but she had spent some careful time in reflection in the last few days, and the product of those thoughts meant that she had sat for more time than usual at her glass this evening.

Thus it was that the four of them arrived, well pleased with themselves and those around them, at Orchard-street, in good time for Lady Dalrymple's carriage to appear. They had come early on purpose so that Sir Walter could offer to escort his cousin upstairs to their box. Lady Russell joined them very soon after, and they stood together in the large hall to survey the company before them and await Lady Dalrymple.

Lady Dalrymple's daughter, the Honourable Miss Carteret, had been solicited to marry only recently, by a rather long-faced, but well-looking gentleman called Annesley, whom Lady Russell, when catching sight of him, considered just the sort of man who might make his already awkward and plain wife even more awkward and plain beside him. However, as much as it seemed an odd match, it was clearly a sensible union on both sides, she thought, for he was in full pockets, by all accounts, and *his* situation would be considerably raised by marrying nobility.

Their happily-situated box was spacious and well appointed, its ten seats neatly set out and the box itself prettily decorated, and with a good view of the royal accommodations not quite opposite. The newly married Carteret and her husband placed themselves behind Lady Dalrymple, each looking as miserable as the other, while the Crawfords placed themselves in the positions they considered most suitable for the pursuit of their prey.

Lady Dalrymple had seated herself in the front row of seats and indicated that Sir Walter should take a place beside her. 'Now do tell me, Sir Walter, what is the Prince wearing upon his head?' commanded she. 'Is it a pigeon? It looks to me just like a pigeon! I cannot tell from this distance. It is no end of amusement to me to see what kind of style that man is setting! Always something new! What is his fashion?'

Sir Walter immediately took up the spy-glass and turned it upon the royal box. 'Ah! I must say, my lady, I must ever look with an evil eye upon the silliest of today's fashions, although it is the Prince, and I cannot say I approve his appearance on every occasion; but tonight, I own myself surprised, for on your supposing a pigeon upon his head I had expected the worst! But it is only a copious dab of powder upon his dark hair! Other than this, he wears a blue coat, a white waistcoat, and white pantaloons - which give rather an odd appearance for they look to be buttoned ornately at the ankle!'

'At his ankles! Are you certain?'

'Quite certain, Lady Dalrymple. After the style of Brummel, I perceive!'

Lady Dalrymple sniffed disapprovingly. 'Brummel, is it? Hmm! And what of his hair?'

'In the style of the Brutus, Madam.'

'And to whom does he speak? The lady by his side must be the Lady Isabella Conway, Marchioness of Hertford?'

'I believe it is, my lady.'

Now Lady Russell came to sit beside Elizabeth as the orchestra began to play in earnest and the room gave its attention to the players. Mary, sitting at Sir Walter's left, provided him with the program, and pointed out kindly the general idea of the action to take place.

Henry, of course, ensured he was at Miss Elliot's right hand, and after a little while of watching her from the corner of his eye said to her in low tones, 'I see you are feeling just what you ought, Miss Elliot; your sensation is the discomfort that must naturally arise when a person of your situation in life is obliged by duty to put aside all the natural aversion to such entertainments in general, in order to do what is right and correct. I do not much like the theatre myself, on the whole, but I confess that tonight I expect to find a degree of pleasure in it, for other reasons,' he added, brushing ever so slightly the hand which lay too close beside him to be thought placed there casually.

Elizabeth, in the company of her noble cousins, and the sole object of Mr Crawford's gallantry, was now content. 'Indeed, Mr Crawford, do you claim to understand me?' She smiled archly. 'That is an intimate claim, and yet we have known each other only a few weeks. What else do you claim, Sir?' Her eyes fleetingly met his and lowered again.

'I can tell you that I am intimately familiar with your...feelings, on several points. For example, Miss Elliot, although I must view the theatre as you do, in general below the notice of a family such as yours, now that Lady Dalrymple has set a precedent, as a guest of the Prince, tonight will do much to forward your Father's interests in Bath, and your own reputation may not be in any way hurt by such an association.'

He could not have reminded her of anything more pleasing, and she allowed her fan to accidentally tip forward so that it was just touching the well-clothed knee only inches from her own, so close they had drawn to talk confidentially.

Henry allowed his finger to play idly over the hard line of little *brisee* fan. He was pleased, he told her, that she would have the opportunity to see the indubitably talented Miss Maria Foote, whom Henry had had the pleasure of meeting in London the season last but one. The lady had condescended to act a scene for some friends, after a dinner one evening to which Miss Foote had been invited. 'I suspect you will be quite impressed by her,' he added. 'Your natural taste and good judgement will, if I might venture to say, be drawn in by her obvious talent.'

'I believe I read of her in *La Belle Assemblee*,' replied

Elizabeth coolly. 'A talent indeed, by several accounts. While I am not one to countenance and encourage the *visiting* of these people to the homes of those who ought to know better, for the association of such women can only degrade the reputation of good families in society – but all the same, one may admire talent, I suppose.'

'You are very right, Miss Elliot, to admire the talent of these people, if not the lifestyle! There is nothing so pleasing as a female with a good voice, a pretty face, and a strong delivery of lines written centuries ago – the greatest of literature – these are characters which have delighted us for centuries – they deserve the talents of these types of women.'

'I remember studying the great plays in my youth, Mr Elliot, as part of my education. It is a great pity there are so many cheap and coarse comedies about these days!'

'I confess, although I have never truly liked a play,' he remarked smoothly, 'when it has been forced upon me, I have always preferred the tragedies. I shall never forget seeing Mrs Siddons do "Lady Macbeth" while I was in town a few seasons ago. She left a great impression upon me! Do you like Shakespeare, Miss Elliot? But, of course you do! You have that innate good taste which comes naturally with good breeding and education.'

Elizabeth, who if she had been more on her guard might have dissembled, allowed herself to be ever more flattered and if she was becoming accustomed to the same compliments which only last year had soothed her into a false security, she gave no heed to the mistakes of the past, so caught up had she become in thoughts of the future, and in calculating the days until she might catch herself a Crawford.

Eighteen

Camden-place, Bath.

Sir Walter at that time had begun to feel looming anxiety and increased solicitousness for his own health. His cough, the usual vestiges left over from the damp Bath winter, had not fully subsided, and still plagued him daily. Poole, by his absence, was a bitter disappointment to him, and the fatigue which was becoming a daily burden to him oppressed him with thoughts of a sooner than expected demise, which had never been a consideration of his, since he was usually so robust.

Miss Crawford was a great comfort to him in the course of these thoughts, for although he could never have been considered a man of great sense, and a squanderer of his money to a large degree, he harboured a great fondness for his oldest daughter, and it had more than once occurred to him that he did not wish to become a burden to her, especially if she was to become mistress of Everingham. Therefore, the kind attentions of Miss Crawford had become a comfort to him, and fancying himself a favourite with her, he began privately to consider the benefits to himself if he were to marry, in relieving Elizabeth of the anxieties of attending a father with failing health, and transferring those to someone who might make him comfortable in his old age.

So it was then, that when the Crawfords had finally taken leave of Camden-place later that same evening after they had come home from the theatre outing, despite his pressing fatigue, Sir Walter felt inclined to make the most of the little intimacy of sharing a final glass of negus with Elizabeth before they both retired to bed. After a small bout of coughing, he submitted to Elizabeth's pleadings to take some of Miss Crawford's syrup.

'What but Poole should not have let me have some before he left,' he complained irritably, after downing the medicine. 'Such are the vagaries of the working class of men, I suppose. All fawning attention one moment, and the next, no consideration for their patrons, if it doesn't suit them!'

'Miss Crawford's potion is so beneficial to you, Father, that you must keep on with it. I fancy your cough is so much better since you have been taking it.'

'Do you think so? I daresay I am a little better, indeed. I am quite often confoundingly fatigued – very inconsiderate of Poole to disappear when I require him – but the cough is almost quite gone away!'

'It was very good of Miss Crawford to bring you such a large bottle of her own mixture; we must find some little way to repay her – a present of some of our pheasant from Kellynch next time Anne comes to us, perhaps. It is too late to send for some now, for Anne is to arrive tomorrow, but perhaps next time.'

'A present?' cried Sir Walter. 'I should think being asked frequently to Camden-place, and the not insignificant attentions they have received from this family, are more than enough thanks, I am sure, for the Crawfords! Besides,' added he, a calculating look upon his face, 'I see that soon enough, my dear, the Crawfords will have all the "present" they might ever wish for, if *certain events* which I have foreseen, come into being.'

Elizabeth slid him a coy, assessing look, then, idly fingering her half-tumbler of negus, said, 'What can you mean, Father?'

He put down his glass and addressed her candidly. 'My dear. I am hardly blind to the growing regard that Crawford appears to have for you.' He strolled to the window and spoke to the night air. 'It would not be difficult for you to bring him to heel, if you can see yourself as mistress of Everingham someday in the near future. It would only take some little encouragement on your part, some cleverness of your own, to bring him to the point of an offer, I believe.'

Elizabeth, faced with this appeal to her vanity, was not easily able to resist. She gave voice to the thoughts which had most pleasantly plagued her for more than a week. 'I must own that such thoughts had not failed to present themselves to me.' She paused, glancing in the glass above the fireplace. She tucked a stray hair into her neat coiffure and spoke to her own reflection. 'To be sure, he is no *Mr Elliot*, but on *that* subject, we shall never more speak after tonight. But Crawford has a considerable establishment, money, and the situation in life which goes with it.' She turned to her father. 'He is not without respectability, and I own that to be the mistress of such an establishment, which, while it is not Kellynch, cannot fail to be respected for its own longstanding position in their family.'

Sir Walter came forward and took both her hands in his own. 'You have the united gifts of the Elliot face, and the Elliot rank, my dear. You are the daughter of a baronet. These, by all accounts, *must* be seen as welcome additions to one such as Crawford. And to unite these gifts of yours with the further blessing of an establishment of the respectability that Everingham must naturally command! Quite apart from the outcome that we once held so dear and were so disappointed in — no, do not be low in spirits, my dear, we shall not mention the business again — now, I could not wish for any better future for my dearest Elizabeth.'

Elizabeth allowed herself to be moved. She grasped the hands which held her own. 'If I have your blessing, then, Sir... I have not lost my looks, and my rank must naturally make the prospect agreeable to him. He is already eating from my palm, and giving me the most meaningful looks!'

'It will only take a little push, my dear, to have him falling at your feet!'

Elizabeth allowed herself a little smile, and pulling away from her father's grasp, now went composedly to sit upon the chaise. 'And, what of yourself, Father? If we are being quite candid with each other, I cannot pretend not to have noticed Miss Crawford's growing regard for you! I know out of affection for me, you have never thought of marriage for yourself, although it was much looked for by our friends after my mother's passing, but if I am to marry Crawford, you may think of yourself now; indeed,' she added most generously, 'it would content me to know you are happy in your old age.'

Sir Walter had naturally given this a great deal of thought in the intervening weeks since he had seen Crawford's regard for his daughter and foreseen the result. For many years he had prided himself on remaining in the single state for the benefit of his oldest daughter. Despite his friends' assumptions that he would make an offer to Lady Russell, he had been most decided in his resolve never to marry again. But now, with such a felicitous prospect before him of Elizabeth sure of being settled so well, he need not scruple to make himself comfortable in his old age. He said as much to Elizabeth.

'Then,' replied she, 'make yourself as agreeable as you may to Miss Crawford. God knows, we will be doing them both a great service, since they will be aligning themselves with the name of Elliot, but I collect Miss Crawford is too sensible a woman to misunderstand the great condescension you will be undertaking in making her "Lady Elliot"!'

Nineteen

Friday 23 June, 1815

Brussels, Belgium.

They had been in Brussels a se'en night, and although Wentworth had not given up the hope of a speedy return to Ostend, he doubted the likelihood of it. As much as the British had won a French defeat at Quatres Bras, the battle fought only hours later at Waterloo had left many casualties from both sides and dealing with the aftermath of the bloody battle would not be an insignificant task. Admiral Malcom had been to the fields of Waterloo on the day of the great battle, commanding Wentworth to remain with the females, but had come back within the day.

'I shall never get used to the sight of a battle field, Wentworth,' he had shaken his head. 'Aye, it gives nothing but heartache even to the staunchest mind, I do not mind admitting. Bloody business. Not an inch of grass in view but was sticky and scarlet with spilled blood. Legs and arms and heads apiece — disembowelled bodies and everything you can imagine, and the worst of it, the local women raking through the remains for coins and what jewels they can carry away — one fellow I saw with a knife, digging a gold filling from the mouth of a poor wretch — aye, tis a devil of a business, is war on land! I'll take the sea and drown for my choice any day!'

Wentworth had seen battles, but the ocean had a way of washing blood from the decks of ships quickly, and gave an insidious, if misguided, notion of cleanliness, even among death and disease. The stench of below-decks could never be disguised, of course, especially when there was yellow fever and typhoid hidden out of sight in the ship's dark belly, but above deck, even in the bloodiest of battles, he had always been grateful for the fresh air, and the relentless waves which washed away the ugliness of pain and death and replaced them with glistening, cool, salt water as if washing away the sins of the world.

'And what of the wounded and prisoners of war, Sir? Did you see Wellington?'

'Briefly, but he has posted to Ostend to arrange for the wounded and prisoners to be shipped back to England. I must follow him, but I shall be back by tomorrow. There are many more ships coming into that port with troops that we shall not need. The Tartarus will remain in port for my use, but I shall commission the Nightingale, Captain, to take wounded back to British soil. I shall need you here for another two or three weeks yet. I am sorry for it,' he added quietly, 'I know you wish to get Mrs Benwick home.'

Wentworth nodded and was resolute since it was what he had expected. Louisa would understand, although she might be disappointed. The admiral posted off instead to Ostend hours later, and Wentworth spent the remainder of the day in carrying out a few small tasks Malcolm had asked him to see to, and in making himself less anxious about Louisa Benwick's state of mind.

Louisa, confined to the hotel, the mood of the town as dark as the mourning gowns she now wore, was resolute as ever, but Wentworth could see that events of the last week had taken their additional toll on her emotional state. Only a week ago she had suffered that ominous day of the battles at Quatre Bras and Waterloo, only miles from the city, the sound of the constant rage of distant cannons permeating their attempts at conversation. The cannons had finally become quiet, late in the second evening, and she had gone up to her bed without having uttered comment. Wentworth had apprehended that with the added burden of her own recent loss, Louisa was now under a great deal of strain, and he wished to see her home faster than he had license to get her there himself. It was a burden to him which weighed upon his conscience.

There were, however, two developments around this time which gave him joy. The first was the much looked for arrival of two letters from home, in the handwriting of his wife. He counted himself lucky to get mail at all, for it was not uncommon for the mail packets to be disrupted in the channel by enemy ships and pirate activity, either making the mail vastly late or causing it to be lost entirely to the sea. Seizing up the letters addressed to him in the handwriting which had become dear to him, he took them to the privacy of his chambers and thrust his knife impatiently under the Elliot seals.

Eagerly he opened the earliest-dated, and read it with rapt attention. The little comings and goings of Kellynch daily life gave him comfort, and a connection he yearned for in the absence of his wife. He read gravely of the bringing of his niece to Kellynch, and in his heart felt again a pride that was natural to him, of having such a sensible and capable wife who did not falter even under duress. He was regretful that he had missed his brother's letter by one day, but Edward would know that Julia was in safe hands at Kellynch in the care of Anne and his sister.

The first letter read over twice, every nuance of her voice absorbed, he then opened the second, written only six days ago, and sent on to Brussels immediately with the first, he collected. In it he found more to give him anxious pause, however, for while his heart was increased in its fond warmth with every word she had written, the name of "Crawford" struck him when it was mentioned, for it seemed too coincidental that there should be a brother and sister Crawford mentioned to him only days apart. It was hardly likely that the two Crawfords were the same people, and yet it made him anxious, for no good could come of any association between the Elliots and this Crawford, if what young Price had told him was truth.

A fortuitous second event at this time however, gave him an opportunity to alleviate his fears. News that a mail packet had very lately arrived in Ostend, which had place for a lady, as well as two other inferior berths which were vacant and might do for a lady's companion or a gentleman, gave him a notion he actioned at once. He sent for Lieutenant Price, hoping he was not too late to catch the young man before he had gone from Brussels. Price had not yet left, and came at once upon receipt of Wentworth's note. Wentworth outlined his intentions and found that Lieutenant Price was agreeable and eager to assist.

'Of course, Captain. It will be my duty and my pleasure to see Mrs Benwick home to England. My sister Fanny will be grateful to see me as speedily as possible and my doing you this small service shall set me upon that path all the sooner than if I had been forced to wait for the Nightingale to embark for England.'

'Then you have my deepest gratitude, Mr Price. I shall inform Mrs Benwick at once, and you will call for her tomorrow morning to escort her back to Ostend. I cannot tell you what peace of mind it gives me to know that you will be at hand on the journey back to England. These packets are speedy little vessels, but there are still lurking dangers in the channel, and although she shall have a servant to assist her, I feel easier sending Mrs Benwick away under your care.'

Louisa, when she heard the news that a passage had finally been secured for her, was resolute. 'You have been nothing but kindness, Captain Wentworth, when I have given you and the admiral only trouble. I have imposed upon you long enough. I am to return to my friends, and it is quite right that I ought to go home. I cannot thank you enough for your arranging it. Poor dear Benwick had a great friend in you, and I shall never forget it.'

As good as his word, Price called the next morning to escort Mrs Benwick and the woman who had been engaged for her comfort, back to Ostend. He was to accompany them on horseback and then see to their comfort once aboard the packet which had agreed to give them passage.

Wentworth personally handed Louisa into the carriage. 'I wish I could have had you home sooner, Louisa, but I hope you will forgive the delay. I own it is a weight from my shoulders to feel that I have discharged my duty to Benwick, and the duty which our former friendship naturally commanded of me.' He paused. 'You have impressed me with the most resolute courage under the greatest adversity, and I hold your character in the highest esteem for it.'

Louisa smiled gently and said, 'I fancy Anne would be proud of me, Captain.'

'Indeed, she would,' he relied gravely. 'If you should want for anything at all, I have given a sum of money to Mr Price to ensure your comfort. You have only to mention any requirement to him.' Wentworth took up a letter from his pocket and held it out. 'Will you see Anne gets this? And give her news of me. Tell her I hope I shall be home within the month, two at most!' He pressed into her hand the note, hurriedly written, and improperly sealed.

Louisa gave him a weak smile. 'I shall give it her with my own hand. Thank you, Captain. Goodbye.'

'God speed, Louisa. Goodbye!'

Price raised his hand in a salute to Wentworth and the carriage drew out behind him, and was away.

Friday 30 June, 1815
Bath.

Anne had entered on the road to Bath a few hours earlier in low enough spirits without needing this further burden of being obliged by sincere friendship and a desire of being accommodating, to accompany the Crofts into a city which gave her no pleasure other than the husband it had gifted her. The tragedy of Benwick and his widow Louisa, of Frederick's glowing account of the woman he had once considered a serious matrimonial prospect, of the weight of the scandal which Julia had near brought upon them, and of all things, her anxiousness for the safety and personal comforts of her husband at this very moment; all these weighed upon her mind. Her thoughts full of these things, she was ill prepared to enter the humid bustle of Bath, stand upon the doorstep at Camden-place and wish herself inside its cold, indifferent walls.

Not much looking forward to enduring four weeks with her family, Anne had been grateful to Mrs Croft, who had divined Anne's reluctance to spend the entire stay at Camden-place and insisted she stay with them, 'if you can be content, my dear, in lesser accommodations than you must have been used when at Bath, but if you do not mind the admiral and me for company, we should be glad to have you with us all the same.'

Anne had not minded at all; indeed, she felt that if she must be for a time in a city which she did not like very much, that she might at least be with Frederick's sister, and find what comfort she could in the undemanding, affectionate company of the Crofts. She would stay with them in the charming lodgings in Gay-street they habitually took when in Bath, which overlooked the fine countryside and which would offer more in unassuming and welcoming comfort than the cool elegance of her father's apartments.

Before making their way there, however, they had first determined on paying their respects at Camden-place. Anne did not expect a particularly warm reunion, her sister always a little cool in manner and her father too conscious of rank to admit the Crofts with the same degree of tolerance as they deserved.

When their little party of four entered the drawing room in that establishment, however, they were met with such a degree of gracious cordiality that she was a little astonished, and somewhat gratified. Although to *her* mind, the Crofts were as genteel and deserving as any two people could be, being Sir Walter's tenants, his manner had always been to overlook them. But now, perhaps since they were her own relatives, her father had begun to soften. She was satisfied to observe it; indeed, she was content. Her father and Elizabeth appeared to be in excellent spirits. It gladdened Anne to see her sister so much recovered from her previous disappointment. Perhaps the visit would not be as trying to herself as she imagined it would be!

It was with genuine happiness, too, that she greeted Lady Russell, who had come on purpose to meet them all as soon as they had arrived.

'My dear Anne, how good it is to see you! How charming you look, my dear; your cheeks are positively rosy! Your condition suits you very well!'

Anne, blushing a little, took her godmother's outstretched hands and allowed herself to be kissed and led to the chaise opposite her father and Elizabeth. 'Thank you. And are *you* well, Lady Russell? How long do you remain in Bath? You must have been here several weeks already!'

They conferred for a time, and when Lady Russell brought up

the topic of Napoleon's defeat only a week or so distant, and asked if Anne had had a letter from Frederick, Anne was composed enough to be able to relate the contents of the letters she had had, and express her expectation of a happier letter soon.

'I can hardly think him in danger, Lady Russell, for he would have stayed well away from the fighting, I am certain. Only, my mind will be a *little* restless until I have confirmation that he is well, and that Louisa Benwick is in the care of her friends here. But I have been fortunate in marriage, for I have gained the very best of sisters in Mrs Croft, and the admiral is nothing but kindness, and daily puts me at ease regarding Frederick!' She did not mention her additional anxiety over her husband's glowing words regarding Louisa's changed character, nor Frederick's taking the widow on to Brussels with their party.

Lady Russell glanced over at Sir Walter who was in conversation with the admiral and Mrs Croft, Julia quiet and grave beside her aunt, and turned again to Anne. 'I confess I find myself not a little put out, my dear,' she said confidingly, 'at a lack of sincere interest in your condition, and in your circumstances, from those who ought to have the most claim to an interest in you and your husband. It provokes me excessively that they do not give you the honour that is due to you, especially in your condition. They do not value you as I do, as the living embodiment of your dear mother.'

Anne smiled and put a hand on Lady Russell's green, taffeta-clad arm. 'You are always so good! My father and Elizabeth have not made mention of the French defeat, or asked after Frederick. But I confess I do not wish to talk of my husband. To talk of Frederick is to remind me of his absence and I confess I prefer to think of him when I am alone, where such thoughts can bring me comfort. As to my condition,' she added, her eyes joyful, 'I feel that I carry a piece of my husband with me; so long as I have my child, I cannot feel so wholly brought down. And Frederick will be home soon, I am sure. Now, how do you go on in Rivers-street, Lady Russell? I may visit you there tomorrow, I believe, for Mrs Croft wishes the admiral to take the waters daily and we shall pass by very near as we go.'

Lady Russell went out of her way to make much of Julia, who had been very quiet since leaving Kellynch that morning. Though having recovered from her first biliousness in the mornings, the girl was yet not quite inured to the future set out for her, and from which there was no escape. She had been charged with silence on the topic of Mr Lyford and her condition. All complaints had been quelled by dint of Anne's promises of taking up some small gifts for her confinement if she behaved herself, and her other aunt's threat to write to her father if she should misbehave. But she seemed now to rally a little in the company of new faces, received Lady Russell's solicitousness with complacence, and partook of tea with a tolerable composure.

Her condition was not yet obvious to onlookers, and Mrs Croft had conferred with Anne and decided that the girl might accompany them for the two or three days she was to remain in Bath before going away with Mrs Haye. Dr. Thorpe had mentioned his going up to Bath very nearly at the same time, and expressed a wish of seeing his aunt, and would 'give her such advice as a medical man might give although she has been at many a child-birth — I confess my own knowledge is far inferior to her own on that point.'

Julia had looked sullen at the mention that he may come to see her, but knew enough of her aunts' dispositions and her own precarious circumstance to refrain from open opposition to the scheme.

Elizabeth appeared in very good looks to Anne's eye, and she was glad. Anne had left Bath before her wedding, with no little anxiety for her sister's state of mind. Elizabeth had been low in spirits then, the knowledge of Mr Elliot's defection to the enemy camp of "Clay" leaving her sister pale and lethargic. Yet the creature before her now was much improved, with a rosiness to her cheek which Anne was pleased to see again. Her father, too, despite a nagging cough, seemed in excellent spirits, and Anne was gratified when he at last spoke of her child, and graciously offered his congratulations.

She made her thanks as warm as she could then asked, 'But how do you go on, Father? I confess I do not like the sound of that cough. Have you had a physician here?'

Elizabeth answered for him. 'I own I have been concerned for our father's health myself, for it seems not to improve as it usually does with the summer months. Poole has gone away to Lyme or some such place, isn't it so, father? Perhaps Miss Crawford's remedy can induce a cure! Miss Crawford you know,' she added for Anne's benefit, 'is experienced in making up a little remedy here and there she says, for her brother. I own I see no harm in a lady making herself useful in such a way, although it is usually the realm of servants to do such things, but she offered so kindly and with such an air of confidence, I confess I put away my doubts and allowed it for our father's sake. Mr Crawford says she is excessively clever in these matters. He relies upon his sister's remedies, and he is such a picture of health himself that I am inclined to believe him.'

'Oh,' cried Anne, a little astonished that her sister could make so many allowances all at once, 'that is excellent news indeed! You might try Miss Crawford's cure, Father, and see how you go on.' She paused then ventured, 'An acquaintance of the Crofts', a Doctor Thorpe, is in town; he might consent to see you, if you wish it? Mrs Croft swears by him for the admiral's gout.'

'Gout is it?' replied Sir Walter, turning to Admiral Croft who sat opposite with his wife. 'Then I am exceedingly sorry for you, Admiral Croft.' He added to his oldest daughter, in tones not low enough not to be overheard, 'Comes of being at sea all one's life I suppose; I have frequently said so, have I not, Elizabeth? Makes one quite decrepit and ill before time! And it quite ruins a once-handsome face!'

The admiral, too good natured to think of being even slightly offended, now interjected amiably, 'Why, that's all very well, Sir Walter; aye, my face might have a little pink about it; but you cannot deny that a stiff north wind will have its way even with the ladies who walk up and down the streets of Bath! We are all subject to a little weather, Sir Walter! But will you have our excellent Thorpe to you? That is the question!'

Sir Walter, having been obliged already to submit to having his notions of propriety and rank squeezed uncomfortably by having to invite the Crofts into his home, and considering a red complexion in his tenant as a personal affront, was on the point of refuting the good of this new scheme, but Lady Russell, listening keenly, at once pressed him to accept the offer.

She was herself, she declared, in no small anxiety about Sir Walter's cough which had gotten no better; indeed, the general decline in his health had been so marked, she could not press them urgently enough to issue an invitation for Doctor Thorpe to call at Camden-place, and she was sure Doctor Thorpe had no red complexion to give offence! Elizabeth now added her entreaties until Sir Walter could not withstand the pleasure of hearing eager concern for his person.

'I thank you but shall not trouble the man until I feel it required,' he replied, coolly. 'These men aspire to get into the houses of those above them for one purpose; to assure their careers! "I have attended Sir this-or-that person", they say. I will not have my name used to such a purpose! I should not have him but merely as a cure for *your* anxiety, Lady Russell, and although I cannot wish to offend, I assure you I am not in need of his services yet. Indeed, I am persuaded I shall be doing everyone else a favour but myself. There is nothing wrong with me that Miss Crawford may not give me an antidote to, I am sure!'

Lady Russell, who was indeed a fair way to being offended by her friend's indifference to her own concerns, nonetheless gave way and changed the topic to something happier.

Anne, Julia, and the Crofts spent a decent half-hour at Camden-place, then excused themselves to go to their own lodgings. Elizabeth seemed relieved to find Anne was not intending to stay with them, and became more easy in her address, so much so as to issue them an invitation to a 'modest card party, tomorrow night, nothing very elaborate, but you shall meet our new acquaintance, whom I wrote to you about Anne — Mr and Miss Crawford, a very elegant set of people.'

Later, Elizabeth said to Anne in lowered tones, 'We have been obliged by common politeness to have the Crofts, but I expect they will want to keep to their own society, while they are in Bath. We can hardly be expected to ask them again — I hope you will discourage them from any further expectations, Anne.'

Anne, her opinion of the Crofts being so high, and feeling keenly the obligation owed them by her father and Elizabeth for proving such agreeable tenants, had little to do but to smile faintly and repress the urge to reprimand her sister. The goodness of her friends, their simplicity of character combined with the most level and commendable common sense and kindness, had long charmed her; kindness had not been, since her mother's death, a great part of her life, and when shown it, she would not stint to reciprocate or defend those giving it.

Julia too, had been included in the party, but when they were taking their leave and waiting for the carriage, Mrs Croft said confidentially to Anne, 'Do you think it wise my dear, to bring Julia again? I own I am reluctant myself, since she is supposed to be impressed by the gravity of her own actions and the scandal she has almost caused in my family.'

'And yet she will be soon be obliged to go with a stranger, to where she knows no one. Let us give her a little diversion, now, Mrs Croft, since she will have so little to look forward to after she leaves here. Besides, it is only a private party. She cannot come to much harm in my father's house.'

Julia was properly gratified to be included, knowing her freedom would be severely curtailed in the coming months, and thanked her aunts with the humility that comes from adversity. There was hope for the girl, thought Anne. If she came through her ordeal and learned from her mistakes, Julia might even find a husband, if her friends could orchestrate it.

Twenty One

The lodgings at Gay-street were comfortable if a little noisy. 'Just what the admiral and I prefer,' Mrs Croft told Anne happily, as they all left the building a little later to walk to the Pump-room. She had insisted the admiral take the waters just as soon as they had seen their things upstairs, and even Julia had expressed a wish to see the famous Baths from the Roman occupation. They had gone out as soon as they had seen their belongings unpacked.

'The admiral and I have so much quiet at home that its quite refreshing and new to see people coming and going, and bustling about. How amusing to sit about by the window and watch people walk by. It is pleasant to be so engaged, after so much solitude at Kellynch!' She wore an elegant turban, in the latest fashion, and a matching day dress in pomona green, and looked as genteel as any fine woman on the arm of her husband. 'A change in scenery is just as good as a rest!'

Even Anne, walking beside Julia, who was demure in her primrose sprigged muslin, unfrilled, and as plain as could be found for her, acknowledged the happiness to be found in a change of scene. It was a beautiful day, and while Anne could take little pleasure in the place for itself, she allowed herself to enter into a certain tranquility of the kind such a day can bestow even upon the most worried and anxious of wives whose husbands are a thousand miles away.

Presently they arrived at the Pump-room, and joined the throngs gathered to take the healing waters. A string quartet played in the gallery of the grand room, and ladies and gentlemen paraded around the room in various groups. They inspected the various pools, which appeared to run into one another, and Julia, upon perceiving the main cistern, exclaimed, 'But surely we do not drink the waters which come from the bathing pools?'

'No, indeed,' laughed Mrs Croft, 'the main fountain from which we drink runs from a different pipe, my dear. Oh, there is Lord Mountford and his wife!'

The Crofts, frequent visitors to Bath, were at once recognised and accosted, and left Anne and Julia for a little while to walk and talk with old friends. Anne now saw Lady Russell approach them and she met her godmother with genuine pleasure.

'Happy coincidence! I had no notion you were to come to the Pump-room directly! Although I ought, as I know it a favourite haunt of yours!'

'I always call on your father and sister before coming here. It is rather a daily habit with me, as you know.' Lady Russell kindly turned to Julia. 'How do you go on, my dear? Have you ever been in Bath before? Is it not a delightful place, with all manner of entertainments for a young lady to enjoy herself?'

'You cannot imagine what a high treat this is for me, Ma'am,' replied Julia dryly, the overtones of sarcasm completely lost on the proper-minded Lady Russell. 'I have never been to Bath before. But I must go away to — to school, the day after next, so I shall not have time to see everything.'

'Oh, so soon? You must be very excited my dear. What a great pity you cannot see more of Bath. But I fancy being sent to school abroad will be a fine adventure for you. The academies for girls these days are far superior to any that we had in my own day. I suppose you will go to a private seminary in France?'

'Where I am going can hardly be called—'

'—it is a very fine place from what I have heard. She is most fortunate to have secured a place!' Anne interjected, observing the rebellious look on Julia's face. She cast her a warning look. 'I believe your aunt beckons you, dearest. I think they are going to take the waters. Perhaps you will like to take them yourself?'

'No thank you, Aunt. But I would like to see if anyone grand is here. May I go and look at the visitor's book? Would it not be diverting if the Prince Regent were in town already?'

'I think we should have heard of it if it were so, dear,' replied Anne, 'but by all means go and look.'

Julia made for the visitors' book, set out upon a table nearer to the door, and Anne stood a moment in conversation with Lady Russell, until that lady, too was called away to give attend to some other acquaintances. Now Anne stood alone and in a most pleasant reminiscence: *there*, just by the fountain, she and Frederick had sat, the morning after announcing their engagement, and held hands; *there* they had walked together and spoken of a future felicity! And then she remembered other occasions, the night of the music concert, in which his manner had seemed to confirm his jealousy, and his possible attachment to her, and all the joyous hope that evening had brought her. He had spoken too, of Louisa, had spoken of her inferiority, his wonder at Captain Benwick's choice, and she had delighted silently in it, so fearful had she been that she had lost him to another. Now she thought again of his new, glowing admiration for the same woman, and wondered where he and Louisa were at this moment, and if he was thinking of herself, or of another.

She was jolted from these dangerous musings by the return of Julia, who approached her looking very pale and unwell.

'Julia! You look ill. Shall I call you a chair?'

'No, Aunt Anne. I am very well. It is only the heat.' The young woman looked so ill however that Anne at once had Admiral and Mrs Croft fetched, and they had a carriage called to take them directly back to Gay-street.

Julia was made to lie down for an hour directly they reached home, but she would not have a doctor called. 'I am quite well, I thank you. I do hate to be fussed over and prodded! I certainly do not need a doctor. It is only the heat which went to my head. A little air and I am recovered, as you see!'

It was providential however, that only two hours later, a servant came with a message to say that there was a Doctor Thorpe downstairs and wishing to call upon them. Julia, who had recovered enough to sit with them all in the drawing room, looked ungracious and as if she would like to make a scene, but Mrs Croft intervened.

'You must remember what you owe to Doctor Thorpe, Julia, and be civil. Your father has given his approval to the scheme, and indeed, we none of us know where you would be without Doctor Thorpe's intervention, and his aunt's assistance. Why you have taken a dislike to the poor man, I cannot think!'

The Crofts greeted him like an old friend. 'Do come in, Doctor! How kind of you to call on us. How is your aunt? Are you just arrived in Bath?'

'I am very well, I thank you, and I arrived only hours ago. Good afternoon, Mrs Wentworth, Miss Wentworth.' He spoke pleasantly and made no particular effort to converse with Julia, who sat in the corner malevolently stabbing at her needlework, as if it were the vilest creature in the world, rather than merely a slip of cloth. Rather less progress was being made on the offending muslin than Anne should have expected, but she said nothing, so as not to provoke her niece.

Thorpe enquired as to their stay and the health of Anne's family, and finally, he spoke in lowered tones of his aunt's departure. 'My aunt intends to quit Bath the day after tomorrow, Mrs Croft, and I shall accompany her up to Herefordshire, as I am in the habit of staying a few times per year. Dr. Green has taken my rounds so I am at leisure to see Miss Wentworth comfortable before I must away to Somerset again.'

At this intelligence, Julia turned as pale as her white muslin and paused her stabbing. 'I do not, if you please, need a nanny, Doctor. I am quite able to travel with Mrs Hayes on my own. You need not trouble yourself on my account.' Her tone was scathing.

Thorpe was openly amused and not at all put out. 'Ah, Miss Wentworth, I see I have offended your pride. Forgive me. All the same, I shall do myself the honour of seeing you safe and sound. I am conscious of a desire to serve my aunt; it is just as much sincere affection for my aunt as solicitousness for your health that prompts me to make the journey with you both. I dare say,' he added laughingly, 'you will grow used to my presence, since I am a regular visitor at Rosedale Cottage.'

'You are certainly the most exceedingly officious, overbearing—' Her countenance was pink, and her eyes dashed at him.

'Julia!'

Her aunts had both spoken at once, and she stopped short, uttered a fomenting syllable or two, then stood and stalked from the room.

Anne was troubled. 'I beg your pardon, Doctor, but my niece is in rather an emotional state. I am certain she would not be as contentious as this if she were not—'

'—in need of a kind word and the relief of the anxiety which must weigh upon her, yes.' Thorpe laughed at Anne's astonishment. 'You have been the best of friends to Miss Wentworth, I perceive, but it must weigh upon her, the seriousness of her situation. I shall deliver her into the care of my aunt and she shall have the very best of care, be assured. I myself will look in on them frequently, and keep you informed.'

Admiral Croft now interjected, 'Aye, Thorpe, you are very right I collect, the girl is quite in an anxious state and does not act herself, I suspect, eh Sophy? We have never seen the like of it. Until now she has been a very good sort of girl, not one to give so much trouble. But then, what do I know eh? An old fellow like me does not understand modern young women, and I never did even while I was a young lad! But I did manage to get Sophie, didn't I my dear, and you must have liked me enough to follow me around the world!'

'Certainly, I did,' replied his wife, squeezing his hand with open, unaffected warmth. 'I daresay she will come around, Doctor Thorpe — she is only quite out of countenance at her own doing and does not like to be sent away, but she will soon own it is best, and come to make the best of things. She has been most fortunate to have a friend in you, Doctor, and your aunt. I look forward to making Mrs Haye's acquaintance the day after tomorrow.'

Thorpe now turned to Anne. 'May I enquire if you have had any news yet from your husband? You must be anxious for his return now that the war is over.'

Anne did her best to conceal the anxiety in her tone, and simply replied, 'I have had no word yet, but Mrs Croft tells me it is always like this when war hampers the progress of ships in the channel. I have charged my sister Mary with sending my mail on to me here, while we are in Bath. I am sure I shall hear from him soon.'

Julia did not appear again in the drawing room until after dinner and when she did, she remained very quiet, saying almost nothing either at dinner and afterward, until she excused herself to bed. The evening party at Camden-place, when discussed, aroused no interest in her, although she seemed to her aunt to be distracted, rather than low in spirits. Anne still wondered at what had so upset her at the Pump-room earlier that day, but putting it down to heat, she put away the subject, and resolved likewise to put away her own anxieties and be content as she could under the circumstances.

Twenty Two

Saturday 1 July, 1815

The following morning, the Crofts expressed a wish to walk in the Sydney gardens. Julia, having but one day left to enjoy her freedom before she was to remove from Bath with Mrs Hayes, was eager for the walk. 'I wish that I might remain here in Bath, even if only for a few more days. It can hardly make a difference,' she added plaintively, as she put on her bonnet and waited impatiently while Anne tied it for her. 'We could walk in the Pump-room one more time before I must go away?'

'No indeed,' said Mrs Croft sternly, who had come through the door just then. 'Mrs Hayes' carriage will be here at ten sharp tomorrow, and you, young lady, will be ready and willing. Do not forget that a very great service is being performed for your behalf, and you owe your poor father the respect of complying without complaint! You have brought disgrace upon your family, Julia — be grateful you are being allowed out at all!'

'Yes, Aunt,' replied Julia moodily, adjusting her lilac-beribboned straw bonnet in the glass on the wall. 'How I wish that odious fellow Doctor Thorpe were not to accompany us north!'

Anne exchanged eloquent glances with Mrs Croft and ushered the young woman down the stairs. 'He has treated you with a great deal of kindness, dear — I think you ought to be more grateful.'

Julia's reply was lost on her ears however as the noise of the street overcame them and they turned northeast to walk to the Sydney garden. It was a day of the brightest sunshine, tempered with a light breeze. Many parties were forming to walk in the pleasant environs of the park, preferring the open air to the Pump-rooms when such weather was to be enjoyed. Moving near to the entrance of the garden, the Crofts now caught sight of Doctor Thorpe, who was already coming to meet them. He bowed to them all, was their servant, and wondered if he might be of any assistance.

'Ha! Is it you, Thorpe?' cried the Admiral, slapping the doctor on the shoulder. 'Sophie and I are always happy to meet friends. Do you walk alone? Aye, and what a happy coincidence, for we are about to walk ourselves. Will you join us? Good fellow, good fellow! We are mightily glad to see you indeed, are we not, Sophie?'

Mrs Croft echoed her husband's sentiments, and within moments, Thorpe had allowed himself to be persuaded, gratified once again of the proof of a friendship which appeared to give them as much pleasure as it did himself.

'You are very kind, Admiral! I am pleased to have found you both at leisure, for I very much wish to get your opinion on something, a pamphlet I have written on the use of nostrums for the treatment of scurvy on long voyages.'

The Crofts, always eager to exercise the powers of their intellects, now engaged themselves in an animated discussion of the topic at hand, while Anne listened from behind them, her mind half engaged by the conversation, but being more preoccupied with thoughts of her husband. Julia had moved ahead, Anne presumed, in order to avoid their unwanted company. Mrs Croft had firmly taken the admiral's arm, on account of 'never feeling quite myself when I have not his hand over mine', but to Anne's amusement her friend did as much to steer the admiral away from the treacherous sides of the river banks, or stepping upon puddles of doughy mud, as he seemed to do in supporting her.

She was just about to stoop to admire a flower, when Julia, a few steps ahead of them, stopped short, and appeared to be staring at one of the little groups who walked in front of them.

Then three things happened at once. Julia uttered a little gasp. She appeared to be staring at a couple who walked a good distance ahead of them. A gentleman with charmingly-tousled brown hair, excessively well dressed, stepped away from his female companion to point at something across the lake, and Julia cried out in great agitation, '*Lyford!* It *was* you I saw in the Pump-room!'

The gentleman and lady together, turning in astonishment, conferred quickly. Then the gentleman was urgently ushering his companion up the path and out of sight. They were too far away for Anne to have made a decent study of them, and she was almost inclined to walk hastily in the direction they had gone. But Julia stood on the path, her face pale, and Anne went to her side, giving up the notion of a chase.

'It was he! It was Mr Lyford!' cried Julia, in a great agitation. 'Why will he not look at me? Who was that woman with him? Why has he gone away? He must be excessively vexed with me, even though I sent him a letter explaining everything! I must go after him!' Her face, as ashen as the fabric of her gown, spoke her agony.

Anne's hand on her arm prevented her. 'Calm yourself,' she instructed in a low tone. 'You must not make known the fact of your acquaintance with him, if it truly is he. And it would do no good to go after him. Do you not see, dear, that he has no further interest in you? Good God, she has fainted! Someone help me!'

Doctor Thorpe however, had already dashed forward, and Julia was laid gently on the grass, both aunts anxious and at pains to make her comfortable. With the application of some hartshorn which Mrs Croft was always in the habit of carrying on her person, Julia began to revive. A little crowd gathered around now, and a half-conscious and mute Julia was lifted up heroically by the doctor himself, and carried to a bench not far from the entrance gates, whereby a passing footman was hailed over and charged with procuring them a sedan chair. A kind passer-by, however, at once obliged them by calling for his own private barouche to be brought to them. Thorpe undertook to thank the gentleman and his lady, and saw Julia into the vehicle.

'It would be wise to get her home at once,' advised Thorpe as Mrs Croft made Julia comfortable. He added in a low voice to Anne, so as not to overhead by Julia, 'She has had a great shock,

Mrs Wentworth. Send for me if you are at all anxious for her. I am to be found in Pulteney-street.' He paused. 'Did you happen to see the gentleman? Could she have made a mistake? Perhaps it was someone who looked like him?'

Anne shook her head. 'I can hardly say. I did not get a good view of the gentleman; they were at distance, and I only had a glimpse. But it can do no good to go after him now. He must be gone away in fear of being recognised. I rather think no good can come of confronting him, since nothing can be proven. It would only harm my niece's reputation more, I collect.'

'I believe you are right, Mrs Wentworth. To confront the gentleman now would do no good. I think it best to put it behind us, and try to salvage what we can of Miss Wentworth's reputation and character.'

Anne was much obliged to him, and said so. 'How dreadful this business is,' she added. 'I am glad my own people know nothing of it; they would not have been so kind to Julia as you have been!'

'Your niece is lucky to have friends,' replied Doctor Thorpe soberly. 'Many young girls in the same circumstances are not so fortunate. Never fear, Mrs Wentworth. She is young, and many girls even not so fortunate have managed to live good lives. All hope is not lost.'

'Thank you.' Anne gave him a weak smile and took her place in the carriage.

In the privacy of the closed barouche, Julia succumbed to her unhappy wretchedness. 'It *was* Lyford, it *was!*' she cried. 'Nobody shall make me say it were not! I know his face just as surely as I know my own! How could he deny me, pretend stranger with me, act as if he had never known me! Who was that woman with him? Oh, Aunt Sophie, I am so angry, but how strange that I weep when all I desire is to rage!'

Mrs Croft endeavoured to relieve her niece's agitations. 'Perhaps you may have been mistaken, my dear; people tend to look very similar when it is only the back of a head in the distance. Are you certain it was he?'

'Yes, oh yes,' cried Julia, emitting great sobs. 'How could he deny me as he did? He loves, me, he said he did! And I loved him! He promised to marry me! He must be in a dreadful temper with me for going away! I must go back and explain everything!'

Anne said gently, 'Do you still imagine, from his behaviour towards you, that he has any intention of marrying you, my dear?'

Julia was unable to answer, doubt and misery alternating across her pale features.

'It is not in the power of such men to act with integrity or honesty. He has played you a fool, dearest, and all the entreaties in the world will not move such a man.'

'I am very sorry for you, my dear,' added the admiral kindly, 'but you must forget him. It is a sad creature he has made of you so far!'

'Perhaps it is for the best that his disguise has come loose, for you to see him as he really is,' added Mrs Croft, patting Julia's arm. 'Time heals all wounds, as the poet says. Soon you will come to feel as little for him as he has no doubt felt for you all along.'

Julia submitted to yet another burst of grievous agitation at these words and alternately wished the vilest evil upon her lost beau, and the sweetest declarations of love, until she gave up altogether, beginning to understand that all was hopeless. Anger turned finally to quiet weeping, until the carriage reached their door at Gay-street, and she was ushered up to her room to lie down. Anne stayed with her for some time, paying her every unobtrusive consideration, until, soothed with some lavender drops and some hot tea, she fell back against the pillows, quiet and spent.

Anne, concerned for her health, conferred with Mrs Croft, and decided that Julia should remain at home that evening rather than attending the card party at Camden-place. Informed of this news, they met with no resistance.

'I have such a sickness of heart that I cannot think of going out! Oh, Aunt Anne, I have been so foolish!' she said sadly. 'I almost look forward to going away tomorrow, out of all the society I once held so vital to my happiness. But look where it has gotten me. My life is ruined, and my reputation along with it. How can Papa ever forgive me!'

Anne took her hand. 'Your father has been kinder to you than he ought; he would never have agreed to have you home when your confinement is over if he did not love you dearly.'

'I have treated him with disrespect, and my new mama too. I deserve only the worst future!' Her voice was lost entirely in exclamations of misery.

Anne endeavoured to comfort her. 'You must earn your place in his house again, my dear, and I am sure you shall. Then, by and by, perhaps something good might come of this, after all.'

Saturday 1 July, 1815

Williams-street, Bath.

Over the vast centuries that have passed since Adam was caught red-handed with the apple, the number of gentlemen who have been unexpectedly confronted with the spectre of their naughty pasts are too numerous to imagine. But there are very few who, caught off guard, could remain unruffled in such a circumstance. This degree of composure and careful concealment belongs to few men, and indeed, such a feat could not have been carried out more smoothly than by Henry Crawford. Upon being confronted with the vision of the very same young woman whom he had enticed from the confines of girlhood seven weeks ago in town, he simply turned on his heel and ushered his sister from the scene, and did it with such creditable aplomb as to allow it had not been the first time; this was why he made it a rule, unless he was with his sister, always to give a non de plume — Harry Lyford, scoundrel, rake shame, and coxcomb, was not Henry Crawford of Everingham, gentleman.

In their cosy Williams-street drawing room, Mary was pouring them tea. She was wearing a delightful lemon silk with a low-cut neckline, and Henry was admiring it from his position across the table, despite the fact that she was in the middle of scolding him.

'I wish you would be more careful, Haro; you know I turn a blind eye to your antics in town – besides, the child is a pea-goose for fancying herself in love with you. No, don't tell me who she is, I don't wish for details. Well, it shall be upon her own head if it disturbs her own peace.' She sighed and stirred her cup gently. 'And I suppose it can hardly signify, even if you were seen. There is no one here who can claim intimacy with you, and therefore I vouchsafe to say you will be untarnished from it, even though you ought to have taken more care over the business. You have been getting altogether too careless in the last year.'

'I can hardly be accused of what any other red-blooded male has not done time and time again!' Henry was nonchalant. 'It is such a bore, dear Mim, to be chased by one's past; I do not care for it at all. However, the girl will do no harm; she cannot, after all, force a confrontation, and I had it from her own mouth that the curate papa is safely tucked away in north of England, so there is nobody who will make a fuss here.'

Henry was composed. He had come and gone from his club in town with never a how-do-you-do – in fact barely a burly eyebrow had been raised at the rumours of his antics in town; such things were *de rigeur* among his own acquaintance, acknowledged, but politely avoided in the drawing room. His reputation, he fancied, had not harmed his standing, and with certain persons, it had even increased. At any rate, he thought as he took up his tea, it was not as if he had been recognised from his evenings spent in Cock's Lane or the gardens behind, and even *that* vice, when it had followed him into the hallowed halls of White's was left at the door with the boot scrapers. He felt himself in no danger.

Mary had already echoed his thoughts. 'You cannot go on as you have Henry! If it was not for your dalliance with the – the wrong side of the street! People talk! There is a certain amount you might be forgiven for, certainly, but after you were seen by our uncle last year at the Mulberry Garden at St James – I only hope he did not mention the matter to anyone. I dare say you are fortunate, but you may not count upon such good luck again.' She had turned away and he discerned in her eyes an unusual glitter.

'I do believe you *are* jealous!' He stood up, approached her, and cajolingly took her hand. 'You are never forgotten, you know!

We go on just as we have, do we not?'

'Don't, pray!' She snatched her hand away, less composed than usual.

'It's all this marriage business, it's getting to both of us. But you will never be less to me than you are now! How says the poet?

' "*Nor believe our love-fits,* **Mary,**
be forgot,
When each the well-looked link-boy
strove to enjoy—
And the best kiss was the deciding lot—" ' he misquoted teasingly. 'Come,' he added coaxingly when she did not smile, 'you do not laugh even a little? Can I not persuade you into a better mood? Don't be vexed with me, Mimsy. Come, my little puss, give me a kiss, your best kiss, so I know you aren't really angry with me.'

Mary, turning now, gave him a careful little smile. She said more measuredly, 'I am not angry with you, Haro. And I am not jealous. Only I don't wish you to undo all the work we have done.'

He helped himself to an apricot tart. 'You know what they say, sis; a blush is more a sign of ill breeding than of guilt. It is quite accepted that a young gentleman ought to test his mettle. I do no less than my peers. Town can be so tiresome if I do not have the project of a heart to work upon! Surely, I am entitled to my little amusements! Besides, I am determined to settle my wife at Everingham within the next six months, and I shall have all the project I desire in playing with her ice-cold heart. Call this most recent incident my "last fling" before I must be shackled by the bonds of matrimony.'

Mary laughed. 'Shackled? I do not think you will know the meaning for long — it is not in your nature! Once your wife is confined with a baby, you will have all the license to which you are used, Henry, while she sits at Everingham nursing your heir.'

Henry tossed a half-eaten sweet, the apricot preserve eaten out of its middle, back onto the plate and licked his fingers. 'She is handsome, but I will need more than a cold-hearted Elliot to entertain me.'

Mary had not finished with him, however. 'But on the back of the rumours we have already come away from Everingham in order to extinguish... and then there is Mansfield.'

'True.' He reached for another tart. 'These are quite excellent. I do love an apricot! Perhaps it *was* a little risky... but think, nothing more can be traced to you, Mim: the servant has taken the blame and been dismissed, and there's an end to it. You needn't worry yourself.'

Mary dropped her cup sharply into its saucer. 'I, worry? What I did, Haro, I did for us both! Pray don't forget your own part in it all! It was you who begged for revenge on that odious pair! I own that I may have found a certain *relief* in the application of a dose of providence, but so did you!'

Henry favoured her with an amused chuckle. 'A dose of providence, indeed! A drop of bitter almond and tincture of black rose, *that* is providence at its finest moment! Poor pious, fawning little Fanny-creature! She deserved what she got in that pious pinch-nose, Edmund Bertram. They both deserve the other!' His tone was bitter.

'That is a change, indeed! It was not so long ago that you were quite in Fanny-raptures,' Mary laughed, relenting. 'And yet, she was too good for you, and you know it! All that piety and goodness! Still, had you married I wager even *she* would have lost her gratitude and devotion after a period — and really, can you truly say that you would have been pleased with such piety? To be sure, it is very endearing to begin with, but to go on with! No, you now have a very just prize within your grasp; Miss Elliot will be a vast challenging project for you, until she gives us an heir. And I shall be sure to give you at least half of my time; I shall be content to spend my winters in Bath and my summers in Norfolk.'

'I won't ever forget what you did, you know.' Henry's voice was low, and unusually sincere.

Mary gave him a bemused look, and then took his hand and gently placed it upon her lemon-yellow bosom.

It heaved fetchingly under his eye.

'Here,' she began, her brown eyes looking into his own, 'beats the heart that has always cared for you. I vowed to protect you when I was eleven years old and orphaned, and you only six years and barely from your skeleton suit. We only had each other then, and it is the same now.'

His voice was unusually soft. 'Sometimes I think it was too much for you. You had so much responsibility — you cared for me like a mother, and yet, you had no mother to guide *you*. You have given up much, for my sake.'

'That is nothing to the point. It was what I needed to do. There was no one else to do it. And I shall always look after your interests, but you must look after mine, too, Haro. We have much work to do yet. You are almost on the point of offering to Miss Elliot, and having her accept, but you must make sure of her heart before you do it. As for me, I believe Sir Walter will need only the prompting of his daughter's being engaged before he will make an offer to me. Everything we have hoped for is now within our grasp; let us not ruin our chances at this most important hour. Family is everything.'

He pressed her hand with his own. 'Family.'

Twenty Four

Evening, Saturday 1 July 1815
Camden-place, Bath.

In the dim evening light, the warm glow from the windows of Camden-place bestowed a more friendly aspect than by day and Mrs Croft said as much as their carriage pulled up. Anne understood that the Crofts knew as many people in Bath as they wished to, and considered their acquaintance with the Elliots mere form, but her friends were kindly and as amiable and willing as they could be to approbate all of Anne's relatives as a way of honouring one whom they had come to love as a sister. Now Mrs Croft excited Anne's gratitude by her commending the appearance of the place, and Anne too glanced upwards as they halted outside. Even without the presence of Frederick, in such amiable company she found herself almost complacent at the thought of an evening with her sister and father.

'You are in very good looks tonight, Anne. I have not seen that gown on you before!' Mrs Croft was handed from the carriage, then watched as the servant handed Anne down after her.

Anne had put on her prettiest chiffon-and-silk, a gift from Lady Russell soon after the wedding, and now she brushed her hands down the rose-coloured gown self-consciously. It barely concealed the growing plumpness of her figure, and she wondered if her father or sister would remark on her condition now that she was unable to hide it.

The polite attention which was, by reason of familial ties, owed to Anne, had been studiously ignored by Elizabeth, but Anne, feeling she could easily guess the pain that this very material sign of her marriage must give Elizabeth, forgave her sister the slight, even though Lady Russell could not. It had long been Anne's share to suffer the inattention of her family, being "only Anne" as her sister and father were so often heard to remark. She had gained a little consequence in the eyes of her father now that she was the wife of a well-regarded naval captain in line for a promotion, but still, behind the privacy of closed doors, this was sometimes conveniently forgotten. But she had friends, very dear friends, in the persons of the Crofts and Lady Russell, who were as prodigiously careful for Anne's state of health as her family was not, and additionally, now that she was come to Bath again, she looked forward to a fond reunion with her old school chum, Mrs Smith, who resided permanently in the town.

Anne had received a brief note from this lady that very morning, entreating her to call the next day, 'being very desirous to see you, my dear friend, after so long a separation, and Nurse Rook has been talking of a visit since we knew you to have come to Bath. Therefore, you must come directly or we shall both think you very cruel!'

Anne had replied at once, promising a visit the following morning, just as soon as Dr. Thorpe had come to spirit her niece away with Mrs Hayes first. But there was this evening to be gotten through first, and the admiral, who had clambered out of the carriage after the women, now took his wife's arm and deferred to Anne to lead the way up the steps to the front door of Camden-place. Mrs Croft had complemented the admiral's choice of naval coat and tails in her own selection of a navy-blue crepe gown set off with gold buttons, clever pleating in the shoulders, and a feathered capote to match. Even a low-spirited Julia had earlier agreed that her aunt looked everything of an elegant gentlewoman on the arm of her husband.

Julia, being now quite wretched in spirits, had taken to her bed and assured her aunts that she did not wish herself with them that evening, and that she desired nothing more than to remain where she was until the next morning when Mrs Haye would take her away. Anne had been relieved to suffer no more of objection and argument, feeling that even if she herself was not tired out from the constant opposition, it certainly did nothing for Julia's state of mind or health either. Julia, defeated in love, however much it might be considered mere calf-love, had finally yielded to the fate her father had chosen for her, and Anne was satisfied that under the care of Mrs Hayes and Doctor Thorpe, her niece would continue as well and as in such spirits as she could hope to be under the circumstances. However much that scandals such as this were not very common, and not easily lived down, Anne hoped with all her heart that Julia's position in life was recoverable, and that she would find happiness, perhaps even in matrimony. The very pretty daughter of a gentleman curate who boasted a not-inconsequential income, might reasonably hope that matrimony was not entirely impossible, even in the particular circumstance she found herself in, provided her father would do his part in the provision of a good income for his daughter.

Their little party was met by Elizabeth with gracious, if restrained, cordiality when they were admitted to Sir Walter's drawing room. Lady Russell was present already on the chaise, and four or five other figures already sat at cards in the soft light of the candles placed about the room. A lady whom Anne did not recognize sat at the pianoforte, playing a popular Scottish country dance. Anne recognized the Edward-Smythes, who were frequent callers at Camden-place, and Mrs Wallis, recently delivered of a child, and whom Anne considered a silly, fashionable woman. Her constant prattle wearied Anne when she was obliged to listen to it, although the lady's beauty and superficial charm seemed to please her father and Elizabeth. A few civilities passed between the various parties over the music, and the Crofts were swept up by Elizabeth and taken to the card tables.

Anne dropped a dutiful kiss on her father's cheek and asked, 'How are you, Father? How is your cough?'

Sir Walter reached for his snuff box and proceeded to take a pinch. 'Poole has left me quite alone, as you know; I was not a little put out! Devilish thoughtless of the man, I must say. However, Miss Crawford has brought me some more of her own recipe and it seems to be doing me some good. It has quite carried away the worst of the cough! But for this confounded fatigue which has plagued me these last few weeks, I would say I was in good health indeed. Miss Crawford says my skin has a much healthier tone these days, although I fancied that she was merely being kind, for I collect I have these dark circles below my eyes which never came over me before. It is excessively distressing, Anne, to suddenly be confronted with one's age, and be forced to see one's reflection in a glass or in a window in Milsom-street and observe changes which must inevitably come but bring nothing but distress! However, I am certain it doesn't signify, and will pass.'

'I am sure it will not be long before you are back to your old self again. It must be the anxiety of the last few months, that is all.'

'I have always been blessed with good health and my friends have always called me a vital man. Lady Russell thinks my fatigue is the consequence of too many late nights, for we have been so much more in company lately, since the Crawfords have been with us so frequently. She and Miss Crawford agree a little more rest, a few constitutional walks, and I shall be as well as ever.'

Anne was doubtful. 'I have never seen you take snuff before, Sir; do you suppose yourself unequal to it powers? You do look a little pale.'

'Nonsense. I have taken up the practice since Mr Crawford gave me this very neat little box from his own collection. Do you not think it a vast pretty piece? I am not in the habit of being a snuff-taker, that is true, but I fancy it helps me with the fatigue.'

'I see.' Anne was thoughtful. 'Well, I hope you feel yourself again soon, Father. Oh, here is Lady Russell — she wants me, I think — will you excuse me?' Anne left her father's side and went to join Lady Russell who was beckoning to her, and already seated upon the chaise in the candlelight, a glass of madeira upon the table at her side.

Lady Russell, who persisted in a silent, if condemning, opinion of the prevailing disinclination of her friends to enquire after her goddaughter's health, began immediately again to be offended on Anne's behalf. 'I cannot say I have not been ashamed by the omissions of your sister and father, Anne, but I daresay, they will by and by recollect what is owed to you as their kin. I wish they would value you as I do!'

Anne would not let her suffer. 'Please do not press the point!' she remonstrated gently. 'You know that I am well used to my sister's ways, Lady Russell. My condition may be a bitter reminder to Elizabeth of hopes unfulfilled, and I am as sorry for her disappointment as anyone could be. As for my father, it is not the province of a man to give notice to such things, and I do not expect to be made a fuss of; it is enough for me that we have been given so cordial a welcome, and that the Crofts have been given the attention due them.'

'As to that, I wonder at Sir Walter, for it is such a change of character in him; it must be the doing of the Crawfords; the company of such an agreeable set of two people as Mary and Henry Crawford, so indifferent as *they* are to rank, and so agreeable in general, cannot fail to have had its effect on your father.'

'And how do *you* find them, Lady Russell? Elizabeth has sent me such a good account of them that I think she must be a little in love with them both!' Anne had made the observation in jest, but she was soon to be astonished.

'Between you and I, Anne,' answered Lady Russell quietly so as not to be overheard, 'I have observed a definite partiality on the part of Sir Walter for Miss Crawford, and I confess I am pleased. You know, at one time, I would have stinted to say such a thing, out of a loyalty bred from long intimacy with your family, but Elizabeth cannot wish her father single all his life — not when he is such a vigorous man in general — but for this cough which does not go away entirely — and you, my dear, are so happily married now, so what little can it matter if your father was to remarry? Yes, you might well look surprised, I daresay it *is* surprising, astonishing, even, but surely you cannot have dismissed the idea that your father might someday remarry?'

'Yes, I confess I *am* a little astonished, but it doesn't come wholly unconsidered, Lady Russell, for you must know there was a time when I thought he might turn his head towards another lady who was only last year my sister's intimate friend.'

Lady Russell sighed. 'I am grateful for Elizabeth's sake, at least, my dear, that such a union never came about; that union could only have been permitted had Sir William Elliot done his duty in turn — but no, I see you are sensitive for your sister — we shall not speak of it, for it is all past now.' She paused, and then added, 'Although, I did even at one time harbour hopes that you and he — but there, you have a fine husband in Captain Wentworth, and it is all just as it should be.'

It was hardly in Anne's power to provide a reply, for she had for some moments been arrested by Lady Russell's extraordinary proposal. Her father! Her father who had come so close to making a match beneath him, and been rescued from such an event by providence, to now so assuredly be in the way of making another! She hoped with all her heart that if such a thing as Lady Russell had proposed was true, that the lady in question was not another "Mrs Clay" who had publicly denounced matches of unequal rank and then promptly defied her own advice!

After a moment, she found that she could not avoid a faint smile to placate her friend, but added more composedly, 'I am in great anticipation then, to meet these paragons — I am surprised they are not already here. I suppose they must arrive shortly.'

'They are always fashionably late; such is the mode of you young people these days,' continued Lady Russell complacently. 'Now, if Elizabeth can get Crawford, it might do much to soften the truth that Kellynch seems now lost to us all. With an estate such as Mr Crawford's Everingham, as much as I feel for your father and sister's giving up Kellynch, it can give no little comfort to either of them to know that Elizabeth might have such an establishment in its stead. Mr Crawford, you know, has four or five thousand a year, and his sister's income exceeds that. You know me to be most direct and honest in my speech, Anne — therefore I will not scruple to say that such an outcome for both of them could be nothing less than most expedient for your family.'

Anne, much astonished at this revelation, searched for a reply.

'I confess this is news indeed, Lady Russell. Are you convinced that my sister is in love with this Mr Crawford?'

'You know Elizabeth gives away very little of what she is thinking, my dear. But I can see that he is positively wild for *her*!'

Anne contemplated this new information. Her sensations had made her speechless. The particulars of Lady Russell's news, and her conviction of its truth, and the very surprising nature of it all — she had not contemplated such a circumstance. It did not wholly surprise her that her father could be drawn in by money, and her sister too. It was in the power of neither of them to be frugal. Then she was ashamed and arranged her feelings quickly. 'If matrimony is truly the object of my father, or my sister, then I shall be very happy for them. It is only that I am truly astonished that my sister would consider anyone other than Sir William Elliot; she once pronounced to me that she would never consider anyone else but he, her equal in rank and in situation — I confess I must see this to believe it myself. Perhaps you have been deceived, or have misread the situation?'

Lady Russell was prevented from answering, for at that moment the doors opened.

'Mr Crawford, and Miss Crawford,' intoned the footman.

Two handsome creatures walked into the room with as much unaffected and unassuming state as could be managed by two people knowing themselves so looked for by others. Sir Walter and Elizabeth went at once to play host and hostess. Looking the pair over with avid curiosity, Anne thought they both had a bright, lively air, and a pleasing elegance, as they plied their compliments to their hosts. When she was introduced to them, Anne saw that they were quite as good-looking a couple as her sister had boasted, with manners as easy, natural, and equal to the pleasing appearances they made.

Lady Russell was charmed. 'Manners always so exactly what they ought to be, and so deferential to your father, Anne, which gives me a great satisfaction in light of what we discussed privately,' she confided after a few minutes. 'I see that Mr Crawford is all attentiveness to your sister as usual — see how he is most attentive to her conversation, and waits upon her hand — and your father so entranced by the beauty of Miss Crawford — and she, showing all her very natural deference — it is all very satisfying, I must own.'

Anne had long ago learned more than a little prudence in her judgements of others and so she tended to follow the inclinations of her heart, and to trust her own instinctive liking or distrusting of a person. While the Crawfords were as attentive as Lady Russell had assured her of their being, and she found nothing immediately to dislike in them, she was wary for her father particularly.

The presence of the Crawfords, however, seemed only to improve their general conversation and spirits, her sister laughing and smiling a great deal more than was usual. Anne soon found herself in the position to examine the character of Miss Crawford, when that lady came presently to sit beside her, and addressed her candidly.

'I see you are in the way of becoming a mother, Mrs Wentworth. How pleasant it must be to contemplate! When is the child due?'

'In December,' replied Anne with a polite smile.

'I hear you have a husband at sea,' noted Miss Crawford serenely. 'I cannot but feel for you, for your natural anxiety which must attend his being gone.'

'You are very kind to mention it, Miss Crawford.'

'Your husband is quite famous, in his own way, you know; he is certainly well spoken of here in Bath, your father tells me.'

Anne, collecting her father and sister had rather grudgingly warmed to her husband only after they had discovered he was considered quite highly in Bath, smiled to herself. Sir Walter had even admitted, despite his dislike of a pink complexion, that he considered Captain Wentworth 'a well-looking man', with 'more air than one usually sees in Bath.' She rather wondered what her father had been telling Miss Crawford. 'My father at one time did not like a naval man,' she told Miss Crawford with a small laugh, 'but I collect there has been a change of heart upon my marriage, for which I am grateful.'

'I confess I myself have a great deal of affectionate respect for the navy; in all things the navy is so much more overlooked than perhaps our regiments, who dwell among us so frequently, and can so easily command our attention by their presence.' Miss Crawford sighed deeply. 'Our brave naval brothers and husbands on the other hand, only come home to us in peace time, and must bear their own absences in the uncertainty of wartime, perhaps even more painfully than their womenfolk do, for the lengthy times they must be separated from their loved ones. It is hard to say which set of people would be more oppressed by such a circumstance.'

Anne, astonished at so much feeling, at once asked, 'Oh, do you yourself have family in the navy, Miss Crawford?'

'Oh, no indeed!' laughed Miss Crawford lightly. 'Unless I count my old uncle, who is ranked an admiral, but has not been active in naval duty for many years — but surely, one does not need a first-hand experience to understand the suffering of those great men, nor must it follow that one must know separation to understand the pain which comes of it.'

'I see,' replied Anne, a little bemused. 'It is very kind of you to enter in to such thoughts on behalf of others, Miss Crawford.'

'I fancy it is, if I do say so myself, but then, I have always been a sensitive creature, Mrs Wentworth, feeling the pain of others just as much I feel my own. And I cannot but sympathise with you in your own circumstance, with a child due and your husband away. It must be trying for you! And yet you bear up under it all very well, I see!'

Anne, very much feeling the absence of her husband, and finding herself applied to, allowed Miss Crawford to be considerate. 'And yet I do not feel my own forbearance, if it could be called that, is anything more than what is a natural and sensible state for any two people united by mutual affection. When one marries the navy, Miss Crawford, both parties know that long absences are likely, and that the best course is to be determined not to be made overly anxious by separation, and to only look forward to the pleasure of reuniting after a period of being apart.'

'And yet it takes, I collect, brave and sensible women to bear the burden of being wives to such men. Heaven knows, I should never have the wits to bear it! When I marry' — here she cast a little glance over the room, and Anne fancied it was directed at her father, '— I shall only find pleasure in the constant company of my husband. Were we to be forced apart, I think I should be very unhappy creature indeed! I am,' she added confidingly, 'of the nature which, once dedicated to one person, cannot find any happiness at all in separation — even my friends will testify to the unusual strength of my affection and attachment once engaged!'

To this speech Anne could add nothing, but smiled politely seeing as agreement seemed expected. If Miss Crawford were guilty of artifice she could not tell, and moving off shortly afterwards to see how the Crofts were faring at Vingt-et-Un, she was gratified to be able to observe the Crawford pair in action as they moved about, first to the tables, then to each other for low conversation, then again to attend her father and sister.

It gave Anne more pleasure to be able to observe than to participate, not being much of a card player herself, but from her quiet position on the chaise, when she wasn't solicited by her sister or Lady Russell to come see this or that little fragment of a letter or resolve an argument as to who ought to be awarded the point for a tie round, she was able to observe what Lady Russell had suspected, and be more resolved to these new and unexpected developments with her father and sister.

Mr Henry Crawford appeared to her in general to be an agreeable man, of good sense and quiet good taste, and much taken with her sister. Elizabeth herself seemed animated and in good spirits, and as much as anything Lady Russell had implied, it was this which impressed itself upon Anne, as to the possible state of Elizabeth's heart. She had not seen her sister so animated since Mr Elliot had renewed their acquaintance with them last year, and it was this, as much as anything she had observed in Mr Crawford's behaviour, which indicated to her the likelihood an of alteration at Camden-place.

And yet, recalling the overt charm with which the despised Mr Elliot had fooled them all, she was reluctant to make a hasty judgment on the Crawfords, either to their credit or their disadvantage. All Anne's prudence came to bear, and although her friend had been enthusiastic for a double love-match, however astonishing or unlooked for, and however good it might be for her father and sister, Anne was obliged to hold back her congratulations until such time as she became convinced that the sleek, too-open charm of Mr Crawford, and the almost throw-away candour of the sister, might be duly dismissed and counted as an error of judgement on her own part. Her natural wariness, her good judgement of people, had exercised their powers over her thoughts, and she was unconvinced that her sister had not fallen for the charms of yet another sleek gentleman.

Upon mentioning her misgivings to Lady Russell she discovered that her friend had not a fault to find in him, and, not quite openly smiling at Anne's careful anxiety for her sister and father, dismissed her cares as 'a natural after-effect of being so wholly brought down by the scandal which entered this family last year, and for which I shall never forgive your Mrs Clay, for while Mr Elliot was not at all right by his behaviour towards your sister and father, hers was by far the more unforgiveable, by her being so below him in rank, and not knowing her place in society!'

While Anne could not wholly agree with her friend, thinking both the actors in that dreadful drama to be as bad as the other, she said nothing for peace's sake, and allowed Mr Crawford, who had come over to ask Lady Russell's opinion on a point in dispute at the card table, to engage them in easy conversation until supper was called.

After supper was had, Miss Crawford begged Anne to play on the fine pianoforte which had been relinquished for her benefit by the young lady who had attended to it earlier, and so, being obliged by politeness to defer to a guest of her father's, Anne played good-naturedly through a Hummel polonaise, two of Beethoven's new 'Scottish Songs', and a popular country reel. Miss Crawford immediately came to stand behind and turn the pages for her, but this had the effect of only making Anne more self-conscious than she might have been if left alone! Begging she might be excused, she was happy to retire into the background and observe the room, and in particular, to watch the Crawfords.

Around midnight the Crofts, having done their duty by appearing in the drawing room of Camden-place, made their well-mannered farewells to Sir Walter and made ready to return home on account of the admiral's gouty foot. Joining Mrs Croft in bidding Lady Russell to call on them very soon, Anne accompanied her friends down the stairs and out into the night, her thoughts still too much engaged to make very interesting conversation on the way home.

Twenty Five

Wednesday 5 July, 1815

The Crawfords had already called, paid the Elliots a long morning visit and gone away again, when a few days later Anne was escorted up the stairs to the drawing room at Camden-place with Lady Russell in her wake. They came upon the two incumbents of the household deep in animated discussion, and when Anne and Lady Russell were announced, both of them turned in some astonishment as if forgetting that there had ever been a set appointment to call.

Elizabeth's face was pleasantly flushed, her pink cheeks more blooming than the roses which adorned the mantel-piece. 'I may as well tell you, Anne, Lady Russell,' she began smugly, as soon as they were all sat down, 'that I have been made an offer of marriage, and have accepted the hand of Mr Crawford.' There was triumph in her countenance, an air of self-congratulation.

Lady Russell was complacently happy for them, and congratulated Elizabeth immediately, but Anne, to some degree grateful that she had had prior warning of the business from her friend, still was not able to conceal her shock. 'This is all very sudden, is it not?' — then, perceiving Elizabeth's displeasure, amended, 'but I am very happy for you, Elizabeth — indeed, I wish you both very happy — I own that you have taken me by surprise but it does not hold that it is a disagreeable one.'

Elizabeth, restored in some part to her former contentedness, consented to submit to Lady Russell's congratulations and flurry of questions as to when and how the deed was perpetrated, and the impending date of the nuptials, while Anne was left to her doubts in privacy. She had not been in company with the Crawfords very many times; indeed, it had merely been but three or four occasions since the card party at Camden-place the week before, but she had quickly come to distrust both the Crawfords. There was a strange intimacy about them, as if they were a pair of gloves which could only each match the other, and, although parted occasionally, always came back together to talk quietly, as if exchanging secrets. Their habit of finishing each other's sentences, too, was as unnerving as much as it was amusing.

Henry Crawford's ingratiating ways with her sister had not been lost on her, and his manner reminded her all too acutely of another man of her acquaintance who had been almost as smooth and accommodating and who had proven as deserving of suspicion as she had found reason for it. But although she owned that she distrusted the Crawfords, she could place her mistrust on no particular incident, and therefore, she must leave both parties to make of each other what they would, and wish them as happy as they could be.

'Your sister,' Lady Russell quietly noted later, after they had left Camden-place and were walking on to the Pump-rooms arm in arm, 'cannot be blamed for taking what may be her last opportunity to marry, Anne. I quite understand your hesitations, and yet you would not have your sister a spinster if she can make what, by all I can see, will be a very good marriage to a man who is not in any way objectionable with regard to his money, nor his circumstances in life; a man of property, of means, and of a generally good disposition, cannot fail to be acceptable to any young woman contemplating spinsterhood.'

It had been some years since Anne had learned that she and Lady Russell, while being the most excellent companions, could often hold very differing views and opinions. While Lady Russell held firmly that there could not be anything suspicious or unseemly in the behaviour of either Miss Crawford or her brother, Anne, having now spent two evenings at Camden-place and walked twice with them all in the Pump-rooms, had just cause to suspect the careful contrivings and manoeuvrings of the Crawfords, which seemed designed to secure themselves each an Elliot. The brother's ambition she could not be sure of; he seemed wholly entranced with her sister, and she could see that the attraction was reciprocated. He could not be after Elizabeth's money for there was not enough of it on her side to make any difference to his, which was endowed more than sufficiently, she collected. It must be a true attachment, or as true as any young man's might be who is on the hunt for a wife.

'I confess Mr Crawford reminds me of Mr William Elliot, in his dealings with me, when he tried for my own hand,' mused Anne. 'He exerts all his powers of pleasing, gives way to her opinion even when his own differs, and goes to great pains to make himself very agreeable. Why, only yesterday when we were in the rooms all together, I heard him tell my sister how excessively fond of a card party he is, although his sister had already mentioned to me privately that they never play at cards or have card evenings at Everingham. I think Miss Crawford must have wished her words unsaid then, for after moment she changed the subject decidedly quickly and seemed to blush a little.'

Lady Russell laughed gently and squeezed her goddaughter's hand. 'And what if he does exert his powers over her as much as he can? Is it not what any young man in love does who wishes to attach his object? Poor Mr Crawford is guilty merely of doing his utmost to please your sister, and now you see the good that has come of it, for she will have a home equal to any she has lost in Kellynch.'

'I am afraid I see more than a mere desire to please, Lady Russell, and yet I cannot say exactly what he has done to offend me!'

'My dear Anne,' scolded her friend, 'I shall not attempt to dissuade you for I can see your mind is entirely made up. You see only the objections, and as to that you are not very specific, for I have seen nothing of the obsequiousness which you claim to have seen in his manner.' She sighed. 'You forget that Elizabeth is not young, and neither is your father. You are still young, my dear, and have not yet faced that which must come to us all eventually;

you have good health and you do not look to the future in the way that we older people do. Sir Walter will marry Miss Crawford, and Elizabeth will be secure for life. With your father's fatigue lately and his health being not perhaps as robust as it once was, on *his* part it is an act of kindness to let Elizabeth go to a new situation, with an income to which she has been used, and I shall not even scruple to say that a little flirtation, a little desire to please instead of being pleased, will not do Elizabeth any harm. It may have the effect of humbling her where she is sometimes wont to a little too much of the Elliot pride!'

Faintly smiling her agreement with this observation, Anne had little else to say. Although she agreed with her friend, she did not want to see her sister set down, nor did she wish to see her made unhappy by a too-hasty union. But Elizabeth was old enough, and cool-hearted enough perhaps, to be safe from any serious harm to her heart. Anne had tried, once, to warn her sister against Mrs Clay and had been set down for it; she collected that there was little she could do or say to persuade her older sister once she had made up her mind.

In the course of the afternoon, Anne consented to walk on the promenade with the Crofts, whose genuine and unfettered delight in meeting every sort of person her father would have announced 'deplorable', made Anne feel as if she was truly at ease in Bath. The Crofts' acquaintance seemed mostly comprised of jolly, good-hearted naval men and their wives who were as robust and fresh-faced as Mrs Croft herself. Putting aside her anxiety for her absent husband, Anne entered into their conversations with an eagerness borne of a vested interest, and found a certain comfort in shared anxieties for friends abroad.

By the time they had returned home, Anne was pink-cheeked and bright-eyed from the exercise, the becoming flush of pregnancy adding a new glow to her usual prettiness. Her good spirits were not marred by the arrival of a letter addressed in Mary's hand, soon after they had convened in the small parlour to take their 'four o'clocks' as Admiral Croft called it. This habit had been consciously instituted by Mrs Croft, more to encourage the Admiral to rest, than to refresh themselves.

'I daresay you think us quite countrified and silly, Anne, compared with your own habits, but the admiral is easily tired these days, and refuses to rest his foot, and if I give him to think that tea and a rest at four is for my own benefit then he cannot refuse me the comfort!'

But with the tea things today came letters, including one from Uppercross, and Anne was waved away to read her letter in peace and give the Crofts any news of Kellynch afterwards. Anne therefore retreated, but only as far as the window seat overlooking the street, and opened her letter.

> *Uppercross Cottage*
> *Monday 27 June, 1815*
>
> *My dear Anne,*
>
> *I would not have written so soon after your departure for Bath, since I cannot but think you can hardly have a care for the doings of Uppercross, when there are all the amusements of Bath to be had, only I wanted to ask you particularly to get some good ribbands from Morcombe's for me, a yard of white and the same of black if they have it, and also to tell you that I am very ill. I have been a poor creature, indeed, confined to my bed these last few days since you left Kellynch. The apothecary prescribed some Sulphur taken in Water for three days, which I fancy did me some good because I felt much better after I stopp't. But I was much afflicted and I thought to write you and beg you to come to me when you can get free of the Crofts.*
>
> *As for my illness, I am sorry to say I expect to suffer some weeks, as this excessive warm weather is making me intolerably listless and heavy. I asked Charles for the doctor to come, but he would not allow it. Charles, as you know, cares so little for my*

complaints, and thinks me so imaginative about my illnesses that he barely blinks when I mention them to him; if only you were here to nurse me! You know you are the only person who can give me any comfort or cure!

I have not yet written to Elizabeth, since her last to me was taken up so much with the particulars of their visits to Lady Dalrymple and Miss Carteret, but no, I must call her by her married name, Hon. Lady Annesley — I quite forgot that she married — can you imagine it! What a droll thought! She is so plain-looking it hardly makes a difference that she is rich! But it is a very good match for her, indeed, so I am told. However, as to writing, I cannot hope to match my sister in news to impart, for so little happens here that there is never anything worth writing about. I can apologise for my letter being so short on that account.

It is very cruel of you, Anne, to not visit more than you do; however, I am good-natured enough not to feel too much offense, for you know my nature is not to complain, but to endure in silence; if you must be in company and amusement at Bath I hope you are enjoying yourself very much and never think of me, for I would not want to burden you with duty when you are gone away to enjoy yourself. But when the Crofts don't want you, I shall depend on your coming to me, very much.

Have you heard from Frederick? — I just now have taken up my pen again, for Charles came in just then and gave me news of the Great House where he has been visiting his father; the Musgroves are in a very wretched state for the sake of poor Captain Benwick, and they entreated Charles to go and fetch Louisa home himself, but he told them of course he cannot and must wait for Wentworth to send her or bring her home. I suppose you do not know any more than we, how she is to come home and when.

Do you suppose Frederick in danger? I can hardly think he could be. We were in very good spirits when the news of the French defeat reached us; the Musgroves had us up to the Great House to dinner, on account of it. I had almost quite made up my mind, Anne, to decline the invitation on account of them not having the civility to give me the time of day until something very agreeable happens and they wish to celebrate, but I relented and now I feel there really was no good reason for me to be going, for a large quantity of claret was put away by them all, and no one took pains to notice me at all! I took three glasses of claret also, for my health, but it did not signify, for I had a worse headache the next day. Perhaps I did not take enough?

Charles caught three grouse yesterday and we will make a very good meal of two of them tonight. Abigail has caught a chill and I have had to send her to bed, so I am very out of sorts, for Jane says she cannot be expected to bath the children and help in the kitchen all at once. When he gets in, I shall get Charles to take the children to a very good bath, in the next field, where the river is shallow, and scrub their necks. Still, it was very ill-considered of Abigail to get a chill now, when I am so poorly myself!

Henrietta is in very low spirits on account of her sister's loss; but I have just had the very good notion to send the children over there, for by their company she must be distracted and brought into a good way again, instead of pining for her sister. A degree of sisterly affection as between those two is quite natural and right, but it can be taken too far, Anne, and from what I have seen of Henrietta's carrying on and talking excessively of the matter, I might say I cannot wholly approve it; I have too often seen natural 'affection' turn into 'affectation', and I cannot approve affectation in anybody, I am sure! I have tried to console Henrietta but she will

*not be consoled. She will take no heed of my telling
her that Louisa has only been married a very short
time and therefore cannot have the attachment for
her husband that a long marriage naturally produces.
She insists on mourning for her sister and has taken
to wearing a black trim on her hat – can you imagine
anything so droll and contrived!*

*Charles says to send his best love. He is just now
gone out again.*

*I shall write to you if I find myself worse; might
you come to me for a month, if Lady Russell can
spare you from her side? At any rate I have
determined to send the little boys to Henrietta for a
week. I may be better off for it. Their noise, you
know, gives me palpitations, and my headaches are
always better when they are away with their father or
aunt.*

*How are Papa and Eliza? Give them all my love
and tell Eliza I shall write only if there is any news of
importance, for I know she cares little for
Uppercross on the whole. I suppose they are too
taken up by life in Bath to give me a thought. I hope
you are in health. I wonder if you are in aprons yet?
I can give you my old gowns which were let out when
I had Walter; I had kept them thinking of Elizabeth,
but that is not to be, it seems. What hopes we all
had, last year! However, they will do for you, if you
are not overnice about such things. At Kellynch you
need not fear being seen in an old dress of mine for
you do not go out much nor have visitors apart from
Lady Russell. Give her my best.*

*Yours in sisterly affection,
Mary Musgv.*

Anne folded this epistolary piece with a sigh. She could not
but find herself wondering at how much news there was when
people write every second or third day, even while insisting that
there is "nothing worth telling". While Anne was glad to receive a

letter from her sister, Mary's lack of sensitivity for Anne's circumstances also gave her a little stab. She would take pains to ensure that Frederick would never hear how little he was thought of at Uppercross! But these thoughts she threw off quickly enough, and she folded her letter and went back to her tea. Since there was nothing of importance to impart regarding Kellynch, she could not satisfy the Crofts' enquiries as to whom had given what entertainments in their absence, and a half hour was chatted away pleasantly on other topics. Mary had not been informed yet of her sister's match, and Anne felt that it must fall upon herself to give the news. The letter was written by that evening, and it was left for Anne to reflect, as she handed it before dinner to Robertson to post, that although she did not dislike writing to her sister, the comparable pleasure of receiving a letter was these days so often far less her portion, than was the duty of writing them.

Twenty Six

Thursday 6 July, 1815
Sydney Place, Bath.

Anne already had been once to visit her friend, Mrs Smith, and was again engaged to her the following afternoon. Previously widowed and left in poor straits by her husband, this young widow, with the assistance of Frederick Wentworth acting on her behalf, had found herself finally the recipient of an income from a property in the West Indies of her late husband's, and had found herself in the way of being able to improve her situation in life. Mrs Smith had originally come to Bath for the waters, since she had suffered poor health, but now, she had told Anne happily, she stayed for the constant employment and occupation it gave her to watch and listen to its inhabitants, for she was a student of human nature and found great delight in studying her fellows.

Her partner in this endeavour was a Nurse Rook, who had tended Mrs Smith when she was first come to Bath a sick widow, and even now remained in her mistress's employ, although her duties were now more to entertain by way of stories and tidbits of gossip than to nurse.

On her first visit in some months, Anne had been gratified to find her friend in far better health than she had left her the previous year, and in a new situation near the Sydney gardens. Now, stepping out of the sedan-chair which had carried her there a second time, Anne was met at the door by the servant and was eagerly greeted when she entered the drawing room.

'Ah, here you are, my dear Mrs Wentworth, and so becoming in this blue silk — why, you are glowing! It is excellent to see you in such health. How do you go on?'

'Very well, I thank you! I was a little fatigued these last weeks, but that has passed almost entirely now.' Anne was gratified to be paid such kind attentions, especially in the absence of such consideration from her family.

Miss Smith was everything welcoming and agreeable. 'How kind you are to call upon me when you must have so many other pressing engagements to take up your time! Do sit down and be comfortable!'

'You are teasing me and you know it!' cried Anne, seating herself on the sofa with good humour. 'How can I be happy in Bath if I do not give myself the pleasure of calling on you at least twice a week!'

'And you know it gives me just as much pleasure to receive you. Now that I am well, we must engage to walk. That is why I have taken a house by the gardens, you know; being prevented for so long from walking without assistance, I am now eager to walk every day in the most lovely of places in Bath, next to the promenade. Will you do a friend a very great favour and walk with me the day after tomorrow?'

Anne was pleased to be able to accept and told her so. Tea was ordered, and, 'we shall have some of Becky's tea-cake; your figure is so slight, even in your condition, that it can hardly signify!'

The tea was poured, and they had just begun a cosy chat when Nurse Rook, intimate enough with her mistress to know that formality with her better was useless, entered the room with a cheery smile, and a warm greeting for Anne.

Anne smiled hers in return. 'Good afternoon, Nurse Rook! Are you still bringing my friend the best of tidbits of gossip in Bath? I cannot wonder that she will not let you go!'

Nurse Rook was happy to oblige. 'I pride myself on always having my ear to the ground, Miss Elliot — I beg your pardon, you are Mrs Wentworth now! — and I have already heard some rather interesting news concerning your family and which must be dear to your heart.'

Anne knew that news of her sister's engagement must be the talk of Bath drawing rooms, although she was surprised that the affair was in so much forwardness that Nurse Rook had heard it already. 'Then you have heard my sister's news, Nurse Rook?'

Mrs Smith added in the kindest, civil tones, 'I believe congratulations are in order, Mrs Wentworth. Mr Crawford is a fortunate man. Your sister is held to be a beauty in Bath, as well as having the blessing of the name "Elliot" to add to her charms.'

'Thank you.'

Mrs Smith added, 'There is much talk of your father and Miss Crawford, too. It is expected that he will offer for her soon now that your sister is engaged.'

Anne could only give a weak denial. 'I have no intelligence of my father's intentions. Perhaps that is the case, but they have not made an announcement yet, and nothing is certain until that happens.'

'He is still a vigorous, well-looking man, and with a fine figure. It is not unsurprising that she may look at him,' mused Mrs Smith. 'And she is a beauty, in her own way, with that fine English skin. He would not be amiss, I collect, in considering her. But how much do you know of these Crawfords?' She exchanged a glance with Nurse Rook.

Anne, intercepting the seriousness of manner with which these glances were exchanged, became a little alarmed. 'Very little, I confess. I hope you have not heard anything untoward? Pray, do not hold back with me!'

Miss Smith replaced her teacup, which she had been sipping, and addressed Anne with a great seriousness. 'I am very pleased for your sister's news, only Nurse Rook here has heard something — something contrary and unpleasant — which might affect your sister's happiness. Is it wrong of me to mention it, my dear Mrs Wentworth? I only mention it with the intention of putting you on your guard, although nothing can be done, I am sure, when two people are in love and determined to marry!'

Now Anne became curious. 'Then by all means you must share what you know, Miss Smith. Is there some intelligence I ought to know?'

Miss Smith took up her teacup again and sipped composedly. 'I would never think of alarming you, Mrs Wentworth, only you and your kind husband have done me so many services this past year, that I feel I cannot let what I know go by without at least bringing your attention to it. This man your sister is to marry, how much do you know of his character, of his past?'

Anne, with conscious awareness of her own unaccountable distrust of the man, quelled these rising thoughts and said mildly, 'Why, very little, I own — is there anything which I ought to find objectionable in the man? Mr Crawford appears to me to be of good breeding and unexceptional manners. I have not spent much time in conversation with him, but I confess he has been, at least in my company, agreeable and civil to all.'

'Then it pains me to tell you anything to the contrary, Mrs Wentworth. Nurse Rook has knowledge of this man, which only she can know, being in a position to hear and see more than sometimes we ladies can from our parlours and drawing rooms.'

Anne began to feel a faint alarm. 'Tell me all you know, Nurse Rook, pray do.'

Nurse Rook began. 'Well, I have some information, which although I am loath to share it, Ma'am, being of a delicate nature and all, might be something you would want to know. I have a friend, in service mind, in a very good household in London. She told me some many months ago now, of a scandal in the household where she serves, involving the younger miss, who was used very ill by a certain gentleman and had to be sent away in disgrace after they was caught in *flagrant delicto*, so to speak. Quite a disgrace, it was, for the whole family and the young girl sent away in shame and her older sister's prospects blighted for it. Well, Ma'am, my friend who works there, says the man's name was Mr Henry Crawford. The family tried to track 'im down, see, and they found him at his club in London.'

Anne was aghast. 'I see.' She was silent for some moments. 'I am indebted to you, Nurse Rook. But it is not uncommon for men to have such pasts, however much we might censure them for it.'

'But this is not all, Ma'am, for the gentleman is known to go under different guises, and he regularly uses the name "Lyford". It was under this name that he seduced the young miss I speak of, and I believe he has a sordid reputation which is known to many folks in London.'

Anne gasped. 'Lyford, you say?'

'Yes, Ma'am. Why, have you heard the name before?'

Anne was deep in thought, astonishment overspreading her features. 'Yes, I am sorry to say I have. I believe I know the name. If what you say is correct, he is an excessively dissolute man, licentious indeed! So, Mr Henry Crawford is Harry Lyford!'

'Yes, Ma'am. This Crawford has quite a reputation, according to my friend. They found that he is well known for his licentiousness; his reputation is for gaming and pleasure-taking, if you get my meaning, Ma'am. He is not at all a good man, if the rumours are correct. They even say,' she lowered her eyes and blushed, 'that he has been discovered in the back alleys of theatres, with the lamp-boys.'

Anne had heard of such things, for she had not reached the age of eight and twenty without knowing something of the world. She blushed a little but was calm. 'I see. And yet, it is my sister's choice. She never would never allow herself to be persuaded by me, for she has a strong will of her own which always prevails in the case. I can try to warn her, but I think her mind is made up. My sister has a very cool head, when she is determined upon a course.'

Mrs Smith ventured, 'For a woman in her time of life, I believe the union is not an unthinkable one, even despite what we know of this Mr Crawford. Perhaps he will tone down his profligate ways and be happy in domesticity, and if he is not, your sister, over anyone, I think, Mrs Wentworth, might have the strength of will to bear up under it. She will benefit by the gaining of a not unmodest establishment of her own, and we cannot any of us say if he really loves her or not. Perhaps it is not wise to bring it to her attention, but I feel only you can be the judge of that. We wished only to warn you to be on your guard, for your sister's sake, and to give her this intelligence only if you feel it is warranted.'

Anne thought for a moment. 'I confess I have known Mr Crawford but a short time, but I have always been uncomfortable around him. Even his sister — there is a certain manner they have about them — yes, he has the most open powers of pleasing a woman. I have seen this for myself, and my sister, I collect, is quite charmed. But at her time of life, I think she feels it keenly that two opportunities have passed her by to marry, and she will not willingly give up a third. I feel she will not be persuaded against a match, and it is not my place to persuade.'

'Did I do wrong, Mrs Wentworth, in bringing these things to your attention? I hope I have not made you unhappy.' Mrs Smith was anxious.

Anne was quick to appease her. 'On the contrary, my dear friend, do not make yourself anxious. You have helped me to understand another matter by revealing this one, and as for any outcome, none of us can really say what might bring this man into line. I cannot hate him, for he is to be my brother, but I shall always be on my guard, for my sister, and know myself the wiser for your intelligence'.

Anne spent many hours in thought after this visit was long over. The fact that the source of Julia's ruin was now known to her did nothing for her peace of mind, and yet, she knew that even while Mr Crawford was making love to her sister, Elizabeth would benefit greatly from the union also. She was reluctant to introduce disharmony into a scene which was set already to making her sister a more happy being than she had been for some time. They could perhaps force Crawford into a confession, and make him marry Julia, and yet, what good would come of a marriage founded in dishonesty and suffering? She would only ruin Elizabeth's own chances of happiness, precarious as they were with such a man. She would not be the source of such information and risk her sister's unhappiness. Wishing very much for Frederick's counsel on the matter, Anne reluctantly resolved to leave the matter alone and let nature take its course.

Twenty Seven

Friday 7 July, 1815

'We must be grateful that Julia never discovered the truth before she went away — and she must be protected from this knowledge at all costs. I suppose it is unlikely that she will have anything to do with my sister even so — Everingham is a long way from Kellynch Hall!'

Anne and Mrs Croft were strolling along the promenade, arm in arm, the admiral having left them briefly to talk with an old naval friend. They paused and admired the views over the river Avon.

'Yes, my dear, she would not bear knowing, I think, that your sister is married to the man who brought her to ruin. Nor would your father or sister bear the humiliation if it was discovered what a man Crawford is.'

Anne paused and turned to her friend. 'To say the truth, Mrs Croft, I am more anxious for my sister than anyone else, for it is she who is to marry him!'

Anne had confided to Mrs Croft her new knowledge of the identity of Julia's "Lyford", and had been gratified to receive the counsel which stemmed from the good sense and consciously right manners she had always depended upon from her friend. Mrs Croft had taken Anne's view on the futility of sharing this knowledge with Elizabeth, but she did not share Anne's concern over her sister's prospects, nor Sir Walter's ever-increasing regard for Miss Crawford.

'Even if what you say is true, I see no reason against their being happy, Anne. It is true that your friend's intelligence has made the prospect of Elisabeth's being happy less certain. And yet there is little you might do for her, if all things are considered. If it were your father in great danger of being duped, I would advise another way, for you must think of the Elliot name, and your father's pride, but as it is your sister... we women must always be weighing the benefits of marriage against the possible harms; we have far less choice in our marital partners, my dear, than men! Your sister, as much as she is an Elliot, cannot escape that fact.'

'Yes. That is very true, Mrs Croft, and it is what has prevented me from speaking.' Anne sighed. 'I confess I am made uneasy by the speed of the attachment on his part. And then, if it were only Mr Crawford, but I see both siblings making love to my father and sister, and Miss Crawford spelling as hard as you can imagine for a proposal. She might well just come out and ask *him!*'

'I have heard the talk of his interest in Miss Crawford, my dear. And yet it must be his decision; he is not a young man, and you must allow him some self-interest at his time of life. It is not unreasonable to wish for companionship, now that your sister is to be married. He is still a well-looking man, and she is very pretty, rich, and of a good family. It would be unnatural for him *not* to think of marriage, in such a circumstance. I would not worry myself excessively, for your father is, for all his self-interest, no mere child. Sir Walter has been enough in the world to be on his guard. Depend upon it, he has more sense that you give him credit for.'

Anne wished that she could agree with this supposition, but she remained silent and could only hope that her friend was correct.

Preparations for Elizabeth's wedding were well forward in execution. Although the wedding was to be in Bath, Crawford had convinced his bride that a small breakfast afterwards might be more tasteful in the circumstances. 'While not wishing to be over scrupulous, my dear,' he had suggested carefully one evening, 'I know you will not wish to give offence, or give rise to that jealousy of feeling in others which may arise from one's seeming happier than one's acquaintances, some of whom are still grieving recent losses on the battle field.'

Acknowledging his view to be all that was right and proper, Elizabeth and Sir Walter found, after only a slight resistance, that their own opinions did after all concur with Mr Crawford's and a small breakfast party, to be given at their own residence, had finally been agreed upon. Elizabeth was in generally excellent spirits, since she had been occupied for some days in ordering her wedding clothes, and was in a bridely fluster of excitement. Anne collected that this was as much as anything else due to the fact that she had finally triumphed over her younger sister, if not in marrying before her, then in marrying better than her, at any rate. What had given Anne to hold this view was the unfortunate overhearing of a few words spoken to Miss Crawford. Anne had ventured past an open door, and had paused as she heard her name spoken.

'...can hardly signify, my dear Mary. Anne may gloat that she has caught herself a husband, but I do not count a mere captain as anything — he has not any property of his own — and if my sister thinks herself in circumstance now that she is married *tolerably*, I do not hold *that* greater than having an establishment of the size and reputation of Everingham; besides, dear Crawford has his own consequence which cannot but precede him, and as his Lady I shall be quite satisfied in my exchanging Kellynch for Everingham.'

Miss Crawford had murmured something condescending and agreeable, but Anne had not stayed outside the drawing room door to hear it; she had coloured, then sighed in vexation at the pride of her sister and the want of familial respect for herself and her husband. Then she laughed at herself for neglecting to remember that if one lingers to hear one spoken of, one is almost always sure to hear something unbecoming!

Despite Elizabeth's habitually dispassionate regard for her younger sister, the frightful alarm of a close call with spinsterhood, at the last minute revoked, had effected to render her, if not an agreeable creature, a much less disagreeable one at any rate. Her usual cold demeanour had been replaced with the dubious enthusiasm of a thawing ice-berg, her once stony features now breaking a long habit of unmovable, cool obstinance, to bask in the warmth of the finally-secured happiness which shone cheerfully upon its surface. She smiled a little more, she laughed occasionally, and she was almost sanguine. Nothing irked or vexed; all was well. After flailing in the great ocean of an uncertain future, with all the humiliation of being an unmarried woman past her prime to look to, she had at the last minute been cast a rope called Crawford, and she had grasped hold of it with all her might.

She was made as suddenly complacent and sanguine as she had been ill-tempered and resentful. The pain of Mr Elliot's defection to camp "Clay" had now been forgotten. She had a wedding, long dreamed of, to plan, execute, and be made happy from. Then she would retire to Everingham to take up the duties of its mistress. Crawford had promised as many visits to town as would give her pleasure, and she could do as she liked with the furnishings. All was to her liking. Her name would now take its rightful place in the volume of honour, her father's *Baronetcy*, thus; *"Elizabeth Elliot, married 20 July, 1815, to Henry Crawford, son and heir of Sir Edgar Crawford, of Everingham, in the county of Norfolk."*

Mary's early marriage had been a sore trial to Elizabeth's shipwrecked nerves, so soon after her first loss of the young Mr William Elliot, and then, to have endured Anne's marriage, too, being recorded upon that hallowed page, was almost beyond what her pride could bear. Seeing the details of her marriage entered beside her birth would give her as much pride as it would afford her father in writing it in. The Book was living, material proof of their consequence in the world. Their forbears had lived and died among its pages. Both she and her father opened that tome regularly and poured over its pages, and their own places in it. The only thing which ever gave her a sour taste upon the tongue was the fact that their family line was so liberally sprinkled with

"Annes", "Marys" and "Elizabeths", the inferior Irish and Scottish ancestors her father disdained, but now these were consciously and selectively dismissed; she was to marry. It was true that Crawford was not a peer; his father had only been conferred a knighthood. But he was of English descent, and of fine figure, good fortune, and tolerable consequence; these were the minimum requirements for happiness, and for a lady who had looked spinsterhood square in the eye, she could not be overnice.

Twenty Eight

Wednesday 12 July, 1815

Anne had not wanted this second visit to Bath in a year to understand the speed with which news carries in that place. It was like a quiet whisper uttered in a great empty room, which is then picked up by the great cold walls and echoed over and over until the hearing of it becomes so irksome that one wishes for silence. So it was in Bath; when any news was to be had, it was taken up and repeated in every drawing room in the city until even the inhabitants of the Westgate Buildings were talking of it over their Bath buns at breakfast.

Anne, upon being congratulated in the street for the seventh time in a morning on the news of her sister's impending marriage, after saying all that was grateful and proper, leaned upon the arm of Lady Russell, and sighed. 'Bath runs mad, I think, for gossip. I declare I have not been in a place more given over to spreading rumours than Bath! Did you note how Lady Everett so boldly hinted at my father's impending engagement to Miss Crawford? Does everybody suspect such an outcome then?'

Lady Russell was sanguine. 'I believe they do, Anne, for he has made no secret of his attachment, and why should he, at his time of life? I am truly happy for him.'

Anne sighed her vexation. 'Well, I shall not be sorry to have it all done with, Lady Russell, and to finally go home to Kellynch and rest! Elizabeth has had me at Camden-place three times this week already, helping her to choose new linens to take to Everingham, and Crawford has promised a new phaeton, to be furnished just as she likes, so you see I have been taxed with every sort of domestic concern until I am tired with the very notion of marriage! I have never been obliged to hear so many congratulations in my life!'

Lady Russell laughed. 'You were so properly frugal in your own ideas of marriage, my dear, if you remember; the smallest of breakfasts, and only a pretty gown to wear — you must allow for a different taste, Anne, to your own, and you know this is the most significant event in Bath since Miss Carteret was married. Your sister must be allowed her celebration, for she has closely avoided a grave future indeed.'

Conceding the rightness of her friend's opinion, Anne contented herself to be escorted down Milsom-street and, after a visit to the lending library and a stop at Morcombe's for Mary's ribbon, she left Lady Russell and took herself home to Gay-street.

When she entered, it was to find the Crofts gone out, and a gentleman in the drawing room awaiting her return. When she enquired from the housekeeper as to the name of this person, she could not have been more astonished.

'*Mr William Elliot? Here?*' She was agape, and vexed beyond measure. She thought she could guess, however, the reason for the visit. She handed her parcels to the housekeeper. 'Leave them on my bed, if you please. Thank you, Mrs Kerry, that will be all.' Watching the woman away, she took a breath, smoothed down her sprigged-muslin day dress, and entered the room.

To Anne, it was most distressing to see Mr Elliot before her, boldly standing in the drawing room as if there was nothing in the past to make him feel the embarrassment he ought to feel. To see him was a painful reminder of all the humiliation of her family which had gone before, and all the distress of those earlier times came rushing back to her. In appearance, he was just as she remembered him; in a well-cut blue coat, and holding his tall hat in one hand, he had the same air of elegance and fashion, but now she could perceive in his eye some surprise as he took in her slightly rounded form. He bowed.

Her resolve to feign gracious politeness was almost unseated as she met his eyes. She felt nothing but disdain for the man who had her ill-used father and sister. If there had ever been any tenderness due to him, any requirement of proper manners due an heir of Sir Walter's, any familial respect owing, she now felt bound by none of these curtailments of rudeness. She was composed, however.

'How do you do?' She spoke coolly. 'You must hardly be surprised by my astonishment to find you here, Mr Elliot, after all that has gone before. You are remarkably calm, Sir, despite it. I wonder you can show your face to me.'

He barely blanched. 'Mrs Wentworth. How do you do? Congratulations are in order I believe — not just for your sister, but on two counts, I see. I trust I find you in health?' He paused but she said nothing and he continued. 'I have come on a matter of some delicacy and I— I rather hope to presume upon an acquaintance which, once, was not so abhorrent to you.'

Anne, remembering her once passing intimacy with the man, was angry. 'How do you leave Mrs Elliot?' she said coldly, in hope of causing him some embarrassment. 'I hope she is in health?' Anne hoped that the reference to the Mrs Clay who had defected from the Elliot ranks in a treasonous act of self-interest, would remind him of her own knowledge of all that had passed.

He did not reply immediately. His expression said clearly, 'Ah, we are going to play it like that, are we?' He moved to the window, his blue-coated back to her. 'I have come to request a favour, Mrs Wentworth. I shall not equivocate. I desire you to dissuade your father from marrying Miss Crawford.'

Anne, who had surveyed the playing board and anticipated her opponent's next move, was ready. She said with composure, 'Really Mr Elliot? I have no knowledge of such an expectation and I think, as Sir Walter's daughter, I might know if such a union is intended.'

'And yet there is so much talk of it among our mutual acquaintance, that I presumed it was almost a decided thing.' His eyes hardened. 'You can hardly think me impervious to such rumours, Mrs Wentworth, when my own interests are so unequivocally tied up in your father's choices.'

She held her anger at bay. 'You would not scruple, Sir, to think of mentioning such expectations openly? You do not think that to mention them plainly is at all ungentlemanly or unseemly? Pray recollect that any inheritance of yours is predicated on the death of my father. And besides that, your inheriting my father's estate was never a certain thing. At any time, he has had the right to remarry and produce a male child, even at five and fifty!

'But I may do all I can to prevent such an event. I even married, far below my own level of society, to prevent such an outcome. You might understand if you were in the same position. I only wish to retain what I have pinned my hopes upon for the past several years — my previous lack of interest in the estate was only, as I explained then, due to a foolish notion that I had somehow offended your father.'

'As I recollect, Mr Elliot, your letters to your friend, Mr Smith, said differently.'

His eyes narrowed. 'Well. Perhaps they did. I suppose his odious wife made sure you saw them. How — *thorough* — of her, to ensure you were so fully informed.' He paused, bitterness briefly playing over his countenance, until his features were smooth again. He spoke more gently. 'Nevertheless, upon meeting you at Lyme, and again afterward — can you truly forget the intimacy with which we spoke, how we shared the same wish for your father? In marrying Mrs Clay, you must own that I safeguarded your father's interests, as much as my own.'

Anne remained unmoved. 'If you expect my gratitude, Sir, for removing Mrs Clay from my father, you are much misled. You were a viper in the bosom of my father, making love to him as earnestly as you could — and only think of your deceit in courting *me*, while at the same time seeking your own interests with my sister's friend! You can hardly expect to incite my gratitude, or soften me with recollections of an earlier time!'

He turned on her a charming smile and said in the most cajoling tones, 'When I made you, Anne, the sole recipient of my interest, and my warm affections, it was because you had stolen my heart — and when your engagement to Captain Wentworth was announced, you could not have hurt me with a colder gesture!'

Anne had been used before to thinking him not always quite sincere, but history had taught her prudence, and now she saw disingenuousness permeate his every word and look. She laughed a bitter little laugh. 'The sole recipient of your affections, Mr Elliot? Was that before or after you had made Mrs Clay the "recipient of your affections" also? May I remind you, Sir, that you have treated the name "Elliot" with disdain, and my father like a fool. You have practiced deception to a perfection, given pain and humiliation to my sister, and deceived even myself — whom you thought to flatter and cajole at every turn — all in premeditated manoeuvring to gain what you had thought lost! And now you would incite guilt in me, when I have done nothing to be guilty of? I own I can have no pity for you. I desire you to leave now.' She moved toward the door to open it.

'Oh, I think it may well be wise for you to hear me out, if you will be so kind as to give me a little of your time. You would not, I collect, wish to responsible for your father's humiliation and your sister's unhappiness.'

'What is your meaning, Mr Elliot?'

Mr Elliot seated himself comfortably upon one of the plump sofas, and placed his hat beside him carefully. 'My wife,' he began, 'has many acquaintances in town. 'One of her friends is a matron who runs a boarding school for girls in Bardley Street. Her name is Mrs Harris. Several weeks ago, now, Mrs Elliot and this female had a most interesting conversation regarding a Miss Julia Wentworth. My wife, understanding at once the significance of the name "Wentworth", mentioned the matter to me.'

Anne paled. 'If you suppose that my brother-in-law's affairs can have any material effect upon my father, Mr Elliot, you are much mistaken in the matter.'

Elliot glanced at her with haughty disdain. 'Pray do not think me a fool, Mrs Wentworth. Once I heard the name "Wentworth", I desired that my wife question her friend more closely, and we discovered some interesting information. Mrs Harris told Penelope that rumours abound that Miss Wentworth had been several times seen in company with a Mr Crawford, in town. Now, that name lit a notion in my head, for I recollected that I had met the man before. I do not know him well, I own, but he is a gentleman of dubious reputation, and known for his, shall we say, fancy for a "petticoat", among other of his fancies, if you take my meaning, Mrs Wentworth. You know he was once outed in the back alley of the St. James with one of the footmen! No, stay if you please, I have yet something further to reveal. It did not take me long to discover that the wayward Miss Wentworth has been sent away to Herefordshire, and not as a part of her education, I shall add.' He got up and strolled again to the window, leaning forward a little to survey the street. 'What a fine view your friends have here.'

Anne spoke calmly. 'Miss Wentworth is merely holidaying with a friend in that part of the world. She will come home in a few months and finish her education abroad, I believe.'

Elliot smiled slightly. 'I kept this information to myself, in case should I find the need to use it. You cannot imagine my interest when two days ago I heard the name "Crawford" mentioned in the same sentence along with Sir Walter Elliot and Miss Elizabeth Elliot! And now, given the talk I have heard, it is time for me to use every tool at my hand to persuade you to disengage your father from Crawford's sister.' He turned from the window to meet her eyes. 'If you do not, I will ensure the circumstances of Miss Wentworth are made clear to all good society in Bath and in town, and I shall reveal Crawford's — *unnatural* — proclivities to all whom your father counts as his acquaintance.'

Anne was silent, for the shock of such revelations had been more than she could take in for the present. But she rallied quickly, and, in some anger on behalf of her father and sister, managed coldly, 'Nevertheless, however it is rumoured to be with Mr Crawford, it is not my place to interfere in my father's schemes. Even if I revealed what you have told me, I doubt that he would be persuaded by me. And if I speak up, my sister's hopes of happiness are dashed. You must resign yourself, Mr Elliot, to whatever the future holds for you; I cannot be an instrument of your evil upon my family.'

Elliot left the window and advanced. His handsome face was hard. 'Mrs Wentworth, I beg your pardon, but allow me to disabuse you of one thing. I would not have lowered myself to marry a woman of indifferent birth, a mere *Mrs Clay*, and take on her *pestilence* of daughters, who make my life a misery with their constant prattle and requests for more pin money, if I was not highly motivated to gain that which rightfully belongs to me! I shall not allow Kellynch, my rightful inheritance, to escape me, now that I have gone through so much to gain it.'

Anne could not pity him. 'I believe you have reaped only what you have sown, Mr Elliot. Perhaps you ought to have considered the consequences of marrying so much beneath you, before committing to a path which by no means has ever been certain. My father has full right to marry whomsoever he wishes, Sir, and produce all the heirs he sees fit.'

'And you will not try to dissuade him from that path?'

'I shall not persuade him otherwise, if I think marriage will secure his future happiness. My father, if he marries Miss Crawford, will be content with *his* wife. I wish you joy of *yours*!'

'Marriage has turned you into a shrew, Mrs Wentworth.'

'Perhaps it has Mr Elliot. But I have no influence over my father all the same.'

Elliot took up his hat grimly. 'Very well, Mrs Wentworth, but if your father marries Miss Crawford, the humiliation and unhappiness that your whole family will suffer when I unveil Crawford's true nature, will be upon *your* head!'

Twenty Nine

To Anne, such a visit could not have been more distressing — to have seen, before her own eyes, the very form of the man who had undone their family so wholly last year. After she had seen him away, she spent some time pacing the room in anxious contemplation. Should she tell her father of Mr Elliot's visit? Until such time as there had been made a definite offer to Miss Crawford, she felt that she could not speak. Anything said pre-emptively would surely raise her father's anger. It was his own business if he were thinking of making an offer. She thought too, of the comparable evils of Mr Crawford and Mr Elliot; she could not say whom was the worse!

Nevertheless, she was determined not to weigh into the case with her own opinions, so little wanted they were by her father and sister. If Mr Elliot chose to expose Crawford for who he really was, she was not sure that her sister would not simply choose to turn a blind eye, given all that she would gain from the marriage. Besides, it was by no means certain that her father would offer for Miss Crawford, and Mr Elliot would do nothing until an offer had been made, of that she was convinced. And if it was made known that Mr Crawford was really the "Mr Lyford" of Julia's ruin, what could be done in any case? He would never be persuaded to marry the girl now. No, there was little she could say without causing harm herself and so she would, for the present, say nothing.

The Crofts were heard coming in, all abustle from their

morning of shopping, and shortly afterwards they entered the drawing room, flushed and happy.

'Why, there you are, my dear.' The admiral smiled widely at her and sat himself down followed by his wife who held a letter in her hand.

'Anne, here you are! I have just ordered some tea. The admiral and I have been shopping in Milsom-street, but he is tired from the walking and his ankle gives him some pain so we are come in to drink tea and the admiral will take his cherry juice. How pale you look, my dear. Are you well?' Mrs Croft hovered anxiously, casting an eye over her sister-in-law.

Anne, rallying at once from her contemplations, smiled and shook her head. 'Yes, I am very well, Mrs Croft, but I think I have been sitting too long.'

'Then you must go out and walk — are you not engaged to sit with Lady Russell this afternoon? But first, a letter has come for you — I know you will wish to read it immediately!'

Anne took the note with pleasure, her heart beating in anticipation of seeing Frederick's hand upon the front of one, but she was disappointed. 'Oh, it is only a letter from Mary — I wonder she can find so many things to write about when she wrote me so recently.' She lifted the wax and read quickly. 'She sends her best regards to you both, and says she is — dear me! Louisa Benwick has come home to Uppercross!'

Amidst the Croft's polite exclamations, Anne scanned the letter quickly. Mary had written very briefly, she said, only to let Anne know that Louisa had arrived, to the astonishment and joy of her parents, at the Great House, three days ago. She had, Mary collected, been escorted there by a young naval officer, whom according to Louisa was a gallant young man who had suffered the loss of an arm in action, and that he was an acquaintance of Captain Frederick Wentworth! No news of Frederick could be gleaned from this short note, other than Mary had written that Louisa had spoken of Captain Wentworth in the most glowing terms and that she had left him in excellent health in Brussels before she had embarked on her journey back to England.

While Anne was hard pressed not to feel a great deal of emotion, especially over Louisa's speaking so well of Frederick, she was at least vastly relieved to hear that her husband was safe and well, and Louisa home at last. But why had he not written a letter to her and charged Louisa with its dispatch directly she had gained English shores? Perhaps there had been a letter and it would soon arrive.

'So Frederick is safe — at any rate, that we must be grateful for.' Mrs Croft sympathised. 'You will hear from him very shortly, I am sure. The war is over, and a letter will soon follow.'

Anne smiled weakly, but in light of all that had passed in that eventful morning, she felt ever more burdened with lowness of spirits. If she had any power over her father at all, should she try to exercise it? Was Mr Elliot right when he said the blame for Crawford's underhanded dealings with them all would be upon her head? Could she countenance the possibility that her sister's happiness, and her father's pride, might be compromised once again because of Mr Elliot, and that she, Anne, had chosen to stand back and do nothing? These were questions indeed, and she wished for nothing more than to confide in her husband and share the burden of her thoughts.

Presently however, she was pleasantly enough distracted by her friends, and allowed their cheery spirits to buoy her own. After another half hour she left the Crofts sitting comfortably, for she had her appointment to visit with Lady Russell. Desiring not to be late, she put on a moss-coloured velvet spencer and hailed her sedan chair in good time.

In Rivers-street she had confidante enough, and after relating to Lady Russell her tale of the morning's unwanted visitor, was gratified that while her god-mother was shocked at the accusations Mr Elliot had levelled at her sister's beau, a great deal of good sense followed, which had the tendency to reconcile Anne to holding her tongue on the matter.

'If Crawford is truly as unprincipled as all that, then I am very sorry for your sister, but it is so with all marriages; women have endured worse husbands, for the sake of security. Happiness in marriage is entirely a matter of chance, my dear, and what if it is all mere rumour? You would not forgive yourself if speaking out led to a breach between Elizabeth and Crawford, and it all proved to be nothing but gossip.'

'But he cannot deny that he seduced my husband's niece, Lady Russell. Of that we are certain.'

'While I own it to be very shocking and evil in him, nothing else in his current conduct can be faulted, Anne. I think it best to leave your father and sister to their choices, and if Mr Elliot is ambitious enough to attempt what he has threatened, they will both of them bear up under it as well as they can, and take whatever action they see fit. I do not think Miss Crawford unfit for your father — if he offers, I shall wish them very happy, and know your father in good hands as he gets older.'

'I own I can find nothing in either of the Crawfords that I have seen with my own eyes, to warrant saying anything to my father,' replied Anne. 'But there is something too smooth, too eager, in Crawford's manner. In his sister too, I detect the same hint of insincerity. Still, they are all of age; my father must be let to decide for himself, I suppose. If Mr Elliot tries to part them, then we shall see the strength of the attachment. My father has never thought of marriage before, Lady Russell; it is Miss Crawford whom I see pushing for the title of "Lady Elliot."'

Lady Russell mused. 'She is not so old, perhaps only one or two years older than Elizabeth. And she is a handsome woman with a satisfactory income. I do not wonder that he may be flattered by her interest in him.'

Anne bit her lip. 'It will be distressing, I own, to have a step mother almost the same age as myself, and yet, I cannot wish my father alone and unhappy now that Elizabeth is settled.'

'You shall see, Anne, that there is little material damage Mr Elliot can do to two people who are determined to wed! And perhaps your father will not offer for Miss Crawford at all, although I would be surprised if he did not, for he looks to be as struck by the lady as she is by him!'

'On one point, I am put at ease, at any rate. Miss Crawford cannot be marrying my father for money.'

'I believe you are right. But neither of us is so unworldly, Anne, to pretend that it could be a marriage of love. He is old enough to be her father. She is after the title; she desires the honour of calling herself "Lady Elliot." And yet, that is no worse than other women have done before her. Let it be, Anne, and let matters take their own course.'

Anne took heart in this advice and determined to follow it. She went up, very obligingly, to Camden-place every time Elizabeth sent for her, and spent several evenings in company with the Crawfords, saying little and keeping her counsel. She was forced to look upon Mr Crawford as a man with no conscience at all, entirely without morals, and the man who had brought her husband's niece to ruin. This truth gave her pain, distressed her beyond measure, and it was difficult indeed to act without rancour to him, to address him without the alteration of manner which her heart urged. Yet she remained coolly polite, guarded, and as agreeable as possible so as not to give rise to remonstrance from her sister. As for Crawford's supposed "unnatural proclivities", such inclinations were foreign to her, but she was not unworldly enough to be irretrievably shocked by them, nor yet to believe them entirely false. But she would not give them countenance, for her own peace of mind.

The days progressed, and so did the wedding plans, until it was only two days from Elizabeth's wedding day. She had gone up early to Camden-place, at around half past nine o'clock, to eat breakfast with Elizabeth, who had desired Anne to go with her into Bond-street, to help the maid carry home some hats and shoes which had been ordered up from town. Miss Crawford, she was told the previous day, 'was too much occupied with her own engagements that morning to assist, and besides, she was of a delicate constitution and could not be expected to lug parcels up Bond-street.'

Anne, being by habit hardened to such affronts, did not point out to her sister that in her own condition she might be considered of a "delicate constitution" herself, but being so used to her sister's general disregard of her feelings, she agreed with only a small sigh, content to be, if unnoticed, at least of use.

Upon being shown into the breakfast-room, however, she was nonplussed to find Miss Crawford sitting alongside Elizabeth and Sir Walter, and looking in high colour. She and Elizabeth had been talking with some animation.

Elizabeth greeted her absently and continued her discussion, but Sir Walter glanced up at Anne and, still chewing his bread, said, 'Oh, Anne. It is only you. Will you sit? I much prefer an even number at table, even if it is only breakfast, and you make a fourth.' Her father only paused a moment to see her settled, then continued, 'I am pleased you have come in, for I have some news. You might as well know that I have offered for Miss Crawford and received her affirmative.'

Anne, for whom such an event was not wholly a surprise, was still a little dismayed. She managed weakly, 'Oh! This is news indeed! I am very happy for you both!' but could for the moment find nothing else to comment.

Elizabeth now said coolly, 'I should think you would be showing more feeling, Anne; our father is to be congratulated, I am sure!'

Miss Crawford smiled as if the cat had gotten a much-coveted dish of cream, and took Sir Walter's hand. 'I am so glad to think that I can be of use to your father and bring him some comfort in his future years. He is more often fatigued these last few weeks, and I flatter myself that I might do him some good, and bring him into better health.'

While Anne searched for something to reply, Sir Walter patted Miss Crawford's hand gently. 'You will do me good, my dear. This devilish bad fatigue which afflicts me is becoming a millstone upon my neck. I declare I cannot bring myself to move some afternoons. It is a great comfort to have you with me.' He gestured to the footman to pour more coffee. 'Mary eats breakfast with us, Anne, since Crawford is engaged elsewhere this morning — wedding business I collect.'

Anne was grave. 'I see. Have you had Doctor Poole to you yet, Sir? You are not a young man anymore, you know. This fatigue of yours may be due to over exertion, perhaps?'

'Poole? Yes, yes, I had him only yesterday, for all the good he did. He could find nothing the matter with me, and would only have me take the waters twice a day. But you needn't entertain the smallest uneasiness on my account. Mary has my cough well in hand, and she says she will give me a little something for the fatigue if it continues. I must be well for my wedding, or Lady Dalrymple will be in a high concern for me!'

Anne rather thought her father might be in need of something stronger than the Bath waters, or Miss Crawford's recipes, and wished Doctor Thorpe were in town to have him attend her father. She placed little trust in Poole, who was as ancient as Robertson, her father's footman. 'And when is the marriage to take place?' enquired Anne carefully, declining coffee in favour of tea and toast.

'We shall not marry until Elizabeth and Crawford have gone up to Norfolk; family loyalty and natural tenderness dictates that I would do nothing to detract from her triumph. No, we shall wait until August, before the cold weather sets in. I do not a like a bitter day for a wedding. I have often said that a cold day renders even the most handsome face as crimson and coarse as that of a sailor! I shall be married before the winter, and Mary is in agreement, are you not my dear? But you may share the news with your sister, if you will; I am sure it is no secret in Bath already, where gossip seems to be the town past time.'

Anne, thinking that it was better if news of her father's remarriage was kept a secret for as long as possible, was quietly relieved to hear the wedding would be a few weeks off, for she had not decided firmly upon any course of action, and welcomed this delay in Mr Elliot's hearing his suspicions confirmed. 'Of course, Father. And Mary will want to attend, I am sure, since she is to miss Elizabeth's breakfast.'

'Mary? Yes, of course — she may come up to Bath if she can get away from Uppercross. I have decided upon a very quiet service here, and Miss Crawford is in agreement.'

Anne could not help speculating at just what Miss Crawford, with her twenty thousand pounds, could see in an aging widower with little to recommend him in common sense, but she kept these thoughts to herself and merely smiled graciously. 'Lady Russell will be pleased to hear the news. Shall I call in on my way home and tell her?'

'Yes, yes, by all means, do. I flatter myself that she will be glad to see me so well situated after Elizabeth has gone away. Mind you,' added he, patting his betrothed's hand again, 'it is no bad match for Miss Crawford, you will agree; a baronet is quite a catch for any young lady, I fancy. And Lady Russell will be pleased that I shall have someone to keep me company and run my home, now that Elizabeth is to be so happily settled.'

Miss Crawford now rose, and impulsively taking an astonished Anne's hands in her own, said very earnestly, 'My dear Mrs Wentworth — may I call you Anne? I hope you will forgive my forwardness, but I am sure you will be very happy for your father at this moment, and I flatter myself that you may, in time, find it in your heart to love me as almost a sister, rather than to see me as any replacement for the mother you have lost. I would not presume it, but I do rather hope we can be friends, all the same!'

With the warmest looks she entreated Anne, and Anne, having composed herself tolerably, kissed Miss Crawford as sincerely as she could manage. 'I wish you both very happy indeed.'

'I only hope that I can do justice to the rank and situation to which I will be ascending, as your father's wife.' Miss Crawford was all humility as she cast Sir Walter a tender look.

Her father took another bite of his buttered toast and noted, 'The superiority of the Elliot name and rank must not be felt at all to be an impediment to marriage, my dear. Miss Crawford brings a superiority of beauty and the manners of a gentlewoman. I have always said one cannot be overnice in these things; an ill-conceived marriage may be the instrument of downfall. It has the habit of bringing into undue distinction, those who cannot hope to live up to the rank and situation they may attain to, and in the male, it must be a carefully considered thing; to bring undue humiliation to the family name would be deplorable in those whom society looks up to in general. However, I am content in my choice. The name of "Crawford" is not without its own good standing, and I am not sorry to be linked to the family.'

Miss Crawford took Sir Walter's hand again and said composedly, 'You are very good, my dear. May I ever live up to the distinction of being called "Lady Elliot."

So long it had been since Anne had heard that name uttered as anything other than a respectful reference to the mother who had been dear to her, that to hear it mentioned now in this way gave her a pang, and she made some struggle to continue agreeable to Miss Crawford, for that lady could perhaps not know the effect her words had had upon poor Anne's living memory of her mama.

Soon after breakfast had been taken Miss Crawford departed, all smiles and flushed cheeks, leaving Elizabeth and Anne to finish their meal alone. Anne shortly afterward accompanied her sister to Bond-street, and on their making their way down the side street towards the milliners shop, Anne ventured to say as they walked, 'It seems you must lose your new friend almost as soon as you have found her, for you are to Everingham and Miss Crawford will stay here in Camden-place.'

'I hope I should not have lost a friend, for Miss Crawford will not be a stranger at Everingham, I collect. But I hope it will be a very happy match for our father.' Elizabeth's tone was warmer than usual. 'I do not feel, at my time of life, that I can harbour any selfish wishes for our father to remain single, Anne. He is not getting younger. He must have the comfort of a wife to attend him, and I cannot resent him for it. He is fatigued more these days, and Miss Crawford is an excessively sensible woman and handsome enough to satisfy his nice taste. She will be a most tolerant and useful wife to him, and manage his household as admirably as I could have done.'

'What do you know of these Crawfords?' Anne ventured carefully. 'Where are they from, what is their history?'

'You yourself heard it from them both. They were orphaned, lived with their uncle, and Crawford has long been master of his estate. They seem well enough liked among their own acquaintance, and the older sister, Mrs Grant, seems by all accounts a decent female. Although I should never countenance having her visit at Camden-place while I live within its walls,' she added with a faint contempt. 'My father may be now obliged to admit relatives of lesser rank than he should have tolerated before, but that is the evil of marriage, I perceive — one may choose one's marriage partner, but one must suffer the relations which come in tow as a matter of course!'

Anne kept her counsel to herself but pressed her sister. 'Perhaps you are right. But your acquaintance with the Crawfords on the whole has been so short — appearances may be deceptive — I should not like to see you or father made unhappy in a marriage you cannot escape.'

'I think it unnecessary in you to be warning me, Anne,' replied Elizabeth primly. 'Besides, what is there to know? Crawford is a gentleman, and English. His appearance and manners are everything becoming to man of his standing. He may not be a peer but I will not scruple over a detail.'

Anne, as much as she felt defeated, was able to acquit herself of not having made at least *some* attempt to encourage prudence. She left off her questions and followed her sister into Bond-street, in a great unease of spirits overall. She was not only disturbed by the recent visit of Mr Elliot and his threats, but felt herself in a growing anxiety for not having heard anything from Frederick for several weeks now. It was with a heavy heart that she finally, after depositing Elizabeth's purchases at Camden-place, climbed into a chair and gave the direction for Gay-street.

As the sedan-chair set off, she considered her position; she must bear up under the burden of knowing her mother's replacement was soon to be ensconced at Camden-place — a new "Lady Elliot" to give her pangs of distress, and one who was only two or three years older than herself! And if Mr Elliot did as he threatened, how she would be forced to bear the pitying looks of those who knew her father and sister!

Then she thought of Frederick, and the dangers he had risked. She chastised herself for feeling wretched; she had merely dealt with family scandals and domestic upsets, *he* had risked his life! She had been astonished and nonplussed to receive his account of Louisa, and now, to have no communication from him after his last, was perhaps the most distressing of all her trials. She had always detected in his manner a lingering guilt for the way he had deserted Louisa a year ago, even though Louisa had claimed Benwick as quickly as her recovery had allowed. And yet, Frederick had always refused to speak of it to Anne, and had changed the topic quickly when the subjects of Lyme, or Louisa and Benwick were mentioned. Could he now be harbouring a revival of that feeling which once had almost tempted him into an offer? Could their being thrown together so much have been the kindling to fuel the fire of his attachment to her?

Below her hand the baby moved, and she absently rubbed the life within, wishing more than ever to have her fears allayed and her husband home safe.

Thirty

Thursday 20 July, 1815

The wedding went off exceedingly well, and the happy couple departed in a small crowd of well-wishers who had come out into the street to see them off after breakfast. Elizabeth looked glowing and exceedingly elegant in a satin-and-French-lace gown of the palest pink, embroidered in rose, which set off her dark hair and eyes becomingly. Crawford, all restrained manners, and condescending smiles for the crowd, had ushered his bride into the carriage-and-four and they had driven off in state, to take up married life at Everingham. The breakfast, which had been held fashionably late around twelve o' clock, had boasted Lady Dalrymple and her daughter, both of whom had come as a particular favour to Sir Walter. After accompanying the older lady to her carriage and seeing her off again, Sir Walter had sent Anne home to Gay-street, where she might lie down. Now progressed to her fifth month, her rounded belly was prominent, and she had been obliged to swap her gowns for aprons which she could let out to accommodate her growing figure.

At home, however, she could not rest. Her mind was full of a thousand thoughts, and none of them to give her any peace in the following few days. No letter from Frederick appeared for which she so earnestly longed, and the thought of the damage Mr Elliot might do to her sister's happiness plagued her. She made two excuses not to call at Camden-place, since she knew that Lady Russell would suffice in her place, for she was loath to look Miss Crawford in the eye until she could better command her feelings. She called once in Rivers-street, but came away again after only fifteen minutes on account of Lady Russell's only wishing to talk of the impending union of her father to Miss Crawford, and Anne found she was not yet equal to such talk.

Doctor Thorpe had called in, the day following the wedding, to see the Crofts. He brought welcome news of Julia to Anne and Mrs Croft. The young lady, he told them, appeared to be doing well, was now in her fourth month, and in tolerable spirits despite her situation. 'She is in good looks, and walks a great deal about the hills surrounding my aunt's cottage. I have given myself the pleasure of walking with them both, and may reassure you that she is resigned to her situation. I believe Miss Wentworth's presence is a comfort to my aunt who lives alone most of the time. They go on together very happily. The arrangement has benefited them both,' he added, with a smile which held back much, to Anne's penetrating eye.

The Crofts had entreated him to spend a few days but he had declined on account of having to return to Kellynch village, but with the promise of giving himself the pleasure of calling upon them all again in a se'en night since he was engaged to attend a lecture on medicine in London and would stop on his way north. Anne was relieved to know Julia was more resigned to her situation, and privately conjectured to Mrs Croft if there might be a growing attachment for Julia on the part of the young doctor.

Mrs Croft was of the same mind. 'It is not unknown for a girl in Julia's situation to be made an offer of marriage, despite her situation in life; a pretty face and a large enough dowry might go some way to attaching a young man who has a liberality of mind and cannot himself depend upon a tolerable fortune to further himself in life.'

Anne was thoughtful. 'True. Eight hundred pounds per year might be a poor incentive to a gentleman of property and means, but to a gentleman in Thorpe's position, any income above five hundred a year would be looked upon with gratitude. She is a fortunate girl if she has fixed his interest, after all. But if Julia is to have Thorpe, she must learn to conquer her dislike for the man!'

Mrs Croft laughed. 'I collect that may never happen! She is a stubborn, headstrong girl, and will have her own way. She has treated our poor friend quite intolerably since coming to Kellynch. Let us see if he will have *her*, before we see if she will have *him*!'

A few mornings later Anne had been sitting at the piano-forte in the drawing room, idly playing a new sonata she was learning, when there was a clear knocking at the door. The Crofts had gone out to walk in the Pump-room, and she herself was not expecting anyone to call. Puzzled, she stood to receive her guest. A moment later a young man of around one or two-and-twenty in naval uniform was shown into the room. One sleeve of his fine blue naval coat, empty and useless, was pinned to the breast of his garment.

Anne understood immediately the identity of the young man. There could not be two young naval officers with only one arm! 'Mr Price!'

He bowed. 'At your service, Mrs Wentworth.'

'But are you come to visit Admiral Croft? Do you have news of Captain Wentworth?' She could not imagine why he had come.

'Oh, no, Mrs Wentworth, it is yourself I have come to see, although it is with very great apologies for the delay. I do indeed have news — that is to say, I have a letter for you, Ma'am. From Captain Wentworth himself.'

Anne's heart rejoiced. 'You have a letter From Captain Wentworth? How is he? When did you leave him? Tell me he is safe!'

Price looked sheepish. 'Ma'am, I regret I cannot give you news of his current whereabouts or situation now, but four weeks ago, when I left him in Brussels, he was as safe as he could be. Here is your letter, Ma'am.' He pulled the now sullied paper, the seal half unstuck, from his jacket and handed it to her. 'I hope you will grant me the opportunity to explain the delay in its getting to you, Mrs Wentworth, but I will give you a little privacy first to read it, as I know you must have been looking daily for it.'

Anne had already torn open the seal. She moved to the window, ignoring the young man, and drank in every word in the short note.

22 June 1815
Brussels

My too precious Anne,

I hope with all my heart that this letter finds you and our child in good health. How I long to be home with you all at Kellynch, and yet I find myself still under orders and obliged to Malcolm, who relies upon me greatly. I cannot say when I might board my vessel and bring her home to England, but I can assure you, if any landscape can command my attention at this time, it is those white cliffs which cannot be sighted soon enough, for they will guide me home to one who means more than life to me. Rest assured I do everything in my means to hasten our departure here, and yet I regret deeply that we must be apart for another few weeks.

I wish to give you a warning, my dear, for it has come to my notice in the most unexpected and strange way, that the name you speak of in connection with your father and sister in Bath, may be in some way connected with an incident which I learned of recently. I shall relate the facts and you shall decide as you please.

Mr William Price, an officer I met here in Brussels quite by chance, spoke idly to me of his sister's wedding to a family of good repute in Northumberland, by the name of Bertram. This family resides near the village of Mansfield, and Mr Price's sister resides with the Bertrams at Mansfield Park, where she is betrothed to one of the sons.

Mr Price spoke to me of a certain Mr and Miss Crawford, and their uncertain part in a tragic drama which was enacted there not so long ago, and which involved the perhaps deliberate poisoning of the son whom was to marry Miss Price. When I heard of the events there, I was shocked, but it seems certain there was foul play, the reason for which I cannot say, for Price did not give me all the details. But when I heard the name, so similar in circumstances to the Crawfords you spoke of, and who have befriended, and perhaps infiltrated, your father's house, I felt a strong urge to avail you of the story, so that you might be warned if they are one and the same brother and sister Crawford.

I can hardly think such things go on in our enlightened society, and yet, my dear, I know you are familiar enough with the world not be totally shocked by such things. If indeed these Crawfords are the same Crawfords previously of Mansfield village, then I now pass to you these facts and entreat you to discover if these two people are a danger to your father and sister.

I send Louisa home at last, in reasonable spirits, on a mail packet which has come to Ostend, and I have commanded the young man, the Mr Price I spoke of, to accompany her home safely. I entrust this letter into Louisa's hand, and will commission her to deliver it to your hand when she reaches English shores. I trust that I myself will not be far behind her, and in your presence within two months at most.

Meanwhile, my dearest love, I remain ever your devoted
F.W.

The effect of such a letter, after a time of the utmost anxiety on behalf of her husband, was not to be borne. Astonishment, relief, and anxiety for her father now fought for dominance in her thoughts, until she became aware of the young man still standing at a respectful distance, awaiting her attention. She wiped away the moisture which had crept onto her cheeks.

'Forgive me, Mr Price, but I have not had a letter from my husband for some weeks and I have been in a little anxiety for his safety — but all is well, and my mind is at rest. You were very kind to bring me the letter. Tell me, you are the Mr Price my husband speaks of? How do you come to have the letter, rather than Mrs Benwick?'

Price bowed civilly. 'Will you give me leave to explain the delay in getting Captain Wentworth's letter to you?'

Anne consented and indicated to the young man to seat himself, which he did rather awkwardly, on the edge of a chair. He laid his hat on his lap and began to speak.

'My sister, Fanny, lives in at Mansfield Park, which is in Northamptonshire, Ma'am. She is engaged to my cousin, Mr Edmund Bertram. That is, they would have been married by now but for Mr Bertram's being very ill. When your husband entrusted the care of Mrs Benwick to me, to see her home across the channel safely, my original purpose was to see Mrs Benwick home myself, and then to go on to Mansfield to see my sister. Mrs Benwick was most eager to deliver into your hand this letter from your husband, since Captain Wentworth had given it to her and commissioned her with its delivery when she reached Kellynch. But when we arrived at Uppercross, to the home of Mrs Benwick's father, it was discovered that you had gone away to Bath and left no fixed date for your return.'

'But I left my sister at Uppercross with the commission to send on my post!' cried Anne, in some vexation. 'It is too bad of her! I suppose she had forgotten where to send it on. Very well, do go on.'

'I fear you will think very ill of me indeed, Ma'am, for I offered immediately to take the letter and deliver it, since I was happy to pass through Bath before going up to Mansfield. I assured Mrs Benwick that I would see it delivered into your hand. Only, the following day, after I had left Uppercross and begun my journey, I enquired from a friend of mine as to the state of things in Mansfield, and learned that my poor cousin had taken a turn for the worse and was not expected to live! Instead of deviating my course to pass through Bath, I made immediately for Mansfield, Ma'am, and have been there some weeks since. It was because of this that the delivery of your letter was much delayed, for which I am excessively sorry, and I only hope you will forgive me.'

Anne was grave. 'I do forgive you, Mr Price, for you can hardly have detoured from your way when such news demanded your presence so urgently, but do tell me, what of your cousin — have you come away from that place now with your sister a widow? I cannot tell you how excessively sorry I am to hear your sad news.'

'Mr Bertram was thought to be in a great deal of danger, but lives still, Ma'am. Fanny thinks it a miracle, but I think it due to her unswerving care of him. Love may be a stronger medicine, Mrs Wentworth, than all the cures in the world! He is out of danger, but still poorly. I think he escaped with his life.'

I see.' Anne remained in thought for a moment. 'My husband mentioned a Mr and Miss Crawford, and says they may be in some way responsible for your cousin's illness. What do you know of these people?'

Price shook his head. 'I am in two minds, Ma'am, as to their involvement. It was Mr Crawford who was instrumental in getting my promotion only a year ago, and *that* must make me grateful to him, since it gave my sister so much happiness to contemplate. But my sister tells me that my cousin was most assuredly poisoned; they have it in a confession by the kitchen maid who says she was forced into it, by none other than Miss Crawford!'

Anne was astonished. 'Whatever would make a kitchen maid poison one of the family? Why would Miss Crawford do such a heinous and evil thing?'

Price shook his head. 'I cannot say for sure, Ma'am, but it is said that Mr Crawford was carrying on indecently with the maid behind the family's back, and when he fell in love with my sister, and tried to get her to accept an offer, and she refused on account of being in love with my cousin, he must have been bitter enough to take revenge. The maid says that he was so taken up with misery and jealousy against Mr Edmund that he had his sister poison Mr Edmund to teach him a lesson, and threatened to out the maid if she told. It is all very shocking ma'am, and the maid has since lost her place there — but why do you ask? Surely these matters can have little to do with you and your husband?'

'Perhaps, Mr Price, but I have good reason to believe that your two Crawfords are the same Crawfords who have infiltrated my father's house here in Bath. I believe there cannot be two pairs of Crawford siblings, both from Mansfield.'

Price was grave. 'Then verily I believe they must be the same pair, Ma'am. What will you do?'

'Very little that I can see, Mr Price, for one Crawford has already made my sister his bride, and they are gone away to live at his estate, while the other is now engaged to be married to my father!'

Price's countenance paled. 'Then you must prevent an association which will, by all that has passed, bring your family into disrepute if nothing else! It means your father may marry a would-be murderess! Or at the very least, align himself with a female of the most amoral character!'

'But this is shocking indeed—' Anne's hand now flew to her mouth. 'God help us! No, it could not be, surely? My father's cough! His fatigue! I had wondered what her object could be in fixing his affections — how she could attach herself to a man almost twice her age when she could so easily have any man of the same consequence — I hope I am mistaken, but perhaps I understand her object, now, after all! Is there no end to the evil let loose upon our family?' She was distressed, shocked, hoping beyond hope that her suspicions were not true, but after a pause, with a great presence of mind she obliged herself to remain calm and asked, 'How do you think, Mr Price? What say you? Do you suspect my father in any danger?'

Price understood little of her meaning, but enough to collect the matter was of some urgency. He advised her to act decisively and warn her father. 'Or I cannot answer that he won't live to regret the alliance, Mrs Wentworth, if all that has been levelled against these two Crawfords is true!'

'Mr Price, you have done me a great service today, and perhaps my father an even greater one. But may I presume upon your first kindness and ask of you another?'

'I am at your service, Mrs Wentworth.'

'Will you attend me to my father's house and give an account of all you have told me?'

Price was most obliging. 'By all means, Ma'am, if you think it will do any good.'

'I have no great influence with my father,' she replied grimly, 'but if you will tell your story, Sir, together we may be able to persuade him that he is some danger of being poisoned to death!'

Thirty One

Tuesday 25 July, 1815

Williams-street, Bath.

Mary Crawford was in high spirits, although she was at all times of a serene countenance in the presence of her betrothed. Sir Walter had been gained; she could want for nothing more at the present time, but to bask, yes bask, in the folly of others, and in the cleverness of her own mind. Poor Sir Walter! He could not be blamed for falling for her charms; she had made them so available — she had fixed his interest with her will. She harboured no resentment for him other than a mild disgust for his belief in the power of his own consequence. Still, if he was hastened off to where he was already going, it was nobody's fault but his own. She would be careful not to be too precipitous, however, but allow at least a year before he became ill enough to alarm his friends for his health.

Henry, before he had gone away, had been admonishing her over it, however. 'Take care, Mim. It is one thing to provoke a little regret by making Edmund Bertram ill, and I will not say he has not deserved it as much as Fanny Price has deserved to suffer to see him brought so low, but it is entirely another thing to take it as far as you mean to. That is another level of playing with lives, and I would not like to see you regret anything you would wish undone.'

'Do not pretend you wish undone what I did for you, Haro. I own I did find a certain satisfaction in seeing Edmund suffer, but my prime object was to hurt pious little Fanny Price; she ought to have learned humility! Silly, simple girl! She thought herself too good for you and now she must suffer for it. It has merely been a small dose of humility that we have served to them both, nothing to cause lasting harm.'

'I hear he has been in a very bad way, although I cannot find any sympathy for him.'

'Edmund will survive,' she said in a bored tone. 'It was only a very *tiny* dose of bitter almond and black rose.'

'And Sir Walter?'

She had shrugged. 'He is not young — a small dose, every now and again, will keep his family in the expectation of his remaining unwell, and when he gives up this life and passes to the next world, I shall have the comfort of knowing I was only hastening what nature would have done in any case. His skin is waxy and his pallor is a sure sign of liver rot — really, I will be saving him from the much worse fate of a drawn-out illness. His cough will be much improved from my tonics, until it returns, and with it a loss of health which only naturally follows one in advancing years. Really, I am doing nothing which nature will not do in a more painful way.'

Henry had not quite been persuaded. 'Then let him decline naturally, sis! You and I of all people intimate with the Elliots know Sir Walter's two greatest weaknesses — a taste for being made love to by means of the most overblown flattery, and second, his weakness when it comes to his belly. Encourage him on both parts, Mim; there is nothing that a pretty woman, armed with compliments and claret and as much liver pate that he can take, cannot do for her own benefit. He is an old fool! You already have him eating from your hand — now have him taking as much rich food and drink as you can, and I will vouch for it he won't last longer than a year or two!'

Mary regarded him with a little moue. 'Yes, I own you may be right after all; perhaps it would be unwise to risk being discovered. His daughters are none of them clever enough to guess — except Anne, who is sly enough to conceal a fine mind behind that simpering acquiescence she affects with those around her, and that disingenuous pretence of modesty with whomever she speaks — but perhaps on the whole, it would be best not to put our hard-won gains into any risk — we have almost everything in hand. I should not like to give up the life I had envisioned for myself and for you, Haro, despite Sir Walter or Elizabeth. We shall succeed, we shall put the rumours which follow us to bed with our respective marriages, and the way will be clear for a life content with our circumstances.'

'*Will* you be happy, dear Mim?' Henry idly drew a finger up the beautiful white skin of her bare arm. 'I should like you to be content. But I cannot promise to be a *very* good boy — a marriage such as the one my bride looks toward, I confess, will not make me very happy for long — I will always need my distractions!'

'You have been too much influenced by our uncle!' She had relented, then. 'But you know I am weak when it comes to you! As long as we are never truly apart, I can be happy enough as "Lady Elliot" so long as I am not required to play that part for very long. Nor should I wish to give my husband an heir. I shall leave that sort of thing to you. But there, I have my recipes — there are ways of making a man lose interest.'

'Then be as prudent as you can in this course, Mim, for if you are discovered, it would mean the loss of every advantage we have gained.'

Mary had reassured him of her discretion, and sent him off to Everingham with the new-made Mrs Crawford. She had no intention of losing all she had gained — she and Henry had done what they both needed to do. The rumours which dogged them would run their course and die away, and once things had returned to peace, she, too, could return to the life she had been cast from — she would not give up her good dinners, her large assemblies, and her freedom to come and go at Everingham without open talk. She would not be forced to go abroad and hide her face and start again, when Henry and all her friends and favourite amusements were to be found right here! No, marriage to Sir Walter was the letter of introduction, the calling card, that would bring to her all that was in jeopardy now, and nothing except Henry himself had the power to curtail her amusement in carrying out the manoeuvers she needed to make in order to secure her comfort, and her future felicity.

In marrying, she did not seek tenderness, nor did she harbour other, more foolish, expectations. She would not love, it was not in her to love; in Henry was all the devotion she required for contentment, and all the object for her tenderness. Love for anyone else was a folly she could not engage in. But she wished to know herself affective — to make her presence felt. As much as Henry liked to put a little hole in the hearts of young and silly girls, she too, wished to sting a little, to feel that she had power in the world — she would make a poor example of a simpering wife to the likes of the Dalbystons and Smythes and Dixons to which Leticia had wanted to marry her off — no, she sought over all things to have autonomy, to have the power to move the chess pieces herself, rather than to be moved about. Life had taught her harsh lessons, and she had been buffeted about in the past; losing her parents at a young age had taught her to safeguard her heart at any cost. But she had not counted on suffering another kind of blow, either.

Mary had recently suffered a blow to her pride — indeed she had come to Bath with a heart iced over with residual bitterness At Mansfield, it had not been the absence of a tender regard which had made her bitter, but the humiliation of finding herself powerless, and by her own stupid mistake. She had suffered a great disappointment in herself for not having been more circumspect. She had thought her prize in hand and found it was not. Pride wounded, she had hit out, both for her own sake and for Henry's. The application of a little revenge had been a powerful antidote to disgrace.

Her object, which had been to marry well and soon, was now at last in hand, and her spirits were revived. She would not, however, make the same mistakes. She had formerly been angry at her own folly in not fixing firmly enough the affections of her chosen prize, but now she had been sure of her maneuvers, and had played her game with a lighter hand, and a more circumspect eye. She had fixed Sir Walter's regard, had formed her aspect to his exact ideal; at three-and-thirty, she had been everything wanted — elegant, handsome, and capable — she had become his lost "Elizabeth".

Her brother, too, had played his part well. Not well enough, however, for Mary to have any anxiety over Henry's being in love with Elizabeth, for she knew his heart belonged to her. She was willing to allow him a little amusement taming his new wife to his own will over time, to bring that haughty cool exterior into some semblance of humility, but even so, he would always be her own. And as for Elizabeth being in love with Henry, it did not signify. If the glacial Miss Elliot had been led to care at all for Henry, Mary consoled her jealousy by contending that her new sister would sooner or later be rendered at least a *little* unhappy by the alliance, for she knew that Elizabeth was as blinded by her own selfishness as anyone could be; her hands firmly pressed to her eyelids, that lady saw only that which she wanted to see. Well, she would see soon enough. She would discover the folly she had committed in believing herself loved by a man who had long ago proven incapable of truly loving any woman but Mary herself. Miss Elliot would suffer a little and finally learn to be content — after all, she had secured Everingham, a husband to keep her in bonnets and gowns and shoes, and in all probability, she would soon have the satisfaction of a child to amuse her. It was as much as any woman on the verge of spinsterhood might reasonably hope for, and more, Mary comforted herself, than Miss Elizabeth Elliot deserved.

Thirty Two

Camden-place, Bath

In the drawing room at Camden-place, Mary sat opposite Lady Russell, who had been called upon to play chaperone for the remaining days until they would marry. Mary had made sure to look her most charming. She had put on a very elegant turquoise silk gown with deep red roses decorating the neckline, which set off her fair English skin fetchingly as she sat beside Sir Walter. She felt with satisfaction his eye constantly upon her form, intently staring, and then looking away again. She had done her part exceedingly well. She returned her thoughts to the conversation. They had all been speaking of Henry and Elizabeth. Mary had been speaking with a great sincerity, of the strength of her brother's affections.

'...and Henry, quite from the moment of his meeting Elizabeth, had taken pains to be on terms with her; I believe, knowing his heart so well as I do, as a sister who has his dearest interests at heart, that there will never be a man more determined in his affections and regard as my brother. Once his affections are fixed, it is impossible for him to regard any other woman with interest; he would not have anyone my sister suggested to him, and he is known to be a confirmed bachelor in town for all his eight-and-twenty years!'

Lady Russell concurred. 'If she can make him as happy as he seems to have made her, then they will both do very well, I believe. Did you give him any intelligence of her before he had met her those weeks ago? Had you not made him familiar with her character?'

Miss Crawford smiled serenely. 'Not at all, for I never like to influence anything Henry does. He is entirely his own man. In point of fact, Lady Russell, I had quite given up on his ever finding someone to meet his overnice tastes; no one was ever elegant enough, or of the understanding which he requires to engage his interest. No, he quite astonished me when after I had brought him to Camden-place to introduce him, he began to question me closely of my dear friend, and enquire as to her tastes, her manner of passing time here, and her history, of which I could tell him little, of course — but it seems there is nothing which he could find any fault with for now he is a man in love, and she will be adored for the rest of her life. What an outcome, and to have Everingham, no small property, to make a home of — dear Elizabeth is a fortunate woman to have won the affections of man like my brother!'

She poured the tea, which she had prepared with her own special brew, adding just enough jasmine to impart a fragrant air. She handed Sir Walter his cup, which he took placidly. 'Cake, my love?'

'Thank you, my dear.' He took a large slice of the rich confection. 'Lady Russell, I hope you will accompany Mary and myself to call on Lady Dalrymple tomorrow morning. I had hoped to ask Anne but she has not been here above twice in the last week; it really is too bad of her! I cannot imagine what business must be so pressing as to prevent her from keeping her duty to her family, to Lady Dalrymple, our esteemed cousin but, in any case, I wish to present Miss Crawford. Lady Dalrymple has expressly encouraged it. May I hope for your presence?'

'By all means Sir Walter, if you wish it. I am always at your service. Anne is only a little busy with some previous engagements, I collect. I am sure you will see her in this house quite soon. But Miss Crawford, do give me the details of the wedding — what are you to wear and eat, and whom shall you have to the breakfast, your first as "Lady Elliot"?'

Mary had just begun a placid reply involving milk-pork, plumb-cake and warm chocolate, when the doors opened into the drawing room and the footman intoned, 'Mrs Wentworth and Mr Price, Sir.'

While Lady Russell uttered a delighted exclamation that her prophecies were so soon fulfilled, Anne, followed by a stranger in a naval uniform, stepped into the room. She was still putting off her bonnet, and she spoke haltingly. 'Good day Miss Crawford, father. Oh, Lady Russell, I am very glad you are here, when I expected — but father, this is Lieutenant Price, a friend of Frederick's.'

Sir Walter, who had become more inured to the presence in his drawing room of a mere naval man, now that his tenant Admiral Croft had been to call there twice, said only slightly impatiently, 'Yes, yes, very glad I am sure, Sir; what is your business with me? Anne? I had not expected you today. What is it that I can do to help your friend, or are you bringing everyone and anyone to congratulate me on my good fortune, now?'

Anne, blushing for her father's manner, replied anxiously, 'I think you had better hear Mr Price's story, Sir, and judge for yourself if I have done right to bring him here.'

Miss Crawford however, whom to Lieutenant Price was not an unfamiliar face, had stood with a sudden rush. Price gave her a polite bow, but she stood looking as if she did not know quite where to turn. Her face was unusually suffused with pink.

Sir Walter looked around in some astonishment. 'You know this person, my dear?'

Collecting herself a little Miss Crawford said with strained gaiety, 'We are somewhat acquainted, Sir Walter. But in no circumstances of great interest. We merely met at Mansfield Park, the home of Mr Price's sister. At one time Fanny and I were intimate friends; I regret that this is no longer the case.' She made a little *moue*, as if in disapproval.

Mr Price stood with his hat in hand and addressed Sir Walter. 'I think, Sir, there is a story which might interest you to hear, and which may have a great significance on your future happiness, if you will permit me to tell it.'

Lady Russell, intercepting Anne's glance, and always aware of her duty to the family since the departure of the former Lady

Elliot, spoke up. She was firm. 'Miss Crawford, I see you are preparing to depart. Would you leave Sir Walter's side so readily now when it is clear you are wanted here?'

Miss Crawford put down the bonnet she had seized up. 'Of course,' she replied in tranquil tones. 'I merely did not wish to intrude upon family business. These things have a habit of becoming sordid, and I know Sir Walter values his privacy. I am not yet "Lady Elliot" and would never wish to assume my presence in private affairs of the family was a matter of course.'

Anne was determined. 'Nevertheless, I should think this particular story will interest you, too, Miss Crawford, if you will be so good as to stay a moment,' for the lady had again put up her bonnet upon her head, as if to take her departure as soon as she might be allowed to slip out.

Miss Crawford's fingers paused, her lips now thinned into a line. 'Very well, if you like.'

Sir Walter, still in some perplexity, waited, while the young lieutenant began to relate his story. Henry's pursuit of Fanny Price was related, and the subsequent illness of Tom Bertram, the older son and heir to Mansfield. When he mentioned that Miss Crawford had exited that house with no hope of ever returning, on account of her cruel and evil speculations as to the impending death of the heir, and his title and wealth passing to Edmund, upon whom she had set her sights, all gazes turned to her.

Miss Crawford now assumed the countenance of one caught out with a hand in the snuff box, but Sir Walter was all in a denial. 'I cannot allow this — your insults to my fiancé — I cannot countenance it — a mistake has certainly been made — but how can this affect me, pray?' His tone was haughty coldness.

'Father, there is more, if you will but listen a little longer,' pleaded Anne.

The final part was told, of the poisoning, the suspicions of foul play, the confession of the kitchen girl, and all the evidence on hand which seemed to expose the real characters of the Crawford brother and sister. All was laid bare. All that was evil and shocking was out, to confront the lady who now sat coldly on the sofa in front of them all.

The skin which had so recently been brushed with pale pink upon the cheeks, had turned waxen. Her lips had been rendered pale, but they now curved into a smile unfit for the circumstances. She gave a sort of cool laugh. 'It was only a little joke we played on Mr Bertram, truly. A small tease, in the nature of any rejected lover — it must be gotten over, surely!'

Anne was angry. 'This Mr Bertram whom you poisoned, has suffered, by all accounts, to an unbearable degree! How can you vindicate your actions as merely an amusement?'

'And if any of this is true, what of it? I did only what duty and tenderness required of me! I was a sister to my brother; I was a champion of the one treated unjustly! Your sister,' she added coldly, turning to Price, 'treated my poor brother with so much contempt that he was barely himself for nearly a year afterward! Now he has found sincere attachment to my friend, the daughter of a fine family, and you come to disturb our peace, expelling your poisonous words, your accusations, and your evil intentions, insinuating yourself into the minds and hearts of those whom you now treat with the injustice that your sister showed my brother!'

Price was bitter, his tone naturally injured. 'Injustice, Miss Crawford? How can you say that for Fanny to refuse your brother was unjust, after he showed his true nature by committing a crime against the family of Bertram by taking his revenge on Maria Bertram, the poor foolish Mrs Rushworth whom he corrupted after making love to my sister? Where was his justice then? And where was the justice when you slipped poison into the hand of a poor innocent child, and bribed her into silence on pain of dismissal, to poison my cousin Edmund? A mere amusement? How can you say it was a harmless joke? Do you call that justice? I cannot but call it cruelty, nay, evil indeed!'

Miss Crawford, deathly white, now had no words to utter up in her defense, but after a moment, managed, 'Of the latter accusation you have no proof, Mr Price. And yet, this is how you repay the kindness of my brother! You dare call me evil, after he secured you an advancement in the navy, going to great trouble on your behalf, yet you then go on to call him a murderer, and me an instrument of murder? Shame!'

'I perceive that your only defense is to invoke the guilt of others, Miss Crawford. Then I shall say nothing, for your defense by its cruel thoughtlessness for my sister and Mr Bertram, is enough to vindicate them yet!'

All that was necessary to be revealed had been revealed, and it had had its evil effect. Sir Walter began to perceive that he might have been tricked, and that he had been a dupe of Miss Crawford. He had never been a man of deep feeling and yet he was not shallow enough to be oblivious to the humiliation to which he had a natural right in the circumstances. He now suffered from great disappointment and regret, and said so to Miss Crawford.

But when Miss Crawford took her leave from the room shortly afterwards, with only the parting remark that she had suffered 'enough pretty lectures to last her a life time, and she would take her leave of another one, and how Sir Walter would regret the severing of ties when he at last became sensible and understood her motives to have been quite harmless,' he had nothing to reply and after she had left, he only turned to the room and said, 'Well. We must, I think, pity poor Elizabeth, to have such a sister-in-law! How I have been duped — a most deplorable female!'

'Do you really think Miss Crawford capable of deliberate harm, Mr Price?' Anne had been doubtful that perhaps it was after all only a case of a little amusement gone awry.

'I only know my cousin has barely escaped a far greater injury, Mrs Wentworth. Poor Fanny might have had more to lament than only a fear of losing my cousin.'

'Then thank God she did not! If it were not for your coming to bring me a letter, Mr Price, we would never have guessed the worst of it. Perhaps we have prevented a crime more horrible than what has already been perpetrated!'

Lady Russell stayed many hours with Sir Walter after Anne and Mr Price were gone away, consoling and offering as much advice in retrospect as she felt might comfort, but in vain did she make any real headway with his damaged pride. He had only to submit, sit upon the couch and be outwardly composed for a few minutes, before he was up and pacing the room, with cries of, 'Whatever would Lady Dalrymple think of him, and she had already been invited particularly to the breakfast, and he hoped keenly that they were not too much out of time to withdraw the expensive order Mary herself had placed for the supply of pheasant and pork and chocolate, for he had no stomach for the stuff himself after the events of the day.'

There were sighings, too, over the memory of the former Lady Elliot of Kellynch Hall, for while Sir Walter had not been a passionate man, and the marriage had not been entirely a happy one, the jolt of the rude transition from single to coupled-up, to single again, all in the space of a fortnight, brought back the memories of a time when he had had the benefit of marital companionship. Lady Russell assured him he would not suffer for want of company, however, for she would be constant visitor to Camden-place while she was at liberty to stay in Bath.

Doctor Thorpe at this time returned to Bath for two nights and made it his chief pleasure to call upon his friends there; the Crofts and Anne received him with sincere friendship and he was entreated to pay a call to Camden-place, as a friend, to look over Anne's father and pronounce him untouched by any ill-effects at the hand of Miss Crawford.

Sir Walter took this visit in a good deal more humour than was expected, and Doctor Thorpe arrived back at Gay-street with the best of news.

'Your father is sound as a horse, Mrs Wentworth, but for a slight touch of rheumatism which is quite natural at his time of life. You have nothing to fear — he is as hale as any man of five-and-fifty I have put my listening cone to. If the lady in question was up to any mischief with her potions, you have caught it in time. Besides a strange aroma of roses, which is an odd ingredient in cough syrup, the bottle you showed me seems only the usual type of "wife's remedy" in common household use.'

'And my father's fatigue?'

'Appears to be improving daily, Mrs Wentworth. All in all, I pronounce your father as fit as he can be for his age.'

This news gave Anne some relief for her anxiety for Sir Walter, for she had been afraid some lasting harm might have been done by Miss Crawford's potions. Whether they contained any ingredients designed to harm, she could not say for sure, and she supposed that it would be impossible to discover it if they had, but at any rate, her father had ordered away the remaining half-bottle of Miss Crawford's cough remedy with as much distrust for its formulator as for its contents.

'Dreadful, intolerable woman! And her remedy did nothing very significant for my cough at any rate; I hold these old women's brews as ineffectual nonsense beside the real wisdom of science! There is nothing to hold a candle to Poole's tincture of Opium and oil of Vitriol!'

Anne was even more gratified to find her private speculations regarding her husband's niece had been firmly grounded. Thorpe had confided in them directly he had entered the house.

'I won't prevaricate, you are too much my friends to do that. I wish to tell you that I have made an offer of marriage to your niece, Mrs Croft,' he advised them gravely, 'and it has been accepted. Julia will become my wife before the child is born, and I shall adopt the infant as my own.'

Amid the astonished cries of, 'But how wonderful!' and '—a lucky girl indeed, fortunate, she cannot deserve such an offer, you are too kind!—' he managed to insert for the benefit of them all, 'I hope I am not so illiberal-minded as to judge a young woman with no knowledge of the world, and no mother to guide her, for being misled by a scoundrel. I know Julia has been a high-spirited girl but I flatter myself that with the right application of wisdom and patience, she might blossom and flower into a very becoming young woman, one whom I shall be proud to call my very own wife — she is exceedingly pretty, and her manners are always pleasant and everything humble these days — I do believe she has turned a new leaf, Mrs Croft, and I count myself lucky — she is everything I regard as necessary in a wife.'

Anne, unlike the Crofts, was not all amazement at this speech, having privately suspected his increasing regard, but she still could not help asking, 'And what of Julia's father, Mr Edward Wentworth — does he give his blessing?' Anne was happy to find that Wentworth was approving of the match.

'He kindly said he could not hope for a happier outcome.' Thorpe was all humility. 'I can only be grateful to have been able to provide one. Still, I would not have done so if my affections for Julia had not long been fixed!'

Mrs Croft had said afterwards of her niece's luck, 'Edward has been prosperous in his own way in life and he has only two daughters to divide his little fortune among; Julia will bring no paltry sum to the marriage, for the daughter of a humble clergyman, and she is perhaps fortunate to have been able to do so. Who can tell if she would have found a husband in her circumstances without such a dowry. But it will be put to the best use, for we believe Silas Thorpe is a man of great talent and may go far in his career, especially if he removes to London. It has not been unknown for a progressive-minded man to make a successful living from medicine in the city, where there are more silly, wealthy women to fancy themselves ill, than country gents too hale to call for a doctor! Besides which, he is as progressive a man as the admiral and I have ever met!'

The greatest relief for Anne's burden had been knowing that Mr Elliot would now never need to reveal the truth about Henry Crawford and harm her sister's happiness. Providence, having taken a hand in the matter, had been kind to her family, and although Anne did not harbour any great warmth of feeling for her sister or father, her own sense of duty to her father, her strong sense of family loyalty, had teased her unkindly with the thought that she might have been somehow implicated in the misery her sister have would suffered if such a character had been revealed.

She was sure Elizabeth would already have enough of her own evils to contend with at home, in the form of a husband who might be more indifferent to her than she had suspected, without any added surplus of anxiety knowing Crawford had a love-child somewhere in the world; but such things were never talked of, and she was confident that Doctor Thorpe would protect both Julia and the Elliots by keeping this intelligence to himself.

As for Elizabeth and Crawford's happiness in marriage — that would rely upon what they would make of it and Elizabeth was not unworldly enough to understand that ignorance is sometimes the least evil to choose, when it comes to one's marriage partner.

To be in harmony, in action and thought, with one's spouse, was a gift which was bequeathed to few, and Anne was grateful above all things that she and Frederick had always been of one mind and one heart. It had been six weeks since she had felt the stirrings of doubt, six weeks since she had been stung at his writing of Louisa with such compliments and admiration as would make any wife jealous for the love of her husband, and because of it, she had been momentarily insensible; weighed down with burdens, she had foolishly let herself doubt. But six weeks had been enough to convince her that she was mistaken and foolish. She wished him home with all her heart, and the life stirring in her belly would lead him back to her.

Thirty Three

Tuesday 29 August, 1815

Kellynch Hall.

Autumn had come unseasonably early to Somersetshire. Eight weeks had seen Kellynch submit to the passing of the seasons in its usual dignified way. The house now stood quietly in the quickly cooling air as its inhabitants went about their business. Trees had decked themselves in oranges and reds all around the house, and the arms of the surrounding great oaks had begun to shed, growing increasingly mighty and bare in their sparse clothing.

Anne walked below their branches, her booted feet carrying her through the piles of bright leaves banked below, and through which she strolled almost daily. She had long since put off her constraining gowns and swapped them for aprons, and even then, the burgeoning life inside her continued to push out her muslins in a way that she marvelled at daily. At seven months with child, she had become womanly as she had never been before, the blush of her cheeks and the light in her eyes more sure of themselves than they had ever been. It had been a most eventful year, and in the autumn of it, she was glad to settle into a newfound peace, in the arms of her dear home, Kellynch.

She had dealt with the alarm of war, with Frederick's going away, Julia's scandal, and the national defeat of Bonaparte at Waterloo. She had been obliged to consider the possibility of

Frederick's still being in love with Louisa, she had born the distasteful and humiliating visit from Mr William Elliot and the subsequent anxiety over his threats, and born the evil of the events and persons which had brought her father into personal danger. Despite all these trials to her nerves, she was content. She looked for Frederick's return every day, but even so, she had yielded to the demands of the child inside her and had given way to the peace only mothers may understand. She felt no anxiety, but a steady peace which told her all would be well and that what would be, would be.

All was well both at Uppercross and at Kellynch. Sir Walter had written to Elizabeth a letter most benign, containing neither a cross word nor an oath from beginning to end, only saying that Miss Crawford, with the first and natural right of refusal had decided upon another course, and had left Bath shortly after Elizabeth's wedding, to marry Sir Lionel Dalbyston, who would provide her with none of the consequence she would have thereafter received as "Lady Elliot", but that he was not bitter, and would be sufficed by the company of Lady Russell and Lady Dalrymple.

At Uppercross, celebrations ensued as Henrietta was announced to be with her first child, and even Mary had written Anne at Kellynch, giving as good an account of herself as she ever had, with no mention of her usual buffet of illnesses and complaints, and only remonstrating once, that it was 'such a great pity that Father had to be sending Miss Crawford away — it was inconsiderate! — how fickle men are, Anne, do you not agree? — and just when I had thought to ask for a receipt for tooth-powder from her; but no matter now, I suppose — I am used to being quite forgot when you are all gone to Bath to amuse yourselves!'

On one point, Anne could not be sanguine however. Lieutenant Price had visited the Musgroves three times, his agreeable manners and handsome appearance making all the females in the vicinity a little in love with him. His conduct was all that must be pleasing, his conversation informed and his high spirits engaging. Even Mary had only good things to say of him. Anne discerned, however, that his object must be Louisa Benwick. She wondered what Louisa's feelings were but if he had visited three times, his interest in her was clear to all.

When Anne herself had gone up to Uppercross for a few days, Mary had mentioned it at dinner. 'Henrietta thinks he will offer for her soon, but Louisa won't say anything on the subject and refuses to say if she has any regard for him. She has gotten vexingly coy since her loss! I think it excessively romantic, do not you, Anne? I must say, it is excessively satisfying to have everything so neatly wrapped up, Henrietta with child and Louisa with such prospects after so much has happened.'

'But it is so soon after her losing Benwick,' mused Anne, 'that I cannot regard *her* affections to be as fixed as *his* appear to be. She cannot have forgotten Benwick so soon! It would not do; indeed, it is unseemly, for it has not yet been four months since. She will wear black at least another two months! If Lieutenant Price means to offer, I hope he is a man of patience, for he must wait for a respectable period.'

'Dear me!' cried Mary. 'Those silly outdated customs hardly signify with young people, and if I dare say so, my sister-in-law is as silly a girl as ever there was, although I have all the filial respect in the world for both of my sisters-in-law. But I have always held that Louisa engaged herself entirely too hastily to Benwick, being so ill, and so far removed from being herself at the time. Mind you, Louisa has always had a fine naval fervour which makes her quite suited to be a sailor's wife. It would not be entirely unacceptable for her to put off her bombazine in perhaps two or three months! I am sure none of us expect her to be miserable for an eternity; after all she was barely married three months before becoming a widow. Such a short period cannot signify at all, Anne!'

Anne had little to reply to her sister, but privately counted herself fortunate that her own husband would never think to replace her with as much speed, nor she him, should tragedy befall them. Time would tell as to the strength of Louisa's affections for her departed husband, and until then, Anne would visit, and do all she could to shore up the young widow. She had seen Louisa only once since she had arrived at Uppercross, and she had been astonished at the changes wrought in the once high-spirited girl. Frederick had been quite justified in his praise, and yet, if Louisa was encouraging the visits of Lieutenant Price, Anne privately found herself disappointed for the memory of the Captain Benwick who had once been her friend.

At Kellynch, however, life was returning to normal. The Crofts had returned home, the Admiral's gout much improved with the application of Doctor Thorpe's new therapies, and Mrs Croft was sanguine and easy in her mind for her niece.

'I can't imagine anything better, in the way it has all worked out. Edward writes to say he is very pleased with his new son-in-law to be, and that Julia is to be married very soon, very quietly of course, and that they will return to Shropshire before the baby is born. Doctor Thorpe's friends are all in other parts, so there will be no questions asked, and as for Julia, they will say she was abroad and married there. All will be done quietly so as to bring no disrepute upon either of them. I think she will make an excellent doctor's wife!'

Anne smiled. 'I collect you may be right! She has the strong will needed to bear his long absences, and will have the pleasure of a child to connect her with happiness when her husband is away in the evenings.'

Mrs Croft took her hand. 'And you, Anne, will have your own child soon, to do the same. I cannot tell you what pleasure it gives me to count myself sister to a woman who has impressed me with her fortitude under so much duress! My brother is lucky to have you, my dear.'

'You are very kind, Mrs Croft.'

'And if you do not give way and call me by my given name, I shall lose patience with you. Have we not shared enough of family sorrows and joys to be sisters?'

Anne could not hold out against such an argument, and consented at once to call her sister by name. 'I shall do so, not to please you, but because if I did not, it would not answer toward myself! I confess it would give me more pleasure than anything — except of course, to see Frederick home again at last!'

'And *that* will not be long, my dear, I will vouch for it. Now, let us to the garden, for you promised to help me with choosing some plants to take up to Lady Russell tomorrow.'

Lady Russell had been returned to Kellynch only a few days, having spent as much of her time in Bath as it was possible, and that time chiefly in the comforting of poor Sir Walter. 'Although I suspect it is more a matter of his pride than his heart which has been the primary victim of Miss Crawford,' that lady noted the next afternoon. 'I only hope your poor sister has found some kind of happiness in her position at Everingham. With such a sister-in-law, I wonder she can be! But then, Elizabeth has always had a strong mind and a strong will. She will find her own peace, I suspect.'

Mrs Croft, now quite decided in her opinion of Anne's godmother, and being quite willing to love all those who valued Anne as highly as she did herself, was happy to engage herself to Lady Russell when invited to accompany her that afternoon to walk.

Anne, however, declined to walk with them both. 'I am always a little fatigued these days,' she smiled, 'and I confess the notion of sitting at home in the morning room with a novel is more attractive to me than walking about. I hope you will both excuse me. The baby is excitable this afternoon. I find myself at the mercy of its kicking feet!'

She was most happily excused, and she returned home, being conveyed in Lady Russell's carriage. At home she took up her volume of Wordsworth and sat upon the sofa in quiet contemplation. Soon her meditation was interrupted.

Robertson had knocked politely and entered, and was holding something in his hand. 'Good afternoon, Miss Anne.'

She smiled. 'I will always be "Miss Anne", I perceive! It is fortunate that my husband takes no offence by it! Ah, I see you smile, because you know very well you have us in your power, George! Very well, what have you there?' She looked with great curiosity upon the paper in his hand, folded into a suspicious-looking shape.

He handed it to her and she took it gently. The little paper was folded neatly into the shape of a boat, the kind which children fold and cast upon a little body of water, as if it were a ship of which they were captain. 'Oh! But where did you find this?' she cried with pleasure.

'Well, Miss Anne, I cannot say I *found* it, exactly, rather I was given it,' he said mysteriously.

Anne eyed him with a bright, coffee-brown eye. 'Is that so? By whom, if I may ask?'

Robertson twinkled back at her. 'By a gentleman, Miss.'

Anne was calm. 'Where was this gentleman, George? Is he still here?'

Robertson pointed out the window. 'There, in the garden, Miss Anne. Behind those trees.'

She perceived he could barely contain his smiles. She bit her lip gravely. 'Very well, George. Thank you.' Taking the little folded paper boat with her, she left the sofa, and ventured out into the garden, a very unusual look upon her countenance. Her cheeks were gently suffused with the pink of happiness. Her white morning dress was not suited to the outdoor temperatures, but she pulled her blue woollen shawl more firmly around her shoulders and made her way along a line of poplar trees and towards the shrubbery, where she could see a flash of blue in the arbour there. Rounding the corner, she paused.

He stood, with his back to her, but when she uttered a small sigh, he turned. Instantly they were reunited in each other's arms.

After a longish time, they pulled apart.

He laughed in joy. 'Dear girl! How large you have become!'

She laughed with him, her brown eyes dancing. 'Is that any way to greet your wife? But I own it is true. It was all your doing, you know, so you must put up with a fat wife now.'

'But not forever.' He kissed her, then ran his hand over her belly. 'How does our child?'

'She is doing well.'

'She?'

'I feel her moving inside me. She tells me all manner of things. She told me you were coming home, you know.'

'She is an astute child, then. Like her mama.'

She sighed. 'Oh Frederick! I missed you terribly.'

'I am home now.' He kissed her tenderly.

After a time, she stepped back. 'And what of Louisa?'

He took her hands. 'She will make a fine wife for someone, if she remarries.'

'I thought — for a little while — that—'

'My dearest girl. I was a fool once, but never more. It is true that in being confronted with Louisa again, I was racked with guilt — my own part in Benwick's death, and her being so gracious in light of all that had gone before — she did not blame me at all, or harbour any resentment, but I own it undid me for a time.'

'And now?'

He laughed a mirthless laugh. 'I suffered nothing but foolish and passing guilt for the past, which receded as quickly as it had taken over me.'

Anne lifted her eyes to his. 'You do not regret your choices?'

'My dearest girl! All I ever valued, the treasures I have claimed in my career at sea, all the gems and valuable things that have passed through my fingers — I would not exchange you for *them*, for all the world. You have seized my soul. When I offered myself to you again, it was with the fullness of my mind and heart, and nothing has changed. You own my soul — do with it what you may, but never say I am unfaithful!'

He bent his head, and after a long interval and many sighs, they parted slightly to link arms, and began to walk back towards the house.

'What will we name her?' Wentworth was smiling down at her.

Anne smiled back up at him, her eyes wide and clear. 'Sophia Elizabeth, if you like it.'

'My sister, and your mother. I do like it.'

At last Anne was content and all there was left was to do was to sigh again, and tuck his arm closer to her side. All the astonishment, the suspense, and the anguish of the past months could be gently dissipated by his being home. She felt that she had never before known such peace as she did now, despite the tumult of the past months. Nothing could compare with the felicity of having him beside her, of knowing that in every breath, in every thought, they were as one. Glowing and lovely in happiness, she entered Kellynch that afternoon, on the arm of her husband, basking in the full worth of the affection of the one who would thereafter spend an entire lifetime endeavouring to deserve her.

The End

I hope that you've enjoyed this book!
After the About the Author section you'll find a preview of
A Bath Affair

About the Author

Kate Westwood is the author's pseudonym. Kate has a background in academic writing and holds a Master's degree in English Literature. Having had a life-long dream to write, she finally turned her pen to regency romance when she turned fifty.

Kate is a huge fan of Austen and her contemporaries, and strives to recreate an authentic 'regency' experience for the reader.

Kate's hobbies, when she is not writing or reading Regency romance, include playing classical piano, and walking and hiking the beautiful Gold Coast Hinterland. Kate has three adult sons and lives in the beautiful Moreton Bay Islands with her partner and cat.

Connect with Kate

Facebook: https://www.facebook.com/katewestwood.net/
Sign up to Kate's email newsletter at :
www.katewestwood.net
to receive the subscriber exclusive story *The Gift* as a welcome gift!

Here is your preview of
A Bath Affair

One

Bath, 1813

'Shan't you get married at all, Aunt Clemence?'

The ten-year-old girl who sat on a chair in the breakfast room with four other members of her family, was charmingly dressed in a white-on-white long-sleeved muslin with embroidered skirts, a pink ribbon to decorate the waist, and a matching pink ribbon in her long red hair. She was, to an outsider, almost a complete replica of the woman who sat opposite – her three and twenty-year-old aunt Clemence. After all, both of them sported pale auburn hair, wide eyes and snubbed nose scattered with freckles. The only difference, and one which was often remarked upon with great astonishment, was that while her aunt's eyes were a brilliant blue, those of her niece were a dark, scintillating brown. Where those brown eyes had come from no one knew, for almost the entire family owned blue eyes, with the exception of two or three pairs of hazel-green. It was supposed laughingly, that the child must be a throw-back from an ancient great ancestor of Lady Hurst's or even Sir Edward's, even though Sir Edward found little humour in the tease.

Of course, as with any family, those who love us the most dearly pay the most attention to details, and to others in Clara Bastable's extended family, most of whom did indeed love her dearly, the similarities between the child and her aunt were not only in countenance, but in character as well. Like her aunt, little Clara Bastable had a sweetness of manner, and a generally amiable countenance. But in her young character was breeding a stubbornness, a disinclination for following, and an inclination for outspokenness which her mother sagely considered a hinderance to her daughter's future happiness. In this point, Clara resembled her aunt, for Clemence openly owned that she had little respect for behaviour as befits ones' breeding, and was always beforehand in speaking her mind and behindhand in consideration of the consequences!

But those coffee-brown eyes of Clara's were now turned upon her aunt Clemence who sat with the rest of the family, partaking of a rather late breakfast as they were wont to do since they were come to Bath. The rather singular smell of smoked kippers filled the room, and mingled cheekily with the scent of the warm chocolate which Bell, the butler, had just served.

Clara's mother, Clemence and George's half-sister, shushed her daughter. 'It is Aunt Clemence's business, dear. Eat your breakfast.'

'Oh, Seraphine, I don't mind her asking, really.' Clemence pushed away her chocolate with a sigh. The conversation which had just taken place had been a rather serious one, to Clemence's mind; she did not like being taken to by George, her younger brother by one year, who seemed as insensitive as Papa for urging her on a course which she had no desire to follow. But because her young niece was in the room, she kept her tone gentle and playful.

'Well, Clara, to say I shall not *ever* marry, I cannot own it for a certainty, but I can say that I am most disinclined at present.'

'But do you not wish to have children, Clemence,' frowned George disapprovingly, 'and run a household of your very own? Why, Isabelle and I cannot contain ourselves for the joy of expecting a child. A child is the making of a woman, they say!'

'You know I am very happy for you and Izzy.' Clemence smiled at her pleasingly plump, fair-haired sister-in-law, who sat next to her husband. 'But to own the truth, George, that is no great temptation to me. I cannot agree that marriage or children "make" a woman. All I have seen of the life of married women is that they become dried up before their time, towing behind them an ill-tempered, ancient husband and six or seven children after a mere five years of marriage, and this all accomplished by only the middle of their second decade!'

Then she looked guiltily at Seraphine. 'Oh, forgive me dearest sister, I hardly meant *you!*'

Poor Seraphine however, at three and thirty years, was just such a woman. She appeared as care-worn as one of forty, with hints of premature grey in her dark brown hair, and that air about her that married women with children frequently take on, of resignation to an unkind fate. Seraphine, more usually addressed by her friends as "Lady Bastable" had married ten years previously. Her husband a peer of the realm, she had taken to heart her duty to produce an heir. Now complete with five of Clemence's predicted six or seven children already, she might have taken umbrage at her younger half-sister's words. But she merely smiled and cut up her Bath bun.

George gave a strained laugh. 'I hope you don't think *me* ill-tempered now that I am married!'

Clemence's eyes glinted. 'No, dear, but you haven't yet been married five years. Let us see how you do yet!'

Isabelle said, in her fine, feathery voice, 'I shall forgive him if he is grumpy, for if it is so, it is only because I have vexed him.' She giggled. 'Although my George is so good natured that I have never seen him ill-tempered yet! But Clemence, do you really intend to go against your father?' Her eyes were wide as they contemplated such a revolt against authority.

'You know, too,' George added in a lower voice, 'that Papa only thinks of your well-being, that he wants to see you settled to a most eligible prospect. Surely you must feel the weight of all that you owe our parents and please them in this?'

'I don't suppose it is my happiness Papa thinks of, as much as the status such a connection will bring to the Hurst family name,' Clemence replied, with a hint of acid in her tone. 'He wants only to boast of a having a 'Lady Underwood of Hyde Hall' for a daughter! You know how fond he is of that sort of thing, George.' She glanced at Seraphine, but her sister remained silent.

'No,' continued Clemence determinedly, 'I am quite content to live out my days as a single woman. I'll live at Grandacres with you and Izzy; why, I can tutor your sixteen children in French and German, and teach them to play the pianoforte so dreadfully that you will beg them to stop!' She gave him a mischievous look, her temper never out of sorts for long.

George however, refused to be in good temper with his older sister. 'Don't be disagreeable for the sake of it, Clem. It is no laughing matter. You are a woman; therefore, it is your duty to marry.'

'What,' replied Clemence, her blue eyes glinting with passion, 'if I have no wish cleave myself to the ball and chain of marriage? Why, a poor woman might need to marry – indeed, she must, if she cannot support herself, but a wealthy one might do very well without a husband; better, in fact, for she has no one to answer to, and no one to displease!'

'Then you do your duty to our father very ill, I must say, when he has gone to great lengths to bring this about for your good. He means to make you accept Sir Richard, like it or not, or he will disinherit you! It is not worth losing your little fortune over, Clem; you will not lose your independence, you know, if you marry, for you will still have money.'

'My husband's money you mean! I shouldn't have any of my own, for you know a husband controls a woman's settlement, and then he will have Mama's money too, when she dies, and ever so generously dole it out to me as pin money! No, I mean to be independent in the world, to move about in it as I wish, to travel and discover! I cannot do such things on the arm of a male to whom I am tethered by an invisible leading rope and who sees me merely as the producer of an heir. You know Sir Ricard is just such a man!'

Clemence looked again to Seraphine for support. She felt quite set upon this morning, and would have wished her half-sister to take her part, but that lady seemed only to have silence to offer. Clemence repressed the vexation which had risen in her and determined to change the subject. 'What time is your mama to arrive, Izzy? Does she come alone? I am not sure we have room for a second maid, but I shall ask Jane to share her bed, if Mrs Harris brings a woman with her.'

'Oh, Mama never goes anywhere without Eliza! She quite considers her indispensable, you know! But the maid is a slight little thing, and could hardly take up much room in Jane's bed. Mama says she underfeeds her, so as to keep her fit for work – is that not excessively droll? Mama says fat maids are sluggish and apt to laziness. She says George and I must only employ thin servants, for a thin-looking maid, Mama says, signifies that they are unlikely to eat one out of house and home. Do you not agree, my dear?' Isabelle looked doubtfully at her husband, who was still frowning at Clemence.

'Clemence, you must not make Sir Richard wait too long, or he may withdraw his offer. Surely you cannot be so—'

Seraphine put down her tea cup loudly, and four sets of eyes turned to her in some surprise. 'That is enough,' she interjected sharply. 'Leave Clemence alone, George. She must make her own decisions. Indeed, that is why she has been sent to Bath, to consider the offer. Allow her to think in peace. Now, who is coming with me to the circulating library? I am bereft of reading material and plan to go directly after breakfast if this rain holds off. Isabelle?'

Seraphine, being the oldest of the three siblings by a great deal, commanded the authority of both familial habit and natural seniority. As for Isabelle, she looked upon her sister-in-law with something akin to a combination of awe and terror, being herself a mere nineteen years and used to being dominated at home by Mrs Harris.

Now, Izzy obediently stood with a rush, ready to depart at once, should her sister-in-law command it of her. 'Yes, I ought to go; that is, I should like a new book, if only I can find one that I can understand – they all seem so learned to me! Even the novels. Why, I tried "Castle Rackrent" last week, as *you* urged me, Clemence, but can make not head nor tail of it.' She tittered nervously into the silent room.

'I am a great enthusiast of the novels of Mrs Edgeworth,' remarked Clemence, eager now to keep the subject moving on from her own tangled affairs. 'I admire Mrs Edgeworth beyond anything! I shall explain the story to you, if you like, Izzy. And I can find you one that is better suited to your taste.'

Isabelle put her hand to her mouth suddenly. 'Oh, but dear me, but I do not have the money for the subscription. How silly I am, but I have spent all my pin already!'

'What? But you had six guineas, dearest! I can hardly imagine on what you have spent it,' answered her husband, a little astonished, 'but here, take another guinea or two; there, that ought to keep you in books and fripperies for at least another fortnight.'

He put away his pocket-book, kissed his wife's cheek absently, and she, blushing guiltily, tucked the guineas into her handkerchief quickly.

The women stood to follow their sister-in-law from the room, and Seraphine took Clemence's arm as they left George mulling over his tea cup. 'Don't mind our brother, he's simply worried about you. He knows what Papa will do if you refuse Sir Richard. You already know *my* feelings on the matter.'

'Oh, Sophie,' was all her sister said. Her blue eyes were eloquent enough.

Clara crept to the side of her aunt and mother, and took both by the hand. 'Don't worry, Aunt Clemence. I think if you don't want to marry Sir Richard, you should tell him so. What does disinherit mean?'

Over the little girl's red hair, Clemence met the eyes of her sister. 'It means that money which is meant to come to you when you marry, or when your parent dies, is given to another brother or sister instead.'

'Oh.' Clara was thoughtful. 'But I still think you ought not to marry Sir Richard if he will only take it all. Perhaps he will spend it all on disgusting things like cigars and port!' She made a face.

Clemence laughed aloud. 'After my own heart, you are, Clarabelle!' she cried affectionately.

Seraphine did not find amusement in her daughter's comments. 'Don't encourage her, Clem.'

It was too late, for Clara, quite delighted she had amused at least one of her favourite adults, added, 'I do not think I should want to marry, either, if my husband was going to take all my money. I'd rather be poor!'

'I think,' said her mother, fastening her daughter's bonnet with more force than was necessary, 'at ten years old, you are far too young to think of marriage yet! Besides, if your aunt has her way,' she added drily, 'she will have had all the laws changed by the time you are ready to marry and wives will manage their husbands' money instead!'

Two

The arrival of Isabelle's mother, later that day, caused a great deal more confusion than ought to be generated by the arrival of one widowed mama and a maid.

Being of somewhat low birth, Mrs Harris had been married for a time to a baker by trade, who had a shop in a good street in London, and by which he was able to make an adequate living and educate his daughter. His death, most surely ill-timed to fall immediately after Isabelle's thirteenth birthday, left his wife with a small house in Cheapside and a modest amount to live on for life, provided she practised a severer economy than to which she had been used. Consideration of her lowered circumstances in life however, brought her quickly to the conclusion that a new scheme was in order.

Ambitious for her own betterment, and for a good marriage for her daughter, through which she saw her own salvation, she had early invested in such a scheme, spending more frivolously than her friends thought wise, to buy herself into a higher society. Her friends, who had been of her husband's set, now were left behind with ill-concealed disdain, in pursuit of higher circles, and with both ambition and shrewd investments, she had been, to some degree, able to achieve her object. There were some, however, who observing her toadying and rising behaviours, and being subject to her vulgar turns of phrase, ridiculed her in their drawing rooms, even though they would not do so to her face.

Spending the great sum which was sufficient to feed Isabelle headfirst into the mechanism of a quality ladies' school, and churn her out the other side ready for consumption by society, Mrs Harris had alternately palpitated at the thought that her extremes might be for naught, and then comforted herself in the knowledge that since her daughter had beauty on her side, all men with eyes to see were equally the same when it came to looking for a wife. Isabelle could just as easily be approached by a Lord as a leper, and Mrs Harris had taken great pains to ensure that all probability was on the side of the Lords.

At any rate, by the time Isabelle had become ready to launch into society for her come-out, Mrs Harris could be well pleased with her endeavours, since they had received the looked-for invitations by the right sort of people, so that Isabelle could be introduced to the right social circles. Mrs Harris had congratulated herself on this achievement, and as a result, fancied herself to be of rather more consequence than others might have thought her privately.

Now, as she ascended the stairs in a great labour of effort, for she was not a small woman, she commanded her poor maid with an air of great authority, so that the girl ran this way and that in a frenzy of panic.

'Why, what an enormous number of steps!' cried the lady, huffing and puffing. 'Be careful with that box, girl! Where is my blue fan? I simply must stop and rest! What an ill-thought notion indeed, to take a house with three flights of stairs! My own dear little house in town has two flights; I suppose it is not quite as fancy as this house, although I pride myself on it's being situated in a better part of town than some! Three flights! But I suppose that is all that can be had in the good parts of Bath!'

This bustle of getting the numerous hat boxes, trunks and other paraphernalia to the guest room, and then the moving of Mrs Harris's ample frame up the stairs to the 'civilized' part of the house, as she called it, took upwards of thirty minutes, during which commotion two boxes were presumed lost, alarm raised, boxes located, and hysteria quieted, so that, when the heaving woman was finally seated heavily on the sturdiest chaise in the drawing room, four or five silent sighs of relief were breathed around her. Her mob cap, which sported so many ruffles and trimmings as to make its wearer an object either of derision or pity, Clemence could not decide which, had fallen to one side in all the fuss, but no one dared to remark upon it for fear of giving offence to the wearer.

'Well, what an agreeable situation you have here, George,' she began to her daughter's husband, as soon as she was gotten comfortable. 'The furnishings are a little worn, I grant you,' she added, looking around with a critical eye, 'but you have no need to feel shame if you receive Quality here. And that window there,' nodding with her head, '*that* is happily placed to give an aspect over the Square, I collect. I would go immediately to see the prospect, but I am so comfortable here I cannot think of moving again until dinner time! Does that window command an agreeable prospect? I only wish I could see it myself!'

George opened his mouth to thank his mother-in-law for the kind observation but was cut off.

'Perhaps it is not so *very* fine as the prospect from the windows at the apartments of my *intimate* friend, Lady Alvers, who is located in the Paragon buildings, and has four flights of stairs, too, but I dare say you don't feel your lack excessively, not having been in the Paragon, since you will have no connections there yet, I should think! I shall introduce you myself to Lady Alvers while I am here, and then you may suppose yourselves thereafter welcome to call upon her, and look out of her windows all you like.'

Seraphine composedly answered for her brother, who was sputtering into his tea. 'Indeed, Ma'am, the view is generally considered to be very fine from that window.'

Although her sister forbore to mention the fact, Clemence could not hold back, and ventured to add with barely disguised amusement, 'And though we are most obliged to you for your kind intentions to introduce us to Lady Alvers, I do believe we have been to one or two of her private evenings, Ma'am. Why, we attended a large evening party only last week. I think, yes, I do believe it was in the Paragon Buildings.' She ignored her sister's warning look and primly studied her tea cup.

However much she should try, Clemence found it difficult to repress the urge to let loose her impertinent thoughts, which flew about her mind like bees, buzzing in her head! She had, in her youth, been called impudent, pert, even shameless, in her tendency to speak whatever came into her head, and she admitted such accusations to be true enough. She had learned prudence with age, however, and now she hoped she had enough wit about her not to allow some of those bees out of the hive, for despite her impetuous nature, she was not truly unkind, and she was sensible of the power of those bees to sting!

Isabelle added breathily, 'Lady Alvers invited us because of knowing George, Mama; was that not very kind? She doted on me excessively and fed me so many cakes that I thought I would be ill!' She giggled nervously.

Under her mob cap Mrs Harris's cheeks grew pink. 'Yes, yes, that is all very well, but what of this weather? How you can stand to stay here for more than a week or so in this wet, I can only surmise at! Isabelle, you must always wrap yourself up if you go out, and in your condition, it don't do to go about in the rain. I shall not hear of it, while I am come to stay. You look quite pale and tired, my dear. But how many weeks is your stay to be here, George? And your sisters, do they continue here for the winter? No, but of course they cannot, I see that now, for I am sure Lady Bastable will need to return home soon to her children and husband, and Miss Hurst will be soon required by her mother. To a father, a long absence can but signify little, but to a mother, it is a trial indeed!'

To this rather surprising monologue, the other occupants of the drawing room could add little, for there seemed, in light of Mrs Harris's great omniscience, nothing to be added. But then Isabelle, a little flushed of cheek, broke the brief silence which had descended over the room, and said placatingly, 'To be sure, Mama, I shan't go out in the rain, unless George or one of my sisters is with me to hold the umbrella over me. It is not so *very* wet, you see, if the rain is only light, and there are so many places we have not yet been to, and George and I have ever so many grand engagements to attend, and you are to come with us, Mama, you know, so you shan't mind a very little rain, shall you?'

George, somewhat eager to make a friend of his wife's mother added, 'Oh, yes Ma'am, we have several engagements of some importance, and we of course wish your company. A little rain won't signify for we have a very good, dry carriage; why it was repainted only last month; paid a pretty penny too, four guineas, for the work, quite as much as the new harness I have got for—'

'Yes, yes,' inserted his mama in law, 'but I hope it don't rain every day, or I shan't get a wink of rest; I could never sleep with the infernal rain drumming about me, you know; Eliza always has to bring me a little drop of sherry about two or three in the morning, when I am not able to sleep. I hope she is not put far from my room, or I will be obliged to have her sleep on the floor, not that but she will feel it for she is quite strong in her limbs and so slight of figure that she can withstand any amount of punishing by a hard floor!'

Clemence exchanged a look with Isabelle, and repressed the urge to suggest Mrs Harris sleep upon the floor and see how *she* withstood the punishment to her limbs, but seeing Isabelle's anxious face, she sipped her tea and schooled her countenance.

Isabelle remonstrated gently with her mother that Eliza could not be expected to sleep on the floor but that she would have a little bed made up. 'And Mama, George knows many important people here in Bath, like the Perrots, who come every winter and are ever so well-looking – such London fashions as would make you quite green with envy! And the Addlingtons, who live in Laura-place and oh, ever so many fine people! You shall be in splendid company Mama, and enjoy yourself so excessively, that you shan't notice the rain at all!'

Mrs Harris's eyes brightened. 'The Perrots, you say? The Addlingtons? Dear me!' Heartened by the thought of meeting 'importance', she patted her daughter's hand fondly. 'If I am obliged to accompany you all and see such grand people as the Perrots and the Addlingtons, why I will certainly do so in good spirits, and not mind at all.' She paused, then added, 'Only I do hate to be out late, for these days I am forced to take to my bed early. It gives some ease to my poor, poor legs! Doctor Finch says I must rest them as much as I can!

Clara, who was staring in open-eyed fascination at their guest, innocently replied, 'What is wrong with your legs, Ma'am? Do you have varicose veins like Grandmama?'

To cover her younger sister's sudden coughing fit, Seraphine quickly offered more cakes to the lady, and hoping to turn the conversation to something more congenial, said, 'When you guessed so cleverly that I must return to my husband, Lord Bastable, you were quite correct, Ma'am. I cannot remain here very long, since my husband has written enquiring after my return to Bastable Hall. I can only stay a day or two more. The children have been asking for me and poor Duncan is quite out of sorts with their naughtiness.'

'I see! Ah well, children can be quite a handful these days!' Mrs Harris cast a stern look at Clara, who looked back at her ingenuously. 'And you will, I hope George, take Isabelle home to Grandacres by her eighth month, for her confinement? It is only two months distant.'

'We intend to return in six w—' George began eagerly.

'But of course you shall. And Miss Hurst,' she added, now finally turning Clemence, 'I hope you will take the waters with me, for I forbid Isabelle to take them on account of how I distrust mineral waters when one is with child. It is quite well known that taking strong mineral waters when expecting can bring on child birth before time.'

'I rather think that is in regard to bathing, Ma'am,' replied Clemence, surprised. 'I collect there is no inherent danger in merely sipping the waters.' She noted that Isabelle's eyes were wide open. She stifled an urge to roll her own eyes heavenward. Isabelle might be awed by her mama, but Clemence was not so timid!

Mrs Harris continued firmly, 'No, indeed, you are quite mistaken, child! Bath's waters are known to be so vigorous that my dear Mr Harris, when he was alive, made a point of forbidding me even to take a mere sip, for fear of their overcoming me. I have such a sensitive constitution, you know. And so does Isabelle. And Mr Harris had a great knowledge of such things. No, my dear, I am quite certain of my facts.'

Is that so, Ma'am? I was not aware of the fact. I wonder it can be so well-known, if no one has mentioned it to me since I have been coming to Bath these four or five years! But then, I never listen to idle gossip, Ma'am. I feel sorry then, for all the women who are to lose their unborn children, who are taking the waters at this very moment! Perhaps we ought to go to the Pump room directly and warn them! At least, that is what Clemence said in her head. Suppressing her impudent little bees, all she truly said aloud was a docile, 'Yes Ma'am, I should certainly be glad to take the waters with you. Perhaps we can go tomorrow, to the Pump room.'

True to her word, Mrs Harris did not move her bulk until the dinner was called, and even when the other three women went to dress, Isabelle's mama was content to sit upon the chaise and wait for them. 'I cannot, at my age, be moving about the way you young things do; it fatigues me to dress for dinner if we are only at home, and besides that, such a fuss is only for younger people. I am sure it don't signify what I wear in my own daughter's house, to eat my vittles!'

When they had gone upstairs to dress, Isabelle was apologetic. 'She is quite determined upon her course, and her way of thinking, that I cannot alter her path, once it is taken. Heavens, she quite persuades me to her own way of thinking, even when I begin on some other path! Sometimes I get quite confused as to what I ought to think! But I am sure she means well!'

Clemence patted her sister-in-law's hand gently. 'Dearest, don't make yourself anxious. We are very pleased to have your mama to stay. I only hope she will enjoy herself and go home feeling as if she has been very much amused while she is here. I daresay a good sleep and an outing will have her quite at ease before the end of tomorrow!' She only hoped that the three weeks of Mrs Harris's visit would pass quickly, or she would be sure to combust from being obliged to be polite!

Read the rest of

A Bath Affair

Get it at
https://www.amazon.com/dp/B07T1GWRN7/
Go to
www.katewestwood.net
and sign up to Kate's newsletter for release notices and more!

Other Books by Kate Westwood

A Scandal at Delford

Beauty and the Beast of Thornleigh

A Bath Affair